NOT MY FATHER'S VOICE

By Starla Ryan

ISBN 978-1-387-02985-3

Designed by: A Mad Lark Rants. Washougal, Washington
               Published by LuLu
2017

Copyright Starla Ryan. All rights reserved.

Not My Father's Voice is a work of fiction. Where real people, events, establishments, organizations or locales appear, they are used fictitiously. Many elements of the novel are drawn from the author's imagination.

Cover art from 123rf.com.

Praying Woman Copyright:
https://www.123rf.com/profile_halfpoint

Grain field Background Copyright
https://www.123rf.com/profile_vencavolrab78

Acknowledgments

To Lois Mae Schellenberg Welton who's faith inspired many; I'm glad I knew you. To LaDonna Mae Kennedy, Sharon Lavonne Layton, Patricia Lorraine DeLashmutt, and Richard Eugene Welton whose lives were transformed by this adventure in its original form; forgive me for seeing it through different eyes. I treasure you. To Mark Christopher Frank Guz who bore with me through computer crashes, tearful nights of frustration and encouraged me to persevere; I couldn't have done it without you. Thank you.

To everyone who reads this story and gets even a glimpse the courage it represents, may your lives be richer for having met Alice Mae.

1   Go

Alice Mae pulled her sweater close and meandered through her small yard. The grass was cold against her bare ankles but she didn't care. The warm morning sun flooding the high northeastern Colorado plains felt glorious on her back after the harsh winter she had endured.

Finding a sprig of early forsythia peeking around the back of the garage, she snapped it off and tucked it into the button hole of her sweater before heading inside to begin her chores. *Lord*, she prayed as she did every morning, *show me what to do.*

She turned the faucet and hot water poured into the old wringer washing machine that stood on the enclosed back porch. Years of wear had loosened the floorboards and they moaned under the weight of the heavy machine. *Nobody still uses these antiques anymore except me*, she thought, and she was right. There wasn't another one like it in Holyoke and hadn't been in a decade, but it still served her family. That was all that mattered. It was all she could afford. She poured in soap and bleach and breathed in the hot, familiar steam.

Pillowcases full of dirty laundry littered the porch floor. With five children, it was endless. She began sorting. She couldn't afford to replace a single item that she might carelessly mix in with the wrong batch and this old machine was unforgiving. Grabbing a mound of faded towels, she lowered them one by one into the water and watched the agitator suck them beneath the suds.

She had been doing the since the age of eight. It was her solitary time and it gave her time to think. She had much to think about.

She had been folding laundry in the living room when the steel gray sedan pulled up in front of her home. The woman she had not seen in years slid from behind the dash and headed toward the front door.

"Alice Mae." The woman called. "Alice Mae, I need to talk to you."

"Aunt Ferggie?" She opened the screen door and stood aside. "What are you doing here?"

Ferggison Currier stepped across the threshold and surveyed the room. She turned to face her niece and without preamble launched into what she had driven several hundred miles to say.

"Alice Mae, you've been on my mind a great deal these past few months. I've tried to ignore it. I told myself that it was none of my business. I told myself a dozen times to turn around and go back home. But I cannot shake the cloud that has settled over me."

Alice Mae blinked, too stunned to speak.

"You cannot stay here any longer." Her voice was insistent. "Holyoke has nothing to offer your children. Nothing!. They need a future and there is no future for them here. You need to leave Holyoke and you need to do it now."

Alice Mae stared, her mouth dry.

"Donna's going to graduate from high school this spring I presume."

The younger woman nodded.

"Is there a man in the picture? Does she have a suitor?"

Alice Mae shook her head. "A suitor? No".

"Excellent! Then I'm not too late." She threw back her head and inhaled deeply. She reached out and took Alice Mae by the shoulders. "You must get her and the rest of your family away from this barren and God forsaken place before they get trapped here." She didn't say *just like you,* but the implication was clear.

"But how?" Frustration and despair burned the younger woman's eyes. For years she had dreamed of leaving, but with no money and no idea where to go, she had no path forward. Her aunt was absolutely right. She was trapped.

Ferggie held her gaze steady. "I don't know how, Alice Mae, but I'm absolutely convinced that you need to get your kids out of here. Your mom would say the same thing if she were still with us." She swallowed hard. "Premilla had such dreams for you."

"Where would I go? I have no car. I have nothing."

"You must find a way." It was not a suggestion. It was a pronouncement. It was a command. It was marching orders. She lowered her voice. "Rumor has it that Gene's brothers are back in the area. Virgil and Kermit were seen in Haxtun a couple of weeks ago."

Fear sparked in Alice Mae's eyes at the mention of the men.

"I've been told they've signed on with the Double D Ranch for the summer. My guess is that Gene isn't far behind. You don't want them to find you here."

Alice Mae nodded, bile rising in her throat while she fought to keep her expression calm.

The two women spoke for several minutes more about family, being careful to avoid the mention of Alice Mae's father who, as far as Ferggie was concerned, had no redeeming qualities. Having exhausted the subjects that they had in common, they walked together out to the car and stood in the late winter sun saying their goodbyes.

"I can't tell you what to do," the older woman said, giving her niece an affectionate hug. "But I know you need to do it soon."

Only twenty minutes after drawing up in front of the tiny house in Holyoke, the sedan pulled away from the curb. Alice Mae watched it roll down Baxter Avenue and turn east to the highway.

The agitation of the towels finished, Alice Mae pulled the plug on the machine and let the black rubber drain hose carry dirty water through the propped open screen door and onto the lawn behind the house. She filled the tub with rinse water and let the agitation resume.

Stepping into the back yard, she stood with her face to the sun and asked for guidance, for courage and for the means to do this great thing. She didn't have words yet, just the desire of her heart and a measure of faith. She hoped that would be enough. *Thy will be done*, she breathed.

2   Bookends

"Hi, girls," Ruth Lynch sang out, pushing through the gate and into the backyard. "Looks like you have already put in a day's work." A fortyish woman with dark wavy hair, except for a streak of gray that slid behind her left ear, shook out the last two towels and handed them over. Four clothes lines sagged under the weight of wet laundry. "Is there more inside?"

"I think this is the last of it." Sixteen-year-old Sharon Wheaton pinned the final two items on the line. Turning the basket upside down, she shook out the moisture from the bottom and slung it onto her hip as she headed to the house. Her long dark hair was pulled back in its customary ponytail, and it swung from side to side as she walked, highlighting her spirited face.

"We wanted to get it done early. We're headed up to the school for tryouts."

The girls in pedal pushers took the two back steps in a single bound and called out in unison as they entered. "Mom. Mrs. Lynch is here."

Laurie was almost exactly a year younger than her sister, overshooting the mark by just four days. Unlike her flirtatious sister, she wasn't much interested in boys. More friends than rivals, the girls were both fine-boned like their mother and bright. Bookends.

Trailing the girls through the enclosed back porch Ruth was met with the earthy odor of soaking beans mixed with the aroma of fresh bread. Heaven. The once white painted kitchen cupboards had been freshly scrubbed and the floor, even with its missing tiles, was clean. Two crusty loaves rested on a cutting board, cooling.

"Ruth?" Their mother popped her head around the corner of the kitchen and smiled, pushing damp hair out of her face. "What a nice surprise. Come in. Come in."

Her ready smile was one of the most likeable things about Alice Mae, not that she didn't have many other exceptional qualities. She was thoughtful. She was compassionate. Above all, she was resourceful. Alice Mae could stretch a pound of ground beef to last a week and could grow a flower garden from a handful of year-old seeds and make it the prettiest flower patch in town. If jealousy weren't a sin, Ruth would have to admit she was just a bit envious.

"I don't know where they get all that energy," Ruth said watching the girls vanish into the bedroom they shared. A moment later with sweaters in hand, the two shot through the house and out the front door leaving the women in peace.

"Bye, Mom. Bye Mrs. Lynch." The call drifted back as the girls cleared the front steps.

"Me either. They've been up since six and haven't even slowed down." She ran her hands down her cotton dress and smoothed the skirt as best she could.

Nodding in the direction of the kitchen and inhaling deeply Ruth smiled. "Nothing smells as good as fresh bread. Makes a house feel so homey, don't you think?"

Alice Mae breathed in the lingering aroma and nodded. "It does smell good, doesn't it? Richie made it for us." She saw the look of surprise on her friend's face and laughed. "He started about a month ago and has a real knack for it. Hasn't had a flop yet. I think maybe I'm finally off the hook. It's still warm. Do you want a slice?"

"No, thanks. I'm not hungry." An outright lie. The smell made her mouth water, but she knew that her hundred fifty pound frame didn't need it and that no doubt the kids did.

Ruth's full figure was the topic of more than a little gossip around Holyoke. Not only was that she well rounded but she carried it in so many of the right places. She enjoyed wearing clothes that accentuated the curves rather than hiding them. As a pastor's wife, she might have been more demure, but she figured if the good Lord had blessed her with the assets, who was she to hide them? And her husband, Joe, didn't mind a bit!

"I figured one of the girls made it."

"I wish." Alice Mae laughed. "I can't get Donna near the kitchen and considering what Sharon turns out I'd rather keep her occupied with another task. Any other task." She shrugged, grinning. "Joyce isn't too bad at it, though. I may have a decent cook in the family yet."

The small living room was comfortable and relatively tidy considering a family of six coexisted in the confined quarters. Cotton curtains covered the one small window and were held back with a wooden clothes pin. The floor of the rental house had been painted at one time, a treatment that was cool and welcome in summer but downright frigid in winter.

"I saw Richie out bright and early the other morning."

"Yeah?"

"He might have been delivering papers but it was hard to tell. Mostly he was having a nice chat with Susie Sullivan." She grinned. "Now that's a cute little girl!"

Alice Mae rolled her eyes and shook her head.

At thirteen, the only boy in the family was a charmer. With dark hair, longer than his mother preferred, and an easy grin that appealed to the girls in sixth grade, he was doing his part to help the family by delivering the News Register on the two mornings a week that it came off the press.

"He's getting pretty good at launching the papers in the general direction of the front porch but I think his accuracy leaves something to be desired."

"It's usually not too bad. I don't mind a little hike in the morning to get the paper. Gets the blood moving."

They laughed easily together.

Ruth appraised Alice Mae and cocked her head. She twirled her fingers indicating for her friend to spin around. "I like the short do. Sort of the Audrey Hepburn look."

"Sharon's work. She's getting better."

"Looks very sporty."

Alice Mae ran her hand along her recently exposed neck. "I'm getting used to it. Think maybe we should have waited till summer though, it's a bit breezy at times."

She draped the tablecloth that she had been pressing across the back of the sofa to cool and sank down with an audible sigh, weary from two hours of bending over the ironing board. She would get three dollars later today when the load was picked up. It would put dinner on the table.

"Oh, that feels good." She breathed stretching her neck and shoulders, working out a kink. "Come on. Have a seat. What's on your mind?"

Ruth perched on the edge of the sofa. "I wanted you to be the first to know that we're leaving," Surprise registered on her friend's face. "It won't be right away. Not for several months. We're trying to keep it quiet. We haven't even officially told the church elders but I wanted to be the one to tell you before you heard it somewhere else."

It was a blow. "Why?"

"Joe wants to be in a bigger town. We've been talking about it for a couple of years, but the position just opened up."

"Where are you going?" She reached for Ruth's hands. "I'm happy for you but I can't imagine Holyoke without you."

"I'll miss you too but life changes. Not here in Holyoke it doesn't change much, but if we let it, it can change and be better." She patted Alice Mae's hand. "Joe's been offered a senior pastor's position in Greeley."

"Greeley?"

"He's wants a bigger church with staff to support his work and to share the load. I'm happy to let him bounce ideas off me, but he doesn't always appreciate my opinions. He wants another man to come alongside him and the church has made him a good offer."

"They'll be lucky to get you both!" She meant it!

"Joe, yes, but I'm not sure Greeley is ready for me." Her grin was wicked. She eyed Alice Mae. "Haven't you ever wanted to go somewhere else?"

The laugh that spilled out surprised them both. It started as a small chuckle and grew till Alice Mae threw back her head and released the tension that she had carried for weeks, months, years. It was contagious. Ruth let out a snort of her own.

"Guess what?" Alice Mae asked when at last she caught her breath.

"What?"

"I'm leaving too."

"What? When?" She sputtered, astounded.

"By the end of summer. I'm taking the kids and leaving."

"Where?"

"I don't know yet."

"But how will you manage? You don't even have a car?"

The laughter stopped and after a deep intake of breath, the conversation took on an air of expectancy. "I don't know exactly, but I have to leave. We'll be gone before school starts next fall."

The women stood and hugged each other. "Good for you. Let me know what I can do to help. Anything!" Sisters in the trenches, they both had a busy summer ahead of them. "Keep me posted. I'm anxious to hear all the details."

"You too. Tell Joe congratulations for me. When are you going to let the congregation know?"

"Not till we have to. Holyoke doesn't do change well."

"Don't I know it!"

3   Look

The sun was high overhead in an expanse of blue sky that felt endless. Alice Mae headed to the town library, a repurposed turn of the century house. It was an easy walk of four blocks, passing several neighbors including Willy Wiggins, the owner and upstairs resident of the Wiggins Funeral Home. A small man with a receding chin and a narrow nose, Willy greeted her with his customary reserve.

"Alice Mae." He nodded.

"Mr. Wiggins." She bobbed her head in return.

She bent to admire the urns brimming with spring primroses that framed his portico. "White's nice but red or pink would be more cheerful," she chided.

"People don't come see me to be cheered up." He returned. "White is dignified."

"But colors would brighten their moods as well as the neighborhood." She plucked a browning petal from among the white blossoms and walked on. "A few orange mixed in would be beautiful," she called over her shoulder

He couldn't see the grin on her face, but he heard it in her voice.

He suppressed a smile of his own. "Not on my watch."

Climbing the short flight of steps leading up to the front door of the library, she was pleased to see that the lilac trees bracketing the entrance were heavy with buds. She inhaled hoping to catch a whiff of sweetness. Not yet. There was a smile on her face, but there were butterflies in her stomach as she pushed into the rich, wood-shelf filled space.

"Good Morning Betty. How's your mother?"

"She had a rough night but I think she's doing better today." Betty Baxter, a tall, lean woman in her late fifties with unnaturally blonde hair, presided over the affairs of the city library from her chair behind the front desk.

"Good."

"How are the kids?"

"Happy."

It was their customary exchange. Betty's ailing mother was the topic of conversation for everyone that crossed the library threshold and had been for more than a decade.

Alice Mae always began her visits in the periodicals. She browsed Life Magazine to see what was new in the country. She read National Geographic, her window to the world. This day, however, she headed to a small section tucked into the back corner of the library's main room.

It took only a few minutes to locate what she needed. After withdrawing several volumes, she spread them across the scarred walnut table, shed her coat and settled in.

"We have in some new magazines," Betty called from the desk. "There's a great spread highlighting President Kennedy's first year and it has some new pictures of the white house."

"Thanks, Betty." Alice Mae didn't even look up.

"You can tell Laurie that the Nancy Drew she was looking for has been turned in. I'm saving it for her."

"Will do."

Walking into the reference area to straighten some already tidy books, Betty tried again. "Donna was in yesterday. That girl sure loves to read doesn't she? I think she's read everything in here at least once."

"Hmmm."

It was nearly three o'clock by the time Alice Mae closed the last of the books and looked out the window, satisfied. She stretched and gathered her notes.

After returning all the material to the shelf, she stepped from the dimness of the library into the bright sunshine. She pulled her coat over across her shoulders and allowed the afternoon rays to warm her bones. "Bye, Betty," she called just before the doors latched.

There was a spring in her step as she walked three short blocks to First Baptist Church to begin her afternoon chores as part time janitor.

Alice Mae walked everywhere; she didn't mind walking. She had not owned a car for nearly four years – since the day her alcoholic husband, had crashed it and then walked away, abandoning both it and his family.

She rarely minded the inconvenience. Holyoke was, after all, no more than ten blocks in any direction.

The central downtown area was exactly two blocks long.

On the west side of Main Street was the Piggly Wiggly grocery store where Alice Mae stocked shelves for a season; the Holyoke Register newspaper office, which currently gave Richie spending money in exchange for an hour of his time twice each week; Shunamakers hardware; and a café whose sign had fallen down years ago that everyone referred to as The Grub.

On the east side of the street stood the stately, three-story, brick Phillips County Courthouse; the fire station with its one engine; the police station with its attached but seldom occupied jail; the local bar that boasted a disreputable pool table; and Sweeties.

Sweeties was no bigger than a broom closet with three bar stools for sitting and a take-out counter in the rear. It looked like a hole in the wall but smelled like heaven. For a meager fifty cents an hour, five afternoons a week, Donna washed up the soda glasses, mixed up the malts and cut up whatever treats had been baked for the following morning.

Three churches served the spiritual needs of Holyoke. St. James Catholic Church with its beautiful red brick and white Gothic columns occupied an entire block just north of the high school. In a mostly protestant community, Catholics were viewed with guarded suspicion.

First Baptist Church, built of sensible brown brick but boasting a grand bell tower that could be seen from all over town, sat just west of downtown. The largest church in the city, it was regarded by most residents as *the* town church.

And lastly, First Church of the Nazarene, a modern, single-story building, relatively new to town was still in the trial stage as far as many of the townspeople were concerned. Ten years was hardly long enough for the residents to have made up their minds as to its doctrinal veracity.

Defining the south edge of the town was Holyoke Elementary School. A play yard and a couple of basketball hoops were all that separated it from the matching brick High School. Beyond those two buildings, flat prairie stretched as far as the eye could see.

The church was unlocked, as usual. Alice Mae laid her coat on the back pew, found the vacuum which seemed to relocate every week and began making order out of the clutter left in the wake of Sunday's service.

Accompanied by the roar of the old vacuum she sang. "I come to the garden alone, while the dew is still on the roses. And the voice I hear, falling on my ear …" She was alone in the handsome old building and her voice carried to the balcony. Praise and prayers filled the sanctuary.

"Alice Mae?" She jumped at the sound of her name.

Pastor Joe Lynch stood in the doorway silhouetted by the afternoon light. He was red haired, shorter than his wife by several inches and had freckles across his perpetually cheery face that would have made Tom Sawyer jealous. "I thought I heard you in here."

"Sorry. I didn't know anyone was here. Was I disturbing you?" She flushed

"On the contrary I was enjoying it."

He settled into one of the back pews, stretched his arms across the top and surveyed the room with its simple stained glass windows.

The comfortable building was a good fifty years old with wood floors that creaked when the congregation rose and squawked when they sat. No one quietly slipped out during his messages. No, indeed.

"I can't help myself. I get busy cleaning and thinking and the songs just spill out. My mother always sang them when she worked. She would be outside feeding the chickens or washing or weeding the garden and she'd sing."

His freckles danced when he smiled. He unbuttoned his jacket and exhaled slowly, relaxing into the afternoon calm. "What else do you remember about her?"

Alice Mae considered the question. Setting her rags and supplies on a pew, she kneeled on the bench and pushed the hair off her face. "She was fragile. She was beautiful. 'Course everyone thinks their mom was beautiful, I guess. She knew what was important and she wouldn't let anything or anyone stop her from getting it."

People that had known her mother said Alice Mae was just like her. She wasn't so sure.

"Beautiful? I'm not sure I could call *my* mother beautiful. Striking perhaps." He appraised his friend. "What did she think was important?"

"Her faith and getting her kids an education."

"Was that a challenge for her? Did she want you to go to college?"

"She wanted me to go to high school." Her gaze went distant, filling with memories.

He waited, but she did not elaborate.

Alice Mae had finished high school. He knew it. He sat in agreeable silence, but the story behind the comment was not forthcoming. Another day perhaps.

Pushing off he said, "Ruth is expecting me for dinner so I'm out of here." The smile on his face was broad and warm. "It's looking good in here as always."

4   Daughters

Masyl Sherwood was just finishing up the supper dishes. With six girls in the family, one might think that she would have help with the clean up but tonight she was alone. Again.

From her kitchen window overlooking the Circle C Ranch, she could see her husband of nearly twenty years tearing across the pasture, herding cattle. A billowing cloud of dust nearly obscured his red pickup but it marked his location. Masyl asked Chuck repeatedly not to drive so fast over the rough range, but he ignored her protests. He mostly ignored her period. Tracy and Sue rode horseback chasing stragglers, two border collies at their heels.

The black rotary phone on the buffet jingled just as Masyl slid the last of the pans into the sink full of soapy water. She wiped her hands and reached for the receiver.

Her distinct ring on the telephone party line was one long and two short bursts. Rural Phillips County had been among the last parts of the country to get phone service and in her opinion it worked just fine. She saw no reason to have one of the dedicated lines that were being offered. How often could one family use the phone anyway?

"This is Masyl," she barked into the handset, louder than she intended.

"Hi Mom," an exuberant Barbara Rae gushed. Tall like her father and blonde like her mother, the seventeen year old turned the heads of most every young man in the county, but there were few who could keep up with her. "Dave wants to take me to a movie. Could you have Jeanie cover for me tonight? Please."

"Where are you going and what are you going to see?" Masyl hadn't been to a movie in years. The television in her front room brought the world to her and after putting in long days, she had no interest in venturing further.

"We're going into Wray. It's a new John Wayne. *The Man Who Shot Liberty Valance.*"

Masyl at least knew who John Wayne was. Everyone knew the Duke. "Okay. Going with anyone else?" She asked, hopeful.

"Not this time. We just want to get away for awhile."

Both kids came from large families. With five sisters and living on a demanding ranch, Barbara rarely got to carve out time alone, especially with her boyfriend.

Dave's father, Clay Riggins, pushed his boys hard, like hired help. Maybe harder. They were up at the crack of dawn to start the milking and worked late into the night – riding the range, herding cattle, bucking bales of hay and branding. He was a nice enough kid, but Masyl worried that he would turn out just as hard and mean as his old man. Like her old man.

"Be careful and let me know when you get in."

"I will. Tell Jeanie that I'll cover her milking in the morning."

⸻

After rinsing the last pot and setting it on the counter to dry, Masyl meandered out into the solitude of her garden. The sun was low in the western sky, but dusk had not yet stolen the last of the light.

Picking up her hoe, she prodded the soil. The sandy loam yielded readily to her experienced touch and the weeds, roots and all came out and were tossed aside like chicken feathers from a hen. Like her sister Alice Mae, Masyl often prayed while she worked. She prayed for strength and endurance. Hers was a difficult life. She prayed for her girls. They were growing up too fast. She prayed, but she wasn't at all sure that anyone was listening or cared.

5 Got It

"I got it!" The screen door slammed. "Mom, I got on!"

Alice Mae looked up from where she was peeling potatoes.

"Got what?"

"Cheerleader! Oh Mom, I can't believe it, but I made varsity squad!" Sharon spun and laughed. "Yippee!" She whooped and dashed through the bedrooms looking for someone else to tell. "I'm going to need an outfit. I'll work for it. I'll do anything!"

She bounded out the back door in search of a sister. Any sister would do. Or a neighbor.

"Congratulations!" Alice Mae called after her daughter.

Sharon had been practicing for weeks. She could do the splits and land almost totally flat, she could kick higher than a Rockette wannabe and she could jump. How that girl could jump!

"What's the racket?" Richie sauntered out from his bedroom, book in hand. "Somebody hurt?" A lone boy in a family of women he had learned that keeping his head down, if not altogether out of the way, was the best way to survive.

"Just your sister. She made cheerleader and is a little excited."

He scrunched up his face, clearly disgusted with such a display over such a stupid accomplishment. "Is that all?"

The look she threw her son said he should not share his opinion with his sister.

"What are you reading?"

"Where the Red Fern Grows. Mrs. Baxter said I'd like it. It's neat!"

"Is it?"

"So far." He turned and ambled back into the back room, to the peace and quiet of his bed. Sharing a room with his little sister was inconvenient but she was rarely there now that the weather was getting warmer. He closed the door tight. *Girls!*

"Wow!" She heard Laurie yell from the back yard. "That's great!"

Joyce popped her head through the back door and called, "We're all going over to see … someone." Laughter trailed the three girls as they headed out to spread the good news.

Alice Mae blinked hard. What would the girls think when she told them that by the time school started, they would no longer live in Holyoke. A shard of panic lodged in her throat. Could she do that to them?

She finished the potatoes and put them into cold water to keep them from browning while she finished her chores. She'd ask Joyce to fry them with some hamburger later. Joyce seemed to actually enjoy cooking. *No idea where she got that.* Being only eleven, she wasn't quite old enough to babysit and she didn't have any social activities yet that took her time. *Social activities. What a strange term,* Alice Mae mused. *Did towns the size of Holyoke have social activities?* Anyway, Joyce was happy to cook and clean and be her mother's little helper. What a blessing. What a joy.

A decade earlier when Alice Mae learned she was pregnant, again, she felt such deep desperation. She had pleaded with God to be spared the burden of a fifth child. She had wept. She had begged. She would have traded her soul to be spared another child had she known how.

She had been only twenty-seven. Laurie had been such a difficult delivery that the doctor had warned her not to have more. Fitting her with the diaphragm and showing her how to use it had been of little value when Gene came home and wanted her. His drunken demands did not allow for the pause needed to secure the birth control. He had no patience for her needs nor memories of his actions. He smashed it out of her hand and ground it into the dirt floor of the shack they lived in before dragging her out of the house into the field and taking his husbandly rights. She had been desperate when she conceived Richie, but nothing like the out of her mind panic that overtook her when she discovered she was expecting a fifth baby.

Now she recognized her little brown haired girl with huge brown eyes as a one of her greatest gifts from God. She thanked him daily and prayed forgiveness for her shortsightedness and lack of faith. She prayed He would forgive her for the anger and bitterness that still resurfaced when she thought back to those days. She could not forgive herself.

———◆◆———

Show me where. It was her first prayer every morning these days. She was convinced that finding a destination was the first step.

During her prayer time and her bible reading which she did faithfully every morning, she had come across several references to the myrtle tree. A passage from Isaiah chapter 55 stuck in her mind. It said, *"For you shall go out with joy, and be led out with peace. The mountains and the hills shall break forth into singing before you. And all the trees of the field shall clap their hands. Instead of the thorn shall come up the cypress tree and instead of the brier shall come up the myrtle tree. And it shall be to the Lord for a name."* She liked the imagery and the promise of it. The myrtle tree: what an odd thing to stick in her mind, but stick it did.

"Oregon." She said it out loud. That was where myrtle trees grew. "Oregon?" She had never even been further west that Sterling.

Oregon was what, twelve hundred miles, maybe more? What else was there? That was the Wild West, right? Were there still Indians? Her mind spun with more questions than answers.

6   In the Wings

On Sunday the sun was high in a cloudless sky and growing hotter by the hour. Stained glass windows on the east side of First Baptist allowed the morning light to flood the sanctuary making it glow with color and warmth. Throughout the gathering, paper fans bearing the advertising note *Courtesy of Shunamakers Hardware* fluttered in the hands of the parishioners.

The pews in the center of the sanctuary faced forward, but the side wings of the church had pews set at ninety degrees that faced the center. They not only gave attendees a good view of Pastor Lynch while he delivered his sermon but also afforded a perfect view of all the congregants sitting in the center.

The wing was where Elvira Davis and ten-year-old Benny liked to sit. From there they didn't miss a thing.

Marsha Culver, for example, had dyed her hair and it was altogether too dark for her age. At fifty, she had a few flecks of naturally occurring gray but instead of wearing them with dignity, she had covered them with something akin to coffee brown.

Elvira scanned the congregation till her eyes rested on Ruth Lynch. Oh, my. Ruth's dress was bright. Most everyone Elvira talked to, and that was a lot of people, thought the pastor's wife should be more restrained. Worse yet, Ruth's bright pink dress made Elvira's pastel suit look downright insipid.

Cindy Jesmenek was reading something during the sermon and it did not look like the bible. Clearly there was a paperback tucked inside the black binding on her lap.

Benny swung his feet. Bored with the service and anxious to be dismissed, he wanted first go at the cookies laid out in the narthex. He checked them out on his way into the service and knew that some of them were chocolate chip, his favorite. With the edge of his paper fan, he scratched at a bug bite while he watched Joyce Wheaton.

Her head was resting against her mother's arm and she was listening, attentively, to the pastor. She was so pretty. After church, he would show her the marbles in his pocket.

When the last notes of the final hymn faded away, Benny and Elvira were the first ones out of the sanctuary and to the refreshment table. They each snatched several cookies and parted ways.

"Joyce," Benny found her in the gathering. "Want to see my cat's eyes?" His voice was whiny even when he was in a good mood. His dirty blonde hair stuck out in several places and the bug bite he had scratched flamed.

She ignored him. A year younger and four inches shorter than her, she found him annoying.

"I'll give you one of 'em if you want." He held forth the orbs for her to admire.

"No, thanks." She turned away.

"You can have the big one if you want." The large one was his prize possession. He had been carrying it around for weeks feeling rich and important just for having it in his pocket.

She didn't look back.

Disgusted with her apparent lack of understanding of the value of what he had, he grabbed two more cookies, stuffed them into his mouth and went outside to shoot his marbles on the steps. *Girls!*

"Alice Mae. Yoo-hoo." Elvira zigzagged her way through the gathering to where her friend was visiting with Ruth Lynch and Marsha Culver. "Wasn't that just the best message? Ruth, that husband of yours certainly knows just what I need to hear."

Pastor Joe had preached from the third chapter of James and had admonished the body to watch their tongues. It was one of his favorite topics.

"Sometimes it just gets away from me and I certainly needed to be reminded." Stepping into the middle of the gathering she continued her greetings. "Oh my, Marsha, don't you look bright and fresh as spring. Love your hair! Alice Mae, how lovely your girls looked this morning. Ruth, love the pink dress. It's so cheery. Well, I'm off. I'm taking Benny to the Dairy King for lunch. I promised him that if he sat through church without throwing anything that we would go. He's just such an active boy!"

And she was gone. The gathering breathed a collective sigh of relief.

Duly admonished by the sermon, the women withheld comment.

7 Send

"I did it." She confided in Ruth as they paused in the aisle of the Piggly Wiggly.

"Good for you. You did what?"

"I sent out college inquiries. Sharon's going to have to apply next year if she is going to get in. I still don't know what to do about Donna." A worried furrow creased her face fleetingly but then she recovered and smiled.

"Wow." Genuine admiration resonated. "Good for you. Where are you looking? Sterling? Denver? Colorado Springs?"

Alice Mae winced at Ruth's lack of vision. "No, I sent for information on Christian colleges farther away."

"Farther? Like Nebraska?" Her eyebrows rose.

With a flourish, Alice Mae announced. "I sent them to colleges all over the country."

It had taken hours of reading and searching, but the results had been worth it. In the end, Alice Mae concluded that her kids not only needed a good education, but it needed to be Christian based. A private Christian college. Once she had made that decision, she felt at peace.

Seven letters had been written to seven colleges. One was in Missouri. One was in North Carolina. One was in Texas. Four were in Oregon. She truly believed that Oregon was her destination but wanted confirmation. Like Gideon in the bible, she considered her letters to be her fleece before the Lord.

Without a car or money, one college seemed as improbable as another so she wrote what was on her heart. After licking the stamps, she said a quick prayer over the envelopes and watched them disappear through the post office slot.

"But how will you get there?"

"Don't have the faintest idea but if God wants us to go there, He'll have to figure it out."

8   Girls

Alice Mae shook her head. "If you want to wear your yellow dress, you'll have to press it yourself."

Sharon put the dress back in her closet and retrieved a blue one that did not require ironing.

It seemed like every client wanted Easter dresses and shirts starched and pressed, not to mention miles of tablecloths ironed. Alice Mae's back hurt. Her neck was stiff from bending over the board. She needed the money, it was what made ends meet, but the work was hard.

"Why don't you see if the green one with the daisies you wore last year still fits? If not, see if it could be hemmed for Joyce. Maybe Donna has something you can use."

For five long months, summer dresses had been pushed to the back of their tiny closet, hidden behind winter skirts and sweaters. Items previously hidden from view were now strewn across the bed in untidy piles. Each piece was being examined to see what still fit, what could be altered and what needed to go to the rag bag.

"Blast!" Laurie shook out a blue print dress with a full skirt that she had worn last summer and found a stain. She held it up to see if the discolored spot fell into an area that wouldn't be noticed and shook her head. "I loved this dress."

"We can soak it and see if it'll come out." Sharon offered and then she looked at the dress again. "Hey, that was mine anyway." She snatched the dress and held it up again in case Laurie's assessment of the flaw was in error. Ink. Impossible. She tossed it onto a pile of scrap to be given to their Aunt Masyl.

Masyl took all the discarded clothes, ripped them apart and then cut them up for quilts. Beautiful quilts.

"When are you going to teach me how to quilt?" Joyce had asked one weekend when she was visiting the ranch.

"When I'm too old or blind to do it myself," Masyl answered, peering over the yards of fabric draped across her lap. "You have to be born with a knack for quilting. You got to have patience. Do you think you have it, girl?" Clearly it was a skill she was not anxious to share.

Barb, Jeanie, Tracy, Sue, and Grace all actively participated in the day to day running of the Circle C. They rode the range. They cleaned the barn. They milked the cows, separated the milk and drove the tractors. They were treated as the sons that Chuck always wanted and worked just as hard as if they were boys. They had neither the time nor inclination to cook and sew with Masyl.

When Joyce came to visit, however, she would sit in the kitchen and watch Masyl cook. She would hover nearby, silent as a mouse when Masyl retired to her quilting corner. She admired her Aunt's talents and wanted to learn everything Masyl could teach her.

And then there was Mary Charlene; Masyl's baby girl. Well, perhaps not a baby anymore; Mary Charlene was eight. Unlike her older sisters who were sun tanned with sun bleached hair, she was slight, raven haired and gentle. She had a sweet spirit and handled life with care.

She gathered the eggs and tended the kittens that multiplied in the barn each spring. She cuddled the puppies too young to earn their keep. When Chuck suggested that Mary Charlene come outside and help with the *real work*, the tongue lashing he got from his wife ended any further suggestions that the little girl follow in the callous-creating footprints of her older sisters.

Mary Charlene sang to her mother and picked flowers to put in mason jars on the window ledge. She was a breath of fresh air in a house that often resembled more of a bunk house than a home.

On Easter morning, Masyl's six girls and Alice Mae's four girls dressed in their Sunday best and, with Richie in tow, descended on the Baptist church en mass. The sanctuary was packed right up to the rafters including the rarely used balcony and the rustling of starched dresses, many which Alice Mae recognized as her work, could be heard when the congregation stood to start the service with all three verses of "The Old Rugged Cross." Men wore crisp, white long sleeves despite the warm weather and hats appeared on the heads of women who, for the other eleven months of the year, would not be caught in one.

Fresh flowers from local gardens filled the platform and bud vases graced the church window ledges adding a sweet fragrance to the air and a joyful spirit to the sanctuary.

At twelve o'clock on the nose, Joe Lynch pronounced his final "Amen" and with great rejoicing the congregation closed the service. "He arose. He arose. Hallelujah Christ arose." When the last notes faded, the brood of cousins spilled out into the April sun.

"Maesy," Masyl shouted at her sister. "Come on. The ham's gunna burn."

She had called her sister, Alice Mae, Maesy since childhood. Together they had grown up Masyl and Maesy. As different as night and day but sisters to the end.

"I've just got to grab the potato salad. Hold on."

"I told you not to bring anything," Masyl said meaning it. She had tasted Alice Mae's potato salad. "Just keep it. You can eat it all week."

"No, no. I got it." In three minutes flat the Wheaton gang had changed into play clothes and was scrambling into the red Chevy pickup. "All of you kids sit down and stay down," Alice Mae admonished as the younger children settled onto blanket covered bales of hay in the bed of the truck.

Masyl shook her head. *Town folks!* Barb, Donna, and Alice Mae, with her unwelcome bowl of salad, squeezed into the cab with Masyl and they headed six miles south to the Circle C.

Fried chicken, baked ham, rolls, coleslaw, and beans; it didn't get better than that. A feast fit for a king was prepared and Masyl hadn't even broken a sweat.

The Easter dinner was spread on a picnic table in the shade of a sprawling tree. The broad walnut branches that sheltered the house on hot summer days made an excellent climbing tree year round. Assorted chairs cluttered the lawn.

"Come and get it 'fore I slop it to the hogs," Masyl yelled using the jargon that she knew annoyed her kids.

"Mom. Really!" Barbara spat with disgust.

Masyl grinned broadly at her daughter. Sometimes the response was worth the effort.

"Smells great." Richie was first in line. Grabbing the top plate from the stack, he asked, "Do we have to pray?"

"Go ahead, Sis, Give it a good blessing."

Alice Mae did. She thanked the Lord for the food, for family, for his son and the promise of his coming again. To the annoyance of her hungry son, her sister, and all her nieces, she made sure to mention family members by name and to ask for safety as they played and worked.

"Amen."

"Amen" was the general outcry.

Richie dug in.

Chatter ceased as eating commenced. Plates laden with a food were settled on card tables, on knees and on quilts spread across the lawn. Everyone cleaned their plates and then went back for more.

As muted silence settled across the yard, Chuck ambled out of the barn. Tall and lean, with natural good looks and charm, qualities that had attracted Masyl to him when she was sixteen, he grinned at the family. "Happy Easter, Alice." He pecked his sister-in-law on the cheek. In his customary dirty overalls, his uniform of choice, he asked Donna about her work at Sweeties. He teased Sharon about boys, knowing most of them by name to the embarrassment of his niece. He admired the muscles Richie had developed on his paper route and chased Joyce, tickling her till she begged him to stop.

After performing his required uncle duties, he ate his lunch propped against the tree, muttered an excuse about checking something in the barn and ambled off again, leaving the family to relax and enjoy the day.

"That man!" Masyl said as if that clarified her thoughts on the subject.

"Yessiree." Her sister agreed.

"Want to see the new chicks?" Mary Charlene scrambled to her feet, grabbed Joyce by the hand. "They're so tiny and soft."

"Sure. Have you named them yet?"

"We can't name 'em but they're cute. Come on." The cousins disappeared around the corner of the house.

"Chuck calls 'em Dumplings and Stew Pot," Masyl laughed.

It felt good to relax for a few hours. The day was bright and warm with a bit of a breeze stirring in the west. Clouds were forming over the mountains, promising a spring shower that would roll through before night settled in. In time, the women wandered from the lawn to the large tilled area between the house and the rangeland.

Green plants poked through the earth behind a wire fence, Masyl's large spring garden was well underway. Tidy rows of new sprouts stretched for more than fifty feet. Well-used tools leaned up against the fence, ready to grab anytime Masyl had a few minutes to devote to the project. The produce from the garden would feed her family of eight most of the summer and well into fall.

"What've you got in so far?"

"Just put in tomatoes and bush beans last week." She pointed to the near corner of the large, cleared patch. "Corn hills are by the far fence. I'm trying to get the cukes and squash in before the calving starts." Masyl worked up a stone from the soil with the toe of her shoe and tossed it out of the tilled area.

"An impressive beginning." Alice Mae bent to the task of tugging up a weed.

"I got the potatoes in a couple of weeks ago and the carrots and peas are already up. Chuck wants to put in more melons this year."

"How about putting in some sunflowers for color?"

"And roses too if you had your way." She snorted. "I don't think so, Maesy, you can have your flowers. I don't have time for such nonsense. The squash blossoms from the garden will suit me just fine." She pulled a thistle and dropped it in place. "Besides, when the clover blooms and the wheat ripens, the fields will be full of color. Come on," she said heading back towards the house, "let's see if the kids left any dessert."

"But you could harvest and dry the sunflower seeds to eat later," Alice Mae argued, trailing her sister.

On saddled horses, the older girls sauntered down the long drive to the mailbox and judging from the voices and cheers, were having a wonderful time. They would be gone for an hour by the time they worked their way around the ranch, through the alfalfa field and across what they referred to as the south forty.

Richie, always hungry for a man's attention, went in search of Chuck in the barn and was no doubt being corrupted by bad language and tall tales, none of which would do him any harm in the long run. Alice Mae didn't even want to venture close for fear she would feel compelled to intervene. The boy would survive.

Sue and Grace lay sprawled in the yard, playing with the two border collies. Everyone was relaxed.

There was nothing left of Masyl's chocolate cake except for a ring of icing stuck to the plate, but there was still half an apple pie sitting on the table. Alice Mae cut a small piece for herself and a larger one for her sister. Settling back into one of the folding chairs, she tested the waters. "I'm thinking we might move again this summer."

Closing her eyes against the bright afternoon sun, Masyl sighed deeply. From years of working in the harsh Colorado weather, her skin looked like fine leather even this early in the spring. "We'll help, of course, just let us know. Whatever you do just don't ever move away." She reached over and took her sister's hand. "I don't know what I'd do without you."

9   Answers

The response came in the mail. It was large and white with her name hand written across the front and a return address from Oregon. Holding her breath, she sat down on the sofa and slowly pulled the cover letter from the envelope.

"Oh, Lord," she whispered before she began. *Is this your answer? Is this the confirmation I've been waiting for?* Although her mind asked the questions, her heart already knew the answer. After more than a month of waiting and watching, this was the only reply she had received. With great anticipation she read,

Dear Mrs. Wheaton,

We would be happy to work with you on a financial aid package for your daughter if her grades are as good as you indicated. We do have several programs that offer work study opportunities, as well as full scholarships for a limited number of students. We have an excellent financial aid staff that can help with academic scholarships, sports scholarships or private funding. We would be happy to talk with you and to answer any questions you may have.

We are strongly backed by and align ourselves with the American Baptist Church and feel our students benefit from their influence. Our students are required to regularly attend chapel in keeping with that affiliation.

I look forward to meeting you and showing you around our beautiful campus.

Sincerely,

T. L. Graves

Linfield College

Her spirit soared. The writing might as well have been on the wall. God was calling her to the land of the Myrtle tree, to the lushness of the Willamette Valley, to the town of McMinnville, to her promised land. She lifted her face to heaven. *Thank you for your answer. Bless you for your faithfulness.*

"McMinnville, Oregon." She spoke the words aloud and allowed herself to feel them on her tongue. "Linfield College." It sounded good and right.

She was amazed. She was relieved. She was sure that she had her destination. Now just a few more details needed to be worked out.

Dad, I wonder if you could drive to Colorado, pick us all up and move us to McMinnville, Oregon. It sounded like a good way to start the conversation except for the fact that every time she spoke with her father he reminded her of what a failure she was and what a disappointment she had been. Maybe she could make it sound more promising.

His philosophy was never ask for help, never give it. A self made man if ever there was one.

Dad, I got a letter from Linfield College in Oregon and they are interested in providing financial aid for the kids to attend there if I can get us there. Could you, please ... Not an outright lie but close. They had not been accepted and most of them were not anywhere near college age yet. Besides, she wasn't going to beg.

Dad, how would you like to take a little vacation and drive all the way from California to Colorado and then on your way back home, just drop us up in Oregon? Lame.

Okay, God. This is your doing. You told me to leave and now you've shown me where to go. Now it's up to you to figure out how to get us there. There. She left it totally in his hands and was not going to worry about it anymore.

God could certainly soften her father's heart. He had done bigger things than that. At the moment she could not think of any, but she knew he could do it. She was just going to have to trust him.

She would eventually have to physically call and talk to her dad about the move, but she was willing to put that off for another day.

Who else should she tell?

Ruth and Joe already knew. Betty at the library was suspicious. She had been back to the library studying maps and college catalogs several times and she knew that Betty was watching.

Family loyalty demanded that she talk with Masyl first.

"Hey, Sis." Background noises reminded Alice Mae that this was a party line, perhaps not as private as she would like.

"Hey, Maesy."

"Are you coming into town any time this week? I want to talk to you about an idea I have."

"No. With the wheat planting and getting the steers ready for sale, I doubt if I'll be in. What's up?"

"Oh, nothing much." Not entirely truthful. "I really don't want to talk to you about it over the phone. I'll just wait till I see you."

"What about graduation? We could talk there."

High School graduation was just ten days away. Donna was graduating with honors although she had declined giving the valedictorian address.

"I'd sooner die," she said, meaning it.

"Sure, that would work. I'll see you next Saturday." She hung up feeling relieved to have been given a reprieve.

10 Plans

"When are you leaving?" The last of the spring daffodils in the church flowerbeds had faded and Alice Mae and Ruth were cutting them back and tying the slender leaves into tidy knots. The afternoon temperature had been in the low eighties, so the women welcomed the shaded protection of a tall blue spruce that shadowed the north side of the building.

"Joe is scheduled to start just after Labor Day, so we're planning to move the last week of August." Ruth was as excited as a school girl. "We've wanted to live in Greeley for years. We love the area. They have good shopping and a theater and several good restaurants. It'll be fun, right?"

"It will be fun," Alice Mae assured her, "but it's going to be hard to go. You've been here a long time." She pulled some errant weeds and tossed them into a pail.

"We have but not as long as you. What's the word on your move?"

"Well, I know where we're going. It's a town called McMinnville in Oregon. There's a college there, a good one."

She looked for a reaction and saw interest.

"I'm going to tell Masyl next week. I'm hoping that my Dad will drive us there." She ducked her head and peeked up at her friend, knowing how this news would go over.

"Your dad? Horrible Henry?"

"Ruth!" She looked around to see if anyone else was within ear shot and laughed. "He's not that bad."

"Not that bad? Last time he was here he had you and half the congregation in tears. Even Joe had to pray for forgiveness after he left."

"He can be a bit difficult." Alice Mae moved and began weeding the east side where the deepening afternoon shade was cool. A few high clouds were moving in and a breeze was picking up.

Ruth scoffed and followed her around the bend and stood, hands on hips. "A bit? How are you planning to pull this off?"

"I'm not. I've given it all to the Lord and asked him to take care of it." She sat back on her heels and looked Ruth dead in the eye. "I believe he will do it. I'm claiming it and thanking God for it and expecting it." She blinked and gave her friend an inquisitive look. "Sounds good, doesn't it?"

"Sounds great." Ruth dropped to her knees and began pulling weeds. They worked in silence for a time. "What is Donna Mae going to do?"

The lack of response spoke for itself. Alice Mae was not yet ready to address that question. She didn't have the answer. Had she waited too long? *Lord, what is Donna going to do?* She asked him that question daily but had not yet received an answer.

"So, when are you and Joe going to tell the congregation that you're leaving?" Alice queried, steering the conversation in a different direction.

"Joe thinks that less time is better. He doesn't want to make an announcement till the beginning of August. He knows how much churches hate looking for new pastors. He doesn't want them to have enough time to talk us out of going."

"You know they will try."

"Truth be told, I'd be disappointed if they didn't," Ruth smirked.

They finished on the east side of the building and moved around to the south where bearded iris had pushed aside the spent daffodils creating a bed of rich purple against the brown brick. Working carefully, they trimmed the yellowing leaves without damaging the young new stalks. Late afternoon shadows gave way to a warm evening filled with birdsong. Crickets started their chorus early. The west glowed with the first hues of the setting sun over the Rockies.

"When are you planning to leave?" Ruth asked.

"Not sure, probably about the same time as you."

"Remember, Holyoke doesn't do change well."

"Don't I know it."

11   Objections

"Are you out of your ever lovin' mind?" Three years younger than Alice Mae, Masyl's voice was strident. "There is no way you can move across the country and just start over in some God forsaken place out west, Maesy. You don't know anything about Oregon. Just uproot your kids and leave all your relatives? No! No! No!" She shook with rage.

Heads turned in their direction. Embarrassed by the attention they drew, Alice Mae fled outside into the city park that bordered the school grounds. Masyl stormed after her.

"What is Barb going to do after she graduates?" Alice Mae rounded on her sister. "What future does she have here?"

"As a matter of fact she isn't going to finish school. She doesn't need to. She and Dave are planning an August wedding. He proposed last week and we said yes. One less mouth to feed."

Her heart sank. "No! She can't."

"They're going to move into the little house on his dad's land and settle down."

"Exactly!" She didn't care anymore who was listening. Let the whole town hear. "In five years she'll have half a dozen kids and work her fingers to the bone just like you."

"And what's wrong with that? She'll have her own place and I'll have grandkids. It'll be okay. It'll be good."

"And she'll be happy just like you are. Right?"

She saw the impact of the jab. In some ways Alice Mae had been the lucky one. Freed from her unhappy marriage by circumstances, she had a chance to create a new life, God willing. Married young, with six children in ten years, Masyl was just as trapped as Alice Mae. In some respects more. The pain reverberated like a slap.

"And if we stay here that is exactly what will happen to my girls. It's not what I want for them. It's not what Mom would have wanted for them."

"You leave Mom out of this." Masyl snapped. "She wanted better for you and look what happened. You did what you wanted. You didn't care what she wanted then, so now you care? Right! What do your kids think about this, huh? Have you told them yet? Do they want to go?"

Her jabs hit home. Alice Mae had asked herself those same questions repeatedly.

"I messed up and my dream died but now I'm going after another. I don't care what the kids think. We're moving to Oregon this summer and we're never coming back. Never!"

She hoped the sting of her words would hurt. She wanted them to wound. Where was her support? How about some encouragement or at least understanding? She turned and walked away from her sister, something she had never done before in her life.

"But it's not their dream. You can't do this to them." Her sister's voice followed her into the darkening night.

Alice Mae didn't look back. She bit her tongue. Hard.

Holyoke had very few streetlights, but enough light spilled onto the sidewalks and alleyways for her to make her way along the familiar streets. She needed time. She needed space.

Meandering past the square house that had been her mother's during the last years of her life, she felt the desperation of limited options. After her parents split up, her mother, Premilla, ran a small, two-room boarding house — never escaping this little town. It had eventually claimed her life.

A decade later, Alice Mae still felt the loss.

Alice Mae walked past the hospital where she had given birth to her children. The one doctor on duty during three of her deliveries was not very skilled; she had almost lost Laurie. He was still only doctor in town and well past his prime.

Willing her anger to dissipate, she sauntered through the courthouse square and down Main Street, stopping to look in store windows. What kind of stores might there be in Oregon? What new adventures? Would she find friends? Could she do this alone?

The night was still and warm. Frogs croaked from the expanse of the courthouse lawn. When she paused, she heard water spilling over the rocks in Frenchman Creek just two blocks to the east. It was a comforting sound. So familiar.

Cars passed her on the street as graduation revelers scattered. Some threw up their hands as they passed. She smiled and raised hers in return. No matter who it was, in Holyoke everyone was a neighbor.

Lord, she breathed his name as she walked. *I have so many questions for you and not enough answers. What do I do about Masyl? If I leave,* she amended her prayer, *when I leave, who will be here for her? Please help her understand that this is not only what I want but that it is what you have asked me to do. Don't let this thing break our relationship. Guide me through this challenging and exciting journey. You have promised that I can do all things through you, who strengthens me. I'm going to need that strength.*

She straightened her back and set her shoulders square. She picked up her pace and turned toward home. Aunt Ferggie had driven all the way from Kansas to deliver the message that was already on Alice Mae's heart. It reverberated with truth. She was leaving town and was doing it within the next three months. When the kids began the new school year, they would be in McMinnville. Period.

12   No

Telling Masyl at graduation had not, perhaps, been a well thought out plan. That was confirmed the minute she walked through the front door of her little house.

"I'm not going!" Sharon announced, her pony tail swinging with the petulant shake of her head. Her eyes were hot and swollen. "Aunt Masyl says you're nuts and cruel to leave her. She says I can come live with her if I want. Barbs moving out. You can go without me." Pausing long enough to draw another breath, she continued her tirade. "How could you even think of such a thing? I am not leaving my school and my friends and the squad. Oh, mother!" She stomped off to her bedroom where Laurie stood framed in the doorway, eyes wide with alarm. The slamming door rattled the windows.

Alice Mae considered turning and walking back into the night.

Richie was sprawled on the sofa watching the storm and looking calm by contrast. The idea of moving across the country to Oregon – wherever that was – sounded like fun.

"Are we really doing what she said? Are we going to get a car?" he asked in anticipation of what sounded like a really big adventure.

"Not now," she begged, heading to the kitchen to tidy up before turning in. "We'll talk about it tomorrow."

He followed. "Can I get a dog? Is Sharon really going to stay? Can I have a room to myself? If we're going to Oregon, can we go to the World's Fair? I want to see the space needle. How far is Seattle from where we're going?" The inquiries shot like pellets from a gun as he shadowed her.

Taking him firmly by the shoulder, she turned him around and maneuvered him into his own room and after turning out the light, closed the door with considerably more control than she felt. "Stay!"

After finishing the kitchen, Alice Mae settled herself into an easy chair, hugged a pillow and mulled the fallout of her not so private conversation with Masyl.

"Richie. Come back in here!"

Reaching for the bundle of newspapers on the sofa cushions. She broke the string and began rolling the Sunday edition of the Holyoke Register.

He reappeared.

"You." She grabbed the rubber bands. "Help me with these. The only place you're going tomorrow is on your paper run."

For twenty minutes, the only sound in the room was the rustling of paper and the snapping of elastic bands. The smell of fresh ink anointed their task. Every time he opened his mouth to speak she gave him a look that plainly said *don't*.

The deal they had was that she would help roll the papers and pack his bag for the larger Sunday edition and then she would get him up at five in the morning to deliver them. On Tuesday nights, he was on his own. After the last roll was stuffed into his bike bag, he could stand the silence no longer.

"Can I quit the paper route?" There was anticipation in his eyes.

"Not tomorrow."

She brushed the hair out of his eyes and gave him a gentle nudge in the direction of his room. "Goodnight."

"Night."

She closed her eyes, exhaustion sweeping over her. *"Oh Lord, this is not the way it was supposed to go. Now what do I do?"* How dare her sister just blab it out like that? She could feel the heat in her cheeks and the stinging behind her eyes.

"You are not staying with Masyl," she called loud enough to be heard in the next room. "And you are not staying in Holyoke. And you are not marrying anyone from Holyoke. Or Wray. Or Haxtun," she added to the list. "And you are not going to yell at me."

The final announcement might have been more compelling had she not made at such a high volume, but she stood by it just the same.

In response, the bedroom door opened and slammed again.

"Where's Joyce?" She opened the door to the room shared by her youngest daughter and Richie and surveyed the girl's empty bed.

"I don't know," he shrugged. "She was here and then Sharon came home all mad and yelling." He shrugged again, "Don't know."

Alice Mae found her youngest daughter curled cozily in her own bed which out of necessity she shared with Donna. Still wearing her clothes from the afternoon, hers was the sleep of innocence – relaxed and at peace. Wrapped in her arms was a yellow long-haired kitten of unknown origin. Oh well.

Nudging both child and cat over and stretching out beside them she wrapped her arms around her sleeping girl. Donna could sleep in Joyce's bed or crowd in with the two of them when she came home from the post-graduation celebration. Alice Mae didn't care.

She settled in for what she hoped would be a good long night's sleep. She hoped and prayed that by morning things would settle down.

She should have prayed harder.

13 Gossip

Sunday morning broke warm and bright. By five-thirty, Richie was on his paper route, burning up energy and earning his two bucks.

It was a good job for a boy his age. Besides the money, it gave him a feeling of contributing to his family. He kept half for himself to buy an occasional comic book or a candy bar, and gave the rest to his mother. It helped.

Donna, tucked into Joyce's bed, didn't stir when Alice Mae came in to wake Richie. The graduation celebration must have gone late. Good. She pulled the quilt up over the sleeping girl.

Alice Mae sat down at the kitchen table with her worn bible and her equally worn volume of Streams in the Desert, her two most cherished books. The myrtle tree passage was marked and she read it again. Then she turned to the 37th Psalm and began reading aloud as she often did. She liked hearing the words. "Trust in the Lord and do good: Dwell in the land and feed on His faithfulness. Delight yourself in the Lord, and He shall give you the desires of your heart. Commit your way to the Lord, trust also in him, and He shall bring it to pass." *Lord*, she prayed, *I do trust you. I believe you will bring this thing to pass.*

At six-thirty, Richie came home hungry. After tossing his coat onto his bed, he headed to the kitchen. "I'm starved."

Alice Mae nodded to the counter where the toaster was already heating up his homemade bread. "Help yourself."

He inhaled two thick pieces of toast without coming up for air.

"The Sheridans got a new car. It's red and really neat," he announced, his mouth stuffed with a huge bite.

He made another piece of toast and slathered it liberally with cinnamon sugar.

"And John Jessop's dog is missing. He asked me to keep an eye out for it."

"Good, maybe you can ride around and look for it after church." Her son kept her apprised of the town news better than the Register. "Do you have any idea where the kitten came from?"

He looked at her. "What kitten?"

"Never mind." Stray cats came and went. This one would too, but she hoped not too quickly. It was a snuggly little thing. She liked it and she didn't usually like cats.

She flipped an egg over the way he liked them. Not too hard, not too runny. Lots of pepper. She scooted it onto a plate and set it in front of her boy. It didn't even have time to cool before vanishing.

"Can I go over to Jake's this afternoon? He has a new bike and said maybe I could have his old one. It's better than mine. It has a bigger basket and it's blue." He pushed back from the table, sated.

She ruffled his hair. "Sure."

He headed for the bedroom. "By the way, Mr. Fleming said he was happy for us. He said you would know what that means." Paul Fleming, the basketball coach and history teacher, was married to Patsy, a one woman town grapevine. They must have heard the exchange at graduation last night. *Lord, this is not good.*

Having done his duty with the papers and filled his stomach, Richie crawled back into his bed for a few more minutes of shut-eye and pulled the blanket up around his ears.

At eight, Joyce staggered out of the bedroom, her hair tangled and her clothes wrinkled. She yawned hugely still holding the kitten.

"Can I have one of those?" she asked eyeing a stack of toast.

"Help yourself."

By nine, the older three girls had emerged from their respective beds, eaten and departed for Sunday school. Nothing was said. Nobody asked any questions. No one made any grand announcements.

The hostility exhibited the night before seemingly passed; Alice Mae decided to give them time to process the news. That was only fair. It had come as a shock. But she would have to talk with them soon. She would need to explain the plan.

Ruth was the first one to mention it. Immediately after the service she rushed over to Alice Mae. In her dress as orange as a California poppy, every eye followed her as she went.

"Well, the rumor mill has begun," she whispered. "They've got you running off to meet up with a man or leaving your kids with Masyl and moving alone. Which one is it?"

Alice Mae gasped, horrified.

Ruth drew her aside, amused. "I thought you weren't going to tell anyone yet."

"Oh no. I didn't. Well, that is I only told Masyl."

Elvira Davis and Patsy Fleming huddled in the corner of the narthex talking among themselves, with knowing glances directed at Alice Mae.

"When did you tell her? I haven't heard this much gossip since Mary Shane came back from Ogallala with her baby." Ruth was enjoying this.

"I just told her last night after the high school graduation. It was the first time I've had a chance to see her face to face and I didn't want to tell her over the phone."

"Who else was around?"

"I don't know. We were standing in the gym having some punch and there were some people around, but I didn't notice exactly who." Who had been there? Half the town?

"How'd she take it?"

"Not well." Alice Mae shook her head and looked away. There was a pit in her stomach the size of a lemon. And growing.

"How not well?"

"You know my sister. Apparently she stormed over and told her kids about my 'foolishness' as she put it. Sharon and Laurie were standing there and they heard. Let me tell you, by the time I got home last night all hell had broken loose."

Ruth's laughter was rich and loud. "That would explain a lot."

"Like what?"

"Well, I noticed your girls didn't sit with you this morning."

"They sat with friends."

"And they bolted right after the last song."

"It's a lovely day. They just wanted to get home."

"Yeah." Ruth was no fool. "Look Alice Mae, you better tell people something.

"Tell them what?" The pit in her stomach was now the size of a grapefruit. "I still don't know exactly what I'm doing."

"You better tell them something before they have you married off and living in California."

"But …" She was speechless.

Her friend nudged her shoulder smiling. "At least your news will distract them and they won't notice when we start to pack up over at the parsonage. Thanks!"

"You're welcome." At last she relaxed and let herself laugh. "It's my pleasure."

14   The Call

"Grandpa called." Laurie did not elaborate.

A reserved girl with a good heart, she reminded Alice Mae more of herself than any of the others. Smart, but not a show off like her older sister. Willing to work but not as eager as her brother. She was an anchor in the storm.

Last night's news was still settling in her. She would talk about it when she was ready. More than anything, Alice Mae guessed that she was hurt that she had not heard it from her mother. That made two of them.

"When? Did you talk to him?"

"About half an hour ago. He just wanted to speak to you. He didn't sound happy." If she was not mistaken, there was a smirk on her daughter's face.

"Does he want me to call him back or will he call again?" The rates were cheap on Sunday.

"Didn't ask." The bedroom door closed quietly.

"What do you think Grandpa wants?" Still wearing her church Sunday dress, Joyce bounded into the kitchen where her mother was making gravy to go with some left over potatoes from the night before. With an apron protecting what was one of the few good dresses she owned, Alice Mae broke hamburger into bits and added salt and pepper.

"I guess we'll find out." Stirring the flour into the browned meat, she studied her daughter and tried to sound casual. "What did Sharon say when she came home from graduation last night? Did she tell you what was going on?"

"Not really. She said she was going to move in with Aunt Masyl. Mostly she was yelling at Laurie. Why was she mad at Laurie? If she does, can I move into her room?" There was a hopeful spark.

"No. Sharon is not going to stay with Masyl. She was just upset by something she heard."

"Like what?" The girl absently braided a small section of her shoulder length hair.

"Well, I think we might move again. What would you think of that?"

The family had moved frequently over the years. Almost every school year started from a different house except this last home. There had been the house two miles north of town where they had no car. That was where they were living when Gene walked away. That had been a challenge.

There had been the house across from the courthouse that wasn't really a house at all, but a basement with a temporary roof that would eventually be a house for someone else. They had been there only about six months. And then there was an upstairs apartment, the home next to the volunteer fireman who ran over several of their stray cats. The list was long.

They had been in the little white house for two years. It felt like theirs. Of course it was not; it was a rental just like every home they had been in, but it felt like home.

The kids embraced the challenge of setting up in new rooms. Their belongings were few so the moves were not complicated and in a small town like Holyoke, addresses didn't matter much. Everyone knew everyone so mail still got delivered and friends knew how to find friends.

"Is that all?" Joyce let go of her hair and began pulling dishes out of the cupboard and setting the table for lunch. "You think Grandpa's going to come see us? Think he'll buy us orange juice?"

Orange juice was a luxury outside of the family budget. Alice Mae was lucky to keep milk around. Frequently the Sunday night special dinner was nothing more than milk on popcorn or milk on bread with sugar. The kids thought it was a treat.

When Grandpa came, he insisted on things like bacon to go with eggs and orange juice not to mention coffee which only he drank. He bought fresh vegetables and donuts. Sometimes he bought steak.

The sojourns tended to last four or five days on the average. He stocked the cupboards just long enough for his visit and not a day beyond, but the kids benefitted from the bounty, temporary as it was.

Upon arrival, he always handed a two dollar bill to each of his grandchildren – Alice Mae's and Masyl's alike. He gave it to each of them with a smile and a flourish and then he was annoyed when they spent the bills, thinking they should save them. A two dollar bill in the hands of children who rarely saw two bits was like winning the lottery. Save? Not a chance.

"Could be. We'll see." Her heart skipped thinking about the phone call. "Do you know where Oregon is?" she tried to sound casual.

"Sure. We studied it in class. It's by the ocean."

"Think you'd ever like to go there?"

"Okay." That was it. No drama. No inquisition. Oh, how she loved this child. She reached over and pulled her daughter into a bear hug.

Joyce hugged her back and giggled. "What was that for?"

"Just for being you."

The call came at two that afternoon. For a moment she considered not answering.

"Hi, Dad." She tried to sound upbeat. "How are you?" Leaning against the kitchen wall, she put a smile on her face even though there was a tempest in her stomach.

"Well enough." His tone was measured.

"Good." She waited.

"Alice Mae? Why the blazes are you want'n to move half way across the country?" Her father didn't believe in small talk. He did not sound happy but, on the other hand, he did not sound as upset as she had expected. It was an open question waiting for an honest answer.

"I'm guessing from your question that you talked to Masyl. What exactly did she tell you?"

"Doesn't matter what she said." There was steel in his voice. "She was carrying on like she always does. Bellyaching about this and moanin' about that. Couldn't make out half of it. Why don't you just tell me what the heck you think you're doing, Oregon?" His voice boomed. She could have heard him without the receiver being an inch from her ear.

Lord, help me. "I want to leave Holyoke, Dad. I can't stay here anymore. There is nothing for us here. I want the kids to have a chance to go to college and they can't get that if we stay here." There it was. Simple and clear. She didn't mention Gene and the brothers being in the area, knowing that would start a whole different conversation that she did not want to have.

"But why Oregon? You got it in your fool head that you got to move half way across the country to find a college for those kids of yours? Aren't there any colleges in Colorado?"

She forged ahead. "I've prayed about it." She knew that carried little weight. The man who had been through six wives had his share of emotional scars. He didn't put stock in prayer. Hadn't she seen that growing up?

"I've read up on it and sent out letters and there is a college in Oregon that has answered me and I believe it is where I want them to go." That said it all.

He harrumphed, cleared his throat and harrumphed again.

She waited. The first one to break the silence loses; isn't that what he had taught her?

He growled.

She waited. She won.

"What's the name of the town? What's the college?" A fair question.

"The town is McMinn …" She was interrupted.

"Will they let the kids go for free or are you expecting me to pay for it?" He bellowed. Now that sounded more like the father she had grown up with. She couldn't help but smile.

"No, Dad, I don't want you to pay for it. I wouldn't let you even if you wanted to. This is something I need to do for my own kids. The school is called Linfield College. It's a small Baptist college in McMinnville, Oregon."

"Baptist! It figures," he muttered with a measure of contempt.

She pushed the hair out of her face and realized she was shaking. "I really believe that if I can get the family to McMinnville, that I can find a way to get them into college. It's important to me. It was important to Mom."

Almost twenty years had passed since her mother had gone to battle with her father for the right for Alice Mae to attend high school.

Every fall for four years he said, "No. I need her on the farm. She needs to pull her own weight. It's a waste of time and money to let her to go off to school every day and just sit around when she could be helping feed the livestock and run the tractor."

Every year her mother stood toe to toe with him and said yes, Alice Mae was going. She had seen fear in her mother and she had seen iron. In the end, her mom won the battle but lost the war, or in her case the marriage.

On the very day that Alice Mae graduated from high school, her mother gave her the same message that Ferggie had delivered to her just weeks before. You need to leave. You need to get out of here. You need to go now.

Fleeing the grasp of her father, she walked two miles to town and found work with a family cleaning and watching their children, believing that somehow she would earn enough money to leave Holyoke and go to college somewhere. Then she met Gene.

"You sound like your mother." It wasn't a compliment.

"You've mentioned that before." Her chest expanded at the rebuke.

"Where are you going to live? How are you going to find a house?"

"I don't know yet. I was thinking of asking you to drive up to McMinnville and see what you could find for us. It should be lovely this time of year."

"Sacramento's just fine this time of year. I'm in no need to see the country. Seen plenty of it." She could hear something in his voice, a curiosity perhaps. "Where exactly is this place, do you even know? Is it big enough that you could likely find a decent job for a change?"

"It's a little north of Salem if you know where that is."

"Of course I know where that is." He was trying to sound gruff again and doing well.

"I've been reading about it. It's in the Willamette Valley and there are lots of crops that can be picked in the summer …"

His tirade started before she could finish her sentence. "If you want to work on a farm you can stay in Holyoke. You've already worked half the farms in the county. If you think I'm going to move you half way across the country so you can do it there you're a fool."

She kept her voice calm. "No, Dad, I don't want to pick crops but it might give the kids a chance to earn money and they don't even have that here. The articles I've been reading say buses of kids from town go out into the strawberry fields and the bean fields and the kids can earn some good money. Not just farm workers but city kids and…"

"That may be but what about you?" She closed her eyes. She could picture him. Unshaven. Wearing a flannel shirt and drinking coffee. Scowling.

"I've been working on that too." She didn't elaborate. "How about it? Would you go check it out for me?"

"Well, I can't have you coming to the west coast without a place to stay. First thing you know I'd find you on my doorstep with all those six kids." She didn't correct him.

He muttered a bit to himself or to his wife, it was hard to tell. "I guess I could make a few inquiries and see what's what. I'm not making any promises. Darn long way to Oregon and with the price of gas." He harrumphed a bit more, made a few unkind comments about her, her mother, women in general, and disconnected.

15   Howard

Howard Howland spent far too many hours in his office. He cared too much about his clients for his own good and his wife reminded him of it regularly. He was a stout man in his late forties with thinning hair and a soft belly. He wore wire rimmed glasses which amplified his gray eyes and had four boys who looked just like him. Peas in a pod.

Alice Mae was one of his favorites. Social workers aren't supposed to have favorites, he knew, but he admired the way her children were clean and bright and an asset to their little town. Not all of the families he managed fared as well.

His spirits always lifted when she walked through his door and today was no exception. A grin split his face when she came in and then vanished when she told him her plan.

"Oregon? Why Oregon?" Everyone asked her the same question.

"I believe it's where I'm supposed to go." It was becoming her stock answer. Sitting in front of his worn walnut desk, in the room that had been a haven for many years, she explained about the town and the college and the letter that encouraged her. Moisture glistened in her eyes as she described the heartache she felt at the idea of her girls being predestined to her same impoverished existence.

He listened intently.

"I've made so many mistakes. I don't want them to make the same ones." Her heart was on her sleeve by the time she finished talking "I need to do this, Howard. Help me."

He nodded. "I think it shows remarkable foresight. It will be our loss."

"So how do I get financial aid? I don't want to stay on it, but I'll need it to get established. I plan to find work just as soon as we get settled, but it may take time."

"In Oregon? I'm not sure. Every state is different."

"Can you put me in touch with someone there who could help?"

"Alice Mae." He didn't want to say it. He took off his glasses and scratched his head. "My jurisdiction is limited to this county, to the state of Colorado at the very most."

Her hand went to her throat and then ran around her neck. "Don't you have, I don't know, some kind of counterpart in Yamhill County?"

From the shelf to the left of his desk he pulled out a heavy volume. Returning the glasses to his eyes he began searching for the section on moving, transferring jurisdiction and every reference he could think of that applied. The large wall clock ticked as he flipped pages. "Aid to Dependent Children funds are federal but they're administered at the county level. Every state is different, even every county."

"Then how do I …?" She leaned forward and pulled her sweater closer. She inhaled, fighting the sting in her nose and blinking away the dampness that threatened her eyes. She would not cry. She would not panic. Not yet.

His fingers trailed across the page as he read. "There is a waiting period while you establish residency." He poured through the section looking for an exception, a loophole, something to offer her. "You can't just move one day and walk in the next day and expect them to start giving you money. You'll have to look for work, show them rent or utility receipts, prove that you are serious about living there. It could take a couple of months."

She paled.

"Do you have any idea what work you might want to do? Any leads at all on a job there?"

"Not exactly. Being a bigger town, I'm hoping there are more opportunities than here. There can't be any fewer."

He snorted. "Probably not."

"I'm hoping to find a job at the college. If I can get on there, the kids would qualify for a staff discount. I read that they are putting in a switchboard next year and when I read about it I just felt like God was telling me that was to be my job. Sounds silly doesn't it?"

"Not at all. Do you know anything about operating a system like that?"

She shook her head. "I'm running mostly on blind faith. For starters, I'll take any job I can get. I'll even go back to cleaning and ironing if need be. I just have to get there."

They spent the next hour reviewing her case history, the kinds of work she had done, the amount of money she might need. There might be resources available, but they needed to locate them.

As her caseworker, he had to caution her that this move was risky. She may not have enough to live on. Her kids might go hungry or even worse they could end up on the street. As her friend, he hoped he was wrong.

"Keep me posted on your plans. I'm sorry to be the bearer of bad news, but there is no way for me to get you the money you need."

She rose and reached for his hand. "Thank you for everything, Howard. I'm still going. I'll figure out a way. I'm going to change our lives."

"I believe you will."

"I'm going to miss you," her voice cracked.

"I'll miss you too. We'll all miss you." He squeezed her small hand in return. He now had two items at the top of his to do list. Find a way to accelerate Alice Mae's funding in Oregon if it was at all possible and tell his son Rodger that Laurie Wheaton was moving. He dreaded the latter more.

16   Hotcakes

On Tuesday evening, Alice Mae made a family favorite for dinner filling the house with the warm, buttery scent of what they liked most. Hotcakes and sausage. She put Karo syrup, cinnamon sugar and butter on the table, the best she had to offer. When a large plate of steaming flapjacks was piled high in the center of the table, she added a bowl of scrambled eggs to the feast and called the family together.

"Come and get it."

"Yeah, pancakes!" Joyce ran into the kitchen, enthused. Wearing one of her brother's old shirts and a pair of cut off jeans, she grabbed her chair and settled into her spot. She had pulled her hair into pigtails and looked younger than her eleven years. "Do I smell sausage?"

"Just a few. One apiece."

"Yes! This is great!" Breathing deeply of the appetizing aromas, Richie pushed past his mother to do a quick wash and rinse of his hands, still black with newsprint from delivering the mid-week edition of the News Register. He wiped his hands on his pants.

Flying to his chair, he reached for the serving plate and stopped only when he saw his mother's arched eyebrow advising him to wait.

Alice Mae opened the oven door and withdrew a plate holding a modest pile of sausage, browned and fragrant. "

His grin spread even wider.

"Smells great, Mom." Laurie bounced into the kitchen, hungry and happy. Her face was flushed with exertion from collecting clean laundry from the lines. She deposited her load on the sofa before joining them. "Good idea. Hope you made plenty. Oh, you made little dollar cakes too, how fun." She was famished. So was Sharon. Both girls eagerly drew up to the table.

Donna walked through the door right on time, home from Sweeties with a bag of day-old cookies to add to the feast. She took only a minute to change from her skirt into comfortable pants and an old shirt. She plunked down in her chair, tired. "Smells good."

They joined hands as was their custom and Alice Mae prayed. "Lord, thank you for good food to eat, a warm home to enjoy and a family where there is so much love. Please bless this food to the nourishment of our bodies. And Lord, please bless our conversations. In Jesus name, Amen."

It never ceased to amaze Alice Mae how quickly food could be devoured. Perhaps that was one of the reasons she did not enjoy cooking. Within five minutes, the sausage and eggs disappeared, followed a few minutes later by the very last of the pancakes, including the burned batch at the bottom of the plate. Sticky drippings and crumbs were all that remained.

As the forks and knives fell on empty plates and she sensed that her children were about to bolt back to their own activities, she began the conversation.

"Just leave the dishes. Let's all go into the living room. We need to talk about a few things."

She got mixed reactions.

Joyce and Alice Mae settled in together at one end of the sofa with Laurie anchoring the other. Donna took what was referred to as the good chair, meaning its springs could not usually be felt, and picked up the still unnamed yellow kitten that rubbed against her ankles. Loud purring ensued.

Sharon sat cross legged on the floor with her back to the gathering and picked up a magazine to demonstrate her disinterest. Richie sprawled across a pillow on the floor.

She had their attention, now she needed their support.

"As you know, for a while now I've been thinking of moving us away from Holyoke."

Sharon buried her head deeper into the magazine causing her ponytail to obscure what was no doubt a frown.

"I'm not talking about moving to another house. We've moved and moved and you've all been great about it. This time I would like us to move to Oregon."

Joyce braided her hair absently. Donna picked at her shirt.

"I wanted to talk to you before anyone else heard about it but after I spoke with Masyl, word began spreading. I guess quite a few people in town know and you may hear some …" she chose her word carefully, "talk."

She knew them well. Curiosity registered on every face. There was apprehension, excitement, and a little fear.

Laurie picked up a pillow and tugged at a fraying thread as she listened. She was definitely interested. Of her girls, Laurie was the most analytical; she would withhold judgment till she heard it all. Tomorrow she would be in the library reading everything she could find on the subject and then sharing her knowledge with the others, especially Sharon. Having Laurie in her corner would go a long way.

"When?" Donna wanted to know.

"Sometime this summer. I've prayed about this more than you can even imagine and have wrestled with it. I know how hard it will be to leave."

"But all my friends are here." Sharon was at last participating.

"All my friends are here too." Alice Mae responded. "I don't know anyone in Oregon." She raised her open palms. "Absolutely no one. Zip!"

Richie asked what several were wondering. "Are you scared?"

She smiled and gave an honest answer. "Yes, I am. But mostly I'm excited."

"How are we going to get there?"

"Are we going to rent a moving truck?"

"How big is the school there? Where will we live?"

"You ask a lot of questions, you know that?" She grinned at the kids, pleased they were at least engaged in the conversation.

"When we get there can we get a dog?" Joyce's eyes twinkled and her shoulder length hair bobbed. "Or maybe just a puppy?"

Alice Mae laughed seeing her excitement. "I doubt it but we'll see." The girl wriggled in under her mother's arm. The snuggling was nice but wouldn't help her get a dog.

"What about me?" Still enjoying the post graduation glow, Donna was content to work at the shop but Alice Mae didn't want to see her settle in. She wanted to see her hungry for adventure, eager to start something new. Having no boyfriend meant precious little in a small rural communities like this one. Farmers and their sons absolutely prowled for girls with a strong back – a sound mind was optional. Donna had both. She was a *peach ready to be picked* as her father would say.

"Is there any chance I could get into a college this year?" The spark of curiosity was there. Yes!

Alice Mae looked at her gentle and intelligent daughter, soft hair falling around her shoulders, soft brown eyes looking hopeful. "I don't know yet. I doubt it." She wished she had more answers.

"Couldn't we wait till I graduate?" She had expected that question from Sharon and was ready. "Couldn't we wait till next year?"

"And then it'll be Laurie's senior year. Would that be better?"

"It'd be better for me."

"Thanks!" Laurie tossed the pillow at her sister.

"You're welcome." The lob was returned with more force.

Pillows pounded into one another. Reserved laughter bubbled to the surface. That was a good sign.

Intercepting the last pillow thrown Alice Mae looked solemnly at Sharon and then at Laurie. "I don't want you to be here when you graduate. I don't want you to think what Barb's doing is okay for you. I want you out of here before you get tied to this place by some boy who you think is cute just because you've never seen anyone better to compare him to." *Like I did.* "I want you to be someplace where you have more options."

The laughter stopped and pain returned to Sharon's eyes. Turning her back to Alice Mae, she hugged a pillow to her chest and flashed the temper that everyone who lived with her knew so well. "I don't want to go! I won't go!"

"I know you don't want to, but you will go. It's my call and we are going to go. Oregon or bust!" She tried to make it sound like fun.

"Do you even know how far away Oregon is?" Sharon rounded on her. "It's on the other side of the country. It's way on the west coast. It's by California for Pete's sake! California!" She bolted to her feet and fled to her room. The slamming of her bedroom door reverberated throughout the house. The neighborhood. Maybe the whole small town.

With the rest of the gathered assembly intact, the conversation lasted a few minutes more with questions and comments and explanations. There was no more yelling, no more door slamming and even a little bit of laughter. It had gone pretty much as expected.

17 The Unexpected

It was nearly the end of June and Alice Mae had stopped to admire a new window display in the hardware store when she saw her coming. Tall and angular, with long red hair and an orange sweater, she was hard to miss and even harder to ignore.

"Well, Alice Mae. I hear you are leaving us." Patsy Fleming gushed after rushing across the street to intercept her friend.

"Hello, Patsy."

Light perspiration glistened on her face, flushed from the exertion. "Rumor has it that there might be a man in the picture." She drew out the word man as though it had several syllables. Her severely plucked eyebrows wiggled up and down in anticipation of hearing all the details.

"There is no man, Patsy." Alice Mae browsed the seed packets and spades.

"But you've been alone for so long." Her insincerity was blatant. "Paul and I were hoping it was true."

Alice Mae leveled her eyes at her neighbor. "I'm not interested in a man, Patsy. We are doing fine by ourselves."

Having spent ten years married to a man who had given her more grief than support she had no interest in getting entangled again. Even before the kids were all born, he had given in to the liquor that had claimed him during what people referred to as The Great War. For Gene, it hadn't been all that great.

After coming home, he couldn't forget what he had seen. Alice Mae tried to keep the marriage together. She covered for him, worked with him and nearly starved with him. Three times he pulled Donna out of school, drove intoxicated with her till he passed out leaving them both cold and stranded in the middle of nowhere. Three times she had begged friends to find them.

Eventually, after his disappearance, she filed for divorce citing abandonment. She had neither seen nor heard from him in more than four years. Frankly, she had hoped to never have to think of him again. She had five kids to raise and her plate was full. No, indeed. She was not interested in a man.

"But is it true? Are you actually moving away?" She was practically vibrating with eagerness to hear the news.

"You have an excellent day, Patsy." Alice Mae walked away.

"But Alice Mae, everyone's talking about it. Is it true?"

Behind her, a foot stomped in frustration. As tempting as it was to turn around and look, just to see the utter aggravation on Patsy's face, she resisted the urge. Smiling broadly, she continued down Main Street.

After stopping at the Piggly Wiggly where she ignored inquisitive looks from the checkout clerk she stepped into the library for a few minutes of quiet.

"Hi, Betty. How's your mother?"

"Been a good couple of days. Thanks for asking."

"Good." She headed to the magazine section to browse the newest additions.

"Got some new college catalogs in for spring."

"Did you?"

She spent twenty minutes perusing the newest *Life Magazine* and reading the thrilling reports of John Glenn's circling the globe and checking out the new style that Jackie Kennedy was bringing to America before gathering up her things. Heading for the front desk she tried to make a quiet get away while Betty was busy. She should have known better. Betty was no amateur.

"Is it true that you are thinking of moving? There's been talk you know. And I've seen you studying the catalogs."

She considered her answer. "I'm giving it some thought." Her hand reached for the door.

"I would miss you but I think it would be wonderful." There was an actual tear in the librarian's eye.

Alice Mae was touched. Actually she was stunned. "Betty, I…"

"If there is any way I can help you. If there is anything I can get for you. If you think there is any way for some of those kids of yours to go to college. I just think it is the most exciting thing I've heard of in a long time." There was a catch in her voice.

Flabbergasted she said, "Thank you. I'm trying not to get the cart before the horse, but I've been praying about it."

Betty nodded solemnly. "I want you to know that I haven't said anything to anyone about it. I know there is talk around town, but it didn't come from me. But I hope you can figure out how to do it. I'm praying for you." Flushed, she retrieved an armful of books and fled behind the bookshelves in the youth section.

Alice Mae followed after her. Touching her arm, she said, "Thank you, Betty. It's nice to have your support. And your discretion."

Betty thrust books into the shelves. An odd and unexpected bond had just formed.

Alice May headed home with a lightness of heart that she had not anticipated when she entered the library. An unexpected blessing. A confirmation. *Thank you, Lord. Bless her.*

18 Set

The call came out of the blue. It was in the middle of the day, in the middle of the week, a most unexpected time for her to receive a call from anywhere. Especially California.

"Alice Mae," his gravelly voice began. "McMinnville is a much bigger town than you have ever seen in your life. Are you aware of that?"

Caught off guard by the call and the question, she inhaled and reached for the back of a nearby kitchen chair. "Hi, Dad. Yes, I know that. From what I read, it's practically a city compared to Holyoke."

"It's a pretty town, though," he offered. "Lots of big trees and a pleasant park. Friendly people too."

"You've been there?" Her mouth went dry. She licked her lips trying to moisten them so that she could speak. "You went? When?"

"Isn't that what you asked me to do?" He sounded annoyed.

"It was. It is. Thank you." She sat down, her legs suddenly feeling shaky. "So what do you think of my moving there?"

"Could do worse. Seems to have good schools. A healthy little business community. The college looks good. The women are good looking too."

"Dad!"

He chuckled.

"And there is a little house I might be able to get for you."

"A house?" She stammered. "You looked at a house for us?"

"Well, yes!" He hesitated. "I just made some inquiries."

"What kind of house? How big is it?"

"Big enough," he barked. "Two bedrooms but beggars can't be choosers, you know. You've lived in worse."

That was true. Some of the places she had lived in hardly qualified as a house. A shack, a cabin, a hole in the wall but not a house. Two bedrooms were doable if that was what it would take.

"And?" She needed more. "Where is it? Within walking distance to schools?"

"Everything is within walking distance since you have no car," he grumped.

"Right. That's right. Wow." Her head was reeling. Her heart was pounding. "I'm stunned. Thanks, Dad."

"You'd probably want to get there and get settled in before school starts."

She was unprepared for this conversation. For months she had hoped for it, dreamed of it but now it was here, she was caught so off guard. "Well, yes."

"And just how are you planning to get there?" The challenge in his tone was familiar to her. *I dare you to ask me*, it said. *I won't offer. You have to ask.* He waited.

She prayed before answering. *Lord, if this is your plan I could use a miracle now.* "I would like you to drive out here and move us." There, she said it. Clear and direct. No begging, no pleading. Just like she had prayed about and dreamed about. Just ask.

There was a very long silence at the other end of the line. "You know Masyl thinks you're crazy."

"She's mentioned it." She held her breath and prayed.

"You know if I do this for you, you can never change your mind and ask me to move you back? Never!" He was adamant.

"I know." She waited.

"You know I think it's a risky thing to do?"

"I know, Dad."

"You know you're a blasted, stubborn woman?"

"You've mentioned that before." At the other end of the line she could hear papers shuffling, throat clearing and a great deal of harrumphing. "Please do this for me, Dad."

A minute passed, then another.

"I've arranged to pay the first two months rent, starting August 1st." He announced it as though he were giving her the weather report. "After that, you'll be on your own. Can you live with that?"

She gulped. Her heart skipped a beat – maybe two. "August 1st?"

"Yeah. You going or not?" He was losing patience.

"You're coming? You're coming here?"

"Yeah. I'm coming and bringing a U-Haul. You be ready to go by the last week in July if you want me to take you. You hear?"

"Yes, Dad. I hear you and I'll be ready." Her eyes glistened. Her chest was so tight she could hardly breath.

"Good." He wrapped up the conversation eager to get away from any emotions that might be coming.

"Thank you, Dad," she said with all the strength she had. "Thank you so much."

"Now call Masyl and make peace with her. I don't want her calling me anymore bellyaching about this. You two sort this out! You hear?"

"I hear. I will."

With a final growl and a harrumph, he hung up.

Alice Mae sat in stunned silence. He was coming. She was moving. In four weeks they were moving to Oregon. She had absolutely no idea how she was going to manage, but manage she would. Her prayer was being answered. She slid down onto her knees and offered a multitude of thanksgivings for her children, her blessings, his faithfulness, his answers to her prayers and his goodness. And then she wept for joy and couldn't stop.

19 Tell

There was so much to do. Every ounce of her wanted to rush into the street and shout the news. She wanted to ring the church bells! She wanted to call Masyl and sort out the hard thing that had come between them but knew that her sister wasn't ready to talk.

She wanted to go over to tell Ruth and celebrate the news. Instead, Alice Mae dutifully finished the task at hand. She pressed the last of the white starched French-cuff shirts that were Mr. Culver's trademark at the bank. She wanted to end well. She would need every last cent she could put aside.

At three o'clock, she headed to the church to finish cleaning the sanctuary before the mid-week service.

Unable to contain her mingled joy and fear, she sang as she straightened the hymnals. "Oh Lord, my God. When I in awesome wonder, consider all the worlds thy hands have made." By the time she got to the closing phrase "How great thou art." she was absolutely belting it out. It felt great to release the tension and express a small fraction of the awe she was feeling.

She heard clapping.

"Well done!" Joe Lynch was beaming at her from the doorway. "I heard the singing from outside and thought a choir had moved into the sanctuary."

She laughed. "No choir. Just me."

She looked him up and down. He was wearing his dark suit. "Been to a funeral?"

"I just finished Mrs. Higginbotham's service. Ninety-seven and sharp as a tack till the day she died."

"Hard-headed as one too from what I heard."

"I heard that, too. She'll give Saint Peter a run for his money when she sees him, I'd guess."

Alice Mae chuckled. "She'll win."

"I'd say you have something to be happy about." He looked inquisitive. "Anything you want to talk about?

"Looks like I'm moving."

He clapped his hands. His grin widened. "How soon?"

"My dad is driving all the way from California with a U-Haul to move us. He said to be ready by the last week in July."

He let out a whistle. "That soon?"

"I'm still reeling."

He saw the conflict in her face. "What is it?"

"Nothing." She shook her head as if to clear the cobwebs. "He says he'll be here so I have work to do."

"You have reason to doubt him?"

She hesitated. "Not this time."

He sat down in the back pew and motioned for her to sit with him. "Tell me about it."

She sat in the pew across from him and looked into his concerned face.

He waited.

She took a long steadying breath. "Growing up he would often make plans. He'd tell us something that he would do for us or with us and then get busy and forget. Or more often he would find some infraction in our behavior and use that as an excuse to get out of it."

"I've met him and somehow that doesn't surprise me." He waited for her to continue.

"And then there was Gene."

He sat quietly, ready to hear what she needed to say.

"You know he drank." She swallowed. "Do you know that he just drove away one day, drove the car into a ditch and didn't ever come home? I had five little kids, lived two miles out of town and he just left us there." Her nose had reddened and her eyes showed the pain that she was reliving. "I called the Sheriff thinking he'd been in an accident. I prayed he was alright but after a couple of days I was told he had been seen in Sterling with another woman. He just abandoned us."

"So you have trouble believing that Henry will come and make this move happen."

"No offense but I don't trust men in general, I guess. But I'm not trusting in Dad." There was resolve in her voice as she stood, smoothed out her skirt and moved away, back to her cleaning. "I'm trusting in God. He'll keep his word." She smiled. "Pray for us?"

"We do. How are the kids handling the move? Have they accepted it?"

"Accepted is a strong word. Joyce and Richie are excited – a new adventure and all. Donna is quiet and seems interested, but reserved. I'm holding my breath. She could decide to stay, you know." Alice Mae sighed, not wanting to entertain that possibility.

"Laurie is willing. She has some reservations about leaving but seems to understand the advantages."

"Good." He waited.

"You know how Sharon is."

"Ruth has mentioned, shall we say, her reticence."

"Good word." Her laughter brought a welcome release of tension

"Well, reticent or not, when we leave here in a few weeks she will be in the car with us if I have to hog tie her and stuff her in."

Now it was Joe's turn to laugh. "If you need help, just holler. I roped a few calves in my younger days. I'm sure I haven't forgotten it all." He turned to leave her in peace.

Descending the front steps, he heard a soft soprano rendition of, "What a friend we have in Jesus." He hummed along as he ambled back to the parsonage.

20   Timing

"You wanted to talk to me?" Masyl jerked open the screen door and strode into the living room where her sister was ironing pillow cases, a scowl line on her face.

"Hi. Yes." Alice Mae forced her face to relax as she waved her sister to come on in. Why some people needed all their linens ironed had always puzzled her. Really? Moving aside the stack of bedding she was working on she motioned to the chair. "Sit. Sit."

Masyl dropped into the chair already having put in a long day. "Barb and Jeanie are getting some things we need at the feed store so I just walked on over. They'll be here in just a few minutes." She was guarded. The last several discussions between them had frayed.

"You want a cold drink?" The summer days burned hot earlier and earlier and the steam iron turned the living room into a sauna. Alice Mae turned toward the kitchen.

Masyl waggled her hand. "I know where it is. I'll get it." She heaved herself up from the chair and made her way to the kitchen looking tired. Curly wisps of summer-bleached hair clung to her flushed face. The country dress she wore was wrinkled and faded. She looked older than her thirty-five years.

"How are the kids?"

"Busy. Chuck's got 'em mending fences but with Barb's wedding coming up they can't seem to keep their minds on their chores. Every time we turn 'round they want to run to town for some fool thing."

"Weddings are a big deal, especially with girls."

"And getting bigger. The dress she wants is a nightmare. Buttons and lace everywhere. I'll be lucky to get it done on time."

"You should have let her buy the dress she wanted." The girls hadn't had a store bought dress in years. Masyl made everything they wore except their underwear – they were lucky she couldn't get the fabric.

"When Chuck saw the price he just about had a heart attack. He just about has a heart attack about everything these days." She shook her head. "Flowers, music, the idea that he might have to wear a suit. It's pathetic!" Masyl huffed. "Wish they'd just elope."

"You don't mean that."

"Yeah, I do. She's givin' her sisters all kinds of fancy ideas. I can see where this is going and it's no place good." She took a long drink of water and let out a sigh. Dropping back into her chair and picking up a magazine, she fanned herself.

"You should have had boys." It was a running joke. They tried and tried for sons and ended up with six girls. The comment got a glower in return instead of the customary chuckle.

This conversation was going nowhere. They were both tippy-toeing around the elephant in the room.

"I know you've been talking to Dad," Alice Mae began.

"Yeah. I told him to talk you out of this addle brained move you're talking about. I told him you need to stay here where you have friends and family."

"He mentioned that." The steaming metal plate slid back and forth over the cotton sheet.

"So what's going on? You're not actually leaving are you? I need you here, Maesy." Her voice was plaintive. In the years growing up together and in all the years of her marriage to Chuck, Alice Mae had never heard that strain in her voice.

She set the iron down and looked straight at her sister. "Dad called yesterday and offered to drive out here and help us move." Plain and simple was best. She watched for a reaction.

Masyl sat, unmoving.

"He's offered to bring a U-Haul trailer and drive us to Oregon."

Her sister just stared, betrayal in her eyes.

"He wants to do it at the end of next month." There it was. All laid out. She watched Masyl as she absorbed it.

"But what about Barb's wedding?"

"I'm sorry but we won't be here."

"Can't wait to get away from us, huh?" Pain gave her words a cutting edge. She pushed out of the chair and stood awkwardly in the middle of the room.

Alice Mae came around to her sister. "Masyl." She reached for her arm, but Masyl drew back.

"How could you?"

"I have to. Please try to understand."

"You want to! There's a difference."

"Masyl, I'm not doing this to hurt you. I'll miss you so much."

The red Circle C pickup truck pulled to the curb and the horn interrupted the moment. The engine revved.

The few feet between Masyl and Alice Mae widened to a chasm. With a face red with fury and pain, she spat, "You just can't wait to get away from us. From me." She backed away from her sister. "So much for family loyalty." Turning she pushed through the screen door looking back only to add her final jab. " Go to hell, Maesy. I already live there."

The blood drained from her face as she stood speechless, watching her sister and best friend walk away.

21 Matchmaker

Howard opened the door at the county office and was pleasantly surprised to find Alice Mae and Joyce waiting.

"Hello, ladies."

"Hi, Mr. Howland." Joyce was at her favorite spot in the office. It contained Archie and Jug Head comics as well as crayons and a paper punch that allowed her to make great piles of little, colored dots from construction paper. Happily, she busied herself and let the grownups take care of business.

"Your move is causing me a lot of trouble, you know." Howard had a spark in his eye as he settled in behind his desk.

"Oh." She raised her eyebrows. "Why is that?"

"Rodger is moping around the house like a lost puppy. He doesn't want Laurie to leave." He chuckled. "Don't worry, he'll get over it."

"Out of sight, out of mind they say." She smiled, seeing in her mind a young version of Howard, minus the glasses and the paunch. "Encourage him to talk with Jeanie or Tracy, Masyl's girls. They're about his age. Nice girls!"

"No, thanks." He snorted. "I'm not playing matchmaker to a fifteen-year-old. He's on his own."

They laughed easily together and got down to business.

"Where do I go from here?"

He pulled a sheet from a file. "There is a new government program there that distributes surplus food staples that you should be eligible for. That will give your family some canned meat, eggs, and milk. You'll need to carry them home from wherever they are distributed and that may be a challenge in McMinnville with no car. I understand they come in big number ten cans and may be heavy. Here's the address where they will be distributed." He slid a piece of paper across his desk. "I don't know where it will be in relation to where you are going to be living."

"Me either but I'll get Richie to help me. We'll manage."

"Probably powdered milk and powdered eggs." His face indicated his opinion on that subject and it wasn't good. "I hear some of the meat is good though. We aren't big enough to get it here yet, but there's talk."

"I'll take whatever I can get." She brushed the hair from her face and tucked it behind her ears as she absorbed the information.

"You can also register with the school system for free lunches for the kids. I can give you a letter that verifies you qualify for those. It might help."

"Okay. Good."

"I've spoken with Yamhill County and got the name of a woman there. Let me see if I can find my notes." He rummaged around on his untidy desk and located a scrap of buried paper. "Audrey Yates. She seemed very nice and assured me that she would do whatever she could to expedite your eligibility. She also told me something that might be of interest."

She looked up, curious.

"They have a training program that you should qualify for. It teaches some basic skills including …" He paused.

"Including?" She waited. She wasn't good at waiting.

He laughed heartily. "Including a multi-line switchboard that you may be able to work on."

"No!" She said so sharply that Joyce looked up from her activities in the corner, alarmed. "That would be great."

"Yes. It's in the courthouse. They use it to train the police and fire dispatch and she's looking for when the next training session might be. She's going to try to get you in. Get in touch with her as soon as you get settled."

"Absolutely." Her eyes danced. *Thank you!* "Thank you, Howard."

Feeling a bit like the goose that laid the golden egg, he continued through a list of forms that she would need to sign and details to address.

"You'll need to find housing before you go. Any thoughts on that?"

"Oh, I didn't tell you. Dad found us a house to rent."

He looked up, surprised. He had heard about Henry and none of it good. "That's good news. How much is the rent?"

"Not sure yet." She had forgotten to ask. After learning that he had paid two months' rent, she was so stunned that she didn't ask the amount and she didn't want to call back to inquire.

"Let me know." His interest was genuine.

"So. It's getting closer." She exhaled loudly and stood. The butterflies in her stomach were now her constant companions. "I'll see you next week. Thanks, Howard."

"Bye, ladies." He extended his hand to the girl and then to the mother.

"Tell Rodger he's welcome to come over anytime."

Howard nodded. He watched the slender young woman walk out of his office with a wisp of regret. He would miss her smile. He would miss her spunk. He would miss her.

Joyce took her mother's hand and they descended the courthouse steps and headed to the church to finish cleaning. At the bottom of the steps, she released the hand and began skipping ahead. "You want some help?" Her sweet voice called back. "I'll run the vacuum."

"I'll take you up on that."

"Can we sing?"

"We can and will." They headed west across the expanse of grass that was already turning brown in the summer heat. Her heart was already singing.

22 Space

Alice Mae left the house and just began walking. She had to breathe. She needed to think.

She had been prepared to make some changes, to sacrifice a great deal but now she had to rethink her strategy.

The evening was warm. Children played kick ball in the gathering dusk, but she hardly noticed. Neighbors sat on their front porches enjoying the summer evening. She waved and smiled absent mindedly. She just walked and talked with the only one who knew the weight on her heart. *How can I do this?*

An hour ago she was planning for the move. Then her father had called.

"Alice Mae," he began with the voice that did not invite discussion. "I've rented a U-Haul and I'm leaving Sacramento on July 24th. I'll be at your house on the 26th and you need to be ready to pack up and leave on the 27th. Will you be ready?" It sounded like a challenge.

"I will." She had been wondering about the exact date, now she had one. "I just need to know what size the trailer is so that I can make sure everything will fit." There were beds, of course, and kitchen items. Clothing and linens. Cleaning supplies and books for the children. A table and chair would be needed for meals and some living room furniture would be needed to get by. She had whittled it down to the essentials.

"I'm not going to pamper you, Alice Mae. And I'm not going to burn up the engine in my car dragging your stuff across the mountains." He had said as much before. "I've rented a five foot by eight foot cargo trailer."

She couldn't breathe. That was small.

"Eight feet long and five feet wide?" She tried to imagine the dimensions. "How tall?"

"I don't know how tall it is." He was annoyed. "About five feet, I think. How much stuff do you want to haul with you? When you mother and I came to Colorado, all we had was a wagon that wasn't half as big as that."

She knew she had to stop asking questions. She had heard this litany before. She had so much. He had so little. She should be more appreciative of what he was doing. If she didn't want his help, he would be happy to stay home. He had better things to do.

"I know, Dad. I'll be ready." She tried to put a smile on her face so that he would hear it in her voice, but her lips trembled. A tear escaped and fell onto her cheek. "Thanks for your help. See you on the 26th."

Passing the courthouse she continued to the bridge spanning Frenchman Creek. The arching overpass provided an unobstructed view of the curving bank. Water bubbled and spilled over rocks, offering a soothing backdrop to the storm raging in her head. A sliver of moon ascended over the sparse trees to the east casting a soft glow on her path.

She needed beds for everyone to sleep in. Joyce could bunk with her while the girls shared. Richie would need something. There would be no room for the sofa. What about chairs? Dressers for clothes? Towels and toiletries? Clothes and boots and coats? The list grew longer. She closed her eyes against the rising panic and prayed.

Lord, I need more than a little of your wisdom. Please show me what to do, what to take, what is important. Give me energy to get done what needs doing. Give me grace in dealing with Dad. Thank you for your faithfulness and your answers to so many prayers. Lord, give me perspective.

By the time she rounded the water tower in the city park and headed home, order had replaced the chaos and she had a plan. Half of what she had anticipated taking was discarded and she was focused on the task.

Passing by the parsonage she was surprised to see Joe and Ruth sitting on the porch.

"Alice Mae." Ruth beckoned her to join them.

"Hi. Enjoying the breeze?"

"Enjoying some of the last evenings in town." The moon was peeking above the roofline of their house and illuminating Ruth's shirt-waist dress that was unbuttoned just a bit more than it usually was for church. Joe's arm draped comfortably across his wife's shoulder.

"How are your plans coming for the move? What is your new house like?"

The couple looked at each other and burst into laughter. "The new house is, in fact, a very old house. The parsonage in Greeley is about a hundred years old. No wonder they were happy to let us have it."

"Oh no."

"As far as we can tell it needs a new roof, a new furnace, and without a doubt new paint throughout," Joe added.

Alice Mae settled herself onto the top step and leaned against the railing. She spread her full cotton skirt across her knees and enjoyed letting the evening breeze ruffle it. "You're kidding. Is the church going to take care of those things for you?"

"Eventually but they say it's not in the budget for this year. They'll give us a little for general fix up like the paint, but that's all. Oh well, the adventure will be good for us. We've been too comfortable here for far too long."

"You sure you're ready for that much change?"

Ruth grinned broadly. "We can't wait."

"That's an admirable attitude." She hugged her knees.

"How about you? What's new on your move?"

Alice Mae couldn't help but smile at their enthusiasm. "I think I need a little of your optimism," she confessed. "I talked to Dad a little bit ago and he told me the size of the trailer he's bringing." Her face told the story.

"Small, huh?"

"Five by eight. Sounds small to me."

"Yikes!" Ruth slid from the old glider and took a seat on the step next to Alice Mae. She put her hand on Alice Mae's shoulder. "That's hardly bigger than a pickup. Can you do it?"

"I've just finished having this conversation with the Lord." Alice Mae put a smile on her face although it was an effort. "And yes I can. I'll prioritize what we need to take and just fill the space. When there's no more room, I'll have what I need." It sounded so good. Reality, however, was going to be hard. In the whole of her life, she had made do with less. Less money, fewer clothes, nothing new. Dad never allowed for anything cute or frivolous. Gene drank away the money needed to buy basic necessities, much less anything personal. With this move looming on the horizon, her hope had been to take at least a few of the belongings she had collected over the years but now that possibility was dashed. Her heart ached with the loss of it even though she did not yet know what she would part with.

Ruth wrapped her arms around Alice Mae. They sat without speaking letting the crickets fill the evening air. Summer lilies mixed with roses made the night air rich with familiar fragrances.

Involuntary but silent sobs shook her thin shoulders. She didn't even realize she was crying till she was offered a tissue. "Sorry," she began.

"Shhh." The older woman comforted. "Hush."

Behind them, Joe rocked and prayed.

23 The Fourth

With the exception of Christmas and the Phillips County Fair, nothing was met with more enthusiasm in Holyoke than the Fourth of July. Alice Mae put on her one and only sun dress and ran her hand down over the full skirt. Yellow with a tiny pansy print, it flattered her delicate features and slender waist. It was a decade old, she knew, and it was a bit thread-bare, but it was still fresh and festive enough for the occasion. She took a final glance in the hall mirror, fluffed up her short hair and stepped into the summer sun determined to enjoy this day.

Parade participants gathered under the water tower that stood like a sentry in the center of the city park. Every child with a bicycle was encouraged to weave crepe paper in and out of their spokes, hang streamers from the handlebars and join the parade. Old cars and trucks newly washed and waxed pulled into line and horses pranced nervously. At eleven o'clock, the high school band struck up a march and the procession began.

Making her way to the front of Sweeties, she waved at Donna who glanced through the large front window and waved back. It was standing room only inside with customers wanting a cold drink and a viewing spot for the parade that was out of the sun.

Howard Howland and his family worked their way through the crowd to stand with her. "Morning Alice. Lovely dress." He tapped the brim of his straw hat. He could be downright charming.

She smiled and nodded. "Morning Howard. Morning Gloria. Boys." They squeezed together so as to not block the shop door.

Behind the flag-waving color guard two of Masyl's girls, Tracy, and Sue, sat astride horses whose manes had been braided with red, white and blue ribbons. With boots polished to an uncharacteristic gleam and cowboy hats shading their faces, they waved and called to her as they passed.

A drill team followed stepping carefully around what the horses had left behind. Cheerleaders and cheerleader wannabes, including Sharon, ran alongside shouting and clapping to the beat of the drums.

Two floats formed the heart of the parade. One sponsored by the local feed store looked like an enormous chicken coop complete with plastic chickens. Or were they painted paper Mache? Or were they geese?

The other float was more dignified if not more original. It was sponsored by the local tavern in honor of the Veterans from the two World Wars. Catering to their customer base, no doubt. Covered in paper flowers and with red, white and blue balloons waving in the summer sun, it had patriotic music spewing forth and uniformed men throwing out wrapped candy. It was a crowd pleaser.

Following the floats, the children pedaled by and waved to the crowd.

Elvira Davis squeezed through the onlookers to stand next to Alice Mae just as Benny rode by on his bicycle, complete with training wheels. Elvira's hand waved wildly. "Keep going, Benny, Honey." Turning to Alice Mae, she confided, "That boy is just heartbroken that you are leaving. He's had his eye on Joyce ever since he was a little kid."

As the town fire truck brought up the rear of the small procession, Alice Mae patted Elvira's hand. "He'll get over it."

Masyl's red pickup truck was parked under an enormous maple in front of the courthouse. Mounted on the side of the truck bed, a sign read *$Circle C Melons–One Buck$*. Masyl was in the back of the truck handing down melons and taking in greenbacks. In her work pants and a oversized shirt, she looked every inch the farmer's wife. Piled high at nine o'clock, the truck was nearly empty.

Barbara and Jeanie were selling watermelon by the slice from a large ice-filled tub. "Twenty-five cents a slice!" They called. Watermelon was always a popular draw at the celebration, but with short shorts and blouses tied up on their midriffs, the girls drew customers as well. There was a waiting line.

"Hey girls. How's business?"

"Hey, Aunt Alice." The girls bloomed in their element, laughing and flirting harmlessly with every male over twelve and a few that were younger. The fun was not limited to the men although they clearly seemed to enjoy it more. High school students, neighbors, and perfect strangers were in a buying mood. "Business is good. Want some watermelon?"

"Maybe later."

Catching her sisters eye she waved. "Hey sis. Want some help?" Maybe today with all the enthusiasm flowing through town things would warm up.

"A dress? Really Maesy!" Her sister shook her head and turned away. Maybe not.

"What's wrong with the dress? I thought it looked nice."

"I think you look beautiful, Aunt Alice." Jeanie gave an apologetic smile and nodded in Masyl's direction. "Don't worry about her, she'll get over it. She's just had a bee up her you know what lately."

"Thanks, Honey." Alice Mae flounced her skirt a bit just for fun and caught a disapproving look from Masyl but a smile from one of the customers. Color bloomed in her cheeks. "Hey, I didn't see Mary Charlene or Grace in the parade. I gave Richie a quarter and told him to take the kids for ice cream cones at Dairy King. Five cents today. Are they here?"

Jeanie cut a large melon into huge sections. "They wanted to go to Wray today with Daddy."

"How fun for him." She leaned in a bit and uttered, "I think their parade is actually a bit better than ours."

"That wouldn't take much."

A welcome breeze was picking up from the west, hinting of a possible thundershower later in the afternoon. An unlikely occurrence for the fourth of July but it would be a welcome relief from the dust of the day. Alice Mae scanned the crowd of men gathered on the lawn and held her breath. Were Gene or any of the Wheaton brothers among them? She thought she saw a familiar head but, no. She turned toward home.

Sitting alone in the shade of the walnut tree in her own small yard, she felt how much she would miss this cozy and comfortable town.

24 Resignation

Two weeks. That was all she had left. Alice Mae opened her eyes to light streaming into the bedroom despite the drawn roller shade and the curtains hanging at the window. She had been awake for an hour, her mind spinning with things to be done. Slipping out of bed so as to not wake Donna, she tried to steal away. She got half way to the door.

"You're awake too?" Donna rolled over and smiled. "I've been trying not to disturb you." She bounced out of bed ready for the day.

"I'm going to open up the house and see if I can get some air moving."

"I'll help."

Together they opened the back door, the front door and every window not painted shut and enjoyed the stirring of fresh morning air.

Alice Mae set up the ironing board and started in on yet another bag of Mr. Culver's shirts. Needing every penny for the move, she was doing even more of what she hated doing in the summer heat, but was thankful for the money.

Donna attacked a pile of clean towels on the sofa that had been brought in from the clothesline. Line drying made them smell great but left them stiff. She shook them vigorously releasing a smell of soap and summer sunshine before folding them into a tidy stack.

"I had an interesting conversation with Mrs. Lynch yesterday," Donna began out of the blue. That is the way news seemed to be coming these days.

"Oh?"

"She told me about the old house they are moving into. Sounds like she'll have her hands full but if anyone can take on the challenge, it's Ruth. She said two of the rooms are painted flat brown over old wallpaper. Can you imagine?" She wrinkled her nose. "Must look like a cave in there."

"She'll turn that house on its ear, not to mention the church ladies. I'd give a lot just to be around to see it."

"The Lynch's are like family, right?"

"Absolutely. Better than family in many ways. Of all the people in town I'm going to miss, Ruth is at the top of the list."

"I'm glad you feel that way." Donna picked up another towel and gave it an even more vigorous shake than the previous ones. She folded it slowly as she spoke. "When I talked to her yesterday, she said that if I wanted to I could stay with them this fall. They will loan me the money to go to North Colorado Community College while you get settled." She watched her mother from the corner of her eye. "What do you think?"

The iron stopped in mid air. Her head began shaking back and forth.

Donna continued. "I know you wanted me to go with you but I can't get into college this year in Oregon. No matter what you end up doing. I would have to pay out of state tuition even if we figured out a college nearby so I cannot attend this year if I go with you."

"But you could get a job till ..."

"If I wait a year and get a job, I'll never go and you know it. Isn't that what you thought you would do? Work till you had the money to go to college?"

Alice Mae's heart wrenched.

"I can't afford to go. You can't help me, but they can."

Alice Mae felt a tears sting her eyes. She didn't care. "I can't imagine you not being there," she whispered. Setting down the iron, she went to her daughter and wrapped her arms tight around her and didn't let go. The ache in her chest was unbearable and yet somehow familiar.

At eighteen, the roles had been reversed. It was the day she, Alice Mae, graduated from high school. After working her way through school, often staying with families in town and working for her room and board so that she could attend, she didn't even get a day to savor the accomplishment. It was her mother who admonished "Alice Mae. Get out and do it now." With pain contorting both of their faces, she said. "Right now! Go and don't look back." Knowing that there was absolutely nothing but back-breaking manual labor and heartache waiting at the farm, she packed her bag and walked two miles into town. Had her father caught her he would have never let her go. Leaving the farm and her sister and her mother so abruptly broke her heart but it was her only chance. The pain was as sharp as it had been all those years ago.

"I don't want to go to Oregon, Mom." Donna returned the embrace, but there was iron in her spine. Her eyes were dry and clear. "There's nothing for me there. The other kids will all be in school. They'll make new friends and you can get them into Linfield. You'll have your job to figure out. This is *my* chance." She drew back and looked at her mother, pleading on her face. "Give me your blessing."

"I assume you've prayed about this."

"I have." She looked evenly at her mother. "Just like you."

"What will I do without you?" It was the same question Masyl had asked her.

"I don't know but I'm staying." She picked up the stack of towels and headed for the bathroom. "By the way, Mom, don't be upset with Ruth. You should know that Mrs. Lynch didn't start this. I'm the one who asked her."

Alice Mae swallowed down her disappointment and picked up her iron to resume her work. Steam rose from the ironing board. Donna had made a choice and it was a good one, even if it was not the one that she herself wanted. "Of course you have my blessing. When are you going to apply?" she called.

"I already did."

She took a long steadying breath before she dared to speak. "You'll have a great time with Ruth and Joe. You'll have to let me know how the renovation goes. Give me all the details."

From the bathroom came a voice filled with relief and excitement. "I'll have a front row seat. I'll tell you everything."

25 Go Figure

She was mentally clicking off the tasks done.

Sharon was finally on board with the move. Not happy about it but no longer throwing around threats and slamming doors. Check.

Laurie had risen to the challenge of whittling down the linens for bed and bath to a single box each. She also took charge of packing up the clothes for Joyce and Richie, as well as her own, ruthlessly making sacrifices where needed. The scrap pile to pass on to Aunt Masyl would be sizable assuming Masyl was speaking to them by the time they left town. Check.

Via his paper route, Richie passed on details of the move to everyone interested and brought back an assortment of comments, speculations, and a few large tips to pad their travel fund. The scuttlebutt seemed to be that there was a man in the wings somewhere although no one knew exactly who or where. Some speculated that she was linking up again with Gene, who was alive and well and living in Oregon. Not a chance!

Joyce was making most of the meals sparing her mother the trouble of coming up with ideas. Peanut butter sandwiches again. Oh well. Check. Check.

The utilities had been notified. Mail would be forwarded, especially any communications from Howard. All her laundry customers had been informed that they would have to do their own ironing from now on – a pronouncement which gave her greater pleasure than it probably should have.

Paper littered the surfaces of the living room where back issues of the Holyoke Register had been procured for wrapping and packing boxes. It was ordered chaos.

Saturday morning was only half gone and the progress was good. Sorting books was next on the list of tasks to tackle. Alice Mae perched on a footstool and began. One for me. One for the kids. Two to give away.

"Knock. Knock." There had been no working doorbell on the house for as long as the Wheaton's had lived there, so when the door was ajar, the familiar call was the norm. "Knock. Knock." She was surprised to see Howard Howland's rounded silhouette filling the front doorway blocking most of the morning light. Behind him, on his right flank, stood a younger version of the man.

"Howard." She smiled broadly. "And Rodger. Come on in." Tossing her head in the direction of the back of the house, she said, "Laurie and Sharon are in their room. Go on back." A grin stole across the boy's face and color swept up his neck as he bolted for the back of the house where a transistor radio was cranking out music by Peter, Paul, and Mary.

She pushed off the stool. "What are you two doing here?" Even though he was fond of her, in all the years of their acquaintance, Howard had only been to her house twice. The first time was when she was deathly ill and he was worried about her. The second was after a particularly bad snow storm; he brought a box of food for the family. She eyed him curiously. "What's up?"

He nodded at his boy. "He wanted to spend a little time with Laurie so I suggested he be useful and give her a hand. Hope you don't mind." He shook his head and lowered his voice. "Changed his clothes twice before coming; he's worse than a girl."

She laughed. "Not at all. We're not proud. We'll take whatever help we can get."

Howard was glad it made her laugh. Holding open the front screen door, he motioned for her to join him outside. "Walk with me for few minutes. I've got something to tell you," he said grinning. "The kids will be okay."

She glanced at the back room and then followed him into the sun. The green grass of early summer had already given over to the semi-brown lawns of July. Dust on the streets peppered the air with the familiar fragrance of drying wheat.

Strolling across Baxter Ave in the direction of the church, she waved to Mr. Wiggins, who was watering his urns. "Mr. Wiggins," she called and nodded. He nodded back.

Howard intercepted a kick ball heading in their direction from some neighborhood children and punted it back. "Thanks," they called in return.

He couldn't wait another minute. Without warning, he grabbed hold of her arm and stopped her in her tracks. He broke the news. No hedging or beating around the bush. "I figured out a way for you to get your money."

Had he not been a married man she would have hugged him on the spot.

26 Boxed

"Knock. Knock." This time it was Ruth calling through the open front door. "Need any help?" In comfortably worn pants and a sleeveless shirt, she came in toting a box of cleaning rags and two rolls of packing tape.

"Come on in," called a voice from the back room. "The more the merrier."

On the living room floor, just to the right of the door was spread a sheet on which a dark line had been drawn marking off what appeared to be a five foot by eight foot area. Within that space, boxes rose in tidy stacks, each one clearly labeled.

Outside the drawn lines, more boxes lined the room. Were it not for the mounds of belongings on the floor outside the boxes, it would have looked organized. Sunlight streamed in through every open window highlighting the happy buzz of activity within.

"Alice Mae?" Ruth called out. "Alice? Donna?"

From the back of the house Donna emerged, her hair tied up with a red kerchief, her face flushed. She wiped her brow with her arm and blew out a deep breath. "Ruth. Welcome to the chaos."

"You think this is bad? This looks orderly to me."

"We're getting there."

"So I see." She surveyed the small house.

No furniture remained in the living room save two floral chairs and a sturdy if not beautiful floor lamp. Both chairs had the legs removed but one was inside the lines. The familiar sofa was missing as was the bookcase that Alice Mae loved. Ruth's heart hitched.

The girl's bedroom had been disassembled, mattresses on the floor, closet mostly empty, dresser drawers stacked. Four open boxes sat on the floor. Knee deep in piles of sheets, clothes, coats and school paraphernalia, the girls sang along to a small transistor radio. *"...Johnny Angel."*

"Those two are for me and those are for Sharon," Laurie pointed out accompanied by Shelly Fabares' song. "You should see how much we're getting in."

"Keep it up girls." She involuntarily began humming. The tune didn't make it to the top of the Billboard Hot 100 for nothing.

Richie was trying with limited success to disassemble his own bed. The mattress leaned up against the wall at a rakish angle supporting half of the frame while he struggled with the bolts holding the other half. At least he wasn't bored.

"You should see our place. Looks just like this times ten. Don't know where it all came from," Ruth confessed to Donna, after surveying the progress. "I wanted to come here just to escape."

"I'll bet! Oh, Mom says to ask you if I can just bring my stuff to your place or if you want me to keep it here till Grandpa gets here on the 26th. I'm all packed up in any case. I do have a bit more than just one box."

"Bring it!" She threw back her head and laughed. "Bring it all. Just make sure it's clearly marked so that when we get to Greeley you can find it again. Now put me to work before I feel compelled to go back home. I told Joe I wasn't coming back till he got all his books packed up. That should give me a good three or four hours."

"How would you feel about tackling the kitchen?"

"The kitchen!" Raising her hand in a mock charge she headed to the back of the house where cupboard doors stood ajar. Drawers were open with contents in need of sorting.

"How much of this are you taking?" Half? Less?

Donna picked up two empty boxes from the Piggly Wiggly. Setting them on the counter with a decisive thump she said. "Just what'll fit in these."

Ruth blanched, then set her hands to the task.

"Where's your mother?"

"I don't know. She was here a few minutes ago." She looked out the back door, peeked around the side of the house and concluded, "I think maybe she and Joyce went to your place to escape."

Ruth laughed. "Good. Joe can use the help."

27   Goodbyes

The sharp ringing cut through her early morning slumber. One short and one long bell on the party line. It was for her.

Alice Mae avoided the boxes stacked against every wall and grabbed the phone. The sound coming across the phone line was mostly weeping mixed with a few words that were almost indistinguishable.

"Mary Charlene ... accident ...Chuck's mother ..." Masyl!

It was only six thirty in the morning. Alice Mae blinked and strained to make out what was being said.

"She's dead."

Oh God. No. It was unthinkable. Alice Mae opened her mouth to speak, but no sound came out.

"Aunt Alice?" Barbara Rae's tremulous voice came on the line replacing her mother.

"Barb? What happened?"

Sobs broke the girl's voice as well but through them the news came. After spending the night in Wray with her grandmother, Mary Charlene and Chuck's mother were driving back to the ranch early this morning when they went off the road. It appeared they swerved to avoid a truck and went into a ditch. "Grandma Sherwood's in the hospital. Mary Charlene was taken to Wray in an ambulance, but she died on the way."

"Has Masyl been to see either of them?"

"No. Daddy went to the hospital. Everything is pretty chaotic around here."

"I'm sure."

"Aunt Alice. Is there any way you can come? Mom needs you."

"I'll try." It was all she could promise. "I'm so sorry." It wasn't enough, but it was all she had. Her heart broke with the sorrow spilling across the line. Images of the sweet girl with the bright eyes and easy smile flooded her mind. She couldn't be gone.

"Mom?" Joyce stumbled into the kitchen awakened by the phone and the sound of her mother. Seeing her mother's face awash in tears the girl wrapped her arms tight around her waist and gave her a big hug. "What's wrong?"

Alice Mae pulled Joyce onto her lap and buried her face in the child's hair. Sobs caught in her throat, racking her slender shoulders. Grief overwhelmed her.

"What's wrong?" Alarm filled her dark eyes. "Mommy?"

She shook her head, unable to speak for a moment. Death had not yet touched her family. Except for her own mother passing a decade ago, they had known no loss. Older townspeople had died, of course. An elderly neighbor man had succumbed to cancer last year and the kids had attended his funeral, but this was personal. This would break their hearts.

"There's been an accident," she began, wiping her eyes with a kitchen towel. "Mary Charlene was in a truck with her grandma and they went off the road." Her throat constricted and she had to get up and get a drink of water. She couldn't bring herself to say the words.

"Is she okay?" Innocence and optimism made any other outcome unthinkable. She reached for her mother's hand and tugged. "She's okay, right?"

"Grandma Sherwood's in the hospital but think she'll be alright."

"What about Mary Charlene?" Wariness crept into her eyes. She squeezed her hand, urgent for reassurance. "She'll be okay, right?"

Alice Mae shook her head.

The girl buried her face against her mother.

By seven, the household was awake and moving in shocked stillness as they absorbed the sad news. Memories surfaced. Stories were shared. Questions were asked.

"Is she really gone?"

"What will happen now?"

"Where will she be buried? When?"

"Could they see her? Did they have to see her?"

So many questions and Alice Mae had few answers. "We'll just have to wait and see."

In all the years she had lived in Holyoke, there had been few times she really wished she had a car. During her mother's last days, she had wanted to go the hospital in Sterling and say goodbye. How her heart had hurt that she could not be there at the end. After Henry sold the farm and moved to California, she wanted to go see the old homestead as it was being torn down. She wanted so desperately to see house and barn razed – to see with her own eyes that it they gone. On neither occasion did a car become available.

More than either of those occasions, today she wanted a car. She needed to go to her sister. The pain of not being able to be with her was excruciating. *God*, she cried out,. *Help Masyl. Comfort Masyl. Be there for her because I cannot.*

Her mind reeled. Who could she impose upon to loan her a car or to take her to the Circle C?

Ruth and Joe. "I'm so sorry." Ruth was devastated. "Joe left for Sterling for a meeting about six this morning. I don't have a car. Let me see if I can find anybody that could loan me one."

Elvira. She dialed. "Oh, Alice Mae, I'm sorry but my car has a flat and I don't have a spare. Charlie over at the station has ordered one for me, but he say's it'll be Thursday 'fore it gets here."

She couldn't think clearly. She couldn't think at all.

Not surprisingly, no one was interested in breakfast and no one wanted to pack. They moved around the house and yard quietly, too shocked to do anything.

When she heard the familiar "Knock, Knock" called at the front door, Alice Mae jumped and swiped at her eyes.

"Come in." She headed out from the bedroom, pulling on a cardigan for warmth. Even though the day promised to be hot, she was chilled.

He was the last person in town that she would have expected to come to her door at nine in the morning, especially on a morning like this, but there he stood. Willy Wiggins with his perpetually pressed dark suit and his seemingly impenetrable eyes stood on the other side of her screen door, hat in hand.

"Would you like to go see your sister?"

She just stared at him, confused.

"What?"

"I know how close you and Mrs. Sherwood are, I mean sisters and all." He seemed flustered. "And I know you don't have a car. I thought that if you wanted to go, my hired boy, Leonard, could drive you."

"But how do you know? That is, how did you find out about the accident?"

"We got a call from the hospital." He sounded almost apologetic. "They asked us to come pick the little girl up. They're going to have us attend to her." His manner was gentle. It was his business to be comforting at times like this, but his concern was more than just professional. It was personal.

She had never thought of Willy as a friend. All the times they had greeted each other, had chatted about his flowers, had nodded at one another after church, she had seen him as distant and cold. Perhaps she had been wrong.

Her voice broke when she spoke. "Thank you, Mr. Wiggins. Yes, I would very much like to go."

He nodded and turned. "I'll send him over in about an hour."

"Mr. Wiggins."

He paused.

What possessed her she didn't know, but she stepped out onto the sidewalk and gave him a solid hug. A sob escaped her. "God bless you."

He straightened his suit, gave her another nod and turned to hurry back and notify Leonard of his errand. A smile tugged at the corner of his mouth as he walked up the steps of his building. He paused momentarily to look at the carefully groomed planters that for years had been predictably the same and shook his head.

28 Leonard

A little before ten o'clock, the black, somber looking Wiggins sedan pulled to a stop in front of the house. Everyone in town knew exactly who owned the imposing automobile although no insignia emblazoned the door, no markings of any kind. A large man whose broad shoulders stressed his neatly pressed white button-down shirt walked to the door. His footfalls were nearly silent. "Knock. Knock," he called softly. "Mrs. Wheaton?"

Taking her arm, he guided her to the car. Wearing a thin cotton dress, she looked frail and tired even at this hour of the morning. Her distress was palpable.

After delivering her to the Circle C, Leonard hesitated. "Mr. Wiggins said to take as long as you need."

"Give me two hours," she met his eyes. "It'll be okay. Come back for me about noon, if you would. If I'm not out here, don't come to the door, just wait for me. I'll listen for you and come out as soon as I can. Okay?" Touching his sleeve, she smiled.

He glanced at his watch. "Two hours." He nodded. "I'll be here. Don't worry about coming right out. I'll wait. I'll wait all day. Mr. Wiggins won't mind."

The ranch was still, the crunch of the departing tires on the gravel echoed in the silence. There wasn't even birdsong. The border collies lay in the shade of a massive tree, their heads pressed against the girl. Their tails beat lightly as Alice Mae approached, but they neither barked nor left her side. The dogs knew their place. Grace sat between them, her long blond hair loose around her shoulders, her arms wrapped around her knees, her back against a tree. She glanced over and lifted her chin almost imperceptibly to her aunt.

"I'm so sad to hear about Mary Charlene." Alice Mae kneeled down and ran her hand down the length of Chester and Hank, their wiry hair rough and dusty. Her hand came to rest on the girl's knee. She squeezed gently.

Hollow eyes looked up at her.

"Where's your mom?"

The girl tipped her head in the direction of the house and then, as if it were too heavy, let the head fall on her knees and stared at the grass, tears spilling silently into the thirsty ground.

The house shades were all drawn against the morning heat. Masyl sat on the sofa in the living room, shoulder to shoulder with Barbara as though holding each other up. Sorrow was etched on their faces, the shock still fresh.

Even at this hour, the kitchen counter was strewn with casseroles and baked goods dropped off by neighbors and well-meaning friends, all devastated by the news. Word of the tragedy reached farms and ranches in the area like a puff of smoke on the morning breeze. Farmers shook their heads and went back to the fields, thankful that their own families were safe. The women cooked. They pulled out their Tupperware and pie plates and they offered what they had.

By the end of the day, the smell of chicken, yeast rolls, desserts, and baked beans would fill the farm kitchen. This would sustain the family during the difficult days ahead.

Jeanie, hair in braids, cowboy boots still on from her morning chores, brushed past Alice Mae and pushed out through the screen door. Her mouth was set, her eyes red-rimmed and angry, the pounding of her heels was sharp against the flagstone path as she made her way to the fence. Without a sideways glance, she grabbed the reins of her horse, swung up into the saddle and with a sharp kick, shot across the driveway and into the field, pushing him to a full gallop.

Alice Mae watched her go and understood. She was dealing with the loss in her own way. An unspoken prayer for the girl washed through her as she saw the rider, horse, and dust trail disappear over the ridge.

Sue sat alone in an armchair petting a cat and idly tapping her foot against the coffee table, disbelief written plainly on her face.

Barbara stood and embraced her aunt and then motioned her to the sofa. "Sit here, Aunt Alice, by mother." The pain etched into the beautiful seventeen-year-old face was deep.

The sisters fell into each other's arms. Overcome with the loss, they clung together for several moments before Alice Mae could speak.

"I'm so sorry." It was inadequate. "Tell me what happened."

The story spilled out. Grandma Sherwood and Mary Charlene were almost at the ranch when a long trailer-truck came around a curve wider than it should have. Grandma swerved to avoid the truck and went into the ditch. Mary was thrown from the vehicle and struck her head.

"The driver stopped, but there was nothing he could do," Masyl said. "He flagged down a car and they went for help but they were too late. He found Mary …" her voice broke. She took a breath and tried again. "He said he found Mary Charlene in the ditch and carried her to the road. He laid her on his coat and then went back for Grandma. The doctor said aside from a lot of cuts and scrapes, she probably would have been okay except she hit her head." She collapsed again into Alice Mae, weeping.

"Funny thing is, I think I heard sirens early this morning and didn't think anything of it," Barbara said as if somehow her lack of alarm had been responsible for the outcome. "I was separating the milk. It just never occurred to me that it could be them." Her shoulders drooped, her self-incrimination visible.

"Don't do that to yourself," Alice Mae said softly. "You had no way of knowing. There was nothing you could have done."

Barb's long sun-bleached head nodded in acknowledgment, but the look on her face clearly said she didn't believe it. "I could have been with her."

"She was helping me in the garden just yesterday morning," Masyl whispered. Fresh tears came. "We were talking about what we would take to the county fair next month."

"Strawberry jelly, I'd guess." Alice Mae allowed a slow smile to steal across her face. "She showed me the red ribbons she won last year, said she would get the blue this year, for sure."

"Yea and she could've won too." Masyl laid her head on Alice Mae's shoulder.

"I know," she soothed.

The memories came in bits and pieces. The pain was unbearable.

"Mary named the new puppies," Tracy said, her voice barely above a whisper. She had entered the room, a basket of fresh unwashed eggs in hand. "Buck, Flank, Pepper, and Shadow. She wanted to keep all four of them." She sat the basket on the counter, kicked off her boots and came over to give and get a hug from her aunt. "She always wanted to keep 'em all." She sat down on the floor next to Sue and said, "Chickens are fed and eggs are done." Just in case anyone needed to know.

Barb nodded. As oldest, she was aware of chores and she was prepared to shoulder the load for the next few days.

"We were talking about getting her a new horse for her birthday in September." Masyl's voice hitched.

"She was supposed to be a flower girl at our wedding." Barb glanced at an unfinished pink chiffon dress hanging on a wire hanger in a nearby doorway. Heads shook, tolling the loss.

So many regrets. So many unfulfilled dreams. Alice Mae felt the stab of loss as each memory surfaced. Joyce and Mary Charlene had been closer than most cousins, more like sisters in many ways. Alice Mae knew the loss was hitting Joyce hard, too.

"Mr. Wiggins told me that she was being taken to his place. Do you know what you're going to do about the service?" Alice Mae prodded gently. The town would turn out. Everyone in the Phillips County knew and loved Masyl's girls. Yuma County too.

"I don't know, Maesy. I can't think about it yet. What do you say?"

Although the weight of the loss was crushing, Alice Mae knew decisions were needed. She took a deep breath and addressed the women, young and old.

"I'm sure Joe will do the service if you want to have it at First Baptist. He'd do a great job of it. It's going to be hard for everyone. She was so loved." The lump that she had been trying to keep out of her throat returned. She cleared it again.

"Not sure Chuck will want it at church. Maybe at Wiggins. I don't know."

"We have to do it at the church," Sue insisted. "Please. Daddy won't care. It has to be beautiful."

"You know the kids and I will help in any way we can. If there is anything special you want, just let us know."

"I know." Masyl nodded and then let her head fell back against the sofa, her eyes closed. "It's just too soon."

By the time Leonard crept back into the yard to retrieve his passenger some decisions had been made. The memorial service would be on Saturday at the Baptist Church. Richie would be one of the pallbearers if he wanted to as well as Dave Riggins, Barb's intended. Mary Charlene would be buried next to Premilla, Masyl and Alice Mae's beloved mother, in the Holyoke Cemetery. Several plots in that section of the cemetery had been reserved for family, but no one had ever imagined it would be used for this precious child.

Before leaving Alice Mac hugged each of her nieces, trying to transfer love and comfort as best she could. "We love you. All the kids send their love too." It was not enough, but it was all she had.

She held her sister for a long time sharing her sorrow and praying silently for her. At last she let go and walked to the front door.

"Love you, Sis."

There was no reply.

She stepped into the harsh afternoon sun. A hawk soared overhead and a few head of cattle bellowed from the distant ridge. Never had the land looked so barren and desolate. From the Dust Bowl of her childhood right through to this view of the rolling high dessert of the Colorado plains, she had endured this unforgiving land. It had taken her youth, her strength, and her mother. Now it had claimed her niece.

In this place she had frozen in winter and baked in the summer, all the time longing to be somewhere beautiful and green. She loved this country with its stark beauty and she hated its merciless harshness. Her heart ached with grief and loss, but her resolve was firm. Despite this unimaginable tragedy, she was leaving.

She rode in silence all the way home. The sunshine that had lit her sister's life was gone. Within a month, Barb would be married and gone. The hope that had once been hers and Masyl's as girls had been replaced by the reality of marriage, poverty and the inevitableness of death. An agonizing cry rose in her throat that required considerable effort to contain.

The following weekend in Holyoke was busy.

On Saturday First Baptist Church, on the corner of Baxter Avenue and Gordon Street, overflowed with families saying goodbye to a little girl they loved. It was one of the best attended services in the history of the church. Flowers filled the sanctuary and spilled out into the foyer infusing the air with the perfume of peonies and roses, lavender and heather. The florist from Wray had made three separate trips delivering vases and baskets and bouquets and the Holyoke florist had run out of blossoms. Those assembled murmured how much Mary Charlene would have loved the flowers.

Unlike most funerals in Holyoke, there were as many children in attendance as there were adults. Cousins and friends, neighbors and acquaintances all came to say goodbye.

After the church service ended, the family drove to the cemetery to lay Mary Charlene to rest beside her grandmother. By the time the black Wiggins Funeral Home car pulled up to the green awning shading the freshly-dug grave, more than two dozen cars had fallen into line behind it. Each car carried an arrangement or two from the church, turning the cemetery into a garden, a fitting tribute to the beautiful little girl.

On Sunday evening, the church was filled again with many of the same families saying goodbye to Alice Mae and her children. Young people gathered in clusters bemoaning the loss of their friends.

"I don't want you to move." Benny babbled as he followed Joyce around like a lost puppy. "Please don't go."

Elvira Davis, Peggy Fleming, and a dozen other women that Alice Mae had known for years wished her well with varying degrees of sincerity. Some were skeptical as to her real motives, unable to understand why anyone would leave the town where she was born – the only town most had ever known. Others were jealous that it was her, not them, taking the plunge.

Nearly everyone contributed to the money tree that had sprouted up on the reception table next to the cake, seeded with a ten dollar bill by Ruth. "You can do better than that," Ruth was heard to say to more than one attendee who tried to clip on a one-dollar bill. "Dig deeper."

Out of earshot of the guests of honor, the assembly was still sprinkled with speculation that she would come back with her tail between her legs. They hated losing one of their own.

For a town who didn't do change well, it was a difficult couple of days.

29   Henry

It was July twenty fourth.

Joyce was the first one to see his car. A long blue sedan towing an orange and white U-Haul trailer was hard to miss in Holyoke. She ran into the house. "He's here. He's here. Grandpa's here!"

"Dad?" Alice Mae pushed open the front screen door, astounded. She embraced him with genuine enthusiasm, grateful for a safe arrival. But, he was two days early!

"Alice Mae. Joyce." He tipped his head in the direction of the girl.

His beard was scratchy. His plaid flannel shirt was cold suggesting that his car had excellent air conditioning. Good. He felt even thinner through the bulk of the thick cotton than she remembered. She inhaled the familiar mixture of after shave and pipe tobacco, fighting the tumultuous conflict the odors stirred in her. "We didn't expect you for a couple more days. How was your trip?"

"Long," he answered stretching the knots out of his tall, angular body. "Left California at dawn yesterday morning and spent the night somewhere in Wyoming. Would've driven straight through but when I left Janet had a hissy fit and made me promise to stop." He didn't have to say it. She heard it in his voice. *Women!*

"Well, come on in. What can I get you?"

He snorted. "Don't suppose you've got beer in there by chance?"

"No, just finished the last one," she joked. "How about some cold water?"

The Chrysler was bigger than Alice Mae expected with wide bench seats. That was good. There would be enough room for everyone without being too crowded. Even without Donna riding with them, six in a car was going to be a challenging trip.

The U-Haul was even smaller than she expected. Much smaller.

Removing his hat he ducked through the front door with Joyce in tow. At six foot four inches he was used to ducking. Not all doorways, after all, are created equal.

"I'll take you up on it. Don't suppose you have any ice?"

From the back yard, Richie and Laurie came running in to greet him. Throwing arms around his tall waist they each gave him a genial hug. He patted their heads and reached into his shirt pocket.

"What do you think I have here?" he teased withdrawing a small stack of two dollar bills. With a flourish, he peeled off one bill and handed it to Richie, then another for Laurie. Folding the remaining bills he put them back in his pocket before grinning at Joyce. "Thought you weren't getting one, didn't ya?" He peeled off one more crisp greenback and a laughing little girl snatched it from him.

"Thanks, Grandpa," they chorused and took off to show their friends their new found wealth.

"Donna's already settling in over at Joe and Ruth's," she offered before being asked. "She's working till six tonight but when she sees the U-Haul, she'll be over to see you. Actually, she's probably already heard you're here. And Sharon's around here somewhere. She's been running errands all over town. I'm sure she'll be back momentarily."

"Good." Cold drink in hand, including ice broken from the one ice cube tray that had been in the freezer for at least a year, he ambled through the house peering into each room.

It wasn't unexpected that he had nothing good to say about the stacks of boxes. She had anticipated that he would find objection to the odd assortment of crates and containers that she had been able to procure from various stores in town. She expected him to tell her that they wouldn't pack well and that she should have found more uniform sizes. She had expected him to start telling her which of the things that she had carefully chosen to take would not be going, that it was too much and that it was too heavy. She was prepared to do battle for each and everything she considered essential. She wasn't prepared for his silence.

He tried to look passive, but she saw the surprise on his face when upon entering the enclosed back porch he saw that it was void of the monstrously heavy wringer washing machine. He had hated that loathsome piece of machinery almost as much as she had and told her for years that she needed to replace it, but had offered no assistance to that end. Looking around as though he expected to find it in the back yard or lurking on the side of the house for him to deal with, he was visibly relieved at its absence.

He turned and faced his daughter. "I'm going to drop the U-Haul here for you to load. Figured you could use some extra time to see what'll fit and what won't. You got five kids who can carry and haul for you. No need for me to stick around. I'll be back tomorrow evening."

He handed her his empty water glass, replaced his hat, and called for Richie.

"Get those cinder blocks out of the back for me."

Happy to help, the boy jumped to the task.

"Now set them down right there." He indicated a place directly in back of his bumper and bent to the task of detaching the trailer from his car. Carefully he settled the neck of the U-Haul on top of the cement blocks, making it level for loading. He rounded his car to the driver's side, opened the door and made his announcement.

"I'm going to go see Masyl."

She had expected that.

"Don't have the first idea of what I'm supposed to say to her. She'll probably bawl all over me. Blasted horrible business." He muttered mostly to himself. "Don't know what she expects me to do."

He tried to sound hard hearted but knowing that he had lost his own sweet girl when she was very young, Alice Mae understood the self-protective nature of his bluster.

"You don't have to say anything. Just go be with her."

He nodded, pulled his pipe from his shirt pocket and clamped it soundly between his front teeth. A sure sign that he was anxious.

She felt the pain in her chest as she recalled the day death had come to her own family.

Alice Mae had been ten. Little Dorothy had been only six. She was a bright, golden haired and happy child who filled their home with sunshine. Her laughter was like music and her gentle spirit was like incense, sweetening the home. Holyoke, like much of the Midwest, was in the grips of the great and terrible dust bowl. For days at a time, there was no light and no fresh air. Sometimes blue sky was not visible for weeks as the dust blew and drifted into homes, towns, and counties burying everything under foot after foot of gray grit. Death hung in the air and families suffered. In the midst of that heartache, Dorothy sang and laughed and shone like a candle in the darkness.

Henry was driving when the accident happened. He had taken Dorothy to town on a rare outing when his truck hit a fencepost that was buried by drifting dirt, making the road invisible. She had been thrown from the truck. By the time neighbors found her half buried, she was gone. Henry had been impaled on a piece of twisted steel that laid his leg open to the bone. Too badly injured and with a raging fever for more than two weeks he was unaware that Dorothy had died. When he regained his senses and found that she had already been buried, his grief turned a hard man into a tyrant. He had never forgiven himself for surviving. He had never forgiven God or his family. He still carried the pain.

Mary Charlene's death brought it all back.

"She'll be glad to see you, Dad. She looked for you at the service even though she hadn't heard from you. She thought you would come."

He looked away and cleared his throat. "No reason to make the trip twice. I'd already reserved the U-Haul and couldn't get it sooner. I made you a promise. Wouldn't have done her any good anyhow." He cleared his throat again.

Turning to face her, he glowered. "Before you leave you two need to make up!" Not waiting for a response, he turned the key and pulled away, turned left onto Gordon Street and headed out to the highway.

30   Cash Money

The walk and talk with Howard had been brief. It had been a miracle.

"If you were going to visit your father in California, your ADC checks would continue while you were out of town. Nothing would change. If you were still in California on the first of the month and asked me to, I could send a check to you there."

Alice Mae stared at him. "But I'm not visiting, I'm moving."

"I know, I know. Bear with me. I read the wording in the section on advancing funds during an absence and it says an absence for any reason for no longer than one year. It also says that you remain accountable to your case worker, me during that time. It is up to me to send you the check or to terminate the funds if I become aware that you have secured another source of income." He was practically vibrating with excitement.

"But I'm not visiting," she repeated. "I'm moving."

"I don't see it that way." He put his hands firmly on her shoulders. "The way I see it is that you are visiting McMinnville *while* you try to figure out *if* you can move there. You are attempting to establish yourself and your kids in a place that will afford them and you the opportunity to find a job, get into college and start over. As far as I'm concerned until you actually get a job that can support them and get them into school, your status there is temporary. You could decide to come back."

She looked at him askance. "That seems dishonest, somehow. I know I'm not coming back and you know I'm not coming back. It could get you into trouble."

He glanced at her and chuckled. "I thought the same thing. So I did some checking. I'm on a firm footing. I'm going to be sending you your check every month for up to one year. Got that?" His face was both set in stone and he was beaming like a kid at Christmas.

"So you're still my caseworker?"

"Yep, for up to one year, till you can make enough money to get off welfare."

She pondered the arrangement trying to find a good argument as to why it wouldn't work. She could think of none. Feeling a huge weight roll from her shoulders, she stretched out her arms and spun like a girl. "Yes, yes, yes." When she came to a stop, she looked up into his eager gray eyes and said. "Howard, you're an angel."

He grinned. "I think my wife might argue with that assessment but thank you."

They spent a few minutes talking figures, strategies and logistics of the money. He explained the forms needed and the procedures they would both have to follow. She assured him that she would keep up her end.

"I've talked with Audrey Yates and explained what I'm doing. She's onboard to help you in any way she can. We both know how quickly a year can fly by so keep her in the loop as well as me with your progress."

"How can I thank you?" Her head was spinning. Her heart was soaring. She was overjoyed!

"You've got one year, Alice Mae. One year to make it happen. Succeed and you'll have more than thanked me."

She grinned back at him. "Watch me!"

31 Masyl

She was standing in her garden, batting at the weeds that over the past weeks of neglect had gotten a foothold among the tomatoes and potatoes when the long blue Ford rolled in. Eyeing it as it passed by and pulled to a stop in the shade, she leaned on the hoe handle.

Henry raised a hand in greeting as he unfolded himself from the front seat. "Masyl," he called. Slipping on his hat against the blazing July sun, he ventured out and waved again.

She continued prodding at the soil and uprooting the unwanted plants.

"Grandpa?" From behind him came the sound of running boots on dry dirt. Grace reached him first and threw her arm around his waist. Sue was on her heels and wrapped her arm around the other side of him. "Grandpa. When did you get here?" The girls smelled of fresh air with a hint of cow dung thrown in. Long blond braids hung down their backs, just like he remembered.

He grunted in protest at the force of the hugs and squeezed them back. "Take it easy. I'm an old man."

"You're not old." They laughed and hugged him again, even harder. "Got to finish our chores," they called out, heading back towards the barn. "We'll be back."

He lifted the latch on the wooden gate and entered what was his daughter's domain. Long rows of vegetation, knee high and taller stretched out before him, a testimony to her diligence. "May I come in?" He did not make a habit of asking permission from anyone, much less from a woman, but given the oppressive sorrow that still etched her face, he asked.

She turned her back to him, wiped her face with the tail of her cotton work shirt and kept digging. She had made it four days without crying but now at the sound of her father's voice she felt her composure crumble. She cursed herself for allowing his presence to hurt. She would not give him that power.

"I'm so sorry about Mary." He took a step closer but then stopped, allowing his voice to span the distance between them. "Alice Mae told me that you hoped I would come, but there was nothing I could have done." He removed his hat and held it in his hands.

Masyl's shoulders fell. "Of all my girls, why did it have to be Mary? She was so young and so happy." Despair rolled off her. "Not that I would have wanted it to be anyone else, but why Mary?"

"She was a joy. Like your little sister, Dorothy. Do you remember?" In thirty years, they had never spoken of it. Her name was not allowed to be spoken in their home after her death. It was a wound that was never addressed, that never healed.

She turned and looked at her father for the first time. "I was seven. Of course I remember. Do you? You weren't there for me then either." The crushing sorrow of losing her sister, just one year younger, had been the hardest time of her life – till now. She had wanted so much to be held and comforted. In the chaos of that time, she was invisible. Alone.

He couldn't argue. She was right.

"Alice Mae was here for you. She and the kids have been with you through this."

The sound that came from her was from a depth that she did not recognize. "Here for me?" she scoffed. "They can't wait to get away from me. You and Alice Mae, you're going to get into your car and drive away and leave me here, forgotten." *Just like before.*

Behind him, the ranch came alive. Word of his arrival had spread and girls in cut-off jeans, cowboy boots, and broad brimmed hats appeared on every side.

Barb emerged from the house, hand in hand with a tall, dark-haired man who she introduced as her fiancé, Dave Riggins. Henry stepped back into the yard and shook the man's hand. He had known Fred Riggins, Dave's grandfather, and a harder man never lived.

Tracy walked out from the barn, set down the pail she carried and gave him an enormous hug. "Grandpa. I'm so glad you came."

Of all the girls, Tracy had changed the most. Two years ago she had still been a little girl and now a young woman stood before him with golden hair down to her waist. Stunning. He felt like he was looking at her mother at fifteen. He blinked hard.

She stepped back allowing him to catch his breath. "How long are you staying?"

"I told your Aunt Alice that I'd be back tomorrow afternoon so I guess you're stuck with me till then." His announcement was met with cheers from everyone under the age of twenty. "Where's your dad?"

Chuck came in from the range just long enough to eat dinner and then he departed abruptly for the barn with pressing matters that needed his attention. The loss had hit him hard. Dark circles under his eyes and gaunt hollows in his lean face spoke volumes.

The girls cleared the table and then headed out for evening chores leaving Masyl with the dishes. Again. Henry turned his chair around, drew out his pipe, knowing better than to light it in this house, and waded in.

"Alice Mae says you're still not speaking to her."

"She was here after Mary Charlene." Hot water filled the deep country kitchen sink making a mountain of suds. She plunged her hand in and began scrubbing pots and pans. "She came to the service, they all did. We spoke."

"Aside from that, she says you two aren't talking at all. God knows it's been hell for you the last couple of weeks, but you two need to make up before she leaves."

She held out a clean pot, dripping with water and suds, and looked expectantly at Henry. Reluctantly he pulled himself to his feet, set aside the pipe and took the proffered pot, picked up a kitchen towel and began drying.

"Anything I have to say will only make it worse. She belongs here! You think she's going to be better off in Oregon where she doesn't know anyone? What's she gonna do when she needs help? Call me?"

"Well, she's sure not gonna call me. I told her that. She'll be on her own. Sink or swim."

"And you're okay with that? You're just going to leave her there not knowing if she has enough food to feed those kids? Not caring if she gets sick? She tells me that the town is big. How's she supposed to get around? You're just going to plop her down and drive away. That's your style isn't it? Just move away so you don't have to think about us or see us." She banged a large pot down hard on the counter. "You really don't care about us at all." Her eyes flashed.

His temper flared. "Look. You've got the farm and Chuck. Your girls have someplace to call home. She hasn't had that in a very long time."

Masyl scoffed. "I've got Chuck. Right."

He said nothing. The strife between Masyl and Chuck was well-known.

"You can still have a good relationship with your sister if you want to, even after she's gone."

"If she wanted a relationship with me all that badly, she wouldn't be going or at least she'd stay till after the wedding."

"She didn't choose the move date. I did, so that's not fair."

She turned back to the sink of steaming water and scoffed. "Life's not fair. You're the one that taught us that, Dad, and you were right."

"So, will you go in tomorrow and talk to her?"

She flung the dishcloth at him, wiped her hands on her apron and stormed out of the kitchen, letting the screen door slam after her. He had his answer.

32 Head 'em up

The U-Haul was loaded. Last minute items were stuffed, crammed and shoved into every crevice. Many neighbors came out to watch the production but few actually helped. The last two items to be wedged in on top of the boxes were the broom and dustpan. The items that remained curbside had not made the cut.

Alice Mae looked around hoping to see Masyl among the well-wishers and was hurt but not surprised by her sister's absence.

"That's it." She forced a smile. "If anybody wants the stuff that's left you're welcome to it."

"I'll keep these for you." Ruth retrieved a stack of books from the grass that she knew were dear to Alice Mae and clasped them to her bosom. "We'll send them with Donna at Christmas."

"Christmas?"

"Yeah, Joe and I decided that a round trip train ticket would be a great Christmas gift for you and the kids. We'll put her on just after finals and you can get her back to us before classes take up in January." With her free arm, she hugged her friend who appeared dumbstruck. "You okay with that?"

Alice Mae nodded, wiping her eyes. She tried to say thank you, but it came out as a squeak. They hugged again while Ruth patted her back. "It's going to be fine."

"I know."

The sun had been up for several hours and the early morning shade provided by the big tree was gone. Even though it was only nine o'clock, everyone was hot and sweaty. It was going to be a scorcher.

Donna walked with her family back through the empty house one more time, opening doors and drawers, reliving memories. The kitchen looked shabby in the harsh sunlight, the paint and tiles peeling, the floor chipped and scarred. The bedrooms looked too small for the five people who had called it home. Without the love and bustle of the family, it was just a little structure that was easy to leave.

"You going to be okay?" Alice Mae took Donna by the hand. "You know I would rather have you with us."

"It'll be just one year. By the time I get there, you'll be all settled and we'll have a real reunion."

"I know." They smiled, each being brave for the other. They both knew the risks. A year could bring many changes good and bad. Donna might, God forbid, meet a man and decide to stay. What if Alice Mae couldn't find a job? What if …?

His bellow brought them back to the present. "You women going to babble on all day? I'm hungry. If you want breakfast, get on down to The Grub and let's get this move moving." Sliding into the sedan, he honked the horn and pulled away from the curb, Richie riding shotgun.

Everyone else walked to the only place in town serving breakfast and waved to well wishers as they passed. Alice Mae noticed that Wiggins Funeral Home had a few judiciously-placed sunny marigolds tucked into the previously all white urns. She smiled at the welcome additions. They had not been there a week ago. She glanced around to see if Mr. Wiggins was anywhere to be seen and finding him absent, she smiled and waved anyway just in case.

"Hotcakes and scrambled eggs all around. And coffee." He barked to the young waitress who dared to offer menus. She pulled them back.

"Blueberry or regular?" She asked with a tremor in her voice.

He glared at her like she was an errant child and growled. "Normal pancakes. Brown syrup. Regular eggs."

She fled to the kitchen.

Eyeing the others sitting around a large table in the center of the room he said. "I'm not wasting time while you all dilly dally over what you want."

This was going to be a long trip!

Between bites, Joyce and Richie peppered their grandpa with questions about California, Oregon, the Pacific ocean, the forest, the Indians, and the Seattle World's Fair. At last he put his hands up. "Enough! Ask me any more questions and I'll just stick you in the trunk instead of the back seat. My ears hurt!"

They giggled, excitement lighting up their faces.

With every plate cleaned – nobody wanting to incur the wrath of the man paying the bill by leaving a morsel – they pushed back from the table.

As they opened the front door, they nearly collided with Elvira and Benny.

"We heard you were here. We just wanted to come say goodbye," Elvira gasped, panting and wiping her face with the back of her hand. "We are all going to miss you so much." She thrust a plate of homemade cookies covered in aluminum foil into Alice Mae's hands and pulled a tissue from the pocket of her red summer dress. "Poor Benny cried all night knowing you were leaving today."

Joyce looked at the pudgy boy with swollen eyes and smiled sweetly before taking a step backward to a protective position behind her mother. She would not miss him all that much. "Thanks for the cookies." She said, hoping they were chocolate chip.

They were burning daylight. Henry made a sweeping motion with his arms and shouted out what every rancher recognizes as the call to action. "Head 'em up!"

They piled into the car and headed north to catch Hwy 6 west. In her purse, Alice Mae had the proceeds of the reception money tree. More than eighty dollars had been generously given. She was giddy with the nest egg and what it represented as far as provisions for her new home since so much had been left behind. Food. Supplies. A blessed beginning. *Make it stretch. Make it last.* In her heart, she sang a hymns of thanksgiving she knew so well. In the car, she just sat and smiled.

33 Move 'em out

With Joyce between them, Alice Mae and Henry settled in the front seat as the grain silos of Holyoke got smaller in the rear window and the silos of Haxtun grew on the horizon. To the south, wheat fields with ripe grain stood combine-ready. To the north, more wheat lay in looping ridges, waiting to be gathered into bales. Familiar white faced Holsteins lumbered across the scruffy rises. "It does have its own sort of beauty doesn't it?" she said, scanning the vastness.

"It does," he agreed, scratching his unshaven face. "But it's unforgiving."

The flat expanse stirred a sense of loss in her that she hadn't expected. Scavenger birds floated on the drafts of hot air looking for prey. She swallowed down a lump in her throat trying not to dwell on Masyl.

Town after town passed into memory as the Rockies loomed ever larger on the horizon. Tumbleweeds blew across their path and the overhead sun lead them west felt like the pillar of fire leading them to the Promised Land.

As they entered the foothills, the shade of the tall Colorado spruce and the fragrance of mountain pine were richer than she had imagined. Cranking down the window, she breathed in the warm summer perfume. Shade and sunlight danced across the car interior.

"Mom! You're letting all the cold air out," Sharon protested as hot air poured into the back seat.

"I like it." Richie sat forward.

"It's too windy." Laurie's hair billowed around her face.

"I'm enjoying the mountain air," Alice Mae grinned, ignoring their outcries.

"I need to go to the bathroom," Richie announced. "I really gotta go."

"You should have gone before we left. Just hold it." Unsympathetic to the boy's distress, Henry drove on. His policy on road trips was to not drink anything so that he didn't have to stop. He had only one cup of coffee for breakfast for that very reason.

"That was more than three hours ago, Dad." Alice Mae gave her father a sideways glance. "I think it's a fair request."

Henry signaled and pulled off on the shoulder of the road and pointed. "Use a bush. Girls, don't look."

"Dad!" She glared at her father. "No. He cannot use a bush! We're all going to need to stop. Please find a gas station or something."

Shaking his head in utter disgust, he signaled and pulled back onto the highway, muttering the word that would become his refrain for the whole trip. "Women!"

It took twenty minutes to locate a facility that actually had plumbing and another twenty to get everyone cycled through the tiny way-side washroom. While they took care of business, Henry slipped around the corner of the building to enjoy his pipe in peace and quiet.

Once everyone was comfortably back in their seats, the journey resumed.

With his two dollar bill Richie had purchased a stack of comic books to read during the trip. The Green Lantern was his favorite. Sharon was given several copies of Seventeen Magazine by a classmate, leaving her money to spend along the way. Laurie found a used Nancy Drew for twenty cents, leaving her with pocket money as well. The tranquility that the reading material provided was a welcome relief from the chaos of the past few days. Joyce was happy looking out the windows, leaning against her mother and soaking in the sights that were all new to her. "Look at that," she said frequently. "Wow!".

"Beautiful."

"I'm hungry," Richie's stomach growled loud enough to be heard from the front seat. "Can we have some of the cookies?"

"Yeah, Cookies!" Joyce cheered.

"Good idea." Alice Mae reached beneath the seat to locate the plate of goodies that Elvira has so carefully wrapped. She stopped at her father's objection.

"Absolutely not! No eating in my car." He looked menacing.

"But I'm hungry," Richie repeated. "Can we have some next time we stop for the bathroom? Besides, I'm thirsty."

"Me too," Laurie added, hanging out her tongue to illustrate her point.

"Me three." Sharon piped in. "It's hot back here." It was a mutiny.

"What do you mean next time we stop?" He grumbled even as he scanned the horizon for anyplace suitable to pull off and get water. Or coffee. "You can't be hungry. You ate enough pancakes to satisfy a lumberjack. Besides, if you eat you'll just have to stop again."

"Aren't we going to stop for lunch?"

"You're just sitting in the car. You're not starving and I'm not wasting my money on more food. You'll survive." The man that Alice Mae remembered was resurfacing.

The entire backseat howled.

The water at the highway rest stop was not cold, but it did satisfy. The cookies were a hit, oatmeal with chocolate chips and walnuts.

"Five minutes. Eat up." They had a schedule to keep.

Watered and fortified, the mood in the car lightened. "How much longer?" someone from the back seat asked, a small whimper in their voice.

"Don't ask." At least Alice Mae and her father were in agreement on that subject.

It was nearly four before the uprising of hungry kids was severe enough that he began to look for a place to eat. Laramie, Wyoming, a decent place to find a meal as he recalled, was coming up. Henry began scanning the roadside for a suitable place to stop.

"Looks expensive," he said, surveying an upscale establishment advertising steaks dinners.

"Looked good to me," Richie mumbled as they sailed past.

"No cars. Must be something wrong with it," Henry muttered as a hamburger drive-in joint with advertised specials became a blur.

"Might have been fast service and they didn't look too busy," Alice Mae's comment was met with silence. Her stomach rumbled loudly.

Neon lights announced *The Chinese Garden,* just ahead. " No," he snapped without explanation.

"It could be fun. Please, Grandpa." Sharon begged. "We've never tried Chinese,"

"Are you paying?" He glared at her in the rear view mirror.

Just two miles east of the Laramie city limits, he finally found a diner whose parking lot was packed with five big rig trucks, in his mind a good sign. He pulled in and killed the engine.

"Everybody out."

One by one the passengers took turns using the restroom and draining their glasses of ice water, refreshed by the change of seating and the cool interior of the restaurant, they were more than ready for dinner. The menu was expansive. Hamburgers, pot roast, spaghetti, and steak. Breakfast served 24 hours. Their mouths watered at the possibilities.

"How about we all have hamburgers?" The response he got was unenthusiastic so he upped the offer. "Cheeseburgers and fries?"

"Can we have spaghetti and meatballs?" Sharon was the first to ask, emboldened by his hesitation when the waitress asked what he wanted. "It smells so good. And can I have a coke?"

He glared at Alice Mae is if she had somehow caused the discontent of her children by encouraging them to be, God forbid, independent. "What do you want?" he asked Laurie.

"The spaghetti sounds good to me too." She responded cautiously.

Joyce nodded her agreement. He looked at Alice Mae and raised his eyebrow. "And you?"

"The burger sounded fine to me. With fries and a malted milk." She might as well go big.

"A hamburger for me too." Richie voted. "With extra fries. I'm starving."

Relieved that the matter had been settled quickly, he placed an order for three spaghetti dinners, three burgers all the way and feeling bighearted, threw in their drinks of choice. Dessert was not an option. They had already eaten a whole plateful of cookies.

His wallet was feeling thinner by the minute.

When every last piece of bread and every last French fried potato was consumed, the six packed back into the car for another long stretch. They still had hours to go before he planned to stop for the night. He wanted to make Salt Lake City before nightfall and although it was looking doubtful, with full bellies he had a better chance of driving through than without.

This cross country trip was an adventure of a lifetime. The further away from home they got and the closer to their new destination the more the excitement grew.

"Tell us about our house. Tell us about McMinnville."

He told them about the town, the Willamette Valley and the changes they faced. He made the new house sound cozy and charming. He didn't know much about the schools or the churches, but he assured them that all the boys were cute and the girls were attractive. They laughed.

"The town is lush and green. The city parks are like forests, shady and full of flowers and ferns and grass. There are at least two of them, one at each end of town. I know there is a bowling alley and a skating rink and a movie theater."

The kids clapped and cheered, anticipation building.

He racked his brain for other things of interest. "Like Holyoke, it's the county seat which means there'll be a county fair."

"What big businesses are there?" Alice Mae wondered.

"There's a dairy and a steel mill on the north edge of town." His efforts on her behalf had been more focused on securing housing and looking at the general layout. He should have paid more attention. "I know there are lots of stores so jobs might be easier to come by for you girls. You already know about the summer crops." The energy level in the car was spiking as the possibilities rose.

"Oh, and I think there is a Purina Mill, too," he added, mentally replaying his quick tour through the town.

As the summer sun finally sank in the west, the lights of the city of Salt Lake lit the horizon. It had been a long day, but the sight ahead drew them forward until they found a motel on the eastern edge of the sprawling metropolis and pulled to a stop.

He got two rooms for the six of them. Richie would bunk with him and the four girls would all have to make do with the other room, somehow. Having never stayed in a motel in the whole of their lives, they saw it as an adventure no matter the arrangements.

Alice Mae reached for the one packed bag she had brought for them to share that night and stopped with a gasp. "My purse! It's not here!" She groped behind the seat, between every crack, in spaces too small for a wallet, much less a handbag and still came up empty. *Lord no.* "No! I must have left it at the diner."

Color drained from her face. She felt like she'd just been punched in the stomach. She grabbed hold of her father's arm. "We've got to go back."

Her dad shook his head. "It's been hours. Even if we went back, it wouldn't still be there. I'll try to call them from the office and see if anyone found it and turned it in, but don't get your hopes up."

"Dad." Her voice broke. "What am I going to do?"

He turned his back and walked away. "I thought you said God told you to make this move. Where's your faith now?"

34 Home

Despite the numbing loss and the exhaustion of a night spent in supplication that somehow her purse would be found, Alice Mae woke with renewed resolve that she would go where she believed God was leading. She turned the matter over to him and focused her attention on her family, her father and the road ahead. It wasn't easy.

With everyone freshly showered, they raided what was politely called a free continental breakfast at the hotel and piled into the car.

In the morning light, the Great Salt Lake was spectacular. The water glistened as far as the eye could see. It resembled an ocean; one that smelled bad. As they drove the kids bombarded Henry with questions.

"Why does it stink?"

"How did the salt get in there?"

"How deep is it?"

Knowing few of the answers, he opted for diversion.

"Years ago when the pioneers were first settling around the Salt Lake, they had a very hard winter. Almost all their food was gone. In the spring, after they had planted their crops, a vast swarm of crickets swooped in and began eating all the new shoots. They ate grass and grain and the leaves off the trees. The pioneer knew that if something didn't happen soon they would all starve." He glanced at his audience. He had them!

"What'd they do?"

"Well, most of 'em were God fearing Mormons and they began praying that the crop would be saved. They prayed and prayed until one day the sky grew dark with a huge flock of sea gulls. They had come all the way from the ocean, as far as the pioneers knew.

They stayed and ate crickets day after day till they were all gone then they flew away. The crops were saved and so were the pioneers. In fact, that's why the state bird of Utah is the Sea Gull."

"Really? Cool." Richie's eyes were as big as saucers. "Tell us more."

"Well," he began, "do you know that the highway that runs across Utah used to be called the Devil's Highway because it was said to be haunted? They called it the most dangerous highway in the world."

"Why?"

"It was said that ghosts appeared to drivers and sometimes showed up in their backseats."

Joyce squealed."Is that this highway?"

"No. That highway was dark and wound through the mountains. They closed it down years ago and built this new interstate."

"So what happened to the ghosts?"

"Who knows? Maybe they jumped into the Great Salt Lake and that's why it's so smelly."

Alice Mae shot him a look but said nothing. At least the kids were entertained.

With a ten hour drive ahead of them, nothing was going to slow them down today. He mashed the gas pedal down and shot across the Great Salt Lake Desert and into Nevada deflecting, as best he could, calls to stop. California lay ahead.

"Past." His voice boomed as he read from the smallish billboard sign alongside the highway.

"What?" Sharon was the first to bite.

"Schoolhouses." He read as the second sign came into view. He pointed to the sign and five sets of eyes followed his finger. "Read the signs."

"Take it slow." Sharon joined him in reading the third sign in the series. "What does that mean?"

Alice Mae laughed as she answered that question although she was not sure where the knowledge came from. "They're Berma-Shave signs. I've heard about them but never seen them. Keep reading."

"Let the little." Laurie and Richie chimed in as the sign came into view and flew past the passenger side window. Everyone craned their necks to see what would come next.

"Shavers grow." Everyone in the car read together.

"Berma-Shave." Henry beat them to the punch line. "We'll pass these signs all the way to California. Keep watching. I'll give a dollar to the first one to see the next set of signs." He was certainly not above bribing his grandchildren if it would keep them occupied and quiet.

"What other ones have you seen, Dad?" Despite the loss of her purse, the beauty of the Nevada landscape and the building anticipation of getting to California and seeing Henry's home was growing. "What other Berma-Shave signs have you passed?"

"Well, as I recall there was one coming across Wyoming that said something like 'Don't take a curve at 60 per, we hate to lose a customer. Berma-Shave.'"

She smiled. "And were you going more than sixty at the time you read the sign?" She could have sworn she saw the color flush his face, but he ignored the question.

"And last time Janet and I went south there was one that said 'Hardly a driver is now alive, who passed on hills at 75. Berma-Shave.'"

The kids all laughed.

"What is Berma-Shave anyway?" Joyce wanted to know.

"It's a shaving cream for men. It was selling like …" he checked himself and revised his description, "wasn't selling very well as I recall. Then they started putting up signs all along the interstates and now everyone at least knows who they are. Still don't know if their product is any good."

"You don't use it?"

"Never have." He reached across the car and opened the glove box and withdrew a rechargeable razor, switched it on and ran it over and over the stubble on his face making a gritty, grinding noise. "I can't use a blade and shave cream in the car. That's why God invented the electric."

"God didn't invent …" Joyce started to protest, but a grin on her mother's face stopped her. Grandpa was teasing and he didn't do that much. She giggled.

"Can I try it?" Richie asked, hopeful.

His grandfather glanced in the mirror and snorted. "How old are you?"

"Almost fourteen."

He shook his head. "I don't think so."

It was barely ten thirty when the familiar outcry of hunger began. As usual it started with Richie.

"I'm hungry."

"You had breakfast at the hotel just a few hours ago."

"I just had a donut."

"You should have eaten more than one."

"Mom wouldn't let me."

"My stomach's growling too." Joyce didn't want to miss the chance to add her two cents worth. "Can we please stop soon? And, I have to go to the bathroom."

"Me too." It was a chorus.

"Here's the deal. We will stop up ahead and you will eat an enormous early lunch 'cause I don't want to stop for food again till we get home. Knowing Janet, she'll have spent the month's grocery budget stocking up for you. She's probably made a pot roast with mashed potatoes, and cookies." Stomachs growled louder. "When I talked to her last night, she said something about fried chicken, I think. Do you kids like any of that?"

"Yeah!" Enthusiastic cheers came from all quarters.

"So there's a truck stop about twenty miles ahead, I think. Do we have a deal?"

"Deal." They chorused, famished.

Burgers with all the works, including fries and malted milkshakes, were ordered with no argument, with an extra order of fries thrown in just for good measure. Full stomachs brought a blissful, if short-lived, reprieve from the incessant banter. Books and comics resurfaced and four children entertained themselves for the best part of an hour.

His mood improved with every mile and with the prospect of his own bed and the silence that would come with it tonight. And he would see Janet. Despite his overt and often pronounced loathing of women in general he had finally found a wife who was his equal. She did not fear him as some had, with good reason. She did not fight him as had others, also with good reason. She was a rock that knew her own mind and put up with him without putting up with his bluster. He respected her. He missed her.

Since the day Premilla had walked out on him twenty years ago, and in hindsight she had been right to do so considering how monstrously he had treated her, he had been looking for a companion. He was not an easy man to know, nor an easy man to love. In the end, he had not looked for love but for respect and he found it in Janet. Her four foot eleven height, well packed that it was, looked comical next to his tall, lanky form but with her he had finally found peace. He smiled.

"Who wants some ice cream?" His question surprised him almost as much as it did his passengers. "We'll drive through and eat it in the car."

Jaws dropped and then grins spread across every face.

Crossing into California the terrain changed from high dessert of the Nevada Mountains to the dense Tahoe National Forest, and then green foothills descending into the Sacramento Valley.

"It's beautiful, Dad." There was awe in her voice. "I've seen pictures of this but they didn't do it justice."

"They rarely do. Look," he pointed north. The tip of Mt. Shasta glowed as late afternoon sun bounced off the snowy peak, white even in July. "We'll go right past it on our way to McMinnville."

She scanned the sweeping vista taking in various peaks and valleys. "Yosemite?" she indicated a span to the south. "Looks like we can see all the way to the ocean. No wonder you love it here."

The first evening lights twinkled in the city below as the setting sun slipped over western horizon. The air smelled fresh and clean. Alice Mae felt like she was driving into a fairy tale. She could only hope it would have a happy ending.

35 Janet

A flash of headlights turning into the driveway brought Janet out of the house grinning and waving.

"You made it! Oh, I'm so glad. I was beginning to get a little worried." The compact woman reached for the driver's door, pulled it open and bent in to give her husband a peck on the cheek.

Six travel-weary people crawled out of the car, stretched and breathed in the rose-scented air. They never wanted to sit down again. The children clustered in the driveway, hesitant to wander into unfamiliar territory.

Sharon was the first to stray. Slipping her sandals off her feet, she stepped onto the soft green grass and sighed with pleasure. Laurie followed. Within minutes, all four children were running barefoot and laughing, enjoying the revitalizing smell and feel of the manicured lawn.

"When you get tired of that I have fried chicken on the table," Janet called.

A collective cheer went up from the dark shadows of the side yard.

Janet gave Alice Mae a congenial hug. "What a long trip. You must be exhausted. Come on inside and let me get you something cold to drink. What do you need to bring in?"

The woman, several inches shorter than Alice Mae, but carrying an additional twenty pounds, had an easy smile. Her blonde, gray-streaked hair was twisted into a tidy bun at the nape of her neck with soft wisps escaping around the edges.

"Just this small overnight bag for now, I think. It has our toothbrushes and night clothes. I'll dig through the rest tomorrow and see what we need." She turned from side to side and arched her back to release tension. She surveyed the comfortable ranch house sitting on a deep, tree lined lot and smiled. "Who does the yard work around here? It's beautiful." She breathed in the intoxicating fragrances of flowers that she couldn't even name.

Janet beamed. "Henry usually does the mowing and pruning, I do the flowers. It's our division of labor."

The home was comfortable with wood paneling and sun washed colors throughout. Miss-matched throw pillows were scattered on the sofa and chairs in the family room. Nothing looked new but rather gently used. She felt a pang of resentment, not for herself, but for her mother who had never known such comforts.

It had been a very long drive since that early lunch and although the ice cream surprise had been nice, it was long gone. The kitchen table was spread like a picnic with a platter of cold fried chicken in the center surrounded by mounded bowls of side dishes that looked incredible and smelled even better. Her stomach growled as she walked past the spread, following Janet down a hallway.

"This room," Janet was saying, "is where I thought you and your girls could all sleep. It has two full-size beds. They're old, but they're comfortable." She trailed Janet into a room sparse of furniture save the two aforementioned beds and a small bedside table. On the table was a sweet-scented bouquet of pink roses, freshly cut from the garden. Gingham curtains covered the east facing window and would be welcome protection from the early morning sun. "There's room in the closet if you need to hang anything up." She glanced at the small bag Alice Mae was carrying. "There's a bathroom right next door for your family to use. Henry and I have our own."

Clean towels hung two-deep on both towel bars in a tiny bathroom where an array of cute guest soaps filled a basket.

"Where will Richie be?"

"The sofa in the family room is comfortable. He can either sleep on it as is or we can pull it out. It is a hide-a-bed but personally I think it's better to just sleep on it as is. Will that be okay?"

"Better than okay."

Finally, allowing herself to relax and let go of the tension she had carried all day, she felt her nose tingling with relief. "This is great." She said meaning it. "Thank you."

The new arrivals fell upon the food like ravenous beasts. Potato salad, fresh picked cucumbers and tomatoes from the garden, baked beans, chicken. It was all delicious and within twenty minutes it was almost all gone. Henry sat contentedly with his arm draped across his wife's shoulder watching the feasting and enjoying his pipe. Nobody objected.

"This is great." Richie pronounced without waiting for his mouth to be completely empty. "Can I have another piece of chicken?" He looked at his mother for permission and proceeded to consume his fourth piece, or was it his fifth?

"Anyone have room for dessert?"

"No, I don't think there could be any room left after this spread," Henry said, straight-faced. "Why don't you just save it for tomorrow."

"Oh yeah?" Richie shot back. "I want some."

"Me too." Laurie chimed in.

"Let's take it out on the patio. Just leave the dishes. I'll do them later." Janet rose and handed Sharon a stack of small plates, Laurie a fistful spoons and forks and Joyce a stack of paper napkins. After giving her husband the tall three layer fudge temptation she had spent the afternoon creating, she picked up a wicked looking knife and took the lead. "This way."

Ritchie scrambled to hold the door open as the processional passed through. He still had room for at least one big piece.

The small patio had a round wooden table under a yellow umbrella. Curved benches provided seating for four. Declining any cake, Henry grabbed a pillow from one of the benches and stretched out on the lawn, content.

Bordering the brick patio, azaleas bloomed in bright shades of red and pink, glorious even in the dim patio light. Alice Mae wandered around examining each variety and checking each one for fragrance.

"What's in bloom in McMinnville?"

With eyes still closed, he muttered, "You'll see soon enough."

It was after ten by the time everyone settled into their seat or a spot on the lawn enjoying Janet's cake. The silence settling over the group reflected contentment as well as fatigue.

Alice Mae was the first to break the calm. "I'm about ready for bed," she yawned. "It's been a long day."

Agreeable murmurs filled the night air.

"Thank you, Janet, for everything. You've made us feel so welcome." She hugged the older woman warmly. "See you in the morning." She picked up her plate to carry inside.

Janet dipped her head and smiled. "My pleasure. Just leave these dishes here. Henry and I'll take care of them."

One by one the visitors said their goodnights and retired. The beds were soft, the house was cool and comfortable and soon the peaceful sounds of sleeping children filled the air.

After the dishes had been rinsed and stacked, his wife led him from the kitchen to their bedroom. "I'll wash up in the morning, Henry. You've had a long couple of days. Let's turn in."

"Home at last," he breathed and followed her to their room.

An hour later when she was sure everyone was asleep, Janet stole out of bed and sat in the glider by the window. It was going to be another long night.

Ten feet away and with a wall between them, Alice Mae lay wrestling with her own demons. She was so sure this was what God wanted her to do. Her prayers had been specific. Her answers had been just as clear yet her heart was heavy with remorse for leaving Masyl. The pit in her stomach ached when she thought of her lost purse. She quoted the verses that she had been given from Isaiah. *"You will go out with joy and be led forth with peace ... and instead of the nettles the myrtle will come up."* She prayed it back to the Lord and claimed the land of the myrtle tree for her family.

36 Be Happy

The lure of frying bacon, eggs and hotcakes on the griddle brought Richie off the sofa and into the kitchen before the first of the flapjacks hit the platter.

"I'm starved," he announced unashamed of the vast quantity he had eaten only hours before. "Can I have the first ones?"

"If you comb your hair I'll give you these." Janet flipped the bubbling discs with a practiced hand while tipping her head in the general direction of the powder room. "And wash your hands." Boys of all ages needed reminding.

"Can I have the next ones?" Joyce was already dressed in short pants and a white sleeveless blouse, her hair tied up with a ribbon when she popped through the kitchen doorway. "Orange juice!" She squealed. "I love orange juice." She pulled back the kitchen chair and settled in. After draining her glass of the golden nectar she held it forth, hopeful of a refill.

"Where's mom?" Laurie trailed the two younger children by a few minutes ready, like her sister, for whatever the day held. "She's not in the bedroom."

"Your mom and Henry are out in the driveway," Janet said, adding hotcakes to the serving platter in the center of the table. Fair game for all. "They already ate. They're reloading the trailer and seeing if they can make room for anything else."

"Do we have to help them?" She eyed Janet hoping for an out.

"I think you're off the hook." A plate of bacon emerged like magic from the oven and was relieved of some of its stack the moment it hit the table. "They're repacking some of the boxes so that they fit better. I'll go see if they need help later. You kids just relax; you've had a long ride." She eyed them over her glasses and grinned. "Have you kids ever picked fresh oranges?"

"I understand that you're not happy about the move." Janet carried a tray containing a glass of orange juice, a couple strips of bacon and two pieces of toast into the bedroom where Sharon, alone, lingered. She eyed the girl. "Since you missed breakfast, I thought I'd just leave this for you. You're welcome to stay in bed as long as you like, just let me know if you want anything else."

The puffiness of the girl's eyes spoke volumes. She eyed her grandfather's wife with wariness. Was this going to be a pep talk? She wasn't in the mood.

"I worked so hard to make the rally team." Turning to face the wall she pulled the covers up over her head. "I'm going back as soon as I graduate and there's nothing Mom can do about it."

"I guess you can do that if you want to." Janet straightened the blankets on the second bed, making a level surface for the tray. "Just for the record, I think you're the one being unfair."

"Me?" The girl came out from beneath the bedspread, her eyes red.

"Yeah." The older woman lifted her head and gazed evenly at the girl. She didn't know this girl all that well and wasn't sure this approach would work, but … nothing ventured … "You haven't even seen McMinnville and you've already decided you don't like it. Henry says it's a beautiful town."

Sharon wrapped her arms around her knees and said nothing.

"And all you can think of is going back to Holyoke because you're scared. Scared that you won't be as popular in a bigger school. Scared that you can't cut it."

"You don't know anything! I can cut it just fine if I want to." She swung her feet to the floor and grabbed a piece of bacon. "Everybody liked me at home. I had a boyfriend. I had lots of friends. If I want to, I can make new ones here too. I can even make the rally squad there if I want to."

"I don't know. Henry says he saw an awful lot of pretty girls there. We'll see." She exited the room trying to act as nonchalant as possible, the grin on her face unseen by her young guest. "Please bring the dishes to the kitchen when you're finished."

Finishing the last of the pans, Janet turned to wipe the counter and was not surprised to see the breakfast tray perched on the end of the Formica. Empty. Sharon leaned against the doorway. Taking her time, Janet drained the sink and began filling it again. She waited for the girl to start a conversation.

"Did you ever have to move somewhere you didn't want to go?"

"As a matter of fact I have. Several times."

Sharon was not rewarded with more information. Her curiosity soon won over her attempt to look disinterested. "How old were you?"

"Which time? The first time I was about thirteen. The last time was when I married your grandpa."

Curiosity piqued her face. "If you didn't want to move here with Grandpa, then why did you marry him?"

Janet picked up the tray, rinsed the glass and put the dirty dishes into the water. "I met Henry when I was out here visiting one of my kids in San Francisco. We bumped into each other at a farmer's market. I was admiring some tomatoes and he was yelling at the man selling them, telling him he was overcharging." She chuckled. "He probably was, but I didn't care, they were beautiful tomatoes.

Sharon tried to look uninterested.

"We got to talking about gardening and farming and found out we had a lot in common. We both grew up in the Midwest, both survived the Dust Bowl, both had grown children. He raved about how beautiful it was in Sacramento." She looked out the window and gave a little shrug. "He said it was the only place he had ever been that actually felt like home."

Sharon remained silent.

"I told him that was the way I felt about Boise and how much I loved it there. It had taken me years to feel settled someplace. I had friends there and some family. I swore I would never move. Even though we liked each other, he said if we were ever to get together that I'd have to move to California. I said no way." She shrugged again.

Having made her way from the doorway to the table edge, Sharon perched on the wooden surface and pondered what she heard. "So he didn't make you move. You should have said no. You could have stayed with your friends."

"Maybe you're right, I guess. But I wanted to marry him more than I wanted to be alone. I chose to move but didn't want to. I *really* didn't want to. I tried everything I could think of to talk him into moving to Idaho." Rinsing the last pan, she held out a drying towel to the girl who ignored it. Her eyes met the girl's and held her gaze. "I didn't know anyone here. I was scared. But I knew he was scared too." She laughed at the skeptical expression that crossed girl's face.

"Grandpa was scared?"

She nodded. "Sure he was. Everyone's afraid of something. He was afraid of being alone for the rest of his life." She didn't know how much of Henry's past was known to the girl and opted for discretion. "He'd been married before and been unhappy. But I loved him and I knew if I moved I could help. That still didn't make it easy. Sometimes the best thing we can do for ourselves is to do something hard for someone we love."

Sharon considered that statement. She picked up an orange from a basket on the counter and began peeling it. "Are you glad now that you moved?"

Janet moved to where the girl was perched and looked her dead in the eye. "I still miss my friends but I'm happy here. I chose to be happy here. You can make that same choice if you want to. You can be happy in McMinnville. It would be your gift to your mom."

The girl slid off the table, her ponytail swinging and popped a piece of orange into her mouth as she exited the kitchen without a word.

37 McMinnville

Unlike the grain silos that loomed on the horizon in Colorado, McMinnville appeared on the horizon as a mass of lush green under a clear blue sky.

The south end of town showcased the college campus, with its stately red brick buildings, open expanses of lawns, and high-rise dormitories. Well, they were only four stories tall but compared to the mostly two-story structures of Holyoke, they looked enormous. Linfield was even more beautiful than they had envisioned.

Driving deeper into the community, borders of bright Shasta daisies, dahlias, and peonies edged yards. Roses bloomed abundantly on arbors and along fence lines. The sights and smells of the town were intoxicating. The new arrivals craned their necks to take it in.

Henry gave them a guided tour. "Power and Water. City Park. Safeway. Courthouse." He gestured as he drove by as if pointing them out would anchor the entire town layout in their minds.

They stared wide-eyed, taking it in.

"High School and Junior High are up there," His arm poked out the open window and pointed vaguely north.

He turned onto the main street of town where clothing, stationary, shoes and hardware stores were decked with hanging baskets of blooming flowers, trailing in the summer heat. Two banks and several offices flanked the street.

He turned right. "Feed store. Grade School. Catholic Church. Groceries.

He made a final turn and wrapped up his tour. "Fire station, funeral parlor and Baptist Church." He glanced at his daughter and suppressed a smile.

Her grin was his reward.

"That's it."

The car bumped over half a dozen railroad tracks before pulling onto a scratch of gravel with dandelions pushing through. He thrust his hand out the driver's door window and pointed. "Here it is. Home sweet home."

There was a collective intake of breath.

It looked more like a shed than a home. If Alice Mae had been worried that she did not have enough furnishings to fill her new home, she would have been mistaken. The miniscule two story structure couldn't have been more than thirty feet to a side. It had a single door in the center of the front, two small windows flanking the door and a peaked roof with one tiny window at each end.

Alice Mae struggled to find something positive to say. It was a challenge. "How did you find this? It's so compact!" It's so awful. She flashed back to the small but comfortable house she left only days before. It was hard to breathe.

The white structure had peeling paint, dirty windows and a mostly dirt yard with nothing growing save weeds. The railroad tracks ran so close to the west side of the house that she could imagine gouges scraped into the siding. *Oh Lord*, she prayed, trying not to panic. *Give me grace!*

"It wasn't easy." Henry pulled a key from his pocket and tried several times to work the front door lock. Finally getting the doorknob to turn, he strode inside and swept his arms wide, clearly pleased with his find. Alice Mae trailed him hesitantly with four restrained children in tow. The interior confirmed their assessment from the street. The house was tiny, dark and judging from the musty smell, had sat vacant for some time.

"Here's the living room." He flipped on the single overhead bulb which cast a weak light. "I made sure the power was turned on before you got here."

A barren room with plank flooring and faded wallpaper engulfed them. "The windows have curtain rods. That's good," she said, desperate to find assets. She could hang up an extra sheet for privacy – if she had an extra sheet.

"Back here is the bathroom and a bedroom." He moved through an opening in the center of the wall.

A room perhaps eight feet wide and equally long had a closet the width of a single door wedged snugly under the stairs. She pointed out a roller shade that hung half way down the one window that, judging from the thick layers of paint, did not open. "Privacy. That's good." She smiled bravely. The bare wood floors seemed solid. She would be thankful where she could.

Although the door was ajar, she could not bring herself to look into the bathroom.

"The kitchen is over here." He led the way through an arched doorway on the right of the living room to a galley kitchen that was, thankfully, furnished with a stove, an old refrigerator, a sunken sink centered on a linoleum counter. The far end of the kitchen opened into the back yard with a door that was so poorly fitted that daylight could be seen on all four sides. The good news was that to the left of the door, wedged into the corner, was an automatic clothes washing machine. Its vintage was newer than the wringer machine in Colorado, but not by much. Patches of rust were visible on one side and it did sit at a distinct tilt but it was a step in the right direction. Skittering sounds came from inside one of the drawers. She pretended not to hear them as they withdrew from the room.

Just to the left of the front door a narrow and very steep staircase led to the upper level which consisted of a wide landing about six feet square and a room with steeply sloped ceilings that allowed them to enter upright but only one at a time. Henry, in fact, chose not to duck in, but stood on the landing which he pronounced to be "a perfect bedroom for Richie."

"It'll be easy to keep clean," the boy said, trying to be positive.

"Is this our room?" Laurie asked, the last of the girls to enter. "Where are we supposed to put the bed?"

"We can wedge it under the eaves and you can use the pegs over there for your clothes." Alice Mae turned away leaving the girls staring in stunned disbelief and followed her father down the stairs and back out into the Oregon sunshine. She needed the air!

Although the house was far from what she had imagined, the neighborhood did have some charm. Orderly homes with well-maintained yards and small flower gardens lined the street. *In all things give thanks*, she quoted to herself from 1 Thessalonians.

The woman across the street waggled her hand in greeting. Alice Mae swept her arm up in return. The loss of Ruth's smiling face across the street hit her like a sucker punch.

"Well, let's get this unloaded. Richie!" Henry called with some impatience, clapping his hands together. "I've got a card party tomorrow night and I have a long drive ahead. Kids. Let's go. Let's go!"

It took less than an hour to unload the entire contents of the trailer, the trunk of his car and find everything that had been wedged under the seats and between passengers. With the larger items distributed to their respective rooms, the remaining boxes made a modest pile in the center of the living room.

"Janet says you need a phone," he said, backing out of the house, making his escape. "I've arranged for one to be installed in the kitchen for you. I don't know if they'll do it on Saturday or if it'll be on Monday, but I've paid the initial deposit and paid for two months of service so you can get settled."

She fought tears. "Thanks, Dad."

"If you go making long distance calls to cry on anyone's shoulders don't expect me to pay for them. I'm just paying for local basic service. You got that?"

She nodded, the reality of her new circumstances hitting her full force. She followed him out of the house, resisting an urge to reach out and grab his arm and beg him to linger a bit longer. "Thank you for everything, Dad."

"When will your first check be here from your Mr. Howard or whatever his name is?"

She swallowed hard. "It should be here on Monday or Tuesday, assuming everything goes smoothly. I'll go talk to the local welfare office here in town next week. Without the paperwork I had, I hope there's no problem." She could feel panic stir in her stomach, the loss of her purse and the dismay of it resurfacing. What if the money didn't come?

He stuffed his hand into his shirt pocket. "Here!" He thrust a worn fifty dollar bill into her hand. "You'll probably need something to feed these kids till you get it all sorted out. You can pay me back out of your first check."

Without so much as a 'good luck' he climbed into the car, backed off the gravel strip that ran between the little house and the train tracks and headed west to Hwy 99.

Alone, she walked around the outside of the house carefully examining what would be her home for the foreseeable future. The paint was not as bad as she first thought. It was mostly just dirty; a good scrubbing might do wonders. Washing the windows would help the outside as well as double the amount of light coming in. Elbow grease was cheap.

There was some evidence of long ago flower beds. She tried to smile. The brown dirt that had obviously once been lawn showed a slight edge where grass had stopped leaving a two foot border almost all the way around the house. She wanted to drop to her knees and clear away the dead leaves and see what might be there, but the job of setting up the house had to come first. The yard could wait.

Heading back inside, Alice Mae noticed what she had missed before. In the black mail box that sat askew beside to the front door, an envelope peeked through the slot. It was addressed to her. The return address was Holyoke. She tore open the letter and read,

> Mom.
>
> *I just watched you drive away and want you to know that I will be okay and so will you. I'm proud of you and will be praying for you. I love you.*
>
> *Ruth says to let you know that she already has my tickets for Christmas. I'll see you in less than five months. Be brave.*
>
> Love, Donna Mae

Tucked inside the letter was the two dollar bill that Grandpa Henry had given Donna on his arrival in Holyoke.

38 Unpacking

The first task had to be cleaning. The worn broom and sponge mop from home that had been wedged into the U-Haul were leaning against the kitchen doorway ready for use. Perhaps with some foreknowledge of what they would find, Janet had insisted on sending a bucket with new sponges, cleaning cloths and a large bottle of her all time favorite, Mr. Clean. *God bless Janet.*

"Girls, let's get to it. This place needs a thorough scrubbing." She called as she tied a towel around her waist.

"Richie, see if you can figure out where the grocery store is. I think Dad said there was a Safeway on Third Street, which is that way." She indicated the direction she believed to be north. "Remember he said the streets are laid out alphabetically and numerically and we are on First. Watch for street names so you can find your way home." To be on the safe side, she wrote down their new address and tucked it into his shirt pocket.

"Okay," He snatched the two dollar bill from her fingers, ready for the challenge.

"If you get lost stop and ask someone for help."

He nodded.

"Bring us some milk, a loaf of bread and some potatoes so we will have something to eat. Just get what you can."

"I'm on it." He looked eager to get our and explore the town. "Wish we could've brought my bike."

"Me too." She ruffled his hair. "We'll try to find you one soon."

"I'll go with him." Joyce offered, head bobbing, eyes begging for permission. "I've got a little money left and he might need help carrying stuff."

"Nice try but no." Alice Mae pulled her youngest girl in for a quick embrace and thrust the broom into her hand. "I need you here. How about you sweep out and wipe down the upstairs? I think we have some ammonia for the windows."

When a frown appeared on her daughter's face, she amended her offer. "Or you could do the bathroom or help me in the kitchen." The girl grabbed the broom vanished up the steps, whistling.

The scratchy sound of Sharon's transistor radio came on in the main floor bedroom, clearly claiming her chosen task.

Handing Laurie the bucket filled with hot pine scented water Alice Mae left her options open, "Go help one of your sisters or tackle the bathroom."

Laurie headed upstairs. "Joyce, I'll help you."

The kitchen cleaning fell to Alice Mae. With the sounds they had heard in the drawers making her more than a little uneasy, she began at the top determined to get it done as quickly as possible. A liberal splash of bleach added to her sink full of hot soapy water made her feel considerably better. The window was painted shut, but the back door stood wide open as she worked her magic on the dingy room.

"I come to the garden alone," she began the old hymn in a loud, clear voice hoping to frighten away any unwelcome visitors. "While the dew is still on the roses." An appropriate song, she thought. Soon the upper cupboards were scrubbed and air drying. Newspapers they had used to pack dishes would serve as shelf liners.

The refrigerator was a welcome relief. Although the small freezer compartment was thickly encrusted with ice, the interior was clean and cold. Alice Mae unplugged it, giving the ice time to thaw and moved on to the stove.

All four stove burners worked – a blessing that had not come with every house she occupied. The drip pans were black with burned-on grease, but she hoped that putting them to soak in the hot water would help. If that didn't work, she would cover them with aluminum foil. She filled her largest pot and dropped in the drip pans to soak. She wiped down the rest of the appliance and felt encouraged. What was left was to open the drawers and lower cupboards and see what was what.

The scream was involuntary. Opening the last drawer, next to the back door, she found what had made the skittering sound. A rat seemingly bigger than some of the cats they had owned, jumped up on the counter, scratched its way halfway to the sink, jumped down and scurried out the back door. She screamed again and backed out of the room.

Three girls yelled from their own corners of the house. "Mom. You okay?"

She swallowed hard. "I'm fine. I'm fine. Just a mouse," she yelled. A bold faced lie! Her chest hammered. She walked out the front door and stood in the sunshine waiting for her heart rate to return to normal. A robin sang from the tree across the street in a beautiful cherry tree laden with late season fruit. Glancing around with what felt like new eyes, she located a walnut tree, two apples and some red blooming, thorny trees that she couldn't identify. She took several long, deep pulls of the clean Oregon air and put a smile on her face before returning to her task. *Thank you for our new home.* She meant it sincerely.

By the time Richie returned with stories about his grand adventure into the city, the kitchen was done. All traces of rodents were removed with as much bleach as she could spare while armed with every implement she could think of including a broom handle and rolling pin just in case the prior tenant had a family. Fortunately for everyone concerned, no more long-tailed inhabitants appeared. First item to be purchased with the money from her father, she determined, was to be rat poison. Lots of rat poison. She would do it first thing tomorrow. If the choice came down to feeding herself or the rats, the rats would win.

"The store is huge," Richie handed over a bag containing milk, bread, a small bag of potatoes as well as two candy bars that had not been on the suggested list. "There is a butcher right in the store that cut meat while I watched. And miles and miles of aisles. It is so cool. Is there anything else you want me to get?"

"How far away is it?"

"Only about five blocks, just past the fire station. There was an enormous truck there too! You'll like it."

She put the milk in the newly cleaned refrigerator, felt in her pocket for the money left by her father, considered the unwelcome rodent that had occupied her kitchen and said. "Show me."

39 Good Vibrations

She woke up shaking. It wasn't only her, she realized, it was the whole house shaking. Again. The windows rattled and the silverware in the kitchen drawer jingled. The wire hangers in the closet clinked together. She pushed her arms into her sweater, quiet not to wake the sleeping girl, and walked into the front room of her new home. It was still dark outside although she saw the faintest hint of dawn etching the tree tops through the bare window. Even in the darkness, she could see the train cars barreling past. Blessedly the train was relatively silent except for the grinding and screeching of the steel against steel. With this, the third train to pass by during the night, she had learned that the whistle usually blew at the south end of the trestle, which stood behind the house, and didn't blow again till it reached the crossing in the center of town. She was thankful for this small kindness that would eventually allow her to sleep through the night. Probably.

That she was not sleeping well was no surprise. The surprises of the day had already come and she anticipated that there might be more. The items that had gone missing from the time she had sorted and packed boxes in Holyoke to the time they unloaded them in the tiny house were numerous. Whether they had been left behind, been mistakenly left at Henry and Janet's during the repacking or were somehow still in a box that had not been emptied she didn't know, but Richie definitely needed a change of underwear no matter what he said.

The upside of having help with the packing was what got put in that she had not expected.

New kitchen towels were the first surprise. "Where did these come from?" she called. "Sharon. Do you know anything about these towels?" She turned them over in her hands and relished the feel of them. "These were wrapped around the glasses in the kitchen box."

The crisp white towels were hand embroidered with a small bouquet of daisies, bright and cheerful.

"I guess Mrs. Lynch put them in when she was packing up the kitchen. Pretty aren't they? How many?"

"Four." Alice Mae wandered back to the kitchen filled with a bit of anticipation.

In the bottom of the box containing food staples from Colorado were six cans of tuna fish, a jar of peanut butter and a canned ham that had not been in her cupboards at home plus a bag of hard candies. Unexpected gifts.

The final containers to be unpacked were boxes that Janet had stuffed in at the last minute. They contained a curious assortment of household items. The family sat in a circle in the middle of the living room floor and took their time removing the items one by one.

"Two decks of cards," Richie called out, happily claiming them. Grandpa taught him to play solitaire and with no television, he would put them to good use.

"A table cloth. Pretty." Alice Mae shook out a sixty inch square of cotton with a red ribbon border and draped it across her lap.

"New washcloths for the bathroom. And here are two new towels." Joyce hugged the soft pink cloths to her chest.

"Garden gloves," Alice Mae smiled, holding the soft cotton to her face.

Pens, pencils, and small notebooks covered the bottom of one of the boxes and were up for grabs. When school started, they would be in demand.

"Marbles." Richie snatched them and appreciatively examined the colored glass orbs.

"A bag of jacks. How did she know?" Laurie grinned broadly. She had won the jacks tournament in Holyoke two years running.

Small bottles of shampoo and bars of sweetly scented soap were tied together in a pastel blue scarf along with new toothbrushes, a package of combs and three hairbrushes. Alice Mae set them aside to put in the bathroom and wrapped the pretty cloth around her neck.

New socks were near the bottom, some for girls and some for boys.

"All the socks are white," Sharon noted with disappointment.

"We will be thankful for them just the same," Alice Mae said, setting the packages aside to wash and distribute.

"What are these?" Laurie held forth a bag filled with an odd assortment of shoelaces, hair ribbons, barrettes, and nail polish. She spilled them on the floor allowing each person to pick up useful items. "I get the headbands."

Sharon held up a small square red book with a tiny lock. "May I?"

Alice Mae smiled and nodded.

At the bottom of the last box were five envelopes, each with a name on them, each bearing the same inscription. *This a 'welcome home gift' from me to you. You must not disclose the amount inside to anyone else. Have fun. Love, Janet.*

"How much did you get?" Richie was the first to open his envelope and find three crisp dollar bills inside. His curiosity was immediate.

"I'm not telling." Joyce closed the envelope and put it under her knee, out of the reach of her brother. "She said not to tell."

"Sharon?" He tried again.

She shook her head.

"Man!" he said, frustrated. "Oh well." He jumped up, took his treasures, and headed for his room.

Alice Mae just stared, stunned by what was inside her envelope. Three ten dollar bills were enclosed with another hand written note. *This is a gift for things you want, not things you need. Spend it with my blessing.* Tucked in the envelope, behind the bills were two packets of flower seeds – Colorado columbine. A weight lifted from her chest.

As the caboose of the early morning train passed, Alice Mae closed her eyes. *Thank you, Lord, for all your provisions. Thank you for a safe journey. Thank you for this house and the safety of these walls. Thank you for friends left behind and new friends yet to be made. Please show me where to go and what to do. Help me change our lives.*

40 Audrey

She found the Yamhill County Courthouse with no problem. The four-story gray marble building with broad stairs ascending on opposite sides was striking. Clusters of large-leaf maples stood sentinel on the grounds and well-tended rose beds bordered the building. She circled all the way around the edifice before mustering the courage to go inside.

"Audrey Yates." Her voice cracked just a little. She tried again. "I'm looking for Mrs. Yates."

A cute blond girl that looked about Donna's age smiled back at her. "Mrs. Yates is on the third floor. Just go up there," she motioned to a flight of stairs in the corner of the lobby. "Take a left at the top and she'll be the first office on your right. Can't miss it."

"Thank you."

Audrey Yates was a tall, angular, bottle brunette who was just as nice as Howard had said. In her navy skirt and crisp white blouse, she drew Alice Mae into her office and offered her a chair.

"Well, you've had an adventure," Audrey Yates said. "From what Mr. Howland tells me you drove half way across the country to make a better life for your children. How admirable!"

"Thank you. Not everyone would agree with that assessment."

"Posh. It shows gumption and foresight." She settled into her chair. "Now let me get my notes and let's see what we can do for you." From a low, lateral file cabinet behind her desk, she withdrew a legal size folder that was already stuffed with what Alice Mae perceived as an alarming amount of information and began flipping pages. "Did you get your check from Colorado?"

Alice Mae nodded. "It came on Monday."

"Good, good. Are you operating on a cash basis or did you open an account at the bank?"

"I haven't actually cashed it yet. I'm trying to figure out how I can open an account, but I don't have any identification with me."

Mrs. Yates raised her eyebrows.

Alice Mae gave her a synopsis of the trip west, the loss of her purse and the resulting dilemmas she faced trying to settle into a new life with no paper trail.

"Well, setting up an account shouldn't be a problem; I know everyone at the bank. After you leave here, just go down and tell them what you need. Have them call me if they have any questions. You can assure them that I will vouch for you."

She returned her attention to the file. "I must admit that I've never seen anyone use that particular *visiting* clause the way your Mr. Howland did but I'm happy for you. He seems particularly dedicated to seeing that you succeed." She eyed Alice Mae curiously. "Was there something special between you?"

"Oh no." She flushed at the suggestion. "I assure you he's just a good friend."

"Well, in any case, my job is to help you succeed. I don't want to be sitting here a year from now trying to get you into the Oregon system. I want to see you off of welfare by then and holding your own." She looked over her horn rimmed glasses and gave Alice Mae a stern stare. "Are we on the same page?"

"Absolutely." Alice Mae tucked her hair behind her ears and sat up straighter.

"So, what can I do for you today? How can I help you get started?" She closed the file and waited.

"I heard there were crops that the kids pick for money. What can you tell me about that?"

"Some of the kids in town make money during the season. You've missed the strawberry harvest and most of the beans, I'm afraid. That's where most of the kids make their money." She slid the folder back into its slot and shut the file cabinet. "Now we're mostly into the filberts. Dundee is just a few miles from here and claims to be the filbert capital of the world. The work's a bit dirty and so most of the kids drop out and leave it to the migrants, but the jobs are there if they want them – or you." Her eyes swept Alice Mae trying to assess just how desperate she was to pick up an extra dollar or two. She leaned forward and rested her arms on her desk. "Busses pick up at the Safeway parking lot every morning except Sunday and usually drop back off about three. They'll need old clothes, a lunch, gloves if they don't want to get their hands stained and good shoes, that is, sturdy shoes."

"Okay. Good to know." She made mental notes.

"When my boys were younger, they did that for a summer. They only made two or three dollars a day as I recall, but it kept them busy and gave them some pocket money. The growers pay cash every day so if any of your kids are interested in trying it, be sure and tell them to be on time. The bus waits for no one."

Alice Mae looked up, interested. "You've got boys? How old are they now?"

"Pete's twenty and Jerry's twenty-two. Living in Newberg with their father." She didn't elaborate. Alice Mae didn't ask.

"Howard said you might help me get some job training. Switchboard training?" She had put this off until the end. Her stomach turned. Could it possibly be true? "I would really like to get started on that."

"He mentioned that to me. I'm told that Olivia will be ready to start training the second week of September if that works for you. I've already signed you up."

"How many people train at the same time?" Not too many she hoped.

"Just you. It's one on one, two or three days a week, whatever you work out. It's sort of an experimental job placement we've been working on. No guarantees. You okay with that?"

"Of course. Yes. That would be great."

"I don't think it's too hard. It's learning to use the new multi-line switching system that seems to be the new wave of communication. The courthouse was the first in town to put it in, maybe four years ago. I still have a direct number, but most of the calls get routed through the switchboard where they can put a call on hold for me or leave me a message." She smiled and stood. "I'll bet you will pick it up in no time but just realize that so far the jobs are limited."

"I am trying to get something at Linfield when it opens up." She eyed Mrs. Yates to gage her reaction.

"So I hear. For now, though, I'd like to see you learn to run it so that you might be able to get on with a local business. Rumor has it that the Shilling Insurance is talking about an upgrade in the next year or two. I've heard that even the high school is considering it next year. Would've been nice for them to have figured that out last year when they were building it, don't you think?"

Alice Mae nodded agreeably, her face bright with anticipation.

"I don't really know anything more than what I've heard via the rumor mill. Even if something does come up, it might be just part time. Would you be okay with that?"

"I would."

"Hmm," Audrey said, looking over her glasses. "We'll see."

Leaving the courthouse, Alice Mae headed west toward the city park. At the entrance, a paved winding road dipped into to a shaded glen. Gravel paths meandered through a grove of rhododendron that were holding on to the last of their summer blooms. Maple trees scattered through the park were fringed with gold from their first autumn leaves. Compared to the modest and flat Holyoke city park, this was paradise.

To her delight, she found the City Library anchoring the southeast corner of the park. She stepped inside. The familiar smell of leather and paper and the hush of the reading room was heavenly. She was home.

41   Baptists

Alice Mae resisted running her hand nervously around her exposed neck. Sharon had taken the scissors to her hair again, trimming her grown out bob into a short new cut she had seen in a magazine. It framed her small face nicely but made her feel unprotected.

The songs were familiar and thank goodness there were no drums. She had read somewhere that in some Baptist churches out west had drum sets in the sanctuary.

The tone of the service was casual and the atmosphere warm. Unlike the first Sunday, when they slipped into the service just as it was starting and fled during the final song, today they lingered.

"Alice Mae Wheaton." She introduced herself, holding forth her hand. "These are my children. We just moved here from Colorado." She smiled as broadly as her nervous lips would allow.

"I saw you here last week but you slipped out before I could get to you." Pastor Wilson Ward held her hand in his. "You and your lovely daughters turned a few heads. I think they were paying more attention to you than to me." His smile was warm. "This is my wife, Patricia."

A petite brunette roughly Alice Mae's age held out a manicured hand to Sharon and Laurie. "We are so glad to have you with us. You girls look about my daughters' age. We have girls seventeen and sixteen, Patsy and Margie. You should meet them." She glanced around the narthex for her girls but came up empty. "Joyce, it's nice to meet you. Richie." She shook hands.

Several women introduced themselves and welcomed Alice Mae to their service.

"Where do you live?" It was often the first question.

"We just moved in a few blocks down the street; trying to get settled before school starts." Her stock answer served her well.

"And what do you do?" The follow up question was inevitable.

"I'm looking for work." She wasn't ready to divulge her situation to perfect strangers no matter how Baptist they were.

"I'm Pastor Jack." A young man in his early twenties introduced himself to the kids as the youth intern. "Come tonight and get to know some of the kids. We've got a great group. The adult service is upstairs at six, and we meet downstairs. We start with games and a sing-along and then break up for bible study at about six thirty. It's casual." He was a charmer with bright eyes and a playful grin. "We have a program for grades seven through twelve." "Laurie. Sharon. Richie. See you tonight."

He turned to Joyce. "Sixth grade, huh? We'll get you next year." As he was leaving he called over his shoulder "By the way, we have snacks so come hungry."

A well-dressed woman made her way through the crowd and took Alice Mae by the arm, drawing her to the side of the throng. "I'm Hazel," she said as if that should mean something. "You must be Alice Mae. You look just like your father described you."

Her heart sank. "How do you know my dad?"

White-haired, in her seventies if she was a day, she was plump in a pleasing kind of way. Barely clearing five foot tall, she wore a little sprig of a hat perched atop her curls.

"I'm the one that helped him find your little house." She positively beamed. "I saw him looking at for rent signs down at the grocery store, you know, posted on the bulletin board. He told me all about you. Proud of you he was."

"Proud?"

"As a peacock. He was so cute." Cute? "Said you were bringing your brood here for an education, something your mother would have approved of, and wanted to find a little place to get you started."

She was dumbfounded.

"He was such a gentleman. We had a cup of tea and he listened to an old woman rattle on about her grandkids." She patted Alice Mae's arm. "He hardly got a word in."

"Really?" Her father didn't drink tea.

"Said you had to get on your feet and needed something you could afford so I showed him the little house. Nobody's lived there for going on two years. A neighbor of mine owns it. Figured you could fix it up." She eyed Alice Mae more closely. "You doing okay in there? If you have any trouble, you come see me. I'll get that old so and so to make it right."

"No, no. No trouble. We're doing great." She smiled.

"Say, do you or your girls do needlework? I just love knitting and wouldn't mind having company sometimes. Or we could crochet." She looked hopeful. Her white head bobbed with excitement. "Or we could bake cookies."

"Never tried any of it. Never had the time or patience for it, I suppose."

She was adorable. She was the grandmother her kids had never known.

"Well, if they have time, I'd love to teach the girls. Your boy too if he wants but …" She looked uncertain. "Do they like oatmeal cookies or chocolate chip? We can make both. It'll be such fun." Her hands did a little involuntary clap.

Joyce, who had been listening, was nodding enthusiastically. "That would be nice." She looked at her mother, hopeful.

"We don't have any … that is I don't have." Supplies. "We don't have anything." She didn't know exactly what would be needed for such crafts, but she knew she had none.

"Oh, I have everything we would need. Needles. Yarn. I live just a few blocks from here." She opened her pocketbook and produced a calling card. Alice Mae took it, charmed. She hadn't seen one of those in twenty years. Black printing on ivory stock, it read, *Hazel P Brandt • 857 Evans St • McMinnville*.

"Here's the address. How about you let this little girl come by and see me tomorrow? We'll have a grand time."

There was nothing to do, but agree. "Thank you. I'll send her over in the morning."

"Wonderful." Hazel headed for the door, waving over her shoulder as she went.

One of the few men that introduced himself to the newcomers, Charlie Townsend, was memorable. Broad shouldered and weathered, he had the look of a farmer about him. After meeting the entire family, he shook hands with Richie. "You should try your hand in my filbert grove on Monday," he said. "My boys are about your age and they are good workers. We have about five acres, a little place just east of town and are always looking for pickers. I'll help you get the hang of it." He gave Alice Mae a broad, reassuring smile and then turned back to the boy. "Be at Safeway by six in the morning and look for a smaller bus with big green letters that says Townsend."

Richie eyed his mother, looking for approval and got it.

"Okay. I'll be there." He rubbed his hands together. Yes!

"Bring a good lunch," Charlie advised. "We have water for you so just bring some sandwiches."

The prospect of some cash in his pocket put a grin on boy's face.

Walking the four blocks towards home, they chatted happily about people they had met and plans they had already made.

"Isn't Pastor Jack dreamy?" Laurie nodded her head at her sister's assessment. "I can't wait till tonight. What should we wear? Do you think he has a girlfriend?"

"Sharon," Alice Mae admonished. "He's your youth pastor, not your prom date. Don't get any ideas."

"Patsy Ward said that there are *several* cute boys in the group, our age." The two girls took off running and giggling.

Joyce skipped ahead, singing.

Alice Mae ambled along the street deep in thought, remembering Hazel's words. '*He's so proud of you.*' Since when?

42 Records

Thursday's mail contained a large manila envelope from the Holyoke Public Schools. Alice Mae ripped it open and was relieved to see copies of report cards for each of the children, letters of achievement from a few former teachers, as well as copies of the the kids medical records and birth certificates. Howard had done it. All the information that had been in her purse had been replaced and then some.

She rushed to the stairwell and shouted up. "Girls, you've got fifteen minutes to get ready. We're going to school."

Sharon in a cotton sundress, wanting to make a good impression, ponytail swinging, and Laurie in her short pants, not caring what anyone thought, walked ahead.

"They'll think we're hicks," Sharon hissed, looking at her dress and wishing she had something newer to wear.

"We are hicks," laughed Laurie. "Who cares what they think?"

Sharon groaned. She cared.

"Would you two rather go alone?" Alice Mae offered. Only two blocks separated the Junior High building from the Senior High. "Joyce and I can take Richie's papers over to the Jr. High and come back by here after, in case you need anything from me."

"No." They said it too quickly, their nervousness exposed. "You might as well come with us."

The school was huge! The sprawling modern structure covered an entire city block and stopped them in their tracks. "Wow!" they said collectively. Alice Mae pulled opened the double-wide front door and nudged them through. "Let's go."

They found the office immediately to their left.

A wiry woman with hair pulled back into a tail that rivaled Sharon's for length and swing smiled at them, moved her eyes directly to Joyce and with a huge grin said, "I'm Vickie. And what year are you? Junior or senior?"

Joyce giggled. "I'm just eleven."

"Oh, dear me. My mistake. How embarrassing. I keep doing that." With a shake of her head and a twinkle of mischief in her dark eyes, she turned to Alice Mae and held out her hand. "It must be you then that is here to register. Are those your records?"

Laughing at her odd-ball humor, Sharon and Laurie stepped forward. "I'm Sharon Wheaton and this is my sister Laurie. We just moved here from Colorado," she said glancing around. It was hard to hide her incredulity. "This place is a lot bigger than the one we came from!"

"There were over thirteen hundred kids here last year," Vickie said, taking the packet of records from Alice Mae. "How big was your old school?"

"Not even a hundred, I think."

Alice Mae nodded. "This will be a change."

"A nice one, I hope. If we're bigger, we probably have more choices for you. What are you girls interested in? Home economics? Art? Languages?" She chattered easily as she glanced over their records. "Our debate team is pretty good, too. Are you two any good at debating?"

Both girls shook their heads while Vicki glanced at their mother.

"They can be. It depends on the subject." Alice Mae chuckled.

"Okay, if you aren't interested in debate, what do you want for electives?" The list of options was long including wood and metal shop not to mention drama, music, and dance. Intimidated by the number of options, Laurie selected typing while Sharon opted for art. And they both wanted French. *French?* Alice Mae grimaced. Where would they use French?

After addressing lockers, homerooms and schedules, the two newly registered girls stepped out into the sunny afternoon both nervous and excited. This was definitely going to be more fun than Holyoke!

Adams Junior High School, although considerably older, was equally impressive in its own way. With wide switch-back staircases in the center and on both ends, the stone three story gray building was massive. Slated for demolition in the upcoming years, all it lacked to fire up the imagination of thirteen year olds was a torture chamber in the basement. Richie was going to love it!

Since he was not with them, Alice Mae chose his electives. "Leatherworking and beginning woodworking," she said without hesitation, scanning the options.

"He can change them after school takes up if he wants to."

She knew he wouldn't change a thing.

The bad news from both of the schools was that the kids needed physicals and immunizations.

"Just take them down to the Health Department," the school secretary suggested. "It's in the basement of the courthouse. They'll give them free exams and shots and I'll bet they can do it today."

Nodding toward Joyce, the secretary added. "She's going to need them, too. You might as well get it done."

"Sure," the nurse told Alice Mae. "We can get them right away. Just have them each strip down to their underwear and put on these." She handed Alice Mae a stack of cotton gowns, ushered her into a cubical and walked away, her rubber heels squeaking on the tile floor.

The nurse started with Joyce. When Alice Mae stepped back into the room, having gotten the other girls settled, Joyce met her with wide eyes. "She says I have to …" She held up a small plastic cup. "I have to go to the bathroom in this." The girl's face burned. "Do I really?"

Alice Mae nodded. "Make sure you wash your hands after."

"That's nasty." The girl made a face and disappeared into the small restroom across the hall from the examination room. Alice Mae felt heat in her own face. City life was different.

She would not let Joyce tell her sisters them about this. Why ruin the surprise?

In Holyoke, the school physical took place in the gymnasium. A volunteer nurse weighed, measured and had each child read from the eye chart that was permanently mounted on the wall. And they were done! No disrobing. No fuss. No lab work. Easier.

"It's just a quick shot, Joyce. Look away and it'll be over before you know it." Alice Mae patted her daughter's arm.

"That's right. It'll only hurt for a second." Looking at Alice Mae, the nurse asked, "When was the last time you had a tetanus shot, Mrs. Wheaton?"

"I don't remember. It's been a few years." *Probably twenty.*

"Why don't you just show her how easy it is? It wouldn't hurt for you to have a booster."

Alice Mae paled. "Oh no, no. Thank you, not today. Just the girls."

"It's free." She held up the loaded syringe and smiled.

Joyce's chin shot up. "If you don't have to have one, I'm not getting one either. Come on, Mom. It'll be over before you know it." Touché.

Forty minutes later four young women walked out of the basement into the summer sunlight. The August heat felt good. After the medicinal smell of the health department, the fresh air was bliss. Fall was coming fast and the crunch of oak leaves under foot sounded downright celebratory.

"How about we go to the library?" Alice Mae suggested. "We have about an hour before Richie gets home."

Squealing with delight, the three girls headed across the grass kicking up leaves and beelined toward the park, their shots forgotten.

Alice Mae flexed her left arm. Ouch!

43   Cook School

Twice before, Joyce had gone to Cook Elementary School to play on the playground, first with her mother, and then with Laurie. The school was seven blocks from home. Four blocks north and three blocks east. Over and up. Up and over. Joyce felt confident she could do it alone.

Billy Reynolds waved when he saw her coming. Living alone with his grandmother, the bony boy with dark eyes and dark hair spent hours at the school yard looking for someone to play with. Today he was hanging upside down on the monkey bars.

"Hey." A lazy grin spread across his face.

"Hey, Billy."

"Want this?" He held forth one of the two sticks of Juicy Fruit he had been keeping in his pocket.

"Thanks." She peeled away the foil wrapping and popped the stick into her mouth, savoring the sweet treat. "Want to play ball?

"Okay." He dropped from the bar and fell in behind her.

For close to an hour, the two children played ball, pumped the swings high in the air and ran around, laughing and enjoying their freedom. When the town whistle blew its twelve o'clock blast, Joyce knew her time was up.

"Gotta go." She announced and turned to flee like Cinderella at the stroke of midnight. Then she stopped.

On the two previous visits, Joyce had come and gone from the same corner of the school yard, the southwest corner where the monkey bars and the bike rack bracketed the sidewalk. From there, she knew which way to go, but today they had run across the field and taken several loops around the building. When the time came to head out, Joyce was in an unfamiliar part of the school grounds.

She hesitated.

"Ya want me to walk you home?" He offered, hopeful. "I could do that. My grandma wouldn't mind."

"No thank you, Billy. I can do it."

Thinking it through, the girl reasoned that she was only one block farther around the building than usual so if she went four blocks south and then went four blocks west she would be at home. Confident, she struck out.

The problem presented itself when she counted the four blocks and turned on what should have been First Street. There wasn't a familiar house in sight. Remaining calm she backtracked four blocks but when she stopped. She was not at the school. Nothing looked familiar at all. Her heart raced.

A tear of frustration slid down her face, then another. She stood on the corner in the city that she found hugely confusing and began to tremble, first her lip, then her hands. A crow called at her from a tree, startling her. Dogs barked, suddenly sounding menacing. The August sun beat down till a bead of perspiration ran down her back. Five minutes passed, then ten.

When the twelve-thirty whistle blew calling the townspeople back to work, Joyce knew she was in trouble. Unable to decide which way to turn, she remained rooted to her corner like a weed, stubbornly anchored where it didn't belong. She decided she should pray.

She was good at saying 'bless this food' and 'now I lay me down to sleep' but now she needed to actually talk with him. That was what Mom always did. *God, I'm scared. Please help me find the way home. In Jesus name, Amen.*

"Do you need some help?" Startled, she spun around and found two girls, close to her own age, studying her curiously. "Are you lost? You've been standing here a long time," the taller of the girls with long dark curls said. "Mom told us to see if you need help." They turned and waved at a woman who was standing in the doorway of a nearby house.

Joyce nodded, distress written on her face.

"Where do you live? Do you know your address?"

She tried to remember but drew a blank. She shook her head and wiped at her face with the hem of her blouse.

"Do you live around here?" the smaller of the girls inquired. "We're in sixth grade and know just about everybody." They smiled and waited patiently.

Joyce found her voice. "We just moved here. I went to the school to play. I've done it before but ... somehow," New tears began. "I can't remember how to get home."

"Tell us what your house looks like. Is it big or little?" This was a game, a puzzle to be solved. "What color is it?"

"White," she said, wiping her face, again. "Next to the train tracks and there's a long warehouse on the other side of the tracks. I know it's on First Street and I thought that was where I was headed but ..." She looked helplessly at the street signs that clearly read Fourth and Kirby. "I don't know which way to go."

"Come on," they said together. "First is this way and we know where the tracks are." They flanked the frightened girl. "Where did you move from? Do you have a dog?" They walked and chatted, putting Joyce at ease. After a few blocks they turned right.

"There it is!" Joyce nearly shouted with relief. She pointed. "That little white one." She turned to the girls and with a relieved smile, said. "Thank you!"

They gave her an awkward pat on the back. "That's okay. Maybe we'll see you next week at school." The girls waved and turned away.

Joyce raced down the block, up the front step and into the house. "I'm home."

"Already? Boy that hour went fast," her mother said, mopping her brow from the steam coming off the ironing board. "I was just finishing these tablecloths for Hazel, she wants them for a dinner party, and then I was going to go out and watch for you. Did you have a good time?"

44 Ring Ring

Letters were her lifeline to her old friends. Ruth kept her in the loop as to their move to Greeley. The deed was done and they were settling in nicely. She had painted almost every room in the house.

> *I used every color that Joe would allow. I think I'm making the ladies of the church guild nervous. I painted the bedroom purple – it's gorgeous. The living room is sunny yellow with white woodwork all around. It looks like the sun is spilling in the window, even at night. And the kitchen is emerald green, well the cupboards are all white, but the walls are green. You'd love it! Come spring I'm going to paint the front porch. Any suggestions? I was thinking of fireman red, but Joe thinks that might be a bit over the top. I'll send pictures as soon as Joe can figure out how to use the camera I gave him last Christmas.*

Alice Mae smiled. She could just imagine!

> *Donna loves having a room to herself. I've never seen a girl keep her room so clean! I'm feeling a lot of pressure trying to keep to her standards.*
>
> *She showed me her fall schedule. It looks like she's taking lots of literature, science, and a couple electives, I can't remember which ones. Classes don't start for three more weeks so she still has time to make changes.*
>
> *She's made some friends through the church's 'college and singles' group and seems to be happy. All is well. No boys calling, yet.*

According to Elvira, Benny hadn't stopped moping around the house since they left. To keep him occupied she had baked cookies almost every day and although it seemed to make him feel better, she had put on at least five pounds. She wondered if, by chance, Alice Mae had changed her mind and might come back.

Donna sent a detailed report about Barbara's wedding which she had attended on behalf of the family.

> *Masyl wore a rose colored suit with white piping along the collar. You would have approved, and she wore high heels. She wobbled a little on them but I don't think anyone else noticed. The girls all looked beautiful in pink. It was probably the only time they had ever or will ever again wear pink, but that was what Barbara wanted. You should have seen them. No braids, no jeans, just curls and yards of organza. I hardly recognized them. Ruth loaned me a little blue suit for the wedding.*
>
> *Chuck refused to wear the shoes Masyl bought him. He showed up in a suit and his dirty cowboy boots. He looked good but still smelled like Uncle Chuck. I hugged him anyway.*
>
> *Barb and Dave, as it turns out, will live in the big house with his parents. The little house in the grove that they planned to occupy isn't fit to live in and nobody has time or money to fix it up. I hope that they don't have to stay there too long.*

Janet reported that she was trying to talk Henry into a road trip north.

> *I told him that he needed to see first-hand how you were doing but as you know, he's such a stubborn old coot. I'm not giving up yet. I want to see McMinnville for myself.*

She couldn't remember ever hearing Janet refer to her father as a stubborn old coot before, but the term of endearment seemed appropriate.

When the phone rang, Alice Mae jumped. The navy beans she was sorting spilled onto the countertop as she grabbed for the phone. Nobody ever called in the middle of the day!

"Hello."

"Mrs. Wheaton?"

"Yes."

"Charlie Townsend, Ma'am. Need to tell you there's been a bit of an accident in the filbert grove. Richie's at the doctor's office."

Her heart hammered. Her hand flew to her throat. "What happened?"

"He was using my big garden rake under some of the old scrub trees, cleaning up the culls for me and whacked himself in the head but good. Doc's stitching him up. Says it's not too serious."

"No! When did this happen?"

Charlie snickered. "'bout an hour ago. He didn't even know he'd been hurt till one of the girls noticed blood and started screamin'."

"He's getting stitches, now?"

"Yeah, Doc says he'll need half a dozen. You want I should come get you or just bring him home?"

"Bring him," she said, walking as far as the phone cord would allow. She looked out at what had been a beautiful afternoon. "What do I need to do about the bill?"

"Never you mind about the bill. My insurance will cover it. I should have been watching out for him, but I think he's done for the summer." He paused and then added. "He's a good boy, Ma'am."

She allowed herself to relax and smile. "Most of the time, Charlie. But he is all boy."

He wore them like a badge of honor. Six black stitches crossed the crown of his head like little black spiders creeping through his hair. It would leave a scar. Cool. It would be a great conversation piece the first day of school. His fingers were stained black from the filberts because he refused to wear gloves, and his arms and face were brown from the sun. He looked every inch the farm boy, wound included. All in all, he thought, not a bad summer.

When the phone hanging on the kitchen wall rang a second time in the same day, Alice Mae grabbed it on the second ring. What now?

"Yes?"

"Alice Mae. It's Hazel." The warm, soft voice slid across the line. Alice Mae took a long breath and relaxed, enjoying the smell of her freshly scrubbed kitchen. After the conversation with Charlie Townsend, she had nervous energy to burn so she cleaned the kitchen. Again. It practically shined.

"Hazel. How nice to hear your voice." It was!

"I was wondering if your family would like to come for dinner on Sunday. I feel like baking a ham and I don't have anyone to share it with. If you're free, I would just love to have you and the children join me. We could enjoy some of the lovely cookies Joyce and I made. I froze the last batch of them and they will be perfect. Just come by after church. What do you say?"

"Yes. Thank you. That would be wonderful. What can I bring?" She held her breath. Her cupboards were bare and her September check was still a week away.

"Not a thing. I'm just so excited. It'll feel like a holiday and I'll use one of those tablecloths you pressed so beautifully for me. Does your family like scalloped potatoes and green beans?" Assured that they did indeed, she ended the call. "Bye, Dear. See you on Sunday."

Sunday morning the family toasted some of Richie's bread and ate nothing more, anticipating the ham and potatoes that Hazel had promised.

After church, not wanting her to feel rushed, they took their time visiting and then ambled the several blocks to her home. C, D, E, they read the alphabetical streets names. Cowls, Davis, Evans. The sun filtered through the trees which were beginning to lose their leaves with the approaching autumn. The smell of late blooming roses assailed them as they passed a garage almost obscured by the creeping tendrils. Even the girls commented on the heady perfume.

Hazel hadn't been in church this morning. She was probably home getting dinner ready, Alice Mae reasoned, appreciating the effort she must be going to on their behalf. With growling stomachs and mouths watering, they rang the bell of her small one story home, smoothed down their hair and put on their sweetest smiles.

The look on their hostess' face was not what they expected. She was wearing gardening gloves and a straw hat and clearly wasn't in the midst of meal preparation. With a 'deer caught in the headlight' look, she stared at them.

"Did I misunderstand? Didn't you say you wanted us to come for dinner?" Color drained from Alice Mae's cheeks. Her heart pounded. She took a step back. "I'm so sorry."

It took only a moment for Hazel to recover herself. She threw back her head and laughter rolled from her belly. "My dear, I forgot you're from the Midwest. You have breakfast, dinner, and supper." She held the door wide. "Come in, come in. It's just that here in Oregon, *dinner* is served in the evening.

45 Expectations

September in Oregon was more beautiful than Alice Mae had ever imagined. As the sun slipped further south, new patterns of shade and light played across the landscape.

She took her time strolling through the grove of stately old oaks that stood across the street from Linfield College's administration building. According to the school brochure, some of the trees had been there at the time of Columbus. With limbs as big as tree trunks, they splayed their arms over the lawn, creating a gigantic canopy.

Constructed of red brick with massive white columns, Melrose Hall was, arguably, the crown jewel of the campus. Its facade graced every college brochure and catalog.

The president's office and the business office, she knew, occupied the east end of the building. Financial Aid and Admissions were located in the west. Right in the center, on the main floor, at the top of a wide flight of stairs, was where the new PBX switchboard was being built. It would be the centerpiece of the building, the first thing visitors would see when they walked through the door.

Alice Mae stood across from the building cloaked in the shade of the trees, closed her eyes and breathed. *Lord, this is where you led me. This is the desire of my heart. When it opens, I want this job.*

Thick plantings of vivid red, white and purple pansies filled the flowerbeds – Linfield colors on display. Ivy crawled up the exterior of stately Pioneer Hall, working its tentacles into the crevices of the old brick, leaving only the white bell tower exposed, gleaming in the filtered fall sun.

Like Joshua marching around Jericho waiting for God to give him the city, Alice Mae walked the campus almost daily, claiming this school for her children and talking to her father, the one that listened.

Not a word from Masyl. Lord. Please heal her pain. Be her friend and her comfort. Her heart ached for her sister.

Keep Donna's eyes on you and on her studies, she prayed. *Keep them away from any boys or better yet, Lord, keep the boys eyes away from Donna.*

Richie has courage. Lord keep him safe. Joyce has grace. Increase her portion. Sharon has a strong will and Laurie has steadfastness. Bring godly friends into their paths. Make them beacons for you in their school. Protect them.

Her prayers were earnest, her desires passionate, her needs real and her faith strong as she poured her heart out to The One who knew her future.

And Lord, be with Janet ...

"Mrs. Wheaton?"

Alice Mae whirled around to see Mike Browning's smiling face. "Mike!"

"Are you okay? You're talking to yourself." He eyed her suspiciously.

She flushed and pushed her hair behind her ears. Had she been talking out loud?

Mike was the first person from Linfield that she'd met at First Baptist and they had hit it off at once. A groundskeeper at the college, he was a stocky man, just a couple inches taller than her, who always wore denim – clean and pressed, but denim just the same. His hair curled around his ears giving him a boyish look.

The morning they met, they had struck up a conversation about the flowers outside the church, then the trees at the college, then the flowers around town. He knew them all. He was a walking botanical encyclopedia. They could have gone on for hours. He was a sweet man but painfully shy.

She smiled. "No. Well, maybe. I was just enjoying the day and your beautiful campus."

"It does look good now, doesn't it?" A bashful smile tugged at his lips and his face added a bit of color. He glanced around, admiring the beds bursting with well-tended blossoms. "Just wait till you see what the students will do to it over the next few weeks." He shook his head. "They'll wear a trench in the lawn over there, cut through the flower beds and trample the shrubs. By Thanksgiving, it'll look like a stampede came through here. Not even that. By Halloween."

"No!"

"Yep." He shrugged. "Nice while it lasts though." He tipped his hat. "Well, nice to see you, Mrs."

"You too, Mike." She watched him dash across the street and vanish behind the maintenance building, probably relieved to be alone again.

Although the campus was a banquet for her senses, her favorite part of the daily walk was the trail that passed behind the President's house and through the park that backed up to the college on the northeast. An arching wooden bridge crossed Cozine Creek allowing water to rush and tumble over rocks and fallen logs beneath. Here she thought she caught a glimpse of heaven. Descending into the cool glen of the park, she added to her prayer list. *Lord, Bless Mike.*

Passing over the bridge and beginning the steep climb up the northern bank she began singing, she couldn't help herself. The old hymns were in her bones. She thought of Joe Lynch and knew he would approve. It began as a private melody but by the time she reached the top of the trail she was in full voice. "Great is thy faithfulness, Lord, unto me."

46   Switches

Switchboard training was scheduled for Monday morning at 9:00 a.m. Eager to get started, Alice Mae ran a brush through her hair till it shined, slid on a trace of lipstick, which she rarely wore and slipped on a blue cotton dress. She hurried out of the house and practically skipped to the courthouse.

The small, windowless space that had been converted to hold the county phone center was about ten-foot square. Corkboard holding information posters covered two walls. It had just about everything except pictures of the FBI's ten most wanted. Bookshelves laden with notebooks and binders flanked the doorway. A large desk in the center of the room took up the remaining space. It was a good thing she had never been claustrophobic.

Olivia Bates extended her hand. "I'm so pleased to meet you. Please feel free to look around. I'll be with you in a few minutes."

Alice Mae worked her way around the room while the woman, twice her width with a full head of red hair and a warm smile listened to recorded messages that had come in overnight and made notes.

Olivia looked up. "Employee rosters. " She answered the question that had not been asked. "Everyone who works here or has worked here in the past several years is in one of those books. It's contact information in case we need to get a hold of them."

"So you don't just answer the phones, you're information central?

"Pretty much. Everyone used to have their own phone number so people would call whoever they needed. Now it all comes through here so people expect us to have all the answers."

Alice Mae nodded and continued browsing books and posters. "And do you have most of the answers?"

"Usually."

She fingered a three-ring binder labeled in large letters SCH.

"School schedules." Olivia offered. "There are five grade schools in town and the two secondary schools." Her hand swept around the room, pointing out information sources. "Office hours of most of the departments as well as emergency information in case we need to contact them. Hospital hours. Yamhill County Fair schedules. Vacation schedules for city as well as county workers. Q I like to have it all."

Olivia shut off the answering machine and stretched. "Ready to get started?"

"More than ready." Alice Mae pulled a chair up next to Olivia and surveyed the control panel that covered half the desk, bright eyed and eager.

The job of a PBX operator, she was told, was twofold.

"Your first priority is to quickly get callers to the person they are looking for without losing them or leaving them on hold too long. Sometimes easier said than done." The board had four incoming lines and a keypad of numbers, symbols and unmarked buttons and two handsets.

Some of the lights were labeled with names or department titles like 'Mayors Office' or 'Sherriff'. Others were not.

Alice Mae pointed to the unmarked buttons. "How do I know who is using each line?"

"Sometimes you don't. When a call comes in and you're the one that put it through, you'll have to remember or write it down. It's easier to just remember."

Alice Mae took a deep breath and pushed her hair behind her ears. "All right. Show me."

After just an hour of explanation and observation, she was put to the test. "You can do it." Olivia traded her seats and turned the handset over to her pupil.

An incoming light lit up and gave a soft beep.

"Yamhill County Court House,"

"Always smile. It can be heard over the line." Olivia whispered.

Alice Mae's smile split her face from ear to ear. "How may I direct your call?"

Olivia muffled a laugh but nodded approvingly.

"Andrew Schneider? Just a moment, I'll connect you." Alice Mae pushed a button putting the caller on hold while she ran her finger down the list of seventy-something county employees to make sure she had the right extension. Tapping the numbers 1-3-2 on the console, she heard the line ring, took the caller off hold and heard the county assessor, pick up his line.

"Schneider."

She closed the connection and let out her breath.

"Perfect!" Olivia beamed. "You're a natural."

Two more calls came in almost simultaneously. "Audrey Yates, please." She had this one memorized. Extension 324. She punched the numbers, grinning.

The second call was looking for the Sheriff whose line was already in use. His light was illuminated.

"That line is busy," she said, glancing at Olivia for confirmation. "If you'll hold just a moment I'll connect you when it's free."

She punched the hold button on line two and tapped the eraser of her pencil on the desk waiting for the line to be free. In less than a minute, the light went out.

"The line is free now, I'll put you through." She released the caller to the Sheriff, heard his deep voice on the line and closed the connection.

"See, nothing to it."

During the afternoon Alice Mae and Olivia traded off answering the phone and answering a multitude of questions. It was like a dance. Your turn, my turn. It was fun.

203

"What time does the planning department close?" It was posted.

"When are my taxes due?" The payment schedule was on the wall.

"When are they going to fix the potholes on my road?" She put them through to the city maintenance department.

"What's the state bird?" Really? She didn't have the foggiest idea.

She looked at Olivia. "How long did it take you to learn all this stuff?" The knowledge base for the job was vast.

"Couple of weeks." She grinned. "Most of it's written down on a cheat sheet." She pointed to a pad on the desk that was more than covered with hand scribbled notes. No help there. "You have to remember that I worked at the reception desk before they put in the new system so I was already on a first name basis with almost everybody in the building."

"Right." Alice Mae ran her hands through her hair, and then ran them through again, tired but exhilarated. Her head was swimming with trivia that she had picked up, schedules she was learning and names she had yet to put faces to.

"I think they gave me this job when it opened up because they wanted someone a little less imposing at the front desk." She ran her hands down her generous hips and laughed, "First impressions and all."

"I'm sure that's not true." *Well, maybe.*

"Suits me just fine." She pulled a clip from her hair and shook it loose, grinning wickedly. "In here nobody cares what I look like."

"What do I do if I can't find the answer to a question?"

"If you get stuck, just punch a key and ask for help. Everyone here is friendly."

"Just any key?"

"Well, almost. The first time I did that because I got stumped I got Judge Herman. Have you met him yet?"

Alice Mae shook her head.

"Big guy, probably six-six. You'll like him. Anyway, he didn't know the answer either but we had a good laugh together. Eventually we figured it out."

Alice Mae's eyes grew large. "The judge?"

"You might want to default to Audrey or someone you know, just in case."

She nodded. "I'll keep that in mind."

During the course of the afternoon, there were as many as six callers waiting at any given time. Only once did she blunder.

After watching a blinking light for several minutes, trying desperately to remember who they were waiting for, she opened the line only to hear dial tone. "They're gone. I lost them." She glanced up, embarrassed, and saw only humor in Olivia's eyes.

"You'll get it. Even I mess up sometimes."

She doubted it.

By the end of the day she had mastered the basics of putting people on hold, tracking who was waiting for whom, and forwarding calls. She even managed a conference call between the building department, the planning department and a caller. Her head was swimming. At five o'clock they switched the system to an automatic answering machine for the evening, took a deep breath, stood and stretched.

"We're out of here. Go get some rest. Transferring calls is only half your job, and the easier half at that," Olivia explained. "We'll practice more on Wednesday and then next week we'll work on customer service."

Outside the late afternoon air was warm. Walking felt good after being behind the desk all afternoon. Passing the grocery store she stopped and picked up some milk and a ham bone for bean soup. When she got home, she would set a pot of navy beans to soak overnight and by the time the kids got home tomorrow night they would have a big pot of soup ready and waiting.

With groceries in hand, she walked down Ford Street, stopping to admire several yards that, in the cooler temperatures of late summer, had fresh nasturtiums blooming. The vibrant yellows and oranges were among her favorites. "Very nice," she said to a woman on her knees, weeding.

The gardener grinned, always happy to have an appreciative audience. "Thanks. They are pretty this year, aren't they?"

"Sharon? Laurie?" Walking through the front door, she knew exactly where Joyce was. The aroma of potatoes baking met her and saw that the table had been set for dinner. Joyce was in the kitchen singing and cooking, making the house feel and smell like home. *Thank you for Joyce. Bless her.*

She put the groceries in the refrigerator, gave her daughter a peck on the cheek and headed upstairs. "Sharon. Laurie," she called.

She found Sharon sprawled on her bed, a lazy grin playing across her lips.

"What's up?"

The girl giggled, sat up cross-legged. "Guess who got a job today?"

Alice Mae sat on the edge of the bed, her eyes wide. "Where?"

"There's a little place on the highway, The Twilight Café, right across from the Junior High. All the kids go there after school. Judy, one of the girls in my French, class, mentioned that she had just quit so I went over and talked to the owner. He looks just like Mr. Howland except with hair." She giggled.

"And?"

"I start on Monday! Just two days a week for now, Mondays and Tuesdays from right after school till they close at seven, but at least it's something. I'll need a nice white blouse to wear, but other than that I can wear any skirt I have. And I get to keep all my tips." She was positively beaming.

She wrapped her arms around her daughter and squeezed. "Congratulations! Spending money!" She started out the door and then hesitated, "Where's Laurie?"

"I don't know. I gotta find a blouse." She came off the bed with the energy that only comes with youth and began pawing through her clothes. "Do you have one I could borrow?"

"You're welcome to look."

47   Boys

Peering through the kitchen window she found Laurie sitting in the back yard on a blanket. With a boy.

"Who's that?"

Joyce shrugged. "Don't know. He followed her home and has been sitting there with that stupid grin on his face all afternoon."

The pale haired boy, probably about sixteen with a fresh crewcut and more teeth than his mouth could easily contain, sat opposite Laurie, enthralled. His arms waved about as he talked non-stop, oblivious to the fact that Laurie was not paying attention. She sat engrossed in the dog-eared issue of Life magazine featuring the recent untimely death of the beautiful Marilyn Monroe.

Famished from her busy day, Alice Mae grabbed a couple saltine crackers and popped them into her mouth before heading out the back door.

"Hi," she said, "I'm Laurie's mother."

The girl looked at her mom and then tipped her head toward the boy, looking bored. "This is Steve. He's in my English class."

Steve jumped to his feet, smiled hugely and flushed. "Hi."

As if having one love struck boy hanging around were't enough, on Thursday afternoon a boy with dark, shaggy, long hair and carrying a ragged cluster of chrysanthemums that looked like they had been picked in haste knocked on her door. With eyes wide, he thrust the flowers at Alice Mae and asked, "Can Joyce play?"

Joyce appeared beside her mother. "Hi, Billy."

The boy's large eyes never left Alice Mae. "Can she come to the school and play?"

His hair needed cutting and his clothes were threadbare but at least his nails were clean. He was polite. "Billy, is it? Where do you live?"

"Yonder by the playground." He gestured behind him in the general direction of the elementary School.

"Does your mother know you are here?"

"Grandma does," he said, his eyes dropping to his feet. "I don't have a mother."

"Would you grandma mind if you played here instead?"

His eyes came back to her and he shook his head, looking hopeful.

"Dinner won't be ready for about an hour. You two can play till then."

Grinning and nodding enthusiastically, he looked like a happy sheepdog.

48   Service

She heard the familiar "Knock. Knock."

"Just a minute." She grabbed a kitchen towel and dried dishwater off the front of her shirt and hands.

"It's just me," Patricia Ward opened the front door a crack and poked her head in. "Hope you don't mind my just dropping by." She set down two large boxes and looked around the small room. "This is a cute little house," she said. Little being the operative word.

It was the first time she had been there and until she walked through the door would not have believed five people could live so sparsely.

Aside from one easy chair and a floor lamp, the only furnishings in the room were the six wooden straight-backed chairs surrounding a small kitchen table, evidently serving as their dining room set. Books, mostly library books, were stacked on the floor, knee high beside the chair. The room was small and dim, but clean. A definite asset.

Patricia pulled out one of the chairs and sat down, crossing her legs and making herself right at home. "Wilson's mother always sends new clothes to the girls in the fall, and we were thinning out their closets and I thought of your daughters." She smiled warmly at Alice Mae. "I hope you're not offended, but I think the girls are about the same size and they're charming things. I hate to just throw them away."

"Offended? No. The girls will be thrilled. When we moved, there was only room for a few outfits each so they had to leave a lot behind. They will love having something new."

"Well, these aren't new but they're in good condition. Take a look and see what you think."

Alice Mae opened a box and whistled appreciatively. "These are so nice." *It was like Christmas.*

"And there are a couple of my dresses in the other box that I thought you might like. I think we're close to the same size. I never wear these anymore, but they're really nice. Again, Wilson's mother." As if that explanation covered it all.

"Thank you. You'd be surprised how tired we are of the same old outfits."

"I can only imagine. Anything you don't want, just give away. No hard feelings." Patricia waved her hands dismissively. "I never know what to do with them every year. One year I just threw them out, isn't that terrible?"

Alice Mae couldn't imagine! She gently lifted the top sweater out of the box held it up. It was a beautiful cashmere cardigan. She peeked through the rest of the stack of clothing neatly folded into the box and caught her breath. There must have been a dozen sweaters, dresses, and skirts. They looked practically new. They weren't the first hand me downs that her family had been given, but they were far and away the nicest.

From the second box she lifted a dress that had been Patricia's.

"These are nicer than anything I can remember owning," she said again with feeling. "Thank you,"

"I'm afraid there isn't anything in there for Richie, but I'll keep my eyes and ears open."

When the girls came home from the library, they fell on the clothes like starving children fall upon food. For half an hour all three girls played dress up, trying on items and then trading and trying on something else. Alice Mae had been almost right. It was better than Christmas.

The following day, Alice Mae wore the first of her new dresses, a blue linen one with inverted pleats and a little black belt and felt like a million bucks. She positively flounced as she walked along en route to the courthouse. She was in such good spirits that she did something that she had not yet done in McMinnville; she deadheaded people's spent blossoms along the way. She didn't care what her girls would say. It felt great!

———◆———

"Customer service is equally important. You need to have a pleasant voice no matter who is on the line. You need to be able to take care of some basic issues. You will be the first line for any incoming complaint; many times people will just begin explaining their issues to you – or worse yet, start screaming at you. The PBX operator must take these calls, calm the customer down, and make sure they are directed to the appropriate department to get their issues resolved." Olivia sounded like she was reciting a training manual. She was.

"I can do that."

Week two of training was underway. Not only would she need the basic skills to run the machinery that made up the PBX system, but even more important, she would need to learn the answers to most of questions she might be asked. She had already had a taste of the variety of those inquiries last week but she knew there would be more.

"How do I learn all this?"

"Just take it a step at time. For starters learn what hours each department is open and who handles what. You'll pick up the rest as you go. You'll only be here for a few weeks so don't worry about it too much. If and when you get a real job, that's when you'll need to learn everything you can about them and their operation."

She worked through a series of challenging calls staged for her benefit, learned how to handle complaints and practiced reciting the basic information about the courthouse that was asked for most often. She had never known work to be so much fun.

By the end of the day she had formulated a plan. In order to apply for the switchboard job at the college she needed to learn everything she could about the workings of the school. To that end, she needed an ally.

"Mike." She ran after the man pushing a wheelbarrow full of fall chrysanthemums. The grounds department was refreshing the college flowerbeds in preparation for homecoming weekend.

Considering that the campus had no fewer than twenty showy beds, it was a huge undertaking. "Wait up."

He set down his load and touched the brim of his hat. "Mrs. Wheaton." His shy smile spread across his face. "Nice to see you."

"You're just the man I was looking for." She caught her breath. "I need a favor."

He eyed her warily.

"I think you know that I hope to eventually get a job on campus."

He nodded. "You've mentioned it once or twice."

"I want to learn everything I can about the school in the meantime. I want to familiarize myself with the staff and faculty. I need a list of all their names."

He nodded.

"I also need a list of all the buildings and what's in them, even phone numbers if you have them. I have a school brochure that they sent to me, but it doesn't have specifics. Would you have access to any of that?"

"I think so. I could certainly get you maps of the campus with all the buildings and what's in them." He took off his hat and scratched his head. "I don't have a list of all the staff and faculty but I'll bet I could find one. When do you need them?"

"Just any time. I'm in no hurry."

He nodded slowly. "Let me work on it. I'll see what I can find and bring it with me on Sunday. Would that be okay?"

"Great! Thanks!" She patted his arm. "You're the best."

The girlish flush in her cheeks warmed his heart. His smile broadened and he tipped his head in her direction. "My pleasure, Mrs."

49 Winds of change

The winds began picking up around noon. By the time schools were let out, the gusts were hitting at forty miles per hour and getting stronger. Walking home, Joyce's dress pressed so hard against her legs that it was hard to move. The sky was dark and smelled like the thunderstorms she remembered from Colorado. "Wheee." Her voice was swallowed by the wind. She liked it!

The National Weather Service warned that this disturbance would likely be the biggest wind storm the Pacific Northwest had seen in the 20th century. Neighbors were worried. Children were called inside. Even pets were brought in to protect them from the pending storm. The town was bracing for a gale like they had never seen before.

Alice Mae walked to the center of the deserted street, held her arm out wide and reveled in the unseasonably warm wind buffeting her. Always craving more freedom and open space than she had, she found the mounting storm invigorating. For ten minutes she stood, turning to catch the drafts and breathing in the turbulent smells, barely staying upright against the force of the wind. Like daughter, like mother.

The first big bough came crashing down about five o'clock. By seven the street was littered with branches and additional limbs that had been torn away and a tree had been uprooted at the courthouse. At nine, the local radio station reported the death of a man caught in his house out on Three Mile Lane when a sixty foot fir tree crashed through his roof. The fun was gone.

The Wheaton family hunkered down to ride out the storm just like every other family in the Pacific Northwest.

Terrified by the crashing sounds outside, Richie, Laurie and Sharon camped out in the living room far from the roofline just in case power lines or trees came down.

"Stay away from the windows," Alice Mae warned.

Every available pillow and blanket was piled in the middle of the living room floor. Three children alternately jumped in terror at the sounds they heard or took turns telling ghost stories to prove that they weren't scared.

Joyce took to her bed hoping to have the comfort of her mother through the night. Snuggled under two blankets, she concentrated on the story she was reading. The flickering overhead light provided a small comfort that she needed in the storm.

Then the lights went out!

As the wires between the poles sparked, the neighborhood sank into darkness with howling wind and flying branches crashing into the house on every side. Power lines fell to the street like writhing, spitting serpents. Flashes of light split the darkness as transformers blew.

"No!" The shout escaped her before she could check it.

"Mom!" Joyce screamed. Her bare feet racing toward the living room huddle.

"Sharon, get the candles," Alice Mae shouted. "There're in the kitchen drawer next to the back door."

"I can't!" The whimper came from the front room.

She headed for the kitchen herself.

Rummaging through the end drawer, hoping no unwelcome four legged visitors were taking shelter there, Alice Mae found the package of four emergency candles, a book of matches from a local merchant, and the two small juice glasses that would have to serve as candleholders. In the dark she used a trick she had learned as a child. She poured a couple of inches of salt into the bottom of each glass to hold the candle upright. With a trembling hand, she pushed one emergency candle into the salt and struck a match.

The flame threw blessed light into the room. Just as quickly a gust of wind swept through the cracks around the back door and blew it out. She tried again.

Five matches later, the wind blocked by her back, the wick flamed and was brought into the front room, set on the floor near the children and the process was repeated. Two points of light illumined the living room where now four children huddled together.

"We only have the four candles," she said keeping her voice calm, preparing them for the stormy hours ahead. "They cannot burn all night."

"Stay with us." Rick whimpered. He sounded five years old.

"I will."

Inspired by memories of her own mother on the dark and windy nights of her childhood during the Dust Bowl, she sat on the floor and drew her children to her, singing a familiar and cherished hymn. "When peace like a river attendeth my way, when sorrows like sea billows roll. Whatever my lot, Thou has taught me to say," They joined her on the refrain, where their voices were tremulous – hers was strong. "It is well, it is well with my soul."

Into the night they sang, first with the flickering light of the candles and then in the darkness. Many of the old hymns from their small Holyoke church were dredged from memory, some with the verses, others with just the melody, but all rich in memories.

"We should have stayed in Holyoke," Sharon said, more afraid than angry.

"No," Alice Mae's calm voice came in the darkness. "We are right where God wants us to be."

"How do you know that? How can you be so sure?" Sharon snuggled up against her mother for warmth and comfort, something she had not done for a very long time.

She hugged her daughter. "He told me so. First in my heart, then by sending Aunt Ferggie and by the many, many ways he answered my prayers to get us here."

Joyce's small voice asked, "Like what?"

"He softened Grandpa's heart so that he would move us here, for one thing. Only God could have done that." *The kids thought that it was great that he had come, but they didn't know the half of it*!

"And of all the letters I sent out, only Linfield answered showing me that this is where he wanted us to come."

A branch slapped against the front window evoking gasps of alarm from the clustered children. They huddled closer.

"But you've never actually heard him, right? You've never seen him?"

There was a long pause. As the storm raged outside, a storm raged inside her as well. She wanted to tell them the truth but was afraid they would not believe her. She wanted them to have great faith but feared sharing all of hers.

"Mom?" Joyce waited for an answer.

She took a long breath and raised her head in the darkness. "Do you remember living in the upstairs of that house in Holyoke, the one with the long outside staircase?"

"Yeah." Several voices answered in the darkness. They were all listening.

"You were all young. I think you, Joyce, were in kindergarten, and I had no work. I hadn't been able to find a job of any kind and I had been very sick for a long time. The doctor told me I had walking pneumonia, but I couldn't afford to get medicine. I was tired and scared and I told God I didn't think I could go on."

She heard in intake of breath somewhere under the covers.

"I wanted to take care of you but I was so exhausted. We had no food in the house. None. Not a stick of butter, not a loaf of bread. I had done everything I could think of. I told God that it was up to him. I was so weak that when I tried to take a step I couldn't move. I just kneeled at the bottom of the stairs."

"What happened?" Joyce's hand clasped tightly to her mother's arm.

"I heard him say *Look at me*."

"His voice?" There was skepticism in Sharon's voice— and hope.

"In my head and in my heart. When I looked at the top of the stairs, there were two angels standing there with their hands reaching out to me. They were beautiful and strong and glowing. They gazed at me and I found I could move. One step at a time. I climbed the stairs and by the time I got to the top they had vanished, but my strength had returned."

Laurie who had been silent gasped. "Really?"

"Really. I felt well and it was only two days later that I got a call from Joe Lynch asking if I would like to be the janitor at the church and within a week I had several ironing jobs."

"Cool." Richie was all into the story. "Were the angels girls?"

"No. In fact, they looked like warriors. Tall and strong. Beautiful warriors."

"Cool." She could hear the smile in his voice.

The windows rattled as winds swept by outside but inside stillness had fallen over the room.

"I felt that same assurance in my heart and in my head when I prayed about moving away from Holyoke. I trust him. I hope you can too."

They had questions. Of course they did. She answered them patiently, one by one; trying to share with them the amazement of that day and the assurance she felt that he had led them to Oregon and that he was going to answer her prayers.

"I wish we could see those angels now," Joyce said in a very quiet voice.

"Me too," Alice Mae agreed, pulling her daughter closer. "Me too."

After the children's voices had turned to soft snores she sang, unable to sleep herself. She felt fear of the storm outside yet felt peace inside that she had told the truth and that she was indeed where God wanted her. A weight lifted off her heart and in a voice that was mostly a whisper she sang, "What a friend we have in Jesus, all our sins and griefs to bear. What a privilege to carry everything to God in prayer."

And then she found the words she had been looking for and she prayed.

50 Aftermath

Morning light revealed a shocking sight. Trees had been tossed like tumbleweeds across power lines, phone lines and cars. Large sections of roofs were missing. As neighbors gathered in the middle of First Street damage reports circulated. The local radio station had lost its antenna. The city parks had been decimated. Several filbert groves throughout the Willamette Valley had lost half of their trees.

"I wonder how Mr. Townsend made out." Richie worried aloud.

"The Salem radio station says the death toll in Oregon is already forty," said a neighbor from down street. She held out her hand. "I'm Maureen Moxley. I saw you move in several weeks ago. I should have come over and introduced myself sooner. These are my two girls, Sheryl, and Cindy. They're twins but not identical."

Two blond girls about four or five peered from behind their mother. Joyce smiled and waved at them. They bashfully waved back.

"Alice Mae Wheaton. Pleased to meet you," she said.

Picking up pieces of what had been her cute white fence, Maureen chatted. "I thought for a while last night that something was going to come right through the windows. Glad it didn't. My husband, Fred, is a long haul truck driver. He's somewhere in Montana. I wish he'd been here." She stopped and turned back to Alice Mae. "They say that the hospital is flooded with injuries."

"We got off easy then," Alice Mae said, seeing relatively minor debris on her lawn. *In fact*, she thought, surveying her little home with amusement, *I believe the house looks whiter.*

"The Potters over on Second lost their dog." A teenage boy wandered down the street acting as self appointed town crier.

"Anyone seen a black lab? His name's Arnold and he's got a leather collar on. John Swenson can't find his red bicycle." The neighbors looked at one another and shook their heads.

"The Baldwins over on Davis said to tell you they have a generator and said they have coffee if anyone needs some. And some muffins and hot cocoa." The boy moved on, calling out his litany to the next assembled group.

Neighbors murmured their appreciation and a few meandered off toward Davis Street, Richie with them. Free hot cocoa sounded great.

"No power means I can't watch the world series." A heavyset man still wearing his bedroom slippers grumbled.

"It was postponed anyway, due to weather," someone said. "Why don't you help with some of the cleanup instead?"

Shaking his head, the man shuffled away. "Ah, man!"

"How's everyone here doing?" Wilson Ward walked up from the direction of the church and shook hands with some of the men before turning his attention to Alice Mae. "You okay? I was checking out the church. Seems to have come through just fine. Patricia was a little worried about you and the kids. She told me to come down and check on you; said to tell you that if you need anything to let her know."

"Thanks but we're good. You walked?"

"Couldn't drive." He surveyed the street. "Looks pretty much like ours."

She nodded, understanding. "Do you have any idea when they might get power back on?"

"None. They'll be working on it, but it could take days."

"Don't you have any connections to the power source?" She gave him a teasing glance.

"No more than you do," he teased back. "I heard that they estimate more board feet of timber were blown down last night than was harvested in Oregon and Washington last year."

Several in the crowd whistled.

"Send Richie over if there's anything you think of that you need. Okay?"

She nodded and waved him off. "Tell her thanks." Then she thought of something. "Hey! Do you know where we could get cheap candles? We used up the only ones we had last night and if the power stays off, it could be a long dark few days."

He threw back his head and roared. "Do I know where to get candles? Send Richie to the church this afternoon. We have more half burned candles left over from weddings than you can imagine. We could supply the whole town. I'll send a box home with the boy. Maybe two."

She cheered!

"I just remembered. Patricia said to ask you if you would like an area rug for one of your rooms. It's brown and really nice, but she wants to get a new shag one." He rolled his eyes with an exaggerated shake of his head. Joyce giggled. "She said with your bare floors she thought you might like the warmth come winter."

Her grin was involuntary. "Yes! Tell her we would love it. How big?"

He spread his arms. "About so big, maybe five by seven feet."

She clapped her hands and so did Joyce. "Wonderful."

"I'll see that you get it as soon as our new one arrives." He lifted his hand in a goodbye salute and was gone.

The front room? No, the girls need it upstairs. My room? Tempting but no. *Thank you, Lord. Please bless the Wards.*

Without music or television or traffic, the street was eerily quiet. Downed power had been cordoned off by the utility company pending repairs. Neighbors picked up branches and tossed them into mountains to be dealt with later. Order out of chaos. It had to be done.

By Saturday night, electricity had been restored to about one third of the town. The downtown was open for business and two of the café's offered dinner for a dollar to anyone without electricity. Patrons had their choice of meatloaf and whipped potatoes plus dessert at one establishment or beef stew and ice cream at the other. They were both doing a brisk business.

The Catholic Church opened their social hall and set up temporary sleeping cots for anyone who didn't feel safe in their own homes.

"Mom, let's go there," Richie said, tugging on her arm. "I want to see all their statues." He feigned a worried expression. "I don't think I feel safe at home."

She gave him a gentle cuff on the shoulder. "I don't think so."

"Jeez," he muttered, disappointed.

By Monday, the entire north end of town had power restored. The south end, unfortunately, did not and First Street was clearly south of the city center. With no hot water, no electricity for heating, and no power for cooking, going to school and to work seemed like outstanding options. Every school in town was opening an hour early and offering free breakfasts to any and all students who needed it. Many did.

"I want to get there really early," said Richie, racing out the door at the crack of dawn. "Maybe I can get seconds."

"Wait for us," Sharon and Laurie were right behind him.

After walking Joyce to school for her free breakfast and wishing the school's generosity had extended to parents, Alice Mae headed to the courthouse, eager to see what the day held.

Even with the relentlessness of the storm, most of the courthouse had enjoyed electricity over the weekend via generators. Olivia stated the obvious. "The jails and the Sheriff's office always make sure they have power."

The switchboard was ablaze with incoming calls.

"We need to listen to all the weekend messages when we have time but first things first. Be prepared for grumpy people who tried to leave messages but couldn't get through."

"Got it."

"They may sound angry but mostly they're just scared."

She knew the feeling.

They opened the lines and calls poured in.

By far the most common question was, "When's my power going to be on?"

They did not have the answer but by four o'clock Alice Mae had learned enough to be sure her power would be off for at least another two days— maybe three.

"Are offices open?"

Yes. Every county office is fully staffed and open for business. In fact, many departments had canceled days off and called in reserves. It was all hands on deck!

"Who is responsible for cleaning up these trees?"

That depended. City streets would be cleared by city workers. Trees down on private property were the responsibility of the homeowner. A list of people qualified to cut and haul wood was made available in the courthouse lobby as well as at the library which, miraculously, had sustained minimal damage. Volunteers had come forward to help the elderly or those without resources.

The city was offering dumpsters for yard debris only. They would be delivered throughout the community on Tuesday morning and picked up on Thursday evening. Locations to be determined.

"Is it safe to go out?"

If there were downed power lines or poles in the neighborhood, residents were advised to stay indoors. Few heeded that advice.

Alice Mae took the calls, routed them to the appropriate offices, answered the ones she knew and generally had just about the best day she could remember. It almost felt like a holiday with all the activity in building. Was she humming Jingle Bells? Certainly not!

By the time she and Olivia stopped taking calls and turned on the answering machine again for the night, they were bushed.

"That was fun!"

"You think so? " Olivia studied her. "You work well under pressure. Think you could handle that kind of pressure on a daily basis?"

"Absolutely, well maybe not every day but I loved the pace of it. Why?"

"Judy Welch trained with me last year and has been the police and fire dispatch ever since. She told me just last week that her husband is being transferred to Eugene. That would leave an opening with the city. You're catching on fast and I think you could handle it."

Her face grew warm. It couldn't be happening this quickly could it? Her heart raced. "Yes! Yes!" Hope that had been pressed down, trying hard to contain itself burst out. "Just tell me what I need to do."

"I'm not sure. Let me talk to Judy again. Give me a couple days."

"Okay." She said, using all her self-control not to jump up and down like a girl. "But if you hear anything call me right away. Okay?" She was practically vibrating. "What should I do in the meantime?"

"Alice Mae," Olivia laughed. "Go home and take a cold shower."

51   Hot Water

On Thursday following what was now being called The Columbus Day Storm by every broadcaster from coast to coast; the family woke to lights, a working stove and best of all, hot water. Sometime during the night power had been restored.

The first clue to this good turn of events was the sound of Sharon pounding down the stairs and announcing "I'm first," as she locked herself in the bathroom.

Richie was hard on her heels. "No. Wait. I've got to go to the bathroom!"

She was given about three minutes to enjoy the hot water before Alice Mae knocked.

"Sharon. Hurry up. There are four more of us waiting."

Given that the refrigerator had been off for almost a week and that the schools were still offering free breakfasts, the house emptied quickly.

Grocery shopping would definitely be on Alice Mae's agenda for the day. She didn't want to look in her pocketbook to see what was left of the last check. Each month the money seemed to run out a few days earlier.

Hot water restored meant she could clean house. She spent the morning scouring out the week old remains in the refrigerator, doing a load of laundry and hanging it in the fall sunshine. On the back of an envelope, she began making a list of what needed done in the wake of the storm.

>   Strip beds.
>   Buy milk.
>   Scrub bathroom.

A rapping on the front door startled her. "Knock. Knock. Alice Mae?"

Wilson Ward, wearing faded blue jeans with a rip in one knee and a faded work shirt with fraying cuffs, stood on her front step struggling under the weight and bulk of two rolled rugs. "Patricia said today's the day. Where do you want them?"

"Them?"

"Two of them and she says she has one more if you want it. It's green, I think."

His load shifted and the top bundle rolled off and landed at his feet.

"Not right in the doorway, if you don't mind." She laughed. She picked up a soft, cream colored area rug that looked almost new and ran her hand over the soft nap.

"Funny." Turning sideways, he wedged his bundle through the door. "Seriously, you want it here?"

"Just set it down anywhere." Her hand swept the nearly empty room.

He let it fall. A beautiful multi-toned brown and tan area rug, trimmed at two ends with fringe, unrolled at their feet. She tugged it flat and drew in her breath. "She's replacing this?"

He shrugged. "It's not really Patricia. It's my mom. Mom insists we need a new shag rug." He looked heavenward and shook his head. "If it's not new, she thinks it's tacky. She's the one that bought these. Maybe five years ago."

He looked down at his clothes and ran his hand over the worn shirt front. She saw the gleam in his eye. "I don't *ever* let her see these. They're *mine*!"

Alice Mae stepped out her back door to take care of her final task, to shake the small rug that blocked the perpetual draft from under the kitchen door. And there she saw it, just one block to the south, standing windswept and empty in the late morning sunshine. In a moment of absolute clarity she knew that this was the day. Today she was going to do what her father had warned her so gravely never to attempt. She was going to walk the railroad trestle.

It loomed in front of her, stretching for what looked like half a mile. As she expected, the structure was narrow, leaving little room to stand and grip the side rail should a train came while she was in the middle. She thought back to the schedule that was now so familiar. A train usually came through just after breakfast. She had heard it, rather felt it pass as the kids were showering and dressing this morning. Another came about two and then there were the three trains that came through at night. Five trains, right?

She was often gone during the day or busy, but she was fairly sure no trains were due for at least two hours. Her heart hammered. How sure was she?

She considered praying for safety but reasoned that it was presumptuous to ask God to protect her from her own folly. Instead she stepped onto the wooden structure, feeling the wind stir her hair and the sun on her face.

The decking boards were old but solid. In her mind's eye, she had envisioned missing slats where her foot might accidently slip through or rotting boards that gave way under her weight. She had rarely been so happy to be mistaken.

She relished the height and the view. Because the trestle spanned a deep ravine, she was a good thirty feet above the treetops. The unobstructed view of fields and church steeples and farms in the distance was spectacular.

She had always loved being up high. As a girl growing up on the farm, she would climb into the hay loft of her father's barn and stand looking out across the fields, wishing she could climb higher. Once she even scaled the farm windmill and thrilled at the vista it provided, but the licking that her father gave her stopped her from doing it a second time.

She could still taste the bile that came with the memory of the beating. She had been only thirteen. The bruises left by his strap had been visible for weeks. It hurt to walk, or sit, or lay down. The sad part was that she understood he had not been worried about her safety, but had been worried about losing her labor on the farm.

She gazed out from the top of the trestle and held out her arms, wishing she could fly. Feeling like she was nearly at the gates of heaven, she couldn't help but start talking to the Lord about all that was in her heart.

She heard it before she felt it. She was standing astride two wide planks, her arms spread, enjoying the breeze, when a train whistle in the distance stopped her heart. She stained to hear the sound again. It had been from the north, of that she was certain.

The boards underfoot were sturdy and spaced close together, but they were not butted against one another, no doubt to allow for vibration, as well as shrinkage and swelling. Pacing her steps, she bolted for the south end of the structure and then picked up speed not daring to look back.

With the first sound of steel on steel, she knew the train was on the trestle. She broke into a run. Fifty feet. Twenty feet. Ten feet. With only three feet to go, she lept from the wooden platform onto the gravelly bank that rose up to meet the span. The loose rocks gave way as she half slid, half scampered down the slope away from the looming locomotive. Sure that she was out of danger, she finally looked back for the first glimpse of what had been breathing down her neck. The single engine followed by a solitary caboose slid by her with hardly a stir. A man dressed in overalls leaned comfortably out the window as they passed and waved. He gave his whistle a small toot. A grin split his face from ear to ear.

She shot up her arm in response, laid back against the rocky bank and started laughing.

52   Lunch

"I don't believe we've met" A slender man with prominent cheekbones, deep set eyes and sporting a leather bomber jacket held out his hand. "I'm Jeffery Adams. My family and I just returned from Africa."

The Sunday morning service had ended, but the worshipers lingered to visit over refreshments. A light rain fell outside and Alice Mae was reluctant to venture out, hoping for a break in the shower before heading home. She took his hand.

"I'm Alice Mae Wheaton, pleased to meet you. Africa?"

He nodded. "It was our second trip. We were there for two years. My son, Ted, tells me that you have two gorgeous daughters and now that I've met you I know where they got their good looks." His eyes twinkled with charm. "We, that is my wife and I, were wondering if you and your children have plans for lunch?"

"You mean now?" Her eyes grew large. This was certainly unexpected. "Lunch today?"

"Yes. My wife, Shirley, put something in the oven to bake just in case we met anyone interesting today and you and your daughters qualify. If the scuttlebutt I hear is at all accurate, you have a story to tell. Coming from Colorado with no car? How bold of you."

She laughed and nodded. It was hard to argue the facts. "Before I say yes, you need to know that I have more than just the two girls. I assume you're referring to Sharon and Laurie, but I also have a son, Richie, and a younger daughter, Joyce. That's a lot of people. Are you sure?"

"Sure of what?" A woman with curly salt and pepper hair, albeit no more than forty, took Alice Mae's hand firmly. "Are you the brave soul that has agreed to come eat my cooking?" She laughed heartily. "I'm a terrible cook, truth be told, but I love having company."

Jeffery Adams looked at his wife. "Ted told me that if I don't talk them into coming he'll mope around all afternoon." His gaze moved to Alice Mae. "We don't want that now do we?"

"Certainly not but as you know, we don't have a car and …"

"No mind. I have our car and Ted has his little beetle-bug. I'm sure we can squash you all in if you're game. Perhaps you had other plans?"

Alice Mae thought of the left over stew that she had intended to serve for the third day in a row and didn't hesitate. "No. No plans at all. Let me find my kids and we'll be right with you."

"Did you see the way he kept watching you?" Laurie giggled. "He was practically drooling."

"He did not. But Ted is cute, isn't he?" The expression of delight Sharon's face was unmistakable. Blushing, she headed upstairs, ponytail swinging, her sisters on her heels.

"That was really cool." Richie came in last, letting the door slam behind him. "All those skins. Did you see those spears?" He pretended to throw one. His eyes danced. "That was awesome. Can we go back?"

"I'm sure we can."

"Mr. and Mrs. Adams have a house on Adams Street. Adams on Adams." He snickered. "That's funny." He took the stairs two at a time. "Hey Laurie, did you see those elephants?"

It had been a lovely afternoon. Shirley Adams was funny and offbeat and unconventional. Her spacious craftsman house was littered with rugs and artwork, none of which matched, all of which, together, made Alice Mae feel like she had walked out of McMinnville and into an international market. Wood and ivory elephants and rhinos covered the mantel in the living room and the center of a large dining room table had painted birds scattered about between colorful serving dishes.

The distinct aroma of curry and spices that Alice Mae could not identify simmered in the oven with what started out as a modest pot roast. It was exotic, wonderful and altogether the most comfortable home they had been in, ever.

Jeffery Adams had entertained them with stories of Africa, of places they had worked, places they had visited and described in detail the people they had lived among. It was National Geographic come to life.

At two o'clock, on the nose, Shirley banished "everyone under the age of thirty" to the covered front porch and turned to Alice Mae. "Now. We want to hear your story." She sat back in her chair with a cup of tea balanced in her lap and waited.

Alice Mae settled into a comfy, over-stuffed chair, took a long breath and began. "You said you felt the call to go to Africa so I hope you can understand when I tell you I felt called to McMinnville, specifically to Linfield." For twenty minutes, she related the tale of Ferggie's visit, of her search for the right college, of the trip with its travails and finally of finding a home and a church family.

Bracketed by fellow believers who were genuinely interested in her story she talked about Masyl and the rift between them. She described the ache of missing her daughter and openly shared with them both her faith and of her fears. Both Shirley and Jeffery listened with rapt attention.

"Tell us what we can do to help," Shirley said. "Let us be your family."

"You've already done more than you can imagine. I had nothing good for lunch and my children and I are having a wonderful afternoon. I cannot begin to tell you what a blessing this has been."

―◆―

From her dress pocket, Alice Mae withdrew a small wooden acorn shaped container about the size of a thimble with a tiny removable lid. "Look at this." Holding it under the light she opened it and spilled the contents onto her hand. Joyce examined the miniature ivory animal forms that had been hand carved. Each one was perfectly detailed and beautiful.

"They're so tiny. How could someone do that?" The smallest wasn't much larger than a grain of rice.

"I cannot imagine." She offered them to her enchanted little girl. "Shirley said I could have it. You want to keep them for me?"

The girl beamed and she nodded.

As she got ready for bed, she found herself humming and smiling. She heard laughter spill down from upstairs—the kids reliving their adventure. What an incredible, unexpected day this had turned out to be. What interesting new friends.

53   Work

"Judy's husband took the job in Eugene." Olivia's announcement hit Alice Mae the moment she walked through the door. "She's giving the city her two-week notice today. If you want the job, you need to go over there now."

"Now?" She froze holding her purse in one hand and her sweater in the other. She glanced down at the dress she was wearing, wishing she had worn a better one, and winced.

"Right now. Run right over there." Olivia was animated, her arms shooing her onward. "Go. Go."

"Thanks." Alice Mae dashed down the hallway and took the stairs two at a time. Pulling in lungs full of the damp fall air, she headed six blocks south, willing her pulse to stop racing and her mind to clear. Was she ready? Her heart fluttered with a mixture of fear and hope. *Lord, let me get this job.*

The bright red building shared by the city police and local fire department, as well as McMinnville's ambulance service, sat on the corner where First Street intersected Highway 99. She admired its contemporary architecture every time she walked to and from church.

The wood-paneled lobby was empty but for a visitor's bench bearing an 'in honor of a fallen hero' plaque. Dead ahead was a set of frosted glass doors with *Police Department* stenciled in black. To the left was a matching set of doors with the words *Fire Department*. She took a deep breath and opened the doors straight ahead.

"You must be Alice Mae." A petite, young woman in her mid thirties, with black hair down to her waist, greeted her as she walked into the heart of the city operations. "I'm Judy. Olivia called and told me you were on your way. Come on in." She lowered her voice. "I just told the chief that I was leaving a few minutes ago so he may not be ready to think about a replacement but, oh well." She raised her hands in a gesture of surrender.

Judy's desk was littered with paperwork and several coffee mugs, not to mention the switchboard panel that defined her job. In the background police chatter was constant with radios squawking with a lot of letters and numbers thrown in. Alice Mae recognized only one of the terms. Her adrenaline spiked.

Like a schoolgirl, her hand popped up. "I know that one. 10-4 means he got it."

Judy laughed. "You've been watching Highway Patrol. Yeah, we use some of the ten-code but not as much as they do on television. They do that because of the delay on the radio. By saying ten before they say the other number, it takes care of that one or two-second lag."

"Really?"

Behind her, the phones lit up. "Excuse me." Judy perched on the edge of the chair and swiveled back and forth as she took the incoming calls.

"Just south of milepost two … Okay. Did you get the license plate?" She listened. "363CDK. Three-six-three-Charlie-David-King," she repeated. She dispatched an officer to the scene.

"Police Department." She listened. "I'll have someone come by and talk to you. What's your address, Mrs. Davis?" She slipped on her headset and called for a patrol car.

"Fire Department … Yes, you need a permit for that … You're welcome."

"Busy place!" Alice Mae leaned on the counter awed. "How long did it take you to learn this jargon?"

"About a month. The first week was the hardest, I just about quit." Her expressive eyes widened. "It was awful! But everyone encouraged me to hang in. They'll help you too if you get the job." Her smile was contagious.

Alice grinned back. "Good. I'll need it."

"Even more than the codes, you'll have to get used to their slang." Judy leaned over the counter and lowered her voice. "The first time there was a big snow last winter, someone from town asked me if I knew how the roads were up on Rex Hill. I put out a call on the radio and was told it was "still and clear" so I passed that information on. Not long after that, the patrolman came in with deep snow on his car and on his boots. When I asked him about it, he informed me that "still and clear meant it was still snowing and the snow was already clear up to his …" she cleared her throat and grinned.

Alice Mae's hand flew to her mouth. "Oh no!"

"Oh, yeah. There's a lot to learn, but you'll love it."

A door opened down the hall. Judy winked at Alice Mae as they heard the sound of boots on wood. "Here comes the chief. Good luck."

A solidly built man of about fifty with a well-trimmed beard and hair graying at the temples, held out his hand and introduced himself. "I'm Fred Bowman. I assume you're Alice?" His manner was easy, relaxed.

"Alice Mae Wheaton. Pleased to meet you." She shook his large, callused hand.

He tipped his head in the direction from which he'd come. "This way."

She followed Chief Bowman into his office and stood, trying to appear relaxed and confident, the trembling in her knees hardly noticeable.

From the seat behind his desk, he gave her an appraising glance.

"Judy caught us all off guard here," he said motioning her, finally, to take a seat. "I'm feeling more than a little pressure to fill the spot ASAP. We're already a man short due to a death in his family." He gave a sigh and straightened some papers on his desk.

"Then perhaps it's a good thing I'm here." She smiled, hoping the nervous tremor in her lip wasn't obvious.

"You've got a lot of people pulling for you, you know that?"

"Oh?" She shook her head and tucked an errant piece of hair back behind her ear. "No, I didn't know that but it's good to hear."

"I've already had a call from Mrs. Yates over at the courthouse. She tells me that you are," he glanced at a note on his desk, "motivated and dependable. Is that right?"

"Yes sir." Her short hair bounced as she nodded. "I'm both of those things."

"Olivia over there's the one who trained our Judy a year or so back. She says you're sharp." Again he glanced at his paper. "Says you're calm under pressure. That's a quality that could come in mighty handy around here sometimes."

She folded and refolded her hands in her lap.

He grinned. "You look like you're feeling a bit of pressure now."

"Just a little." She grinned back at him.

"I'm feeling a bit of pressure to let Judy go as quickly as a replacement could be found." I know her husband. Good man and in a hurry to leave us."

She sat forward, "I'm available." What else could she say?

He slapped his hands on his desk top and rose. "How about we give you a trial period of, say, sixty days to see how it goes. Minimum wage, four days a week."

She nodded and rose with him.

"By then we'll know if you're cut out for this job."

"That would be great." She took his hand and shook vigorously. "Thank you."

"How about you start day after tomorrow? Nine o'clock. Judy can train you on days till she leaves."

"And then?"

"It'll be baptism by fire." He laughed. "We'll move staff around and you'll take the graveyard shift, usually our quietest time of day. You'll have four days on, three days off. Think you can handle that?"

"I'm sure I can." Not exactly true. She let out a breath that she realized she had been holding a long time.

She practically ran all the way back to the courthouse.

"I got it. I got it," she cried bursting through the door.

Olivia grinned. "I know. Judy called."

"So does this mean that our training is over? I want to go up and tell Audrey."

Shaking her head and letting her red hair fly, Olivia scoffed. "Over? You know how to run a switchboard, but dispatch is a whole new game. Have a seat! I've got two days to teach you what should take us a week."

———◆◆———

Heading out into the late afternoon, she pulled her sweater close. Even though in the middle of the week the rates would be high, she was going to make a phone call. "*Howard,*" she would to say. "*You won't believe this. I got a job!*" She practically ran in the direction of the little white house on First Street as excited as a girl on her first date but as she got closer to home, she slowed down and reflected. Actually Howard won't be all that surprised. She couldn't help smiling. *God bless Howard.*

54 Acronyms

"Mom, I'm freezing," Laurie whimpered from the top of the stairs

"Me too." Richie's teeth chattered.

The humidity of Oregon that made everything so green and beautiful was now, in November, chilling everyone in the house to the bone. It seemed like the sun never broke through the cloud cover long enough to dry anything. Winters in Colorado had been colder according to the thermometer, but the ever present moisture made the fifty-degree night in McMinnville feel like thirty. With the winter coming, it was only going to get worse.

According to what Alice Mae read, the Willamette Valley didn't usually get below the mid thirty's in the winter months but with the humidity even that was going to be miserable. If the temperature dropped into the twenties or teens, which was always possible, they would be in real trouble. The little house had no insulation and only three small baseboard heaters. One was in the living room, one in the master bedroom, thank goodness, and one in the bathroom – a blessing on cold mornings. There was no heat in the upper room nor floor vents to allow any warm air to rise.

Crawling out from under her own covers where she tried to get a few hours sleep before heading out to her shift at the station, she folded up the one quilt from Masyl that she had brought and hauled it upstairs. "Here." She tucked it around her shivering boy. "This should help."

"Where's ours?" Laurie croaked, throat sore from coughing.

"Put on some socks and snuggle closer to Sharon." It was the best she could offer.

"We already have on socks, two pairs."

"I gotta go, Honey. You'll be fine." She heard a moan from the girls room but no argument.

Downstairs she folded the remaining blanket on her bed in half and covered Joyce with a second layer, praying it would be enough and then added her sweater for good measure. She kissed the sleeping girl on the cheek, hoping that the warmth she felt wasn't a fever coming on, and slipped into the bathroom to dress. At least the station was warm. If it weren't for the cold, wet walk in the dark to get there, she would look forward to it.

"Morning, Alice."

"It's not morning yet," she said glancing at the clock. "Five minutes till." She hung her dripping coat on a rack and slipped off her wet shoes, setting them near a heat vent to dry. No shoes under her desk were better than wet shoes, she reasoned.

"Anything exciting going on?"

Ron Wells sounded slightly disappointed. "Nah, It's been a quiet night. One DUI got picked up and an APB out, but nothing else going on. Couple of speeding tickets. The usual." Part time student, part time fireman trainee and part time dispatch, Ron filled in wherever needed. He looked at her soaked shoes. "You got to get some boots or something. You're going to catch pneumonia like that."

She grinned back. "Too late. Already had it."

"Maybe some of mine would fit." He looked at his size eleven boots and then at her size six flats. "Or not."

"I appreciate the thought," she said, running her hands under hot water in the small lunchroom sink to warm them. Briskly drying her wet feet with a dry towel she padded back into the main room. "Okay. I'm ready."

He put on his coat, pulled up his hood and with a wave, dashed out into the night. "Have a good night, Alice."

In nearly a month, Alice Mae had picked up most of the jargon. She could issue an APB or a BOLO with no trouble. She knew a DOA from a DID, which was a good thing because the first meant someone was dead on arrival while the other was simply a driver in the ditch. Big difference! She knew when the officers were talking about the department of Justice, DOJ, or the county jail, CJ. All in all, she was feeling reasonably confident about her abilities, but she had yet to encounter a real emergency. She had yet to roll the fire trucks or send an ambulance when a real life and death situation was in her hands. She continually prayed that when the time came she would keep a cool head.

"I got a call from somebody named Howland. Says he wants me to verify your wages." Chief Fred Bowman strolled in at six o'clock, morning coffee cup in hand and eyed Alice Mae with a scowl. He was not a morning person! "Says he needs to know exactly how much you make. You okay with that?"

"That's fine." She smiled at him despite his grumping. After his second shot of caffeine, his mood would improve. "He's my caseworker from Holyoke and he needs to know how much to deduct from my ADC check. Please send it to him ASAP." She liked using acronyms!

"So how much do they take out?"

"All of it."

"What?" He almost spit his coffee.

"For every dollar I make here, they deduct a dollar from my welfare check."

"That's absurd! No wonder no one wants to get off welfare." His face reddened as soon as the words came out. "Sorry, Alice, I didn't mean that the way it sounded."

She smiled and ran her hand over her neck, weary from a long night. "Don't worry about it. A lot could be said for that argument."

"So if I can ask, how much do you get?"

She told him.

He whistled. "That's all? You live on that? My wife wouldn't make it a week and we only have one kid."

"We don't live too well, but we survive. We rely on a lot of services like free lunches at school and the surplus food but it's tight."

"I've heard that stuff is pretty good." He eyed her over his mug. "True or false?"

"Well, the canned meat is good. Makes great stew or beef and noodles, but the powdered eggs and powdered cheese …" She made a face. "And the dehydrated potatoes taste like cardboard. Let's just say it beats going hungry but not by much."

"Got it." He walked into the small lunch room and filled the percolator with fresh coffee grounds and plugged it in. The gurgling sounds began.

The chief walked back into the room and leaned up against the doorway. "So, with a minimum wage job how are you going to get ahead. You'll earn money from here but lose it from your relief check. Right?"

"That's one way of looking at it. But the point is I earned it here." She spoke with conviction. "It's my money and if I do good, eventfully you'll give me a raise and I won't be making minimum wage. Right?" She was counting on that.

He said nothing.

"Besides, my welfare benefits end next July so I have to make this work."

He walked into his office shaking his head. "I'll send Howland the information but it seems like a stupid system to me."

She couldn't argue with him.

55   Knit One

"Alice Mae, you okay?" Hazel squinted through her thick glasses. "No offense, Honey, but you look like something the cat dragged in."

"None taken." She laughed. "You're probably right. The graveyard shift is harder on me than I thought it would be. Guess it's showing."

The older woman raised an eyebrow. "A bit."

What could she say? "Thanks for having Joyce over again. And thanks for the cookies. They didn't even make it to dinner."

Hazel laughed. "She's a joy, and speaking of cookies, she's a smart little cookie."

"She brought home the pot holder you helped her make. It was good for her first try."

"Not exactly square but she's catching on. We're going make another one." The older woman's easy smile faded. She lowered her voice and glanced around to see if anyone was within earshot. "Joyce tells me your house is always cold. Is that right?"

"The kids think so."

"And you? Do you think so?"

"Maybe a little." That wasn't an outright lie. The downstairs was warm enough during the days when some sun cut through the clouds and warmed the exterior walls or when someone was cooking. At night it was cold. "But we're doing fine."

Not one for letting go of a worry, Hazel persisted. "Joyce was telling me about her Aunt Masyl and her quilts. She loves those quilts. Says you used to have lots of them."

Alice Mae nodded and swallowed down the lump in her throat. She hadn't had a word from Masyl in four months, even though she had written several times. "They're beautiful. She likes piecing them and sewing them, but I think her favorite part is the quilting. She spends hours stitching intricate designs." Her hands moved up and down, mimicking the stitching as she talked. "She's won ribbons at the county fair every year for as long as I can remember." Her eyes gave her away.

"You miss her?"

Alice Mae nodded, not trusting her voice.

After a moment, she cleared her throat and smiled. "She used to cut up the kids old clothes and make crazy quilts for their beds. We had a dozen of them. When we moved, we had to leave most of them behind. The trailer Dad brought had," she chose her words carefully, remembering that Hazel knew and liked Henry, "very limited space." She could feel an unwelcome sting and felt her nose redden.

The church was nearly empty by the time Hazel pulled her car keys from her coat pocket. She hesitated. "I've never had the patience for quilting, all that cutting and puzzling them out. But as you know I do love knitting and crocheting and I have trunks full of afghans I've made. All my family is sick of them and don't want any more, but I still like making them. Gives me something to do while I watch Perry Mason, you know." She gave Alice Mae a mischievous glance. "I just love Della Street and oh that Paul." She giggled like a girl.

It must have been the expression on her face because Hazel put a hand on her arm and said, "My dear. Why didn't you say something sooner? I'll drop some off this very afternoon."

She eyed the younger woman's feet, still soaked from the walk to church and asked. "What size shoes do you wear?"

———◆◆———

When at midnight, Alice Mae slipped out into the rain, she walked easier knowing that each of her children slept under the weight and warmth of a bright, homemade afghan. In addition, a box of bulky, hand knit scarves, hats, and slippers of assorted sizes sat in a bag by the front door.

"Nobody wears these." Sharon had announced after Hazel's departure. "I'm not wearing them."

Richie scrunched up his face. "No way am I wearing pink."

Nobody wanted them tonight, and that was fine, thinking they were too old fashioned. She suspected that by Christmas, they would all be in use, albeit in the privacy of their little home. The cold floors and damp shoes would give way to warm feet and she was thankful for every last item. In fact, it took a great deal of persuasion to get Hazel to go home with the rest of the items that she had offered, but enough was enough.

Except when she passed under the streetlight, no one could see that on her head she sported a cute, fuchsia, crocheted beret that she thought looked rather fetching. It kept the top of her head dry and warm. On her feet, over her thin shoes, she wore a pair of very old-fashioned but very dry plastic slip on rain boots. They were ugly as all get out and she wouldn't ever show them to the kids but, oh, her feet were so dry! *God Bless Hazel.*

56 Table Talk

It was after two in the morning when she slipped the envelope out of her pocket and spread the letter across the police dispatch desk. She stared at the looping penmanship and read it again although it was not necessary. She could recite the section from memory.

> *As we talked about the night you stayed with us my sight is continuing to deteriorate. Henry is still in denial and insists that I just need new glasses, but I find it increasingly difficult to drive and tasks around the house are getting harder. I worry about your father and what he will do when I am no longer able to take care of him. He acts tough, but the truth is he needs someone looking after him.*
>
> *How is it that you have been through so much and yet you have such faith? I find myself angry with God for allowing this thing. I have never known him the way you do, but I wish I could. I find losing my sight frightening but as I get older I recognize that I have more to lose than just my sight.*
>
> *Please pray for your father and pray for me.*
>
> *With much affection,*
>
> *Janet*

Alice Mae had never actually shared the gospel message with anyone other than her children. Her heart pounded as she considered what she might say.

The night she stayed in Sacramento she slipped from a troubled sleep and went to the kitchen in search of a drink of water. Janet heard her and tiptoed out to see what she needed. In the peace of the darkened house the two women chatted and, to the surprise of both, found mutual companionship and comfort.

Sitting at the kitchen table, Alice Mae confided. "I had everything I needed in that purse; addresses, copies of legal documents, school records. You cannot imagine how much."

"No! Henry didn't say a word about it."

"I think he figured it served me right, somehow, for putting him through all the trouble of the move."

Janet shook her head.

"I'd gone to the courthouse and gotten copies of all our birth certificates just in case we needed them." Her shoulders slumped. "I even had some of my mom's letters to me when she was …" She couldn't say the word *dying*.

Janet sat still, hurting for her.

"I hadn't carried a purse in years, usually just had a little cash in my pocket for necessities, so when we left the café last night, I didn't think to reach for it." Her hand went to her lips. "I thought it was safer to keep them all with me than to pack them. They would have been better off in a box, locked inside the U-Haul." She wiped an involuntary tear from her cheek.

Janet nodded, knowing.

"I trust God. I really do. I know I'm doing the right thing, but it's still hard." She looked out the large kitchen window and could see the lights of downtown Sacramento in the distance.

"I admire your faith and courage. I could use some of it," Janet began. It took a couple minutes before she could say the words. "I'm going blind." It was the first time she had said them aloud. She took a deep breath. Her lip began to quiver.

"No! How?" Words failed Alice Mae. By contrast, her troubles suddenly seemed trivial. Now it was her turn to sit and wait.

"It started about six months ago but I can feel it progressing. My night vision is almost gone and my vision is rapidly fading." Her voice quivered. Her fear was plain. "A couple nights ago, when Henry was gone, I went into the garage to put away some things and I realized I couldn't see which box I needed. I couldn't read the labels. I think that was the first time it really hit me. I find myself sitting up at night, unable to sleep, and trying to imagine what it will be like to live in the dark."

Alice Mae started to reach out a hand to Janet and was surprised to find that they were already clasping hands, Janet's plump hand sandwiched between her own thin ones.

"Have you told any of your kids?"

Janet shook her head, allowing the long blonde and gray hair, which had been so neatly tucked away earlier in the evening, to settle around her shoulders. "No. I don't want to bother them. They weren't too happy when I married Henry and moved here and there's nothing they can do about it. Eventually, I'll have to tell them, of course, but I'm not ready yet."

"I'll pray for you," Alice Mae promised, meaning it.

The police station was quiet at this hour. Radio chatter from patrol cars was intermittent, but nothing needed her immediate attention. Alice Mae lowered her eyes against the light of the room and began talking to the one who had all the answers. *Lord, how many times over the years have I prayed for my dad? I've prayed, but I don't know that I actually expected an answer. Now I pray earnestly, wanting answers. Janet is in need of your help, your strength. Lord, she needs you. Give me the words she needs to hear.*

Like a big *Amen*, the phone rang and a light on the ambulance dispatch panel lit. "City of McMinnville."

"I think my husband might be having a heart attack." The woman's voice was high pitched and anxious.

Her training kicked in. "What's your name?"

"Sandra. My husband is Mike, Mike Martin. He slumped over on the side of the bed and I can't get him to answer me." She was crying but she was not hysterical. That was good. "I think I need an ambulance."

"What's your address?" She got the information, dispatched the paramedic to a neighborhood at the west edge of town and heard the doors closing and the ambulance roll out into the night.

"They're on their way. You should see them in about two or three minutes. Sandra, stay on the line with me till they get there, okay? You did great calling. You'll have some help in just a couple of minutes."

"Okay." She could hear the breathing on the end of the line ease. "Thank you."

In three minutes flat, Alice Mae heard someone pounding on the door and the commotion of the paramedics taking charge of the situation. "Good luck Sandra," she said but there was no one was on the line. She disconnected the call.

She felt like a kid on a roller coaster. Adrenaline surged through her. Her heart hammered in her chest. She was shaken, but she had done it. Actually, she had loved it. Her board lit up with calls as one patrolman after another, having heard the on-air chatter and the siren checked in with her for updates and instructions. She had it under control.

She stood and paced the office offering up prayers of thanks for being with her. She prayed for Sandra and Mike. As her racing heart returned to normal she realized she knew what she needed to say to Janet.

57   One for All

Her fever registered 101.4 degrees. For three days everyone in the family had been coughing, sneezing, blowing their noses and generally been under the weather but on Wednesday mayhem broke loose. It started with Laurie.

"I'm not going." Her throat was raw, her face flushed. "I'm not going to walk to the health department. I'm too sick."

"You probably need medicine and they won't give it to me without seeing you."

"I don't care." She pulled the blanket up over her head, trying to get warm. "I'm staying here. Could you get me another blanket?"

Alice Mae pulled an afghan off of Richie's twin bed and spread it over Laurie.

Feeling her own muscles aching and suspecting her temperature was also on the rise, she considered who among her recent and still tentative friends she might call to ask for help.

There was Hazel, of course. She didn't doubt that the old woman would be willing to come but she did not want to expose the woman to whatever ailment that she and the children might be sharing. No, indeed.

Mike Browning came to mind. He was hearty and probably had immunities built up by virtue of the fact that he spent a lot of time outdoors, not to mention he was around the college kids who doubtlessly spread germs. Her friendship with Mike was cordial, but she was uncomfortable asking a single man, a very reclusive man at that, to come haul her and her sick kids somewhere.

Patricia Ward might be willing. She had daughters of her own and knew how difficult it would be to see then sick and have no way to get them to the doctor. She, however, could not bring herself to call

Patricia who always looked like something out of a fashion catalogue and smelled like lavender, to come pick up a sick, germ laden girl and transport her to the county office. Although she knew that pride was a sin, she was too proud to ask.

In the end, she chose to wait it out. Perhaps it was just a twenty-four hour bug and she would be better tomorrow.

By midnight, as she dressed for work, she knew she was in trouble. Chills ran down her back and her muscle ache was fierce. Calling in sick was not an option. Chief Bowman did not like last minute shift changes. Besides the station was almost deserted during her shift. Her job required her to just sit. She could handle that. *One more day*, she told herself. She would give it one more day to run its course. *Or two.*

The night, however, was anything but quiet. By one o'clock there had been two accidents on Hwy 99, one with an ambulance dispatch, one without. The Chief came in at four, not happy to be called out at that hour. John Williams, a young officer and a single dad, had kids who dared to get sick and the Chief had to cover his shift. His grumbling reinforced Alice Mae's earlier conclusion. She had been through worse. She would survive.

By the time she dragged herself home through a torrential downpour, aching and tired; she found that everyone in the house was running a fever. Everyone had chills. There was not a soul healthy enough to get up and take care of the others. That task fell to her.

She called three schools, reporting four kids sick. She called Audrey to see what, if anything might be available for her family as far as getting transport to see a doctor. She should have known better.

She took drinks up and down the stairs to the kids, offered them dry toast and fell into bed, too exhausted to move and slept for four hours straight till Joyce's racking cough woke her.

When she called the Health Department a little after noon and explained her situation, the nurse who remembered her was sympathetic. "Do you think you could make it down here?"

She wanted to say no, no, no! She didn't think she could drag herself to the bathroom, much less through the rain to the Health Department.

"Yes. I'll be there in about half an hour."

"Good. The doctor can see what's going on with you at least. We'll go from there."

Her shoes were still wet from the walk home and felt like they weighed ten pounds each. The dress she wore last night lay across the foot of her bed. She put it back on, pulled on a sweater and her only coat, also still damp from the walk home, and trudged to the courthouse hoping nobody she knew would see her. No such luck.

"Alice Mae?" Olivia stuck her head out of the office, took one glimpse of her associate, wrinkled and pale, and gasped. "You look terrible. Where are you going?"

She tried to smile, but it came across as more of a sneer. She motioned down the hall. "Health Department," was all that came out.

"You walked down here?" Olivia shook her head in disbelief. Her hands went to her hips and she scowled at Alice Mae.

"No car."

Like a whirling dervish, Olivia flew to the phone, called the Police Station and told the Chief that Alice Mae would not be at work tonight. "The woman is too sick to be out in this weather. I don't know how it is that nobody there noticed how sick she was when she left this morning. Now, you need to send a patrol car over here to the courthouse in about half an hour to take this poor woman home." She was on a roll. "If you cannot find someone to take her shift tonight, I'll come myself."

"Of course." The chief knew when he was outmatched.

"And," Olivia added for good measure. "It will probably be several days before she is well enough to come back, so if you need help on any of her shifts, I'm available. Gratis." She hung up, looking smug, and nodded.

Alice Mae stared in utter disbelief and relief. "Thank you," she mouthed.

Thirty minutes later, laden with enough free pharmaceuticals to relieve the fever and most of the symptoms of mother, son, and all three daughters—Alice Mae rode home in a blissfully warm patrol car. The young officer walked her to the door, carrying her bag of relief.

"You take care," He insisted, seeing her inside. "We'll see you when you're all better. Chief says there's no hurry."

She stayed on her feet long enough to give all four kids a dose of medication, tucked them in as best she could and then crashed back into bed. As she drifted off to sleep, her mind replayed a nursery rhyme. It went something like:

> There was an old lady, who lived in a shoe
> She had so many children, she didn't know what to do.
> She gave them all broth, without any bread
> And kissed them all soundly, and then went to bed.

58   T'is the Season

The Christmas season was supposed to be cold and crisp. In the high Colorado plains, the snows often began around the first of November and by late December Holyoke was, what was euphemistically called, a winter wonderland. Bundled up in gloves and boots and festive scarves, shoppers braved temperatures that frequently dropped into the teens. Generally they greeted one another on the sidewalks with white puffs of breath accentuating their words.

The temperatures in McMinnville, however, hovered in the mid fifties and the shoppers toted umbrellas. *Walking in a soggy wonderland*, Alice Mae thought as she stepped around puddles on her way home from work.

On the plus side, there were camellias in bloom. Flowers blooming in December! Extraordinary. The first time Alice Mae saw the showy pink camellia blossoms she thought they were roses.

"Roses at Christmas?" She pulled a pink flower from her coat pocket and showed it to Mike as they lingered after church. "They're blooming outside my house and I've seen them in other yards too. Is that possible?"

The reclusive man laughed. "They're not roses. They're camellias. They're evergreens and they bloom year round. Haven't you ever seen them before?"

"Never."

"They're beautiful but they turn brown almost as soon as the rain hits them so if you like them, cut them and bring them indoors."

"I will. I'll cut some as soon as I get home." She was giddy with anticipation.

The bush grew on the northwest corner of her house and was regularly buffeted by the passing trains. It had been little more than a dried, brown tangle of branches when she moved in. Being one of only a few signs of growth around her tiny house, she pruned it back and dug around its base hoping that, come spring, it would revive. To her delight, when the autumn rains began, the green leaves grew in shiny and variegated with golden veins and then glorious camellia bloomed.

She had to admit that what McMinnville lacked in snow and frost, it made up for with Christmas spirit. The downtown area was ablaze with lights and holiday music spilled from shops up and down Third Street. *Merry Christmas* banners hung between light posts.

"Merry Christmas," someone would say.

"Merry Christmas to you," came the reply from neighbor and stranger alike.

Fresh cedar, fir, and juniper swags graced windows and doors from the East end of Third Street to the West. Fragrant candles burned in stores and warm cider was handed out to shoppers by merchants all along the street. Candy canes were free at the bank to children. Christmas music spilled onto the sidewalk as doors opened and closed. It was a banquet for the senses.

Walking into the police station in early December, Alice Mae was delighted to find a six foot Grand fir gracing the lobby. It had deep green, shiny, flat needles, and was covered with red balls and silver tinsel. During her shift she kept wandering over to better enjoy the fresh cut fragrance and allow herself to be infused with the Christmas spirit that, despite the merchants' efforts, she was struggling to find.

Besides work, December was promising to be a memorable month.

The invitation made of red construction paper, laden with glitter, was on the refrigerator. Every time the door opened, sparkles reigned down like snow.

Parents, Grandparents and friends of Cook School children.
Join us on Friday December 14th, 7:00 PM for our annual Christmas performance.
Cookies and punch will be served after.

And then there was a church pageant in which the Junior High age students, including Richie were singing. The bright green bulletin insert with large bold type was hard to ignore.

Don't miss our live nativity with our own choir of angels

December 19th. 6:00 pm.

Refreshments after.

And Donna was arriving in Portland via Amtrak. Arriving December 21st, 8:14 PM. Her note was short. *Can't wait to see you. Who will be there to meet me?* Alice Mae had no idea. The only link between Portland and McMinnville that she knew of was Greyhound and their service didn't run that late at night.

If that weren't enough, both Sharon and Laurie had birthdays, Sharon's on Christmas Eve, always a challenge, and Laurie's on the twenty-eighth. And, of course, there was Christmas.

Oregon was more expensive than Alice Mae had anticipated. Rent on the little house took an enormous bite out of her monthly check. She was five dollars short on the water and power bill last month and although they had been nice about it, she knew she couldn't fall short again. The surplus food was the only thing that kept the family fed and even it ran low towards the end of the month.

After Christmas, the phone would have to go!

She had no money for a tree and almost no money for gifts. Thankfully, the kids each had bit of spending money that allowed them to enjoy the season.

Sharon was still working two days a week and getting good tips. Laurie had picked up a few babysitting jobs through the church and Richie still had some of his summer nut picking money. Even Joyce had watched Maureen's girls a couple of afternoons while their mom ran errands. With the added expense of having another mouth to feed, Alice Mae knew she would have to ask them to chip in. They would.

The Christmas envelope containing the two-dollar bills from Grandpa arrived, as usual along with a five-spot for Alice Mae. It was always welcome, but the two dollars didn't go as far as they used to.

Exhausted, she fell into bed. Lord, *I'm not short of faith, just on cash.* She was glad he knew her heart because she was asleep before she could think of anything else to say.

59 Cash

"Ted says he'll drive me to Portland to get Donna." Sharon bounded into the kitchen, her face alive with excitement. "He says we can leave right after school on Friday and he'll buy me dinner in Portland. If it's okay with you we could take Laurie with us." Her head was nodding, her ponytail bouncing. She was absolutely glowing. "Please, Mom, please. I've always wanted to go to Portland."

Alice Mae threw her arms around her daughter. "Yes. By all means yes! That would be wonderful. Tell him thank you for me."

Relief washed over her. Donna would be home in less than three weeks, all the way home. Her mind raced. She had so much to do and no choice but to ask for help. She dialed a number she knew by heart.

"Hi Shirley."

"Alice Mae! I'm so happy to hear your voice." Her enthusiasm and sincerity was heartening. "Ted just told me he gets to be the first of us to meet your older daughter. He's so excited."

"We are too." The smile on her face could be heard across the line.

"Do you know what she might be bringing? Ted can take our car if he needs to. It has more trunk room you know."

Alice Mae laughed. "If she brings everything she owns it'll still fit in just one suitcase. No, his car will be fine, I'm sure."

"Now, with her coming I know there are things you are going to need. What can I do for you?"

She hardly knew where to start. "Do you know anyone at the church that might have a single mattress we could borrow? And

261

perhaps some extra bedding? We don't have a sofa and there's no place to put her …"

"That's right. You don't have a sofa? Do you not want one or did you not have room to bring one?"

"There wasn't room."

"I'll work on that. And no bed for her? Is there room in the girls' bedroom for a twin bed if we can find one? They have a full size in there now, I assume."

"Actually, they have a three-quarter bed. It's halfway between a twin and a full. It's an oddity, but it was all we had and all that would fit in …" Every time she talked about the tiny U-Haul trailer she felt her throat constrict. "It's a good fit for their room though. It has slanted ceilings," she added as if it explained everything.

"I'm sure we can find you one. Jeffery knows just about everybody. Let me talk to him and see who has what. What else?" She waited, but not long. Patience was not her strong suit. "Do you have your tree?"

"Not yet." She hedged.

"We are going to go cut our own this weekend. Do you think Richie would want to go with us? I'll bet he'd love it. Jeffery has an old school chum who lives up in the hills above Sheridan so we go there every year and just whack away at whatever suits us. They're not always perfect, but I like the whimsical look. What do you say?"

Her eyes stung with the merriment of it. "Yes. I know he'll be thrilled. He's never done anything like that before."

"I'll give you a few days to think about it but I want a list of things you will need for Donnas' visit. Remember, we're family."

Enclosed with the December check from Howard and the Phillips County Welfare Department, was a hand written Christmas card.

Alice Mae. I am so proud of you. I knew you could do it. Please keep me updated on the work situation as well as any progress you might make on the college front. On a personal note, Rodger sends his regards to Laurie and asked me to send her a sprig of mistletoe.

I declined.

Please accept a small gift for a personal holiday treat from our family to yours.

Howard Howland.

Enclosed was a ten dollar bill. She read the note again and smiled. Alone in her home, feeling blessed and refreshed by the encouragement, she did what she so often did. She sang what was in her heart. "Great is thy faithfulness, oh God my father …"

60 Lights

After a twenty-five minute performance, forty children holding construction paper candles with glitter-glued flames wrapped up their performance. "We wish you a merry Christmas. We wish you a merry Christmas. We wish you a merry Christmas, and a Happy New Year."

Everyone applauded!

"Good job." Alice Mae hugged Joyce at the rear of the gymnasium where cookies were being served. "You did great."

"Hi, Mrs. Wheaton." Billy Reynolds sidled behind the girl.

"Hi, Billy. You did great, too." With hair that still needed a trim and mended clothes, he stood before her, looking like a lost waif. "Is your grandma here?"

"Nah, she doesn't like to go out in the dark."

Her heart hurt for the boy; he looked forlorn. She glanced at Joyce and hesitated for just a moment before asking. "How far is it to your house?"

He shrugged, "Just a couple blocks."

"Would you like to walk with us? I thought we might look at some Christmas lights on our way home." From the corner of her eye, she saw Joyce nod enthusiastically.

Billy's eyes met hers and grew wide as did his crooked grin. "Yeah! That'd be great."

"Grab a couple cookies while I speak to your teacher. And get your coats."

With a girl on her left and a boy on her right she led them through the night, looking into lit windows, admiring a makeshift manger scene and laughing at a plastic Santa already climbing into a chimney. The lights were bright. The children were carefree.

When finally they stopped in front of a home no bigger than their own, they said goodnight to the boy who skipped up to the door and waved hugely. "Goodnight Joyce."

"He seems nice." They walked in the direction of First Street. The sky was clear for a change and a few stars were visible even with the lights of town ablaze.

"He's okay." A comfortable silence settled between them for a block. "He thinks I'm pretty."

"He's right." Even in the darkness she could see the smile crawl across the girl's face.

Joyce began softly humming. *Silent night, holy night."* There was a skip in her step. Alice Mae took her hand and softly picked up the carol. "All is calm. All is bright. Round yon virgin, mother and child. Holy infant, so tender and mild. Sleep in heavenly peace. Sleep in heavenly peace."

———◆———

The house smelled like a forest. Stepping inside she stared, transfixed. Dominating her living room was a five foot tall Douglas fir. A lit strand of large blue, green and red lights tangled in its branches, glowed.

"Beautiful," she breathed.

"I cut it myself." Richie beamed. "You should have seen the one that Jeffery, I mean Mr. Adams cut for them. It was twice as big." His arms reached for the ceiling.

"It's kind of crooked," Joyce observed, walking around the tree, "and it's got a broken branch back here."

"It's perfect," Alice Mae pronounced hugging the boy.

"Mrs. Adams asked if we had any decorations. I told her no, so she gave us the lights. Ted and Sharon put 'em on before they left."

"Left for where?"

"Basketball game at the high school, I think. Ted drove."

She nodded and surveyed the empty living room. "Where's Laurie?"

"Said to tell you that she's at the Heinrichs, babysitting. Mr. Heinrichs called and asked her sort of last minute. He picked her up about fifteen minutes ago."

"So it looks like it's up to the three of us to get this tree decorated," she said, slipping off her coat and tossing it on her bed. "Who wants to string popcorn?"

"No need," the boy pointed to a cardboard box sitting on the table. "Look! Mrs. Adams said we could use these." He ran to the table and began pulling out an assortment of ornaments along with several packages of icicles. "She said they were going to have an African Christmas tree this year and didn't want these. Can we go see their tree when it's done?"

"I think we should. I'll bet it will be beautiful."

With Christmas carols scratching from Sharon's small transistor radio and colored lights blinking and flooding the living room with cheer, they examined each ornament in the collection and selected the ones they liked. By the time they were done the tree was decked from top to bottom.

"We can use one of our new towels for a tree skirt," Alice Mae said, dashing to the bathroom to find a large one. Carefully she wound it, turban-style, around the base to cover the wooden stand. "Perfect."

As a finishing touch, they tossed on lots tinsel to mask any flaws. It was a thing of beauty.

"Now off to bed with you two," She gave then a final hug and patted them on their backsides. "It's late and I'm tired. I have to be up in two hours and I need some rest before I go."

Once the giggling and the patter of feet stilled, she settled into the living room chair opposite the tree, bathed in the glow of the colored lights. Rather than nod off as she was tempted to do, she took a pen and a piece of stationary and began writing.

Dear Janet,

I am sorry to hear that your eyes are getting progressively worse. I cannot imagine the distress this causes you. I continue to pray for you faithfully.

I pray for your courage and that you might find peace, but the peace you are seeking will not be found with your doctor. Your eye sight will probably fail you. My father will most likely fail you as well. I'm sorry for that. But if you put your faith in God, he will not fail you. The peace you seek can only be found in a relationship with the One who can give you sight with your heart, not your eyes. The peace you are looking for can be found with Jesus.

When I was only six, my dear mother led me in a prayer that changed my life. It gave me hope and faith and a relationship that has sustained me all my life.

It started with a basic admission that I was a sinner. I was born that way. I needed to ask God to forgive me for my sin and to take charge of my life. I gave him my heart freely. I asked him to be the Father I needed and later the husband I needed. Even now, often feeling alone in this new place, he is my constant companion and best friend.

Since that time when as a child I prayed and asked him into my heart, I have had a relationship with him that at times is just as real and vivid as with any loved one on earth. I have needed that love because as you know, my life has been difficult.

I encourage you, my friend, to invite him into your life. Let him give you spiritual eyes to see that will ease the loss of your sight. His gift will not only allow you to enjoy peace during your years on earth but will give you a glorious peace with him for eternity.

Jesus wants to hear from you. He waits with open arms.

I wish a very Merry Christmas to you and my dad. I pray for you both, often.

Love, Alice Mae.

With that letter folded and put into its envelope, she began another.

> *Dear Masyl,*
>
> *I miss you.*
>
> *Christmas is almost here and it will be the first Christmas without you and your family in many years. My heart aches with the knowledge that we are not only far apart but that you are still hurting and I cannot put my arms around you.*
>
> *When I left Holyoke, I thought that distance and time would ease the pain of not seeing you. It has not.*
>
> *I know that you do not have the faith that our mother lived out so well when we were children. You have struggled to believe that God cares for you, especially during this challenging year. I promise you that he does.*
>
> *I do not understand why He saw fit to take our little sister, so sweet and young. I don't know why he took Mother when we both needed her so much. I still miss her daily, even after ten years. I cannot begin to understand why he allowed Mary Charlene to die. I do know, however, that I can trust him with my life, with my future because He loves me.*
>
> *I will continue to pray that you will write or call me. I want to know what is on your heart and to share it with you. I will only have my phone till the first of the year but would love to hear your voice.*
>
> *I pray you and your family will find peace and joy during this season.*
>
> *With much love,*
>
> *Your sister, Alice Mae.*

61 Donna

It was almost ten when Alice Mae finally heard the little beetle-bug stop in front of the house. Two short beeps of the horn announced its arrival. Even though she knew Donna's train wasn't scheduled to arrive till after eight and they were an hour away, every car that drove by since eight had been scrutinized.

She opened the front door wide. As Donna came through the door, she grabbed her oldest daughter and hugged her hard and long. "You're home," she breathed, rocking from side to side. "You're home."

When she finally let go, she took a step back and examined the girl she had left standing in the middle of Holyoke five months ago. She looked the same, except for one thing. "Donna? Wow." She didn't trust herself to say more.

"I thought I'd take after you." The girl turned her head this way and then that, showing off her new, very short haircut. She took off her coat and threw it on the couch. "Do you like it?" The long, soft hair that she had always worn, that Alice Mae had loved, was gone.

The new cut was right out of a fashion magazine. Long bangs, short at the nape of the neck and cut short around the ears. It was cute, but it wasn't Donna. She swallowed hard and turned her daughter around.

"Ruth talked me into it. She said I needed a new look for my new life." With her fingers, she fluffed the top of the hair and tucked short strands behind her ears. "What do you think?"

"I love it!" Sharon clapped her hands with glee. "Doesn't she look just Suzanne Pleshette? It's adorable." From behind Sharon, Ted nodded enthusiastically, eyes bright with pleasure and set a large box he was carrying on the floor next to the tree.

Ted pecked Sharon's cheek and she blushed. "I'm out of here. It's late and you all have catching up to do." He waved at Richie, who was bounding down the stairs at the sound of the arrivals, and to the assembled family said. "Bye Laurie, Mrs. Wheaton."

"Thanks for the ride, Ted." Donna grabbed his hand and squeezed. "It was really sweet of you to go all the way to Portland to get me."

"Believe me, it was my pleasure. Another nice-looking Wheaton sister is a great addition to our town." His grin was effortless. "Bye Sharon. See you Sunday if not before." He pulled the door shut behind him and a minute later and with a short toot of his horn, drove away.

"Mush." Richie teased Sharon. Her blush deepened.

Laurie set down the box she was holding and stripped off her coat. "I hardly recognized her when she got off the train. I looked right past her and wondered if she'd missed it. Then I heard Sharon yelling and hugging this complete stranger before I realized it was Donna." She laughed. Everyone was laughing.

"Another box? What did you bring?" Alice Mae pointed at the two boxes now stacked next to the tree and felt a charge of alarm. "No gifts I hope. We told you not to."

Donna shook her head. "They're not from me. They're from Ruth and Joe and Masyl."

She saw the surprise on her mother's face and nodded. "Well, just one thing is from Masyl. It rattles. I think it's her peanut brittle."

Alice Mae felt her heart skip a beat.

Every year in December Masyl made peanut brittle, packaged it into tin canisters and delivered it to family and friends alike. It was her only Christmas offering outside of her immediate family. No fudge. No cookies. Only brittle. She was up to about twenty cans per year. It took her days to slow cook the confection and more days to package and deliver, but she loved doing it. *Mary Charlene always helped her.* She swallowed down the memory, not willing to allow the loss to dampen the reunion.

"How did you get it?"

"Barbara and Dave dropped it off last week. They were on their way to Denver; they took me out for hamburgers. It was fun." Donna dropped to her knees and began unloading the boxes that were filled with packages. Joyce and Richie were happy to help. They read each nametag with glee. Inside of a couple minutes, the boxes were empty and the tree looked like something from a Christmas card, laden with wrapped gifts. Donna handed her mother the canister from Masyl.

Alice Mae hugged the can, thankful for the connection. *Was it her imagination or did it smell like Masyl?*

"How are the kids doing?"

Sitting on the floor in the light of the tree, Donna played with her hair, tucking it again and again behind her ear. "Barb's anxious to get a house of her own, as you might imagine. She mentioned it several times but for now they're still living with his folks."

"Really?" She wasn't the slightest bit surprised.

"Yeah. Barbara's dropped some weight since she got married. She's thin, but I think she's doing good. They seemed happy."

Alice Mae said nothing but felt a weight on her heart. *Masyl's life all over again.*

"Anyway," Donna nodded at the can, " apparently Masyl said it wouldn't be Christmas without it. Let's open it and see."

With the hub-bub subsiding, Donna finally looked around the room, noticing for the first time those things that had never been in their home in Holyoke. "This place looks great."

In two weeks time, from the bringing in the Christmas tree, to a few days before Donna's arrival, Shirley Ward, Hazel Brandt, Patricia Ward, and several other ladies from the church, had been busy 'fixing' the little white house. By raiding garages, attics and basements, they had transformed it into a real home. It had a fullness and warmth about it that prior to their efforts had been missing.

A green and gold sofa, covered with yet another of Hazel's knitting projects, graced the east wall of living room. A small black and white television on a stand of its own sat next to the door, complete with rabbit-ears. A painted bookcase filled the south wall, filled to overflowing with books, and Patricia Ward's fringed rug warmed the floor.

A dining room table large enough to actually seat six comfortably, rather than the kitchen sized one that they had been using, filled the west end of the living room. The chairs from Holyoke looked much better tucked under the warm wood veneer. With the lit Christmas tree shining at the window nearby, the place was truly festive.

The kitchen table took its rightful place in the kitchen, providing a badly needed work surface that was an alternative to the lacerated linoleum counter tops that came with the house. In the center of the table sat a large plate of Hazel's cookies.

Upstairs a twin bed on a Hollywood frame had been added to the tiny bedroom leaving just enough space to slip between the beds if one turned slightly sideways. Nails had been added to the pegs on the wall making room to hang additional clothes. To say the room was snug was an understatement. On the plus side, both beds had new sheets as well as plump pillows.

"Wilson's mother," was all Patricia had said, handing a folded stack of nearly new linens to Alice Mae.

A soft rug runner filled the small gap between the beds which would make getting up on cold mornings less shocking.

"You can sleep up here with us," Laurie said, tugging Donna to the new bed and pulling her down to sit on it, "or Joyce can move upstairs and you can stay with Mom. It's up to you."

"Donna." Richie grabbed her hand and pulled her out of the bedroom and into his hallway room. "Look at these. They're real African spears." Propped beside his bed were two impressive wooden poles, intricately carved with running cheetahs and chiseled to a wicked looking point. "Cool, huh? Mr. Adams said I could keep 'em."

She ruffled his hair. "Yeah, Kiddo. Cool."

By midnight, the house was quiet. With Joyce tucked snuggly in the new upstairs single bed, and the other kids settled in for the night, Donna and Alice Mae fell onto the sofa and pulled the knitted blanket from Hazel over their laps. They laid their heads back and breathed in the smell of warm fir. "I can't believe I'm finally here."

"I know. We've missed you," Alice Mae said, nibbling a piece of peanut brittle and savoring its familiar sweet and salty mix. "I've missed you."

Donna slipped her arm through her mothers. "I've missed you too, but Ruth's been great. I never realized she was so funny."

Alice Mae chuckled. "I know. I remember one year on April Fool's day, she took a week old newspaper, substituted the front page from the April 1st paper, and rerolled it. When Joe started reading it, he was so mad that the Register had reprinted the same stories. He was going to call them up and complain. He practically read the whole paper before he realized what she had done."

"I can see her doing that."

Five months of separation and the girl that had been left behind had matured into a poised young woman. College had opened her eyes and her mind to possibilities bigger than Holyoke. For that Alice Mae was truly thankful. "So, you're happy in Greeley?"

A lazy smile curled her lips. "I am. I'm content there. I could stay there another year and Ruth says I am welcome to if I want. They would front me the money."

Alice couldn't breathe, but she keep her face composed. "Do you want to stay?"

"I thought I did. I've got a few friends. I'm loving school. But what I believe I'd really like to do is go see Linfield." Alice Mae exhaled. "Let me see what a good school looks like and see how it compares to North Colorado. I didn't realize how much I missed you guys till I got off the train and saw Laurie and Sharon."

Alice Mae nodded. "We'll walk up there on Monday and have a look around. When we first moved I walked up almost every day but it's been a while."

"What do we do if it's raining?"

"We walk anyway."

"In the rain? Don't you get soaked?"

"I suppose we do; we hardly even notice anymore."

62 Melrose

The Columbus Day Storm left scars on the campus. Linfield's oldest oak, its landmark tree, had a new steel brace supporting an enormous lateral limb that had been damaged, but not lost, to the gale. The tree was estimated to be about five hundred years old and its loss would have been distressing. Three bare-dirt patches, each about six feet in diameter, scarred the grassy lawn where trees had gone down.

Morning mist clung to the campus, creating a damp, earthy aroma that Alice Mae had come to love. Winter sun cutting through the haze created a halo effect on the buildings. The sight was splendid as the two women climbed the steps of the administration building.

"Donna, it's a pleasure to meet you." Theodore Graves, Dean of Admissions, came out from behind his desk and shook her hand warmly. "Mrs. Wheaton. I remember your letter well. Please have a seat." At six foot plus and slender, he oozed charm and confidence like a used car salesman but with better clothes. His smile was white and his manners were practiced. Within minutes he had extolled the virtues of the college, explained the admission process and summoned an intern.

"This is James. He'll show you around campus and answer any questions you might have. When he's done, he'll bring you back here and introduce you to our Financial Aid staff. They'll be expecting you."

James was a tall, blonde, senior with natural good looks sporting a navy jacket emblazoned with the Linfield logo led them on a tour of the school. "We have an excellent academic program. Business, Mathematics, Sociology, and Psychology are in these buildings." He pointed out the respective building. "Biology, Chemistry, Physics." He continued the list. "Philosophy, Physical Education.

"We just began offering an Art major last year. Renshaw Hall is the newest building on campus. It caused quite a stir when it was built." He directed their attention to a striking, modern building on the south edge of the campus. "I'm a Political Science major myself with a minor in French. I'm hoping to go into international relations, to work at the United Nations after I graduate."

"So what was your take on the whole Cuban missile situation? I'll bet you would have loved to be in Washington during that standoff."

He grinned and nodded. "I would have indeed but I think President Kennedy handled it well. I sure would like to be there if there's a next time." His eyes danced. "What are you interested in studying, Donna?"

"Literature." She didn't hesitate. "American, European, I don't care. I love to read anything and everything I can get my hands on, especially the classics."

He spun on his heels, heading back across campus. "Then let me show you our English Department. Can't believe I missed that one," he said, chastising himself. "Perhaps we can find one of the professors and introduce you."

As promised, at the end of the tour, James delivered them to the staff of the Financial Aid office and made introductions. "It's been my pleasure to meet you both," he said. He was a charmer!

"You might be eligible for the American Baptist Association Scholarship or the Conservative Baptist one." Norma, one of the clerks riffled through a lateral file, pulling out this form and that. A jolly woman in her mid fifties, with white-blonde hair, she was professional and efficient and had, apparently, consumed too much coffee. She chattered as she scanned folder tabs. "Was your father a war veteran? Many of our students qualify for this one." She pulled a form. "Are you partially American Indian? I'm part Cherokee, I'm told, but not enough to do me any good."

She shut one drawer and opened another.

"Your grades are good so you might qualify for these." The stack was growing. "What about National Honor Society? Do you know anyone in Kiwanis or the Moose Lodge?" By the time she finished going through the list, an envelope stuffed with no fewer than a dozen possible funding sources was assembled.

"Good luck." Her hand fluttered as she watched them head down the hallway. "You call me if you have any questions."

The last stop before leaving Melrose Hall was to check on the status of the new switchboard. The construction appeared to be mostly complete. An electrician was taming a tangle of wires protruding from the wall and attaching outlets and switches. The drywall mud needed to be sanded before paint could be applied and flooring was not yet in, but it looked promising.

"Look at the view from here," Alice Mae whispered, turning toward the building's entrance.

Above the massive double-doors glass windows, each one about three feet square, were arrayed four high and eight wide. They made a wall of light and provided a window-pane view from the landing that went for miles. The two women looked out across the oak grove, the downtown buildings in the distance and the rolling foothills of the Oregon Coast Range beyond.

No foot traffic moved through the hallway as they stood transfixed by the view. Late morning sunlight etched the valley with a golden glow, softened by wafting clouds brushing the treetops.

Besides the panoramic view, the building smelled of books and history. Subdued voices behind doors and the rapid-fire staccato of typewriter keys in the nearby offices were like music, the smell of mimeograph ink and wood polish was better than perfume. It was intoxicating.

Lord, Alice Mae prayed with every ounce of her being. *Let me get this job.*

She was told, when she inquired, that they were pushing for the construction to be completed by the end of April. If all went well, they planned to hire by the first of May so that the system could begin trials and be up and running by summer. They said they were not taking applications yet. Yes, she was welcome to check back.

63   Waves

"Ted's taking us to the beach!" Sharon jumped up and down with excitement. "He's going to pick us up Thursday morning about eight and he'll take whoever wants to go." She twirled, unable to contain her excitement. "He says it's his birthday gift to me and Laurie." She jumped again and landed in a split that Alice Mae hadn't seen since the cheerleader trials of Holyoke. "He's taking his dad's big car so we can all fit. Who wants to go?"

"Count me in." Richie was on board. He pumped his arms in the air.

"Absolutely." Donna spun around. "What should I bring?"

"He says to bring a coat, tennis shoes for the beach and a change of clothes for after. He says it's going to be cold and wet, but I don't care. I can't believe it. We're going to the beach!" She shrieked and ran upstairs to see what she had to wear.

"Mom? You coming?" Her voice trailed down from on high.

Few things were higher on her list of things she wanted to do than to see the Pacific Ocean. When the decision to come to Oregon was finalized it had been one of her dreams to run into the water of the Pacific and feel the pull of the sea and the sand on her feet. She dreamed of the sound of the waves crashing on the rocks and the cry of the sea gulls against the open sky. She could taste the salt spray. Yes, she wanted to go. Of course she wanted to go.

"No. You kids go ahead and have fun." She tried to sound nonchalant. "I'll do it next time." *Next time? Of course there would be a next time.*

The reality was that working from midnight till eight in the morning left her exhausted to the bone. With the added challenge of having all the kids home every day during the Christmas break, the extra meals, the chaos of the house not to mention the laundry, she needed the day to catch up and to sleep.

At nine o'clock Thursday morning she walked into the house, weary. It had been a busy night and her replacement was late. She was soaked from walking home in the rain and she felt another sore throat coming on. What met her was a most unexpected sight. Order.

The kids had obviously risen early. The kitchen was clean. Towels from yesterday's laundry were folded and there was a fresh batch of clothes in the washing machine. Outside the back door newly washed sheets fluttered in the early morning breeze. *They must have hung them in the dark.* She smiled. The fact that they were hanging in the rain didn't matter a bit.

Peering into the tiny room next to her bedroom, she discovered that even the bathroom had been scrubbed and the rug shaken. Her heart nearly burst.

On the kitchen counter, a large batch of freshly made dough was cresting the top of a large bowl, risen and ready to be punched down and formed into loaves. Richie's work, no doubt. A note beside the bread read: We know you wanted to come but felt you needed to stay. Get some rest. We'll bring you something from the beach. The kids had all signed their names. Tears stung her eyes. She would get the bread into the oven and put her feet up while it baked. "Lord, bless those children!" she absolutely shouted. She didn't care if the neighbors heard her or not. "Bless them all!"

She awoke to the sound of someone rapping on the front door. They knocked again, louder. Through the fog of her sleep deprived mind she heard a voice. "Alice Mae. Knock. Knock."

The small wind-up clock sitting on the window ledge showed it was 3:30 in the afternoon. She had been asleep for four hours. Slipping her shoes on against the cold floor, she blinked hard and made her way through the living room and peered through the window.

Shirley Adams was waving madly from the front step. "Alice Mae. Did I wake you?"

Yes. She wanted to go back to bed.

"No, I was just resting. Hold on a minute." She ran her hands through her hair, tried in vain to smooth her rumpled clothes, put a smile on her face. She opened the door. "Shirley, what on earth are you doing here?"

Dressed fashionably in tan slacks and an African motif sweater, topped with a rain slicker, the woman smiled. If Alice Mae was not mistaken, she had carved ivory rhinoceroses hanging from her ears. *Rhinos?* "I know the kids are gone for the day and I wanted to talk to you about an idea we have. Can I come in?"

Alice Mae opened the door wider. "Come on in and have a seat." The room was spotless with every surface clean. The house smelled of fresh laundry and-baked bread. She felt a stab of pride. "Can I get you anything? Richie made bread this morning. Would you like a slice?"

"No thanks." Shirley slipped off her wet coat, hung it on the back of one of the dining chairs and gave Alice Mae a quizzical look and inhaled. "Did you say Richie? He's your baker?"

"A good one at that." She beamed. The stupor in her brain clearing as her blood began moving again. She yawned hugely and covered her mouth. "I'm so sorry."

Her guest laughed. "No matter what you say, I know I woke you. Yawn all you want."

Alice Mae's eyes blinked away sleep. "Sit. Sit." The two women settled in on the sofa. Alice Mae tucked one foot beneath her and picked up a pillow and pulled the edge of the afghan across her legs. "So what's on your mind that we need to talk about without the kids around?"

Shirley leaned in towards Alice Mae and looked at her with a curious mixture of excitement and nervousness. "Well, as you know, Jeffery and I came back to the states so that Ted could finish high school here. He doesn't have any desire to stay on the mission field with us. He wants to go to college in the states."

Alice Mae nodded. "Understandable. He's young."

"We are planning to go back to the Congo just as soon as he graduates and we can get him settled. We have acquaintances in Seattle who will welcome him and some here in town who have offered to let him stay. He just has to decide what he wants to do."

"It sounds like he's got some good options."

"What I'm trying to say is, sometime before next fall we are planning to go back. In the past, each tour has lasted two years. Now with Ted gone, we feel free to work there till we feel God telling us to leave. It could be several years. God only knows."

"That sounds exciting." It did. Odds were good that Alice Mae would never see Africa, but that didn't stop her from being gripped by the adventure of it.

"We want to keep the house. It's where we hope to retire someday. Each time we've left the states we have felt that God had given us the right person to live in our house, to be a caretaker of our things till we return."

Alice Mae felt a tingle run up her spine. She held her breath.

"We've prayed about it and wondered if you and your family would like to live in our house till we return."

Alice Mae's mouth went dry.

The Adams house was large. It had three bedrooms and a full bathroom upstairs. There was a bedroom and another bath on the main floor as well as a fully equipped kitchen—with a dishwasher. There was a formal dining room, a comfortable living room and a front porch with a glider swing. It sat on a spacious corner lot and had a garden area the size of her current house. Best of all, it had a furnace that kept the house warm in winter.

She pushed her sleep-tangled hair off her face. "I could not possibly afford your house. I can barely afford this." She spread her arms. "It is wonderful for you to think of us, but we couldn't."

"We aren't asking you to pay more. We feel like God has told us that you should have our house. He didn't tell us what rent to charge you, so as far as we are concerned, you can pay us whatever you are paying here."

Alice Mae stared at her, blinking.

"You have a job. I know you can't be making much, but your wages have nowhere to go but up. We're not sure when we're going to be leaving. It might be July and it might not be till September. We don't want to keep you in limbo, but we just don't know yet. By then you might be able to afford the higher utilities that our house will run you. We'll fill the sawdust bin before we leave. Did we mention we have a sawdust furnace?"

Alice Mae shook her head.

"Well, we do."

Alice Mae wasn't exactly sure what that meant as far as heating the house. She'd dealt with many heating sources over the years but sawdust was a new one.

Shirley stood. "I don't want you to say anything today. There would be drawbacks for you. The location for one thing. You'd be three quarters of a mile from work and church, even farther if you ever get on at the college. That's a serious amount of footwork, especially in the winter." She reached over and gave Alice Mae a hug. "Just think about it. Okay?"

Alice Mae seemed unable to do anything but nod. She felt unwelcome tears gathering in her eyes.

"Summer is still a long way away and there are lots of things to work out. We've just learned over the years that when God tells us to do something we need to act, so here I am." She looked at the poor woman, blurry eyed and stunned by the unexpected offer.

She pulled Alice Mae to her feet, turned her around and guided her back toward the bedroom. "Now get back to sleep and don't let any more visitors in. You hear? Honestly, the nerve of some people calling on your one day to rest." She grinned, waved goodbye. The front door latched behind her.

Alice Mae could not go back to sleep. Her mind raced with questions and possibilities. *Ruth. Lord, you gave me another Ruth,* she prayed into her pillow. *Thank you.*

64 Spring

After a dreary, damp and dark Oregon winter, spring arrived. It felt like one morning the rains simply changed from the gray, ever-present downpour to soft showers interlaced with sunshine.

"Alice Mae," Chief Bowman called from his office one morning in early March. "Come in here." She was just putting on her coat when his baritone voice stopped her cold. She ran her hands through her hair and stepped into his office.

"Yes?" Her hand automatically flew to her neck.

Nursing a cup of coffee, certainly not his first of the day, he was frowning at a mass of papers spread across his desk.

Since hiring her in October, the chief had sported a full beard, a goatee and now he was working on a handlebar mustache. Despite his general good temper, he could be intimidating and this morning he had that edge. He fingered his new facial hair.

"When I hired you, what did I tell you about your salary?"

She squirmed. "You said I would get minimum wage, four days a week. Right?"

"Did I tell you that I would give you a raise at any point?"

"No." She hesitated. She had assumed that if she proved herself that it would happen, but it was never spelled out. In fact, she realized, there was nothing at all in writing about her pay—just their verbal agreement.

He raised his head and set her with his eyes. "This Howard of yours, this case worker that wants to know everything about you," he grabbed a piece of paper from his desk and shook it at her. "He says that I should give you a raise."

Color drained from her face. "What? No. I'm sorry. We have an agreement and it's not his place ..." She was horrified. She was embarrassed. She was scared. It was true that she was hoping for an increase but now, she just wanted to keep the job. "I'm sorry." She was repeating herself.

"What do you think you're worth?"

"Well," she swallowed, her throat suddenly dry. This was her moment. She shot up a quick prayer and cleared her throat. "Minimum wage is $1.15. I agreed to work for that and I'm willing to continue doing so. An agreement is an agreement and I'm a woman of my word." She hedged. "I do think, however, that this job requires a bit more skill and responsibility than say a stock boy or a clerk, so I think it might be reasonable to pay a little more than that. Not because Howard says so, but because I think I'm doing a good job."

His expression didn't change. He nursed his coffee, listening.

"It's been about six month. Perhaps you might bump me to, say $1.20 or $1.25 if you think I'm doing well." She was holding her breath. She felt her knees going weak but locked them, determined to not let him see her sweat.

He scoffed. "I don't think so."

Disappointed, she said. "Okay. You asked."

"Tell you what I think, Alice Mae." He stood, his imposing size taking up a lot of space in a suddenly small room. He strode around the desk and perched on the front edge, crowding her space.

She took a step back and felt the wall behind her. She splayed her hands against it for support.

"I think Howard is right. I think you're doing a good job and I should move you to five days a week and not wait till April. How would you feel about that idea?"

She swallowed and nodded.

"I think we should raise your wages to $1.30 an hour for now and then at a year, consider another bump. How about that?"

Her face broke into a grin. She could have hugged him. "That would be wonderful."

"As a matter of fact," he reached around to his desk. "I already told the department we were going to do that and here's your paycheck reflecting the increase." He handed her a pay envelope, smiling. "You handled that well. Olivia was right. You do good under pressure." He chortled. "Congratulations."

She took the envelope with only a small tremble in her hand and turned to go.

"One more thing," he said. "Ron Wells is wanting to come on full-time this summer. How would you feel about switching to days then?"

She didn't even notice the rain on the way home. She ran and skipped and jumped over puddles all the way to the little house. If she still had a phone, she would have called Howard. Instead, she picked up her pen and paper and wrote him a long, newsy letter and thanked him for his interference. She hardly noticed that as she wrote she was humming, *Great is they faithfulness* ... When she got to the last refrain, she sang with gusto. "Great is thy faithfulness, Lord, unto me."

The following Thursday, the McMinnville's local paper featured a piece showing the completed and soon to open PBX switchboard at Linfield College. Seated at the desk was the President of the college. *It was completed more than a month ahead of schedule and more than $2500 under budget. This state of the art communication system is another way Linfield continues to be at the forefront of private colleges. The college is eager to have it open and operational by the first of May.* Alice Mae's heart stopped. She reread the article. That was her switchboard, her job and she had lost track of it. She had been so busy with work and inconvenienced by the constant rain that she had failed to do her part.

She went home from a long eight hours of work, and changed into a gray shift dress with matching jacket, one of the dresses Patricia Ward had given her. She stuffed her one pair of good heels in a bag, donned her coat and flats and walked in soaking rain to the college.

For nearly an hour she sat in a chair outside the comptroller's office, shivering from the wet walk, and waited to see the man in charge of hiring for the position. She filled out the application form given to her by the clerk but declined to hand it in, determined to do so in person. She had rehearsed and rehearsed what she would say. She had studied every list, brochure and map of the campus that Mike Browning had given her. Nobody in town was better qualified for the job. She was experienced, motivated and had children who wanted to attend the college.

"Mrs. Wheaton?" A balding, overweight man stood before her, looking bewildered at her presence. Suit jacket off, shirt already rumpled, he had the look of a tired banker overdue for a vacation. He sighed. "I'm Aaron Miller. Jill tells me that you did not want to give her your application for the switchboard job. Says you wanted to see me in person. She says; that you've been here since we opened at nine o'clock." He looked at the clock that showed it to be almost ten. He sized her up and reached his hand out, expecting her to put the paperwork in it. "It's not our policy to interview a candidate who applies for the job till we've checked their qualifications and references."

She stood, still holding tight to the application. "I understand that. But I believe I am uniquely qualified for this job and I want to talk to you about it. I could save you a lot of time and trouble searching for someone else." Her heart was pounding so hard she thought he could probably see the vein in her neck throbbing. She put on what she hoped was a smile although as nervous as she was she couldn't be sure. "I moved all the way from Colorado for this job."

"Really?" He looked the slender woman over from head to toe and with a resigned sigh, stepped aside. "Well, you better come in and tell me about it."

65 Policy

"It is the policy of this college to hire from within," Mr. Miller explained after she had finished her remarks. "Although your argument for being uniquely qualified is impressive, it would be against our policy to offer you the job without first seeing if there is anyone already working at the college who wants the position."

Her heart sank.

"I have had only two applications submitted so far, so the list isn't long, and we will have to check out qualifications and references before making any decisions."

She nodded. "I understand."

He studied her application. "Aside from the recent work in town, you don't have any experience with reception or office work. And you've only been with the police department for a few months. It seems rather unprofessional and impetuous to consider leaving after such a short time. It makes me wonder if you would do the same to us." It was apparent from his condescending glance that he did not want her to respond.

"Anyway, as I said, the position is being offered in-house. I fully expect that a member of the Linfield family will be interested in the post. Perhaps when there is a clerical opening you might want to look into that." He stood and gave her a patronizing smile. "Thank you for coming to see me anyway." He didn't even offer his hand for a farewell shake.

She had been dismissed, unceremoniously dismissed. Not knowing what else to do, she picked up her bag containing her wet flats, thanked him for seeing her, and departed the office, devastated.

The walk home was cold and long. The path over Cozine Creek that last fall had been so gorgeous was now barren of new growth except for the moss covered, rain soaked trees which felt more menacing than beautiful. The water raged under the bridge, full of its spring run.

Disappointment crushed her. *Lord,* she cried out. *This was why I came. That job was the one you led me to. What happened?*

The incline going up from the creek bottom seemed almost insurmountable. Several times her foot slipped on the wet leaves. *I could use a couple of your angels now.*

The house felt smaller than usual. Alice Mae hung her coat, took off and hung her good dress and set her wet shoes by the heater knowing she would need them dry before work tonight. She pulled on her worn robe and a pair of Hazel's warm slippers and slid under the blankets of her bed. Her eyes were hot, her limbs felt like they were filled with lead. She closed her eyes and fell into a sleep of exhaustion and disillusionment. She didn't stir at the sound of the afternoon train. She didn't hear Joyce come home from school and peek in to find her mother with the covers pulled over her head. She didn't stir till Richie came in and let the front door slam.

The small clock by her bed read almost six-thirty. Dusk had settled around the house, leaking only thin light around the window shade when she pulled her still exhausted body from the bed. All four children home and occupied with homework. She headed for the kitchen to see what she could rustle up for dinner when she saw the thin stack of mail on the table. Alice Mae's heart quickened at the sight of the letter from her daughter. She sliced it open with a butter knife and read,

Dear Mom,

I've made a decision.

You told me you believed that God sent you to McMinnville so that you could work at the college and we could attend there. If that is true, then I am willing to trust him too. I have decided that I will come home to McMinnville only when you get the job. Until then, I'm staying in Greeley.

I'll write again later when I have more time.

Love, Donna Mae

Her legs buckled and she landed hard on the edge of a chair.

66   April Fools

If March was supposed to come in like a lion and go out like a lamb, so far Alice Mae hadn't seen any lambs. Spring daffodils and crocus that had dared to peek through the soil and smile at the world had, in the last weeks of the month, been buffeted by pounding rain, hail and even a thin dusting of snow. April Fool's Day arrived with a trick of its own. A late season ice storm encased branches, twigs and leaves with a shimmering sheath of ice. The glass-like streets were perilous.

"Two hours," Sharon shouted, feet pounding down the stairs. "The schools are on a two-hour delay." She slammed into the bathroom, absolutely giddy. "Two hours, two hours, two hours." Her jubilant singing carried through the door.

"Good!" Richie called from the top of the stairs. "I'm going back to sleep. Tell Sharon to be quiet."

Joyce was still in bed, snuggled under the blankets, her dark hair a bird's nest of tangles above the edge of the bedding. "Mom, It's too cold. I don't want to go."

Since turning twelve last month, Joyce had lost some of her childish whimsy. For one thing, she had decided that Billy's attentions were more annoying than fun. First Benny, now Billy; she was going to be a heartbreaker. Alice Mae smiled.

"Yesterday at church, Ted said that if the weather was bad he'd come pick me up for school," Sharon yelled through the bathroom door. A teenage boy driving on ice or her daughter walking the fourteen blocks to school on the ice-rink street. Alice Mae thought it a tossup.

"Take Laurie with you," she called. "Richie too."

"That would be great," Laurie said having come down stairs for her turn in the bathroom.

"Mom, no," she heard the whine.

"Then you can walk."

"Why can't Laurie get her own boyfriend." The petulant comment was not meant to be heard, but the thin walls left little privacy.

"Because I don't want one." The resolve in Laurie's voice was steady. "I'm going to be like mom. We don't like men."

The statement set Alice Mae aback. She felt the blood stop in her veins. What attitude was she conveying to her daughter? What attitude was she projecting to her son? *Oh, God*, she said, *I don't want to deal with this.*

She walked into the empty kitchen and leaned her forehead against the cold window, gazing into the back yard. The freezing glass felt good against her hot face. The empty trestle beyond called to her. For a moment she remembered the short lived feeling of freedom she had enjoyed from that vantage point, just before the little engine and caboose sent her diving off the platform. If it were not iced over she would walk out again.

"Mom." Joyce's voice threaded through the house.

"Just a minute." She walked contemplatively into the bedroom she shared with the girl and stretched out beside her. "It's nasty and cold outside. If you don't want to go today, I'm okay with that."

"Really?" Huge eyes looked at her with incredulity. "I don't?" She snuggled up against her mother, grinning. "I love you."

———

By Wednesday, the ice was a memory. Green had reclaimed the landscape and branches hanging heavy two days before danced in the spring sunshine. Forsythia speared from fences as she passed them on her way to the Adams Street house. Shirley wanted to talk about the house. Alice Mae needed a sounding board.

"So every morning before you leave for work or whatever you are going to do, you have to shovel the sawdust into the hopper here," Shirley demonstrated using a huge snow shovel. "It takes a dozen or more loads to fill it. You have to damper it down or open it up, depending on the barometric pressure. You'll get the hang of it. I must warn you," she confessed sheepishly, "I've singed my hair more than once with this thing. It can backfire."

Alice Mae took a step backward.

The mountain of sawdust had been pumped into the basement through a window. It filled a walled-off space the size of a small bedroom and it looked like an old fashioned haystack from her childhood. It was aromatic and made the basement smell like a walk in the woods. That was a bonus.

"How often do you fill this and what does it cost?" Alice Mae shook her head in bewilderment. She was totally out of her element. "Who do I call?"

"Once a year. Sometimes less if it's a mild winter. We'll leave you the number. It's actually about half the price of oil and here in Oregon sawdust is readily available. It's just a lot of work, so most houses have been converted. We like it though."

Besides the furnace which was like a gigantic boiler with octopus legs crawling in every direction, the basement had a workbench and a laundry room complete with a washer, a dryer, a folding table and a soaking sink. She couldn't ask for more.

"Now, enough about the house," Shirley said after giving her guest a tour of every room. "Tell me what's going on with you. How's the job situation?"

"The job at the station's going great. I got a bit of a raise and I'm on full time now, so the money is pretty good."

"Excellent." She clapped her hands with joy. "And the college?" She looked eager. "Any news on that front?"

Alice Mae looked down and shook her head. The smile on her face buckled. "In-house. That's the term Mr. Miller used. They're filling the position from in-house. He basically dismissed my application without giving me a chance."

"No! So they've filled the position?"

"According to Mike Browning, my inside source," she glanced up sheepishly, "they've had some issues with the phone lines and so they've put off hiring for a few more weeks. He thinks now that they're going to wait till mid-May before filling the slot. He says they are actively encouraging women on staff to apply for the job."

Shirley leaned forward. "But they haven't filled it yet. That means you're still in the running."

"You should have seen his face when I talked to him. He thought my story was," she paused to find the word she was looking for, "audacious. He said it was presumptuous of me to think I could get on at the college just because I had come a long way for the job. He implied that hiring me would be risky since I had just started at the police station."

"Hogwash!"

Alice Mae looked at Shirley, taken aback. "What?"

"Hogwash. Hooey. What a bunch of twaddle!"

"Such language! I thought you were a good Christian woman." She laughed.

"What gibberish. In-house just means they have first chance. But none of them have your training, I'll bet. You have experience. You have spunk."

"That's what the Chief said." Her confidence was resurfacing. "He said he liked spunk."

"So show some of that spunk. Aren't you the one that told me that when you first moved here you used to walk around campus claiming the job? Didn't you say you believed that God was calling you to Oregon, to the land of the Myrtle tree, as you put it?" She was on a roll.

Color rose in Alice Mae's face. "I am and I did."

"Did Joshua stop marching around just because the first day he saw no cracks in the wall?"

Alice Mae stood. "No."

"Did Joshua give up because someone in the town laughed or told him he couldn't have the city?"

Alice Mae's chin went up. She could feel her pulse picking up.

"Did Joshua eventually take the city?"

"How far did you say it was from here to the college?" The flush on her face was unmistakable. "More than a mile?" She glanced down at the cotton skirt she was wearing, thread bare and with a stain on the pocket.

Both women were revved and ready to go.

"From your place it's less than a mile. Let me drop you home. You might want to change before you start marching."

They headed out to the car. Alice Mae was ready to fight for her Jericho.

"I'll be praying for you," Shirley said, sliding into the driver's seat.

67   Numbers

Correspondence from Howard was usually good news. Besides keeping abreast of her ADC account and various papers that had been filed on her behalf, he often included tidbits of news about Holyoke.

Once he sent an entire copy of the Holyoke Register so that she could see what she was missing, little that it was. Twice he had included clippings of obituaries, knowing she would be interested to know of someone's passing. So, it was a comfort to see an envelope with his return address laying on the table at the end of a long and demanding night shift.

She took the packet, stretched her legs out on the sofa, eager to see what he had sent, and withdrew the contents. There was his hand written note and another sealed envelope within. She could feel a tired grin tugging at her lips as she inhaled in anticipation and read:

> *Dear Alice Mae,*
>
> *I hesitated to send this to you but feel that you have the right to know. At first when the Sheriff told me about it, I wanted to leave it alone. After a few days, however, I decided it would be better that you know and be prepared, just in case anything came of the information.*
>
> *Know that I have faith in your ability to handle whatever might come.*
>
> *I hear from Chief Bowman that you are doing well and that he gave you a small raise. I told him it was about time and that the raise should have been bigger. I don't think he likes me!*
>
> *With best wishes to your family,*
>
> *Howard*

She stared at the second envelope trying to imagine what it could be. It bore the official stamp of the sheriff's department. That seemed ominous. She turned it over. Her hand trembled. Laying her head back on the arm of the sofa she closed her eyes. Fatigue was becoming her constant companion and at this moment it swamped her. *What now?*

She allowed the heat that was gathering behind her eyelids to dissipate before sliding her thumb beneath the glue-sealed envelope flap and prying it open. It took a minute for what she was looking at to register. She read every word; the body of the document, the fine print, the illegible signature of Sheriff Ellis, and she examined the date.

It was written two weeks ago so Howard nor Sheriff Ellis had deemed it urgent. The weariness she felt a moment before gave way to mild panic as she reread the paper.

In her hands she held a copy of a request for information issued by the Oregon State Police to Phillips County Sheriff Department asking if they had any information on or knew the current whereabouts of two men. One was named Gene Leonard Wheaton and the other was Virgil Frank Wheaton, both former residents of Phillips County.

The significant part of the form, for Alice Mae, was that the request was sent from Oregon. Their last known address had been in Salem, Oregon, some thirty miles from McMinnville.

Alice Mae let the letter fall to the floor. It couldn't be possible. After fleeing her old life to this promised land, she could not come face to face with Gene. Worse yet, as if anything could possibly be worse, was that his brother Virgil might be that close. A numbing panic swept through her body and she thought she might be sick. Laurie's comment rang in her ears. *I'm going to be like Mom. We don't like men.*

Sharon had been a babe in arms. Gene and two of his older brothers, Virgil and Buddy, were working the wheat harvest south of Wray running farm equipment six days a week. With seven boys in his family, Gene and his brothers were often more like a pack of dogs than like self-sufficient men. The relentless heat was oppressive; temperatures hovered in the nineties. Hawks floated overhead on the waves of heat like the fingers of death looking to pluck life itself from the fields.

The shack behind the main house was nothing more than a one room structure with a roof, a rough-cut plank floor and a solitary door. With no windows for ventilation and only a few bunk beds built into the wall, it was not fit for a family but it was all they had. The dust from the fields and unmerciful heat made it hard to even breath. Alice Mae wanted to take her bare hands and smash another hole in the wall, just so that air could move. Had she the strength she would have. With two year old Donna, an infant to feed and the dull knowledge that she was probably pregnant with another child, bone-thin Alice Mae worked in the laundry room of the farmhouse during the days, children at her feet, in exchange for food. Her only relief came in the pre dawn hours when temperatures dropped into the seventies and she could stroll through the fields, breathe air that was not clogged with wheat chaff, and talk to her God.

After twelve hours of running a combine, sweat pouring from their baking bodies Gene and his brothers could barely stay on their feet. They each stayed upright long enough to swig a few beers, concealed from the boss because drinking was grounds for immediate dismissal, and eat the bread, potatoes or corn Alice Mae had managed to rustle up, before passing out on a blanket in the yard.

On a particularly torrid morning as she ambled through the field enjoying the few minutes of solitude, she heard rustling behind her in the field. Turning with a wisp of anticipation of seeing her husband, she was jolted to see Virgil coming after her, loathing and anger flashing in his eyes. Instinctively she knew she was in trouble.

Her feet tripped over the field, trying to circumvent his path and return to the relative safety of the yard and the cabin. She rushed, then hearing his feet pounding behind her, she ran. He caught her when she was still two-hundred feet from safety. With angry-hot breath mixed with a vice-like grip of pent up furry, he pushed her to the ground and began groping and tearing at her thin cotton work dress. Alcohol induced or battle fatigued from the war or just plain driven by jealousy, she didn't know, but every ounce of him was determined to take what was his brothers for himself. Cursing and mumbling gibberish about what was in the family belonged to them all, his intent to rape her was clear.

Terror gave her energy to fight. Knowledge that she would rather die than allow this repugnant man to have her, she clawed. She struck at his face and kicked with her legs and at the last moment as he was struggling to pin her while freeing himself, she wrenched free and fled.

Bruised from his blows and with lacerations from stubble in the field, she ran back to the house and closed the door, leaning against it as though its thin, slatted surface could protect her. She panted, she cried, she prayed and she collapsed onto the floor, a pile of bones covered with tattered cotton.

In the morning when Gene came to from his drunken stupor she told him what his brother had done.

"You're lying. He would never do something like that," he muttered, eyeing her as though she was untrustworthy. He then snorted, "He probably just figured it was all in the family."

She never told anyone else about it but resumed her life, such as it was, and bore the trauma and pain alone.

Oh God, she prayed ardently, *please keep them away from my family. I can't face them again. I can't face him.*

Drawing up her legs and wrapping her arms around herself, she curled into a ball, pulled the afghan over her shoulders and allowed herself to feel the sorrow and pain of that night all over again.

She needed to have a long talk with Laurie.

68   Trumpets

When Aaron Miller came out of his office, he saw her, again. Alice Mae Wheaton was unobtrusively sitting on the bench outside, smiling. He tipped his head in her direction. "Mrs. Wheaton." He said, agreeably.

"Good morning." she said pleasantly.

This had become their new dance. Two or three days a week, she walked to campus after her morning shift at the station, circled the building and then took a seat outside his office so that he could not avoid seeing her. She did not want him to forget her.

"As far as I know he hasn't filled the position," Mike Browning whispered on Sunday morning as he shook her hand after church. "I know one person has talked with him about it, but for some reason he is still not hiring." He winked at her and then blushed. "Don't give up."

She had no intention of giving up. How many days had Joshua marched around Jericho before the walls crumbled? Seven? She had been walking around the campus more times than that. After the march, Joshua blew trumpets and shouted before the walls came down. *Maybe I need a trumpet.*

———◆———

The end of April finally brought sustained spring-like weather. Azaleas burst forth in brilliant reds and pinks. The smell of sunshine was heady as the winter chill gave way to fragrant tea roses.

The flower seed packets from Janet said to *plant in warm soil after the last frost* and although Alice Mae knew overnight temperatures occasionally dropped to near freezing, she couldn't wait. Wearing her garden gloves, she reclaimed the flower beds outside the south facing back door and lovingly scattered the Colorado Columbine seeds into the long barren earth.

The promise of summer just around the corner also brought Patricia Ward back to Alice Mae's door.

"Knock. Knock."

Alice Mae held the door wide. "Wilson's mother has been here again?"

"How'd you guess? Doris showed up last weekend and took the girls to Portland for an all day shopping spree." She shook her head, amused and set the boxes down.

"I win!" Alice Mae announced, hand in the air as though she had just crossed the finish line of a race.

Two boxes filled with last season's spring and summer clothes for the girls as well as a couple new things for Alice Mae were unloaded onto the table. As before, they were nearly flawless.

"She bought the girls the most horrid A-line dresses." Patricia held her arms slightly out from her body in a stiff triangular shape. "They look like tents. She says that's what the kids will be wearing this year. And pants. She wants them to start wearing pants to school! I told her about the dress code. She scoffed and said we needed to get more modern."

"Well, I guess we know what's coming. I think my girls might be a bit behind the trend."

"Lucky you! She wants me to look like Jackie Kennedy. Honestly! I like our first lady as much as anyone, but I don't think I need to start wearing a pillbox hat just yet." She laughed and sat down. "It's nice to just sit here. She's stayed with us five days and I was just about ready to pack my bags and run away."

"You're always welcome to hide out here."

She looked around the room, pleased with the changes she saw and then said, "If she has her way, next year I'll be replacing my drapes."

"Don't look at me. I'm happy with the thin curtains I have. I like being able to see out the windows. Never have liked closing them off."

Patricia nodded.

Heaving herself to her feet, she rolled her shoulders. "I'm out of here. Wilson wants to meet up for lunch and then I have an appointment at the school to discuss Margie. Something about skipping class, I think. Maybe while I'm there I'll inquire about the dress code." She grinned wickedly, "Maybe I can stir the pot."

The afternoon mail contained just one postcard. She turned it over and immediately recognized the large looping scrawl.

Dear Alice Mae,

Persistence pays off. Henry says he'll drive up to Oregon this spring. He wants to wait till he's sure the pass is clear. Thinking of June. Looking forward to it.

My eyesight is still getting worse, but I'm chatting about it with someone who might be able to help. Keep praying.

Love Janet and Henry

Infused with hope that Janet was talking with the Lord, Alice Mae pulled on her sweater and closed the back door behind her. The afternoon train had passed while she and Patricia were visiting. With quick steps she bounded onto the boards of the railroad trestle, nimbly tripped across the planks till she reached the middle of the span, held her arms out to catch the wind, raised her head to catch the afternoon sun, and sang.

69 Chance

An advertisement in the local paper caught her eye.

Open a new account with us today and get a
new toaster or percolator — your choice.

Just last week, after nearly two decades of service, her old toaster had died. Two pieces of Richie's homemade bread went down into the slots and stayed down. No heat. No pop. No toast.

Alice Mae already had a modest checking account into which she deposited her checks and out of which she paid her very few bills. She struggled to keep enough money in it at the end of each month to keep it open. She had no savings account nor any money to save. Nonetheless the prospect of getting a new toaster without spending her hard earned five dollars was appealing. If she saved no more than a dollar per paycheck, by the end of the year she would have amassed a small fortune. She felt the thrill of financial independence, albeit miniscule. In the relative quiet of the police station, she began making a list of things to do.

- Walk to Linfield, see Mr. Miller
- Open new savings account, get a toaster
- Return library books
- Check on Hazel, three weeks of silence
- Write Masyl
- Write Ruth
- Write Janet
- Pick up surplus food

The phone rang. "McMinnville Police."

"Alice Mae?"

The familiar tone was immediately recognizable. "Pastor Ward?"

"I thought I might catch you there. Are you busy?"

"Not at the moment." She glanced at the clock. Six-thirty. Shifts would be changing soon and activity would be picking up, but for now things were calm. "What's wrong?"

"It's Hazel. I'm at the hospital. Knowing that you two are cronies, I thought you would want to know she's been admitted. It's her heart."

She felt her heart constrict. "How bad is she?"

"Not too bad I think. Her daughter brought her in because she has been having some discomfort and then she called me. Hazel asked if I would come pray with her."

"Of course,"

"Not being family, they're not telling me much but I think they're calling it angina. They're going to keep her for a day or two. I just I thought you might want to come by and since you don't have a phone at home, I thought I'd call you at work. Hope that's okay."

"Absolutely." She ran her hand along her neck and through her hair and then reached for a pen. She drew a circle around Hazel's name. "I'll stop by and see her this morning."

A letter from Ruth was always a welcome sight. This one was long and looked promising so Alice Mae withdrew to the relative quiet of her bedroom, kicked off her shoes and stretched out on the bed to read.

Dear Alice Mae,

How time flies. Donna is getting ready for her finals and has blossomed here at school and with us. I think she could be happy here another year if that is what she decides to do. Know that we love her as if she were out own.

Alice Mae pulled Masyl's quilt up over her legs and settled in for a good long bit of news.

Joe still hasn't figured out the camera so I cannot send you pictures, but I did indeed paint the front porch red. The neighbors were nervous when they saw me start it but eventually decided they like it. Actually the railings are white and only the deck is red but I love it. Joe's withholding judgment for now, but he'll come around.

Last weekend we played hooky from church and went back to visit Holyoke. The new pastor's name is Willard Weed, can you believe that? He has a wife and four kids. I'm sure he's good, but his name makes me laugh. Anyway, while we were there we ran into Elvira Davis who caught us up on all the town news.

She's put on some weight since you left and says it's your fault. What's that all about? Something about cookies?

Your little house has a new coat of paint, white with blue trim. It makes our old parsonage look downright tacky, but your little house looks wonderful.

Peggy Fleming is pregnant! How's that for a shocker? Apparently she made the doctor verify it twice. Her youngest is just turning ten and here she goes again. I don't think it was planned. I didn't see her but would love to see how she looks with a little paunch to go with her red hair. Oh for a working camera!

Speaking of who's expecting. I assume you know that Masyl's oldest, Barb, is due next month. They wasted no time starting a family and I wish them well. You haven't mentioned Masyl in your recent letters so I'm guessing in your case no news isn't good news and she's still not speaking to you. Anyway, you're going to be a great aunt. Congratulations.

Oh, you'll love this. Wiggins Funeral Home has yellow flowers in the urns. After all the years you bugged him about adding color, he did it. I think they're primroses but not sure. Who knows, maybe next year he'll go crazy and opt for red. Ha Ha.

All the flowers we cut back around the church are in full bloom. It looks beautiful. We did good.

I told Joe that writing letters is good but I miss hearing your voice. He has agreed that we should see if we can encourage you to reconnect. Enclosed you should find a check, if I don't forget to put it in, for twenty five dollars. We would hope you would use it to have the phone hooked back up. We will call you and save you long distance expenses but would love to have you just a call away. Donna would like it too.

If for some reason, you need the twenty-five for something more pressing, know you are welcome to do with it as you see fit. We trust your judgment.

We love you and miss you.

Your sister in the Lord,

Ruth.

A check for $25.00 was taped securely to the bottom of the letter. By the time she had finished reading the letter, her heart was soaring. Good news on all fronts.

70   Aaron

"Mrs. Wheaton." Aaron Miller walked past where she was sitting outside his office, again, and let out an audible sigh.

"Good morning Mr. Miller." She stood, collected her coat and then paused. For some reason, she felt like she needed to say more. "Any word yet on the switchboard position? Has it been filled?"

He stopped in his tracks, his back to her as he was prepared to enter his inner office. He turned and leveled his gaze at her. "Step inside," he growled, motioning for her to follow him.

He dropped his heavy frame into his chair and waived for her to take a seat. Eyeing her over his desk he looked tired, his comb-over didn't help. "Are you just trying to wear me down or do you honestly believe you are the best person for this job?"

She didn't hesitate. "I *am* the right person for this job."

He cleared his throat and reached for his coffee cup which, considering she had been sitting outside the office waiting for him for twenty minutes, had to be cold. He took a sip and grimaced.

"Two women said they were interested. Both have changed their minds. Said they would rather stay where they are. Something about being restricted out at the switchboard, not being able to move around." He watched to see her reaction.

She held her breath and sat very still, trying to keep a pleasant but interested look on her face instead of the adrenaline-pumped, bug-eyed anticipation that she was feeling.

"My goal was to have the switchboard up and running before school got out for the summer. I wanted to have time to work out the bugs before the major influx of new students that come in August."

She nodded.

"If we want to try it out while at least a few of the students are still here we need to be up and running in the next two weeks."

She sat forward, "Sounds reasonable."

"*If*," he repeated the word. "*If* I were to give you a trial period, when could you start?"

She was ready for this question. "I currently work the graveyard shift at the police station. That means I get off at eight in the morning."

It was his turn to nod.

"I could come here directly from the station and work for you."

"You can't work two eight-hour shifts back to back."

"I wouldn't be the first person to do it."

"What about your family."

"Mr. Miller, I'm doing this for my family."

He shook his head and looked out the window.

"You're a stubborn woman, aren't you?

She grinned. "I've been called that before." After moment she added. "You should know that I've already spoken with Chief Bowman about this possibility. He's willing to work with me on whatever shift change I need to make if you're willing to give me a chance."

The surprise registered on his face. "Presumptuous of you."

"Perhaps, but I honestly believe this is meant to be my job. Everyone seems to know that except you."

She had him. The grin or grimace or whatever the expression was that spread across his face was uncontrollable. "What is today? Wednesday?" He riffled the calendar on his desk. "Make whatever arrangements you need to and I'll give you a one week trial. Come next Monday morning after you get off work and we'll see what's what. No promises."

She bounded to her feet and reached across the desk to grasp his hand in both of hers. "You won't be sorry."

"Spunk," he mumbled as she bolted from his office. "She's got spunk."

71   Connections

"So, if you don't make money here for a week, your ADC check will compensate you for the lost wages and they won't be deducted from your check. Right?" Fred Bowman sat behind his desk, scratching his new beard that was filling in.

She plopped down on the front edge of a chair in his office and stretched out her legs. Her hands were animated, her eyes blurry from her shift yet bright with hope. "Right. I'm not sure exactly when the adjustment will be made, it might be that I'm short for a few weeks and then they'll make it up."

"If that happens, can you live with it?" He didn't know how she was making ends meet as it was. He leaned forward. "You're doing good here Alice Mae. You could have a good job here. Are you sure this is what you want?"

The determination on her face was unmistakable. "I'm sure. If I have to miss payments or be late for a few weeks, so be it. I want this job!" Her shoulders were squared, her jaw was set.

The chief picked up the phone and snapped at Kristen Anderson, the dispatch that had just relieved Alice Mae, "Get me Ron Wells on the line."

"Right Chief."

"You can't go there sleep deprived if you want to prove you're the one for the job. Yes, you could probably function, but you wouldn't shine. Alice Mae, you need to show them how you can shine." It was the fatherly pep talk she had always wanted. "So here's the deal. Ron's going to take your shift next week. You will fill his weekend spots, giving you Monday through Friday free to show Aaron Miller what you're made of. I've met the man. He's a mean, stubborn son of a gun and you'll need everything you can bring to the job. By the end of the week, we should have a good idea where this is headed."

She was a butterfly emerging from her cocoon, ready to try her wings. She was a bear emerging from a long winter of hibernation. She felt such anticipation that her chest hurt from the compression of it. She was ready to fly.

◆◆

When the phone rang, Alice Mae jumped. Since getting it reconnected, she had made a few quick calls to tell friends and family that she again had phone service, but nobody had called her back. She set down the book she was reading and ran to snatch the receiver from the kitchen wall.

"Hello."

A thin but cheerful voice was on the other end. "Hi Alice Mae."

"Hazel. It's good to hear your voice. How are you feeling?" She leaned against the kitchen counter, ready for a much anticipated chat.

"Right as rain," the words were upbeat but the punch behind them was missing. "I was so happy for your visit. I'm old, but you made me feel like a girl again."

"You're not old, you're well seasoned."

"Then somebody's been using too much pepper because I feel downright spicy today." Laughter rolled across the line. "I've wanted to write a little note to Henry but I cannot for the life of me find his address. Would you be good enough to give it to me again?"

She hesitated. "You want to write to my father?"

"Yes, your father. When he was here I promised him I'd let him know how you were doing and I've never gotten around to writing. Now that I'm taking it a little easier for a few weeks, I thought I'd catch up on some of my correspondence."

She recited the memorized address. "He and Janet may be coming to McMinnville this summer. I'm not sure, but there's been some talk."

"That would be nice. His wife must be a saint and I'd love to meet her." Her laughter was light, almost ethereal. "I know I told you he was charming and he was but I know men well enough to know that holding up that halo he showed me were probably a couple of horns. I'll bet he can be cantankerous without even trying." They both chortled agreeably. "Well, thank you, Honey. I'm going to write this before Perry Mason comes on." A smile was in her voice. "Bye."

"We've got our reservations to return to Africa," Shirley and Jeffery told her as they stood in the narthex, enjoying a cookie. "Ted is going to Seattle for the summer and then in the fall he'll begin studies at the University of Washington."

"So when are you planning on leaving?"

"June 4th. We're going to take a detour to Spain to see some associates for a couple months and then head back to the Congo before fall." She laughed easily. "Actually in Africa it will be spring. It's beautiful there in the spring. The grasses turn this beautiful green and crimson color and quiver in the breeze." Her face was lit with anticipation.

"So soon? And the house?" *We're talking weeks, not months!* Her hand flew to the back of her neck.

"Well, now. That's up to you. I know we were talking about later in the summer or even closer to fall before we had to settle this. Why don't you come over for lunch and we can talk about it? I've got a tuna casserole in the oven."

"Sounds like a good idea. It's a gorgeous day. How about you and I walk? I'd like to see just how much of a hike it will be." She looked down at her flats and then at Shirley's low heels.

"Jeffery, honey," Shirley called across the room. Heads turned. She didn't care. "Alice Mae and I are walking home. Round up all the kids will you? See you at the house."

Her husband shot up his hand in acknowledgment.

She shamelessly blew him a big kiss and grabbing Alice Mae by the sleeve grinned and said, "Let's go. Maybe we can beat 'em."

Jeffery Adams blushed and grinned from ear to ear.

72 Rock On

At a good clip, the walk from First Baptist to the Adams house took twenty-two minutes. From the house to the college would take a good forty to forty-five. In good weather that would be a hike. In winter. When the rains were heavy and the wind and the traffic along the highway kicked up spray, it would be a challenge.

The flip side was that from the Adams house to the high school or junior high school the walk would be less than fifteen minutes, half the time it currently took her kids to get to school. That was significant.

After the tuna casserole had been consumed and lunch cleared away, Alice Mae stepped out onto the wide covered front porch and leaned against a painted column. She looked around the quiet neighborhood filled with mature oaks and dogwoods in bloom. A great Queen Anne cherry tree at the end of the porch was raining the last of its pink blossoms. It was a snapshot of the American dream and yet she knew what was holding her back. Fear. Doubt. A sense of unworthiness that she had rarely verbalized. She could hear her father's voice in her head.

"You'll never amount to anything." How often had he said that to her?

"Worthless girl." Somehow it was her fault that she had not been the son he needed.

"You got exactly what you deserve." She heard that more times than she could count. Every time she failed at something or got hurt, it was her own fault. It was under her skin and imbedded in her mind. She had accepted it as truth.

The sins of the father are carried to the next generations her mind paraphrased a verse from the old testamant. Henry blamed his dad for his actions, she blamed Henry for hers. Was she going to allow the voice in her head to keep her from accepting this offer?

The porch swing creaked as it received Jeffery's weight. "Alice Mae, what would it take to convince you to move here? Is it the utilities? Is it the move itself? What can we do to make this work?"

Shirley came to stand beside Alice Mae and let her hand slide across the thin woman's back. "You and your kids could be happy here. You've been struggling alone long enough; let us help you in this."

"I don't deserve anything this nice." Her voice quivered as she spoke the words aloud. "My father has told me that my whole life." She felt the tears coming and drew in a long breath trying to quell them. "Everything here has happened so fast and has gone so well. I'm afraid." She faced these two gracious people who had taken her in like family and who were making this open-hearted offer. "I'm afraid that this is some kind of a dream and I'll wake up. I'm afraid that I won't get the job and I'll end up having to move back into the little house. I'm afraid that my father is right. I can hear his voice."

Shirley wrapped her arm around Alice Mae. "That's not your father's voice. I know your real father and He says to trust him. He says he desires to bless your family for your faithfulness. He told us that this should be your home."

From behind the women, Jeffery moved back and forth in the swing, the creaking swing adding a sort of music to the conversation. "In fact we are so sure that he wants you to have this house that we are not going to rent it to anyone else. If you aren't ready to move in now, we'll leave it empty until you are ready." He glanced at his wife who smiled and nodded her assent.

Alice Mae turned and drew in a tremulous breath. "It shouldn't sit empty. It's more than I ever dreamed of, but I can think of nothing I would rather do than move in here. Can we talk about what will be left and what you will store?"

Jeffery sprang to his feet. "Let's not just talk about it, let's walk through and you can tell us what you would like us to leave. We're wide open to suggestions."

"Let's start in upstairs and work our way down." Shirley took Alice Mae by the arm and tugged her into the house. "We'll go see what mess Ted has left in his room. You can decide who gets what room and we'll go from there."

"Oh, I should let the girls choose."

"Phooey. This is to be your house. You get to choose and set up the house any way you want. They can always change rooms later. Do they know we have talked about this?"

Alice Mae shook her head. "I haven't said a word about it."

Shirley absolutely hooted. "Won't they be surprised!"

"That's an understatement!"

Monday morning Alice Mae took great care to dress in her good gray sheath, fix her hair, and add a dab of lipstick. She took her time walking to Linfield, wanting to savor the lilac scented spring air and wanting to get there crisp and fresh, not sweaty from the hike.

"The men's dormitories are Hewitt, Frerichs, Anderson and Campbell." She spoke the names aloud, letting them rolling off her tongue. In her strolls around campus she had walked past each of the structures so she knew them well. "The women's dorms are Failing, Latourette, Miller and …" She drew a blank.

She started on another list. "Dana Hall is where married students live. Cozine is maintenance and Dillin Hall is dining," She got all of them on the first try.

She had been over the faculty roster that Mike had provided and the kids had quizzed her on names. She could list them forward and backwards. She could practically recite the college brochure and felt well prepared. "Bring it on," she declared as she rounded a bend in the highway and the beautiful brick buildings of the college came into view. Her heart was soaring.

She marched up the steps of Melrose and opened the double doors wide. At the top of the stairs, the new PBX room was illuminated.

A manual that rivaled the Webster dictionary sat on the desktop and Aaron Miller was seated in her chair, flipping through the pages.

"Good Morning." The glow of spent energy spilled from her.

Mr. Miller glanced up at the large wall clock above the desk and noted that she was three minutes early. He appreciated punctuality. "Good Morning, Alice Mae." He appraised her. "You look awfully chipper for having just come off an eight-hour shift."

She flushed. "Don't be. I would be dragging just a little if that were the case. The Chief moved my schedule around so that I don't have to pull double duty. For the next few days, I'm all yours." She gave him a broad smile.

He thumped the book and stood. "Why don't you have a seat and spend an hour or two going through this manual and see if it makes sense to you. The company that installed the system has offered to come give us training if we need it." He turned and started towards his office. "But I told them no. Said we have this hot shot operator who assures me that she's up to the job." She heard the challenge in his voice as he headed down the hall.

She swallowed hard, the adrenaline high from the walk settling down to meet the reality of the challenge.

Everything that Olivia had taught her had been via demonstration and first-hand practice with her standing nearby. The police station was handed off to her after Judy had showed her the ropes. Learning from a book might be quite another matter. She eyed the tome feeling a bit of alarm at its mere size. "Let me have a go at it. I'll let you know," she said to his retreating back.

Hanging her coat behind the door, she settled in behind the new desk and breathed in the fresh wood finishes. Her fingers ran gently over the switchboard keys. She picked up the receiver and felt the weight of it in her hand.

Aside from the encyclopedic-sized manual, she found that she had at her fingertips lists of phone numbers, department extensions, staff and faculty rosters, sorority and fraternity lists and sports schedules. Aaron had provided the resources she would need. *This is just like the courthouse.*

A total stranger to everyone in the building, save one or two, she drew curious stares from staff and faculty who wandered past the desk.

"Morning." Most gave her a cursory greeting.

"Good morning." She returned as professionally as she knew how.

For two hours, she studied the material left by the system installers and was comforted to realize she did indeed know what to do. She figured out how to turn the system on, how to retrieve messages left in her absence, and how to transfer calls. The basics. Her confidence rose.

Currently, there were dozens of phone numbers at the college. Each department had its own number as did each administrative office. If someone wanted to talk to the cafeteria, they had to know the number. If one wanted to reach one of the coaches in the athletic department, they had to dial that number.

With the new system there would be only one number for the college. Every brochure, every catalog, every poster for the college would list a single phone number. How simple. Anyone using that number would reach the switchboard that in turn would route the caller to the department they were trying to reach. It would, over time, save the college thousands of dollars in phone expenses and recoup the cost of putting in the system.

In addition, it put Linfield at the cutting edge of technology, showing the public that they were ahead of the curve and giving them a marketing advantage. It was a game changer.

There were exceptions. Each dormitory also had a direct line so that in the evenings or on weekends when the switchboard was not manned, parents or professors could reach students. Fraternity houses had their own numbers as did the President's residence and a few key faculty members. In the event that someone needed to reach those individuals during the week days, however, the switchboard could connect them. It was an impressive system.

"You think you have it all figured out?" Aaron Miller's jarring voice startled her. "You're ready to take it out for a test drive?"

"I think so." She was ready. She was excited. "Let's give it a try."

"We're going to try it in stages, just in case there are any glitches. I've asked the phone company to roll over the numbers associated with Melrose first. By this afternoon your phone should start ringing. We'll see how it goes."

By five o'clock when she closed the system down and engaged the after-hours answering machine, it was all she could do to not dance. The calls had come. She had fielded them. She hadn't missed one.

"The Registrar's office." She nailed it.

"Admissions, please." Bingo.

"The Business Office." Connected.

"Mr. Wallace." She knew his extension.

Because the trial group of phone lines were contained, she could hear the connections being made. She would answer "Linfield College, how may I direct your call?" punch the keys and hear the phone ringing in an office down the hall. She followed the lights and learned quickly what was what and who was who.

She practically ran home, excited to go back on Tuesday and do it all again. *Thank you, thank you, thank you,* she sang over and over again.

73 Phyllis

On Tuesday, she hurried to the college looking forward to expanding her network and making connections all over the campus. Confident of her ability to handle the job and excited to prove herself, she skipped up the front steps, pulled open the heavy doors and got halfway up the stairs before it registered. Sitting in her chair was an attractive woman, ten years her senior, professionally dressed and chatting amicably with Aaron Miller. Alice Mae slowed.

"Ah, there you are." Mr. Miller gave Alice Mae his most patronizing smile. "I'd like you to meet Phyllis Lassiter."

Ascending the last few steps, she surveyed the woman. Dark hair with a few flecks of gray was pulled into a tidy chignon, a slim skirt and heels made her look very professional. Suddenly the dress Alice Mae had chosen with care felt dated and too casual for the position.

She extended her hand. "I'm pleased to meet you, Phyllis." Not true.

The woman had a pleasant smile. "I'm so happy to meet you. I've been watching them put this project together and I'm so excited to actually see it up and running." Try as she might, Alice Mae found it difficult to dislike the woman.

"Phyllis works in the Alumni office," Mr. Miller said by way of an explanation. "I would like you to teach her how to run the system. Show her what you did yesterday."

Thunderstruck, Alice Mae stood staring at the man who yesterday had seemed pleased with her performance. She inhaled and said evenly, "I don't understand."

"It's not hard to understand, Alice Mae. I want you to teach her how to run the PBX system. Can you do that?" He had lost the small amount of charm that she had seen less than twenty-four hours ago and was all business. "By this afternoon I want you both capable of connecting calls all over campus. I've instructed the phone company to roll over about half the phones on campus during the course of the day. Everything except the residences, the fraternities and for now the President's house will be routed through here." His gaze was direct and challenging.

"Of course." She forced herself to smile, trying hard to keep her face composed. "We'll get started right away."

He huffed and swaggered towards his office without a backward glance. "Good."

Alice Mae turned to Phyllis and said as pleasantly as possible, "Let's start at the beginning. Every morning we need to turn the system on and listen to calls that were left during the night." She flipped a switch and typed in a series of numbers to activate the system. Pulling up a second chair that had not been in her office the day before, she began pointing out the buttons and switches involved.

"This wasn't my idea." Phyllis was the first to break the awkward pause that lingered between instructions. "I had talked with Aaron about the job a month or two ago, mostly out of curiosity. I wasn't really interested. I prefer more face to face interaction with people than I think this position will offer. He telephoned me last night and asked if I would come in today and learn the system." She looked uneasy. "I don't want the job; I'm just intrigued. They're putting in a new IBM punch card reader system over in Graf Hall and I've been over there poking around at it too. I like technology." She shrugged.

"It's always a good idea to have more than one person qualified for the position." Some tension released that she hadn't realized she had been holding. "I was surprised more than anything to see you sitting here when I walked in. Did it show?"

"It showed." Phyllis tipped her perfectly coifed head back and laughed quietly. "Trust me it showed."

"Guess I shouldn't take up poker."

"Guess not." The atmosphere in the room warmed as Alice Mae realized she had found not an adversary but a friend.

During the morning hours as the phone company rolled more and more extensions into the switchboard, the number of calls picked up. Alice Mae handled them for half an hour and then turned the console over to Phyllis. Back and forth they fielded the calls; they made a good team. As at the courthouse, questions came out of left field and although Alice Mae was prepared for many of them, there were some surprises that Phyllis knocked out of the ballpark.

"Is Professor Elkinson still with the college?"

"He retired three years ago. He and his wife, Bonnie, are living on the coast," Phyllis said, knowing.

"Can I pursue a double or triple major at the same time at Linfield?"

"About fifteen percent of our students graduate with a double major, only about one or two each year will try for a triple major. Let me put you through to Admissions, they'll be able to address that question much better than I can." She whispered to Alice Mae, who was staring, impressed. "I've been here nearly fifteen years. It comes with experience."

"How far is Linfield from George Fox? We're heading up from Roseburg and were hoping to visit both campuses on the same trip."

"There are only about twenty miles between our two schools. It will be easy for you to tour both schools and still have time to spare. But come here first. Once you see how beautiful Linfield is you won't even need to go to Newberg."

Phyllis was a natural. Her relaxed manner and extensive knowledge of the college made Alice Mae realize that even with her studying, she was still woefully unprepared. Unlike the courthouse or the police station where it was about efficiency and speed, here the job would require more than head knowledge. It would require that she know and love the college.

When the massive bell in Pioneer Tower began striking twelve Phyllis pulled a couple dollar bills from her pocket and held them out to Alice Mae. "Why don't you go get us some lunch. They make a mean turkey sandwich over at the student center. I've got this covered. Surely you need a break by now. I'll go after you get back."

She tipped her head inquisitively and asked, "What did you do yesterday? Without someone to cover for you, what did you do when you needed to, you know?" She wiggled her eyebrows with an impish twinkle in her eye.

"I didn't, you know." Alice Mae wiggled her eyebrows in return, her face flushed. "I just waited till I got off."

"No way! That's unacceptable." She looked aghast. "Aaron has to arrange for you to have breaks and lunch. Don't let him take advantage of you. He's good at it. If you get this job, you tell him what you need and if he doesn't work with you, you let me know. He may be the big scary business manager, but I know where the deep pockets are. Remember, I'm connected to all the alums." She gave Alice Mae a mischievous wink. "Now go. Take a break. Breath some fresh air."

74 Brothers

By Friday afternoon Alice Mae had settled into the job and could handle most any call that came through the system. All the phones on campus had been rerouted to the one main number and she was swamped with calls yet was fielding them like a pro. There had been a few minor blunders but no major missteps.

During her week on campus she had learned a great deal about the advantages of being employed there. For starters, her children would automatically be eligible to attend. That was huge considering the number of applicants that Linfield received each year and the limited numbers of slots available. With their grades falling well within the academic guidelines, any of her children that wanted to enroll would be automatically accepted. Her heart skipped.

If she were to get the job, during her first year of employment any dependant of hers would be eligible for a twenty-five percent reduction in tuition. That wasn't a lot but they could also apply for scholarships and grants, not to mention they would be eligible for the work study program. With all those resources, they might still have to take out student loans, but it was workable.

Her second year at the school would raise the discount to fifty percent. The third year she worked there seventy-five percent of their tuition would be covered. Year four and beyond meant that if she still had any children in school they would have a free ride. There would still be fees for books and labs and miscellaneous expenses, but they could go to college. She was absolutely giddy with anticipation.

"Alice Mae." At the sound of Aaron Miller's voice, she turned in her chair and looked up with anticipation. Her face was flushed from a busy afternoon and her spirits were high. This was what she was waiting for, his approval and a job offer.

"Yes, Mr. Miller." She tried to look professional and keep the grin that was tugging at her mouth in check. "What can I do for you?"

"I need to talk to you. I've asked Phyllis to take over the board." His expression was cold, his jaw set. "As soon as she comes, please step into my office." He turned and without the slightest trace of a smile headed down the hallway.

A gasp caught in her throat. "Yes, sir." When the phone rang she answered with what felt like unmoving lips. "Linfield." Her suddenly hot eyes blinked hard to see the buttons she needed.

Ten long minutes drug out before Phyllis Lassiter darkened her doorway, a shadow against the bright afternoon sunshine.

"Aaron said you need a break." Her cheery disposition gave no hint of anything more than a typical afternoon. "Take as long as you need. Things are dead in our office. I'll just sit here and enjoy the view." She turned and scanned the sun bathed vista. "You know you have the best spot on campus." Her smile was warm and relaxed.

Nodding, Alice Mae fled to the ladies' washroom to regain her composure and pray for courage before facing what Mr. Miller had to say. All her father's hurtful words came back like weeds in a garden, pushing out the faith and confidence she had been enjoying.

She tapped on Chief Bowman's door. "Do you have a minute? There's something I need to ask you." Her hands were shaking, but her resolve was solid. She had to know the truth.

"Come in." His face with its neatly trimmed beard relaxed at the sight of her. He closed the file folder he was working on and rolled his shoulders, releasing tension. Reaching for his ever-present coffee cup he smiled. "I always have time for you. Come on in. What's on your mind?"

"I have a favor to ask of you and don't know exactly what the protocol would be. I need to know if someone that the Oregon State Police were looking for has been found."

His eyebrows went up. This was hardly the question he had been expecting. He sat back in his chair and studied her. She was anxious. Tiny lines around her mouth were tight. Her eyes were dilated. She was scared. He got up and closed the door.

"Have a seat."

She sat, hands in her lap, looking down and waited. Despite her best efforts, her lip trembled.

Settling back into his chair, not wanting to crowd her, his radar was on high alert. "Who are we looking for?"

"Two brothers. Gene Leonard Wheaton and Virgil Frank Wheaton." She raised her eyes to meet his.

"Wheaton." His pen was poised to write down the name, but it not necessary. The name registered immediately. He watched her and waited for more information. She offered none. "Your ex-husband?" It was a fair guess

She nodded.

"Why are the police looking for him? Are you in danger?"

"I don't know what they may have done. I don't believe I'm in any danger, but I have reason to think they have been in this area. I need to know if there is any chance of my running into them." There was a catch in her voice. She withdrew the letter from Howard along with the enclosure from the Sheriff Ellis and laid it on his desk. She returned her hands to her lap and laced her fingers together. "I got that in the mail."

He unfolded the papers and read them carefully before looking up. "Which one was your husband?"

"Gene."

He studied her and considered his question carefully before asking, "But he's not the one you are afraid of, is he?" Abuse? Child abduction? Assault? Worse?

She shook her head.

"Do you want to tell me what happened?"

She shook her head again and rose. "I just need to know." Her eyes were pleading.

The chief stood and reached for his hat. "I'm headed right now to the State Police office out on the highway. I'll see what I can find out and let you know. Do you want me to come by your place?"

"No!" She started, alarm on her face. "Please don't! I don't want the kids to worry."

He nodded. "I'll let you know what I find out. Okay?"

The relief that flooded through her was apparent. She nodded and then whispered a hoarse, "Thank you."

75   Blue

Her small mailbox was jam-packed full. She tugged the bundle of paper from the metal box, trying not to rip it from the house. On top of the stack, a postcard was scrawled in a large looping hand.

Dear Alice Mae,

Your father and I are planning to come to McMinnville on May 30th. We will get a hotel so don't worry about putting us up. We will plan to stay a day or two. Looking forward to seeing you and all the kids.

Love, Janet and Henry

With all the changes in her life, she had almost forgotten about the pending visit.

The kids were out of school. Now she had two children that had graduated high school and needed to be in college, one still in Colorado and one at home. She still had no guarantee that they would be attending Linfield.

Sharon was working four days per week, sometimes more, at the Twilight Cafe and Laurie had taken a summer job babysitting for Maureen Moxley who decided she liked working retail.

Joyce and Richie were in the strawberry fields every day earning 'pin money', as her mother called it, and having the time of their lives. Out the door before six every morning and home before the heat of the day settled in. How much profit the growers got out of the throngs of young pickers she didn't know but was grateful for the income opportunity it provided.

The move to the Adams house was coming around the corner and she was too tired to worry about what her father might say or do.

"Let 'em come," she said aloud, tossing the postcard back onto the table.

The letter on official welfare department letterhead from Howard was brief.

> *Dear Alice Mae,*
>
> *According to my last communication with Chief Bowman, your wages are almost exactly the same as the ADC allotments for your family. The last two checks that have been issued to you have been for less than thirty dollars each.*
>
> *Audrey Yates tells me that with the income your children are contributing, which, fortunately, does not affect your allotment, you are faring well. I cannot begin to tell you how pleased I am to hear it.*
>
> *In two more months our relationship will end. Of the many single women I have been privileged to know over the years, yours will remain my favorite success story.*
>
> *Please keep in touch*
>
> *Howard Howland*
>
> *Phillips County Welfare Department*

The last letter in the stack, under the water and electric bill and snagged in the fold of a flyer from the hardware store, was a letter in a blue envelope she recognized. Her fingers slid over the textured paper. It was from a box of stationary she gave Masyl for her birthday several years ago. She had never known Masyl to use stationary, but it was a color their mother had loved. She clearly remembered the look when Masyl opened it. *What am I supposed to do with this?*

She took the envelope to the back step and sat down on the cool cement, next to the flowers from Janet that were growing in the reclaimed flowerbed. Allowing the afternoon glow to warm her skin, she sniffed the envelope trying to catch a whiff of Masyl. Holding her breath, she fingered the blue embossed tab and tugged it open. The single page of matching *blue paper slipped out easily. Unfolding it she read.*

Dear Sis,

I miss you too. It's been a hard year.

You have probably heard that Barbara and Dave had a little boy. That makes me a grandma. Baby Randy is adorable. Randy Reginald Rigging. How's that for a name?

The house feels almost empty without Barb and Mary. Four girls still home and yet it is hollow.

Chuck keeps busy on the ranch and says little. He never was much of a talker.

I don't know exactly what to say to you. I am still hurt that you left, but time has given me some perspective and I hope you are happy and doing well. I ran into Mr. Howland in Holyoke the other day and he says you have a job and are good. I'm glad.

Masyl

Alice Mae clutched the letter to her chest and lifted her face to the afternoon sun. *God bless Masyl. Hold her tight and don't let her go. Amen.*

The talk with Aaron Miller on Friday afternoon was brief, so brief, in fact, that he didn't even offer her a seat. "Alice Mae, I think you could do a good job for us. You have shown diligence and punctuality and have shown your willingness to learn what you need to know to do the job."

Her pulse picked up.

"Nevertheless, as I mentioned before, our policy is to hire from within. It is my opinion that now that it is up and running we will find someone from the campus that is interested in the position. Many people have come by to take a look and several have talked to me about what is required for the job so I'm not prepared make you an offer."

She felt her heart stop.

"I'm going to ask Phyllis to man the board for now till I can make a final determination as to what we want to do. I thank you for your work this past week." The meeting was over. He handed her an envelope. "Here is your pay for one week of service. I'll be in touch with you when we have made our final decision."

76 Yes!

Working days for the police and fire dispatch was much easier on Alice Mae than working nights had been. She was getting a decent night's sleep and her head was clear. Even though she was disappointed to be back with the city instead of at Linfield, she counted her blessings.

"Any news?" she asked the chief when he came in. He was getting used to the question. She didn't have to elaborate. They both knew she was still worried about the Wheaton brothers.

He shook his head. "Charlie Swenson is making some calls. He's a good man and will keep things under the radar. He said he should have something for me today."

She nodded. Waiting was difficult.

She was waiting on Linfield to make a decision; it had been more than a week and she had heard nothing from Mr. Miller.

She was waiting for word about Gene and Virgil; she found herself uneasy that she might turn around and meet one of them face to face.

The family was waiting to make their move to the new house; trying to imagine settling into all that vast space. She felt like her life was on hold.

When at nearly five o'clock the call finally came from the State Police. She put it through to Chief Bowman and held her breath. For ten minutes the line stayed lit—an interminable time.

When he finally opened his door his face told her nothing. "As soon as Ron relieves you, come see me. I have news." He retreated back to his office and closed the door.

There was good news and there was bad news. Such was life.

The good news was that after talking with the officer in charge of the case, he was certain that Virgil had left the area. Two weeks ago he had passed through Ogden, Utah and last week he had been traced to Cheyenne, Wyoming. He was definitely heading east, away from Oregon.

The bad news was that Gene was in custody and probably headed for the Oregon State Penitentiary. He had been arrested and pled guilty to bouncing checks and would most likely be a guest of the state for the next three to five years. He would not be walking the streets of McMinnville any time soon.

The relief Chief Bowman saw on Alice Mae's face told him everything he needed to know.

The following morning, with two minutes before she needed to run out the door the kitchen phone rang. She hobbled on one shoe to grab the receiver while trying to zip up her skirt and practically barked into the phone. "Hello!"

"That didn't sound as professional as I might have expected," Aaron Miller said coolly.

It took a moment for the voice to register and when it did, her face burned. "I'm sorry." She glanced at the clock and sighed. She was going to be late.

The clock hands had never moved so slowly. After rushing into work, a full ten minutes late, she had watched the hands on the clock move at a glacial speed. Where was he? Where is the chief?

Two traffic accidents before noon and one ambulance run should have been enough to keep her mind occupied but it was not. When at 11:59 a call came in announcing a fire behind an apartment building on North Baker Street, she rolled the trucks. She watched the hands creep past one o'clock.

By two in the afternoon she had heard him on the radio once but had still not seen him in person. He was tied up with some problems out at the migrant labor camp and wouldn't be in till late afternoon. She had to talk to someone. Chief Bowman should be the first person, but she was about to burst. She dialed the only person who she was certain she could trust with the news and not have it spread.

"Shirley!"

"Alice Mae. We were just talking about you. We were trying to decide if you wanted us to leave all the dishes or if we should pack them up. What do you think? Do you want some of them?"

"I don't know. Let me think about it. I have something I want to tell you." She whispered, "Are you alone?"

Shirley Adams froze. "Is something wrong? Yes, I'm alone. What is it?"

"I got it." She said it so softly that Shirley asked her to repeat it.

"I got it. I got the job at the college."

Shirley absolutely shrieked. "Yes! Yes! Yes! I knew you could do it. I knew you'd get it. Yes, yes, yes." At the other end of the line, Alice Mae could hear her dancing around and shouting. "Jeffery! She got it!"

"No, Shirley. Hush. You can't tell anybody. I haven't told the chief yet."

"Fiddlesticks. What time do you get off work? We're going to all go out and celebrate. Where are the kids? Do they know yet?" She was on a roll. "What did he offer you? No, don't tell me over the phone. I want to see your face when you tell me."

Alice Mae couldn't stop grinning.

She dialed again. "Olivia?"

77   Shift Change

At the end of an exhausting day, the chief of police dragged through the door uncharacteristically disheveled and weary. At the beginning of the harvesting season trouble often stirred in the Eola Hills south of town where migrant families moved into shacks not fit for dogs—the kind Alice Mae remembered too well. The heat and lack of sanitation raised tempers and fights were unavoidable. When those disputes were carried into the McMinnville city limits, Fred Bowman and his men stepped in. By four o'clock two men were in lockup for wielding knives and one man had been sent to the hospital. Tomorrow would likely be just as bad.

"Anything I need to know about?" he asked as he heaped Folgers into the coffee basket and plugged in the percolator.

He didn't even have to look at her to know that Alice Mae was smiling. He could hear it in her voice. "As a matter of fact there is. You got a few minutes?"

The office around her was a flurry of activity with officers doing paperwork, the radio alive with chatter, and one of the fire trucks returning from a car fire and bringing with it the inevitable mayhem. Even amidst the uproar, when the chief heard the excitement in her voice he knew exactly what she was going to tell him.

"Schallock," he barked to a young officer working on his report and motioned to the dispatch desk. "Cover the board. Alice Mae, in my office!"

He dropped into his chair and heaved a sigh.

She stood in front of the desk and waited for him to get settled. The fatigue on his face was unmistakable as was the dirt on his usually impeccably clean uniform.

"You got the job, didn't you?" It wasn't even a question. "You're leaving us and going to work at Linfield."

The grin that spread across her face was unstoppable. Her head bobbed and her hands opened and closed in an attempt to contain her excitement. "He called me this morning just as I was walking out the door. He wants me to start as soon as you can find a replacement for me. I told him I needed to give you two weeks. I told him that you would probably need me to train a replacement."

She was saying all the right things. She was being professional and respectful of the opportunity this job had provided for her, but the expression of absolute elation on her face clearly said she would like to leave today.

The Chief pushed back his chair and did something she had never seen him do before. He put his boots up on his desk. He raised an eyebrow. "Two weeks?"

Her grin slackened. Her hand went to her neck and she nodded. "That's customary. I believe that was what Judy gave you when her husband was transferred." She was starting to babble but she couldn't stop herself. Tiny stress lines crept around her eyes. "He said he could wait that long if need be but that he absolutely had to have the position filled by the end of the month."

"Do you know anyone who might be qualified for this job? Have you by chance talked with Miss Olivia to see if she had someone waiting in the wings for this position?"

She brightened. "As a matter of fact I spoke to Olivia today. She has a woman that has been training for just one week, but says she might do nicely for this position. Her name is Nancy Browning and she's young and very bright. She has two small children and is highly motivated."

"So you talked to Olivia about this before you even told me?" A frown creased his face. "Don't you think you should have talked to me first?"

Exasperation was creeping in and spoiling her jubilant mood. "You were not available and I thought Olivia would be a useful resource. Besides, I knew she would be excited for me." *Even if you're not.* Her chin went up and her back straightened. "If you had been in I would have told you first thing this morning but I felt like it was incumbent on me to not leave you high and dry so I tried to see what was available. Yes."

Spunk. There it was, that spunk he had seen in his first encounter with her. He grinned. "Good for you! Olivia was the perfect person to tell and as a matter of fact I've already spoken to her too. When you were doing your one-week stint at the college, I talked to her about training someone just in case. I've met Mrs. Browning and am willing to give her a go. How about you give me one week. Ron Wells is on summer break and would love all the extra hours I can give him."

She could have hugged him. "Thank you, Chief." She reached for the desk calendar on his desk and turned it so she could read the numbers. "So May 25th will be my last day."

"May 25th." He heaved his weary body to his feet. "Speaking of things going on in May, don't you have a birthday in May?"

"I guess I do. I had completely forgotten about it."

"According to your file it is May 19th. Does that sound right? And if I am not mistaken, that is today."

Her mouth dropped open. She stared at the date on his calendar and inked into the square that had the number nineteen were the initials AMBD, Alice Mae's birthday. Today was in fact her fortieth birthday. How could she have lost track of that?

He reached into the top drawer of his filing cabinet and pulled out a small box from the bakery containing a cupcake with a candy candle on top. "Happy Birthday, Alice Mae."

Lilac trees were in full bloom and the air was sweet with their perfume. Apple blossoms drifted across street and lawn dusting the street with a carpet of white. Tulips, daffodils and lily-of-the-valley filled flowerbeds that just a few weeks ago were still brown from winter.

Taking the long way home, Alice Mae wandered past the little house where Hazel had welcomed her and her children and made them feel like family. She knocked on the door and shared her good news. The hug she got in return was frail but genuine.

"Have you told Henry yet? He'll be so proud of you."

"I thought I'd surprise him when he gets here. I want to see the look on his face." *I want to see if he's proud of me or shocked. I want to hear him say now that I got exactly what I deserved.*

The old woman nodded and patted her on the arm. "For what it's worth, I'm proud of you." It was worth a lot.

She walked up to the college and around the campus hoping to find Mike Browning. Although he was nowhere in sight, she saw his handiwork. All over campus the lawns were groomed and the smell of fresh fertilizer stung her nose. Since her trial week at the college, new beds of pansies and primroses had been planted and were thriving. She snatched up a tiny blossom and held it to her nose, enjoying the sweetness. She was home.

Heading past the president's house, she began the descent into Cozine Creek Park and saw the Trillium peeking through the ferns and stopped to pluck a spent flower from the stem, making room for new growth.

The song bubbled forth on the descent into the glen and as she stood looking down at the water flowing freely under the bridge she sang what she had so often heard her mother sing when God had answer her prayers. "Amazing grace. How sweet the sound that saved a wretch like me. I once was lost, but now am found; was blind but now I see." She didn't care who heard. He had been faithful to her and her heart could hardly contain the elation and gratitude she felt.

She climbed the path leading back to the highway and to home, anxious to see the faces of her children when she told them. They would be proud of her. They would all go out with Shirley and Jeffery and celebrate; maybe to the new Shakeys Pizza that had just opened out on the highway east of town. She had never had pizza, but Sharon swore it was delicious and tonight Alice Mae wanted to try something new. As she neared home her feet flew, skipping over the sidewalk like they had wings.

78   Contract

The paperwork waiting for her was more than she could have imagined.

He stood in front of her riffling through a stack of stapled papers. "Just fill them out and hand them to one of the women in the office."

He dropped the first stack in front of her. "This is wanting to know how much you wish to contribute towards your retirement fund. The college matches your contribution up to three percent of your wages."

She looked at the form, stunned.

"These are asking for your designation for medical insurance, disability insurance, and life insurance. You need to read over the forms and make your selections. We can do automatic withdrawals for you so you don't have to worry about paying premiums."

She nodded, taken aback at the number of options laid before her.

"This is a schedule of paid holidays, vacation day choices and days the college is officially closed. You will accumulate vacation days beginning today but will not be eligible to take any vacation days for at least six months. They accrue monthly and can be carried forward for up to two years."

She said nothing. *Vacation? Paid vacation?* In all her life, she had never had a paid day off. She felt a flutter in her stomach.

"And lastly, this is the actual contract of employment. Here is your monthly salary before any deductions." His finger ran across a number that she assumed was an error. "These are the estimated deductions based on having four dependants. We may have to make adjustments to these after you fill out your W-4. Any questions?"

He had to be kidding.

"Yes. Let's go back to the number you pointed at. What exactly is to be my hourly wage? We've never actually talked about it. I've been so anxious to get the position that I failed to ask." She could feel the color rising on her neck.

He gave her the patronizing look that she was coming to realize was his customary expression when dealing with women in the office. He pointed to the number again. "Your starting salary per month. Only the students are paid by the hour. Everyone else on campus is salaried. Reviews are annual and pay increases are usually one or two percent."

She swallowed hard and looked up at him. With a face that was as composed and professional as she could manage, she smiled. "Great. I just wasn't sure."

After he walked away, she scanned the papers he left behind. Most of them were confusing and would require study. She had never before had to deal with insurance companies or deductions. She had never considered a vacation schedule nor a retirement fund. One page, however, was abundantly clear and that was the first page of the employment contract. After staring at it for a long time she closed her eyes and let the tension of the past year melt away. From the time she walked out of the police station last Friday to the time she walked into her position as the new switchboard operator at Linfield College, her monthly income had just about doubled.

◆◆

Life was repeating itself. Many of her belongings were sitting in boxes when her father showed up—two days earlier than expected. Walking home from her new job she was stunned to find Janet sitting on her front step, basking in the late afternoon sunshine.

Janet saw the look of disbelief. "I told him we should call you and let you know, but you know your father. He woke up at five this morning and said he was ready to leave. Fifteen minutes! He gave me about that long to throw my clothes in a suitcase and get in the car or he swore he'd go without me." She shook her head, apologetically.

Alice Mae laughed weakly. What else could she do?

Janet gave Alice Mae a curious look. "Hazel Brandt wrote to Henry and said you have things to tell us. She wouldn't say much."

Alice Mae heaved a sigh and tipped her head back and allowed the late afternoon rays to flood her face. She rolled her head from side to side and ran her hand along the side of her neck, stretching. The smile that spread across her face reflected her contentment. "It's a long story."

◆◆

When a little blue Renault sedan pulled into her driveway, Alice Mae got up and started toward the unknown car but then stopped when her father unfolded his long legs and practically crawled out from behind the dash. She stared, dumbfounded. The little French made automobile was not what her father usually drove. He had always been a Ford man. In fact he has chosen a long bed Ranchero the last two times he had traded up. Now a Renault?

"Dad?"

Scrambling from the miniscule backseat, Joyce ran up to her mother and danced a jig of excitement. "That was fun! Grandpa took us over to see Hazel. She gave us cookies!" Clutched in her hand was a bag filled with mostly whole cookies. "She said she'd see us at dinner." She dashed around the side of the house, giggling.

Richie emerged from the passenger door. "Grandpa let me shift. He worked the pedals and let me move the stick shift. It was cool." He followed his sister around the house. "Hey Joyce. I want some of those."

Smelling of pipe tobacco and wearing his customary flannel shirt, Henry gave his daughter a tentative embrace. "Hazel tells me that Sharon works at someplace called the Twilight Cafe. Ever eaten there?"

"Never. It's about a mile from here and I've never felt that flush, but Sharon says it's good. Mostly burgers and sandwiches, I think."

"Well, Hazel's coming by here in a few minutes to pick up some of the kids. We won't all fit in my car. What say we all go check out the place?"

"That would be great. Let me get changed." As she disappeared into the house she called out. "After dinner I'll show you where I work."

"I've seen the police station, Alice Mae. Remember. I'm the one who showed you where it was the day you arrived."

She smiled, amused. "I remember."

79   Stick Shift

They were sitting in the cool of the evening while the kids played kick ball in the street. Dinner had been wonderful with Hazel and Henry trading jabs and keeping them entertained.

"Mine?" The hair on her arms tingled. Her eyes widened.

"If you want it."

"Of course I want it. But I don't understand."

Henry stretched out his legs and pulled the pipe from his shirt pocket. He flicked the bowl of the pipe with his finger and scuffed at the contents. Eyeing his daughter he considered carefully what to say.

"Dad?"

He cleared his throat and looked at his wife of five years.

"A year ago when you told me you wanted to move I thought you were just going on a wild goose chase. I expected you to call and say you had changed your mind; that you wanted to stay in Holyoke. After Masyl lost Mary Charlene, I assumed you would have second thoughts and remain with her."

"I considered it."

"I know. But when you told me you were still planning to move Oregon, I began to see how serious you were." He shifted in his chair and pulled out a match. Striking it, he lit his pipe, a gesture she had rarely seen. He drew a satisfying pull and blew it out.

She waited, praying for him. *Lord, he's searching isn't he?*

"You seemed so sure that it wasn't just your idea to go west but that God was telling you to go. You sounded like your mother." She saw pain in his eyes for the first time.

"You've mentioned that before."

"But I don't mean it as an insult. Your mother was a better woman than I gave her credit for. She had faith that I could not understand. I hated her for it."

Alice Mae felt her heart wrench. She had loved her mother, had loved her faith.

"When you lost your purse I felt smug. I thought he had failed you and that you would turn around and go back like a whipped pup, but you didn't. You still had your faith that he would take care of you."

She nodded.

"I don't understand it. I've been a self made man all my life, never asking for help, never needing anyone or anything. Till now." He took Janet's hand and squeezed it. "You know about her eyes. She's been praying like you and she says he's giving her peace."

Janet laid her head on his shoulder, her eyes closed. She was praying too. Alice Mae could see a tear of joy sliding down the side of her nose. There was an unmistakable tranquility to her countenance.

"I've tried to talk to him too. So far, I haven't hear anything back. It wasn't his voice that told me that you needed a car, but I'm allowing Janet and Hazel to speak for him." He winked at his wife. "They both told me that you needed a car so I found this little tin can with wheels and thought I'd leave it with you. I certainly don't have any use for it. Think you can figure out how to drive it? It's a stick shift you know."

"It's been a few years but I think it'll come back to me." She studied her father. There was a stillness about him as well. "How are you two getting home?"

"Hazel's picking us up at the hotel in the morning and taking us to the bus station. We told her we'd buy her breakfast if she'd be our taxi. 'Go Greyhound and leave the driving to us.'" He repeated the familiar radio jingle. "We'll be home in time for me to get to my Canasta party tomorrow night."

―◆―

The box was sitting on her desk when she arrived at work. Inside was a tiny, hand hewn bud vase about four inches high with a neck opening, barely deep enough to hold a single sprig of greenery, and a stack of Polaroid photographs.

The enclosed note was short and sweet.

> *Dear Mom,*
>
> *I knew you could do it. Congratulations.*
>
> *Ruth and I found this little Myrtle wood vase in a store here in Greeley. It was made in southern Oregon. When we saw it we couldn't help but think of you. We thought it might look nice on your new desk.*
>
> *Ruth is enclosing some pictures of her house. Joe finally figured out how to use the camera. Please note the orange flowers in the planters on the porch. She planted them with you in mind and said Mr. Wiggins would hate them. What does that mean?*
>
> *Let me know what Dean Graves says about transferring my credits to Linfield this fall. NCCC says they should all transfer without problems. My plan is to be home well before orientation.*
>
> *Love, Donna*

The note from Audrey Yates was even shorter.

> *Dear Alice Mae Wheaton.*
>
> *After consulting with Howard Howland of the Phillips County Welfare Department and talking with you to confirm your gainful employment, I have closed your case file.*
>
> *It has been my pleasure to work with you and I offer you my sincere congratulations. You have successfully been removed from the welfare rolls.*
>
> *My continued best wishes to you and your family.*

Her name was scrawled across the bottom of the page.

80   New Beginnings

The calls never stopped. With classes taking up in less than a week, Linfield's switchboard was lit up like a Christmas tree. Alice Mae connected and transferred calls as fast as her fingers could fly. "Linfield College. How can I help you?" Olivia was right. The grin on her face did indeed carry over the line.

When can students move into the dorms?

"Starting Saturday at eight a.m."

Where do we go to change schedules?

"Registrar's office, Melrose Hall starting Monday morning at 10:00"

When does Dillin Hall open for meals?

"They will be open for paid meals starting Saturday but the meal plans don't begin until the first day of classes. No cash, no food."

When does George Fox College start?

She didn't know that one. The college in the next town was on their own.

When Donna and Sharon stopped by to say hello, their faces were alive with exhilaration.

"Any luck? Did you get your work study assignments?" she asked.

"I got the library," Donna said with more animation than she usually exhibited. "I start next week working from four to ten, Wednesday through Saturday. I can't wait." She sniffed the sprig of heather nestled into the small wooden vase and eyed her mother. "From Mike Browning?"

"He said I could pick whatever I wanted. Considering the size of my container, I don't think he's worried about my taking too much."

"The only campus job left by the time I got there was the dining hall." Sharon scrunched up her nose in distain. "I didn't want to do that especially since I'm not even on the meal plan so I declined. But I was told that the phone company in town hires students so I'm heading down there to apply. Pay's supposed to be good and they are always looking for people willing to work holidays and weekends. I'm up for that." She spread her arms wide, ready to embrace the opportunity.

The lines behind her blinked and the phones rang. "Gotta go." Alice Mae waved goodbye and turned back to her task. "Linfield College, how may I direct your call?"